THE LION MISTRESS:
BOOK 1

Other books by R. A. Steffan

The Complete Horse Mistress Collection
The Complete Lion Mistress Collection
The Complete Dragon Mistress Collection
The Complete Master of Hounds Collection

Circle of Blood: Books 1-3
Circle of Blood: Books 4-6
(with Jaelynn Woolf)

The Last Vampire: Books 1-3
The Last Vampire: Books 4-6
(with Jaelynn Woolf)

Vampire Bound: Complete Series, Books 1-4

Forsaken Fae: The Complete Series, Books 1-3

Antidote: Love and War, Book 1
Antigen: Love and War, Book 2
Antibody: Love and War, Book 3
Anthelion: Love and War, Book 4
Antagonist: Love and War, Book 5

Diamond Bar Apha Ranch
Diamond Bar Alpha 2: Angel & Vic
(with Jaelynn Woolf)

THE LION MISTRESS:
BOOK 1

R. A. STEFFAN

The Lion Mistress: Book 1

Copyright 2016 by OtherLove Publishing, LLC

ISBN: 978-1-955073-28-8 (paperback)

For information, contact the author at
http://www.rasteffan.com/contact/

Cover by Deranged Doctor Design

Third Edition: March 2022

AUTHOR'S NOTE

This book contains descriptions of violence and graphic sex, including—but not limited to—sex between men. Additionally, it deals with underage prostitution and miscarriage in a character's past. It is intended for a mature audience.

The Lion Mistress series takes place five years after the events of *The Horse Mistress: Books 1 - 4*. It is not necessary to have read *The Horse Mistress* series first. However, *The Lion Mistress: Book 1* does contain broad spoilers for some of the previous series' events.

TABLE OF CONTENTS

ONE

It was strange that someone as quiet and timid as Vesh would leave such a noticeable hole in the world once he was gone.

Almost a week after the mob caught up to Vesh on the outskirts of Rhyth, Kathrael still occasionally found herself turning to speak to the space next to her where he was supposed to be. Each time, the person-shaped *emptiness* there jolted her back to that horrible evening spent hiding in the shadows, watching the fanatics jeering and laughing as they paraded the slender, battered corpse through the streets. Every such occurrence brought with it a tidal wave of fresh grief, along with renewed determination to succeed at her impossible, self-appointed quest.

Kathrael would have liked to place the blame for Vesh's carelessness — which ultimately turned out to be fatal — squarely at his own feet. It would have been easier to mourn him if she could work up a decent level of anger toward him at the same time.

But of course his death had been her fault, not his. Never his.

If she'd still been able to work, Vesh would never have started accepting riskier clients in order to earn enough money to feed them both. As a eunuch who had escaped the Priests' Guild, Vesh had been in high demand as a prostitute. However, he had also been a target of hatred.

With the foreign god Deimok gaining a foothold on the island of Eburos, the Priests' Guild no longer held the power they once did. The new faith — originally brought over from the continent by traders and visiting nobles — was a vicious and vengeful one. As the cult of Deimok grew larger and stronger in and around the city of Rhyth, practitioners of the traditional religion were increasingly singled out by groups of angry young men intent on venting their frustrations. These groups would harass anyone the cult leaders told them was responsible for Rhyth's current political and economic woes. Any poor soul unlucky enough to be accused of using witchcraft or having magical abilities was in immediate mortal danger — but eunuchs were also a popular target.

All of the priests of the Old Religion were eunuchs, but so far the rabble-rousers had not gained enough confidence to attack any of the temples directly. Vesh, though, had run away from his temple shortly after he'd been castrated. Without the protection of his Guild, he'd been easy prey. Lured to a secluded spot with the promise of generous payment for his services, Vesh had ignored Kathrael's pleas for caution. He'd been hungry. Desperate. They both had been.

So he'd gone off with a silver-tongued stranger, who doubtless had a gang of his friends waiting in secret. And now he was dead, leaving Kathrael alone in the world, without any means of income or support. No food, no home except whatever convenient doorstep or overhang she could find for shelter at night. Nothing, in truth, except for the clothes on her back.

But she couldn't afford to let that stand in her way. Because Kathrael had made a solemn vow to lead an uprising against the corrupt leaders and slave masters who held Rhyth in an iron grip, even as the city slowly rotted from within, descending into chaos and rioting.

First, though, there was one other thing she had to do. She was fucking well going to murder the cowardly bastard of a shape-shifter who'd been prophesied to lead them all to freedom, and hadn't.

The man who'd ruined her life.

The morning dawned gray and stifling, matching Kathrael's dark mood precisely. Her stomach felt like an empty pit—a yawning chasm that ached for sustenance. She unwrapped her threadbare shawl from around her shoulders and contemplated the same question she had asked herself every day this week. What was it to be today? Begging, or stealing?

Of course the gods couldn't have been thoughtful enough to afflict her with some infirmity that people would find pitiable, but non-threatening. Lameness, or paralysis, maybe, or a missing limb or something. No, that would have been too bloody simple.

Instead, she sat at the crossroads with her shawl laid out in front of her in the dust to receive alms. Hours later, after countless passersby had glanced at her face, only to look quickly away and increase their pace until they were out of her immediate vicinity, she had only a single grubby coin to show for the morning spent abasing herself to complete strangers.

Once, she could have made ten times that much in the space of ten minutes, servicing some rich fop in a shadowed alley, fluttering dark eyelashes up at him as she pretended that his perfumed prick was the most delectable morsel that had ever passed her lips during the course of her short life. Now, she trudged to the nearest market, where an elderly, kind-hearted vendor would occasionally give her some of his damaged produce in exchange for such a meager sum.

Today, it was a pair of spoiled ground tubers, blackened on one side and reeking of mold. She accepted them silently, her face downturned, and scraped away the squishy parts with her fingers. Happily, someone had finally fixed the crank handle on the well at the edge of the square. The starchy white blobs were marginally more appealing after she'd rinsed them off, and it gave her something to drink with her pitiful meal as well.

With her stomach temporarily quieted, Kathrael found a shady spot to sit and think. Grief had dulled her wits. She'd allowed it to distract her from her goals. It was time to move, before she slipped into complacency and gradually starved to death, or was caught pilfering some insignificant item or bit of food.

She shuddered. Being thrown in the cells beneath the garrison would surely be a death sentence for someone like her... or, at the very least, a sentence that would make her long for death.

No. She had to find a new way. She had to move. If she didn't move now, she would never be able to. She wracked her mind, trying to think of fresh options. Her thoughts were cloudy, unfocused. Lack of sleep and decent nourishment was affecting her ability to think.

Think now. It will only get worse later, she reminded herself. A snippet of verse that her sister had used to croon, late at night when Kathrael couldn't sleep, wafted through her memory.

All who seek shelter shall find it.
All who grieve shall be comforted.
All the gods' children will receive solace.
Ask at the temple and gain the help you need.

Vesh would have laughed aloud at her. The temple had never meant solace for him, but rather, pain and suffering. It was, however, an avenue she had not tried before. The glimmer of a plan began to form, and she chewed absently at a thumbnail as she contemplated the possibilities.

She needed to act, while she still had the strength.

Vesh's old temple was further inside the central part of the city than she really liked to go these days. There was no getting around it, though. She arranged her shawl over her head and shoulders in such a way that it draped across the left side of her face, obscuring it in shadow. Her dress was in tatters, but there was nothing she could do about it. She would not be the only beggar girl inside the city walls, after all. Far from it.

Her bare feet were aching by the time she reached the city gate nearest the temple. The guard gave her a look of disdain and shoved her as she walked past, knocking her into a tall man wearing plain, well-mended clothing. He cursed, caught by surprise, but helped steady her as she staggered. It was on her tongue to thank him when she realized her shawl had slipped from her face in the confusion.

The man gasped sharply and jerked his hands away from her shoulders as if she had suddenly become red-hot. He stammered something and hurried away, wiping his hands on his tunic as if he feared she had contaminated him somehow.

Kathrael hurriedly covered herself again and made for the nearest alley where she could escape notice from others in the crowd who might have seen the man's reaction. The stab of hurt she had felt at his look of horror took her by surprise — she would have thought she was immune to such things by now. Perhaps it was because he had seemed as though he might be kind. Once upon a time, she might have used him somehow, playing on his sympathy for a poor, beautiful girl fallen on hard times.

Now, though, she was very much on her own. After regaining her bearings and making sure no one had taken any further notice of her, she rejoined the crowd trickling through the gate and headed in the direction of Vesh's temple, keeping her head down.

The sun was high in the sky when the impressive structure of wood and stone finally came into view. The new temples dedicated to Deimok were mostly shining white, built of polished marble and financed by the Emperor of Alyrios, sitting safe in his golden palace on the mainland across the channel. By contrast, the temples of the Old Gods still looked to be part of nature, made with local materials and designed to blend in with their surroundings.

Vesh's temple was dedicated to Naloth, god of rain and male fertility. Kathrael had always felt more of an affinity with Deresta—the goddess of the sun, fire, death, and warfare—but one did not go to Deresta's temple to beg for succor. Indeed, by rights, she should be visiting the temple of Utarr, Naloth's mate. For it was Utarr's Prayer of Solace that had risen earlier from the depths of Kathrael's memories, promising the chance of aid.

However, what she would be seeking was more than a simple meal or a handful of coppers to pay an irate landlord. To have any chance of success, she would need to find someone there who had cared for Vesh and might place value on their shared connection with him. Given that Vesh would have been stripped of all his titles and associations within the temple immediately upon running away, it was admittedly a gamble. That said, Vesh had been the kindest and best person Kathrael had ever known. She was confident that *someone* here would remember him in the same way she did.

The doors to the temple had been thrown open to let in fresh air. Kathrael was pleased to see that there were few people coming and going, and that the entryway was attended by a pair of acolytes who were barely more than boys. She approached them, eyes down, clutching her shawl over her scarred face so it would not slip free at an inopportune moment.

Addressing the younger, softer looking of the two, she said, "Please, brother, my situation is desperate and I have nowhere else to turn. I cast myself on your mercy. I beg you, can you take me to the kindest of the novices? I can barely bring myself to speak of the terrible thing which has befallen me."

From the corner of her eye, she watched the boy's expression transform from one of pleasure at being addressed as if he were in a position of power, to concern and sympathy as he took in her words and the way she hid part of her face as if ashamed. Without saying a single untrue word, she had conveyed to him that she had been assaulted, probably raped — perhaps impregnated. He would assume that the shawl over her face hid signs of a beating.

Most such victims chose to appeal to Naloth, as the arbiter of male behavior, so the situation would not be an unfamiliar one to either of the two acolytes. And, indeed, the youngster immediately moved to reassure her.

"Peace, sister," he said. "You have come to the right place. There are many here who can help you."

Kathrael hunched as if cowering, hiding her face further. "Only, I cannot — I cannot bear the thought of speaking to some gray-haired priest who would remind me of my f-father. Please, it must be someone young. Someone gentle, who will not judge me."

Those words, spoken in a voice quavering with suppressed emotion, perfectly described Vesh. She could only hope that like had called to like during his time here.

"Of course," said the acolyte, placating. "I know just the person. Come with me. I will take you to Novice Hameen. He is young, and he has always been kind to me."

"Thank you," she said, allowing relief to color her voice as she laid her free hand on his forearm and squeezed. "I didn't know where else to go. *Thank you*."

"We are all here to serve, sister," the boy said, obviously pleased by the fawning. "Come. Follow me."

Kathrael allowed herself to be led into the relatively cool darkness of the temple. The acolyte guided her to a small, comfortable room with several seats and a low table holding food and wine. As soon as he left her to fetch Novice Hameen, she fell on the bread and fruit as if it might disappear at any moment, washing it down with wine straight from the jug.

How long had it been since she'd had access to as much fresh food as she could eat? She couldn't even remember. At the sound of approaching footsteps, she quickly rearranged everything that was left so that it looked a little less like the aftermath of an attack of gluttonous rats. When the novice entered, she was seated on the low wooden settle with her hands twisted in her lap, waiting quietly.

She glanced up at him, trying to gain an impression of his character—a skill she had cultivated during her days as a prostitute, and one that had stood her in good stead. Physically, Novice Hameen was Vesh's opposite in every way. Obese where Vesh had been skinny, even-featured while Vesh's features had exhibited a slightly asymmetrical character that served only to make him more interesting to look at. Hameen's eyes were also an unusual shade of pale gray, very different from Vesh's rich brown.

All of that was unimportant, however. Like Vesh, Novice Hameen projected an aura of compassion—a soul-deep kindness that could not be hidden or dimmed. He was also more or less the same age as Vesh had been. Kathrael let out a silent breath of relief, suddenly and irrationally certain that the two must have known each other.

"Welcome to the temple of Naloth," Hameen greeted in a clear, pleasant voice. "I am at your service, sister. What troubles you?"

Kathrael's heart pounded for a moment as she chose her words. "Brother Hameen, thank you for speaking with me. I believe we share a friend. Were you, by any chance, acquainted with a young novice who went by the name of Vesh?"

Hameen raised his eyebrows and regarded her in surprise. "Forgive me. That is not at all the subject I expected us to be discussing." He paused for a moment. "Surely you do not mean Novice Ta'vesh?"

It was Kathrael's turn to frown. "I knew him only as Vesh. A slender person, with a small gap between his front teeth, and his nose slightly bent as if it had once been broken?"

Hameen drew in a sharp breath and sat down rather abruptly in the chair across from her. "That describes Ta'vesh exactly, yes. His nose was broken when he was fourteen years old, by one of the other slave boys. I helped him set it, but it never healed quite right."

Kathrael swallowed hard, surprisingly affected by being here with someone else who had once called Vesh a friend. It had seemed since his death that without her to remember him, Vesh would disappear as if he had never existed. To know that others remembered — that others had been affected by him — was strangely comforting even as it made her grief rise once more.

"Do you know where he is?" Hameen asked eagerly, before bringing himself visibly under control. "I'm sorry. By rights, I should not even speak of him. He was formally cast out of the temple after he ran away."

"He is dead," Kathrael said. "Stoned to death by a mob last week, outside of the city."

Hameen's eyes closed in pain. "I had feared the worst, ever since he left. Yet even so, it's somehow worse to know that he survived so long, only to perish in the end." When he opened his strange, pale eyes again, they were wet. "Tell me, sister, how did you come to know him?"

"He befriended me when we were both living on the streets. We looked out for each other... or tried to." She lifted the shawl away from her face, meeting Hameen's gaze with her own. "He kept me alive and nursed me back to health after this happened."

The novice examined Kathrael's face without flinching, though his dark eyebrows drew together in sympathy. Although she avoided her own reflection like the plague, she knew perfectly well what he was seeing—scarred skin that had melted and run like wax, framing her useless, milky left eye. The burns extended down the left side of her neck and over the top of her breast, thankfully covered by the high neckline of her tatty, threadbare dress.

"What happened?" he asked kindly, and she suddenly realized that, aside from Vesh, he was the only person who had ever cared enough to ask.

She raised her chin. "I was a prostitute. We both were," she said, daring him to make an issue of it. "We were *good*, too. I could always tell if a man was safe to go with or not. This particular man was a good client. He always paid generously, and he never wanted anything too strange or distasteful in return."

Her attention turned inward, sliding back to that awful day the previous winter. "I didn't take his wife into account, unfortunately. She found out that he'd been spending the household savings to visit me. The man was a metalworker. One evening, his wife came to the inn where I always serviced him. She burst into the room and yanked me away from him by the hair. Before I could push past her and get to the door to run, she threw a vial of something at my face. I learned later that it was green vitriol. It's used to dissolve metal when making etchings."

Hameen winced.

"I didn't stop to think—I just ran. It wasn't so bad at first, but then it started to burn everywhere it had touched me. I couldn't get it off. Whenever I tried to wipe it away, it just spread the fire. I don't know how I managed to get back to where Vesh and I were staying, but somehow I did. One of the other women there wanted to soothe the burns with oil, but Vesh wouldn't let her. I remember that he dragged me out to the well and kept pouring buckets of water over me until I thought I would drown. At some point I must have passed out, because that's the last thing I remember from that night."

Novice Hameen had raised his hand to cover the lower part of his face in dismay as she spoke. When she finished, he took a deep breath as if centering himself, and returned it to his lap. "Ta'vesh's father was a metal smith. He would have known that oil would only make it worse. You are correct that he probably saved your life."

"Whereas I was unable to return the favor and save his."

"The friend I knew would no more have blamed you for such a thing than he would have blamed the sun for rising in the east," Hameen said.

Kathrael was silent for a moment. Vesh might not have blamed her, but she still blamed herself.

"He grew careless of his safety in his attempt to earn enough coin to keep both of us fed," she said eventually.

"If that is the case, then he must have thought you worth the risk." The young priest settled back in his chair and regarded her frankly. "Now, tell me what has brought you here. As appreciative as I am of knowing Ta'vesh's fate, I don't believe you sought me out solely to exchange memories of our beloved friend."

"No." Kathrael looked down, and then up again, preparing herself to lie to the first person who had shown her real kindness since Vesh's death. "I am utterly destitute, Brother Hameen. I have no means of making a livelihood. I cannot even beg—my face repels everyone who sees it. And yet, I am compelled to undertake a pilgrimage."

Hameen's brow crinkled again. "What sort of pilgrimage?"

"I must travel north to seek out the Wolf Patron, and try to convince him to aid us here in Rhyth," she said, forcing herself to meet Hameen's gaze squarely as she spoke.

There was a pause as the novice digested this.

"You speak of High Priest Senovo, the wolf-shifter of Draebard?" Hameen asked.

"He was Rhytheeri long before he fled over the mountains to live as a northerner," Kathrael said.

After the war five years ago, everyone in the south knew the story of the Wolf Patron, though numerous wild tales had grown up around the central truth. Senovo's parents sold him to the Priests'

Guild as a young boy, when they could no longer afford to feed all of their children. He had grown up a slave, but he showed the intelligence and temperament required for eventual initiation into the priesthood.

Or so his owners had thought. When the High Priest ordered him to be dragged into the temple and forcibly castrated, Senovo changed into a wolf and tore his tormenters limb from limb. Only one survived to tell the tale, though he died of his injuries not long afterward. The wolf ran off and escaped into the wildlands, only to surface years later in human form as the powerful High Priest of the northern Draebardi tribe.

Along with the Draebardi Chieftain—rumored by some to be the Wolf Patron's lover—High Priest Senovo commanded an army of wolves that repelled an attempted invasion by the Alyrion Empire. Rhyth, situated on the southern coast of the island of Eburos, had maintained a lucrative trade partnership with the Empire in the years before the Emperor of Alyrios attempted to expand his reach by conquering northern Eburos. Since the unsuccessful incursion, however, the north had all but cut ties with Rhyth, turning instead to new, far-flung trading partners on the continent. Rhyth's supply of ore and gemstones from the productive northern mines had been strangled until it was a bare trickle.

Without valuable raw materials to trade, Rhyth was falling out of favor with the Empire, and now the city was struggling for its very survival.

"Perhaps the tales of the Wolf Patron's southern roots are true," Hameen allowed. "But what you propose is still an immense undertaking. Beyond the central fact that a young wolf-shifter did escape from the Temple of Deresta some years ago, the story is more legend than not."

"No," Kathrael said. "You're wrong. It is true. Being a prostitute puts a person in a position to hear a lot of talk. After a while, you gain a sense of what is truth and what is wishful thinking."

She didn't add that she had made it a lifelong mission to ferret out all the information she could about High Priest Senovo of Draebard. She also had one additional advantage that no one else knew about—she'd met the spineless son-of-a-bitch personally, on a sweltering summer day almost six years ago when her life had first begun sliding toward ruin... all thanks to *him*.

TWO

"Nevertheless," Hameen said, "you must be aware that the Priests' Guild does not give credence to the so-called prophesy of the Wolf Patron."

"Well, *of course* they don't," replied Kathrael. "The story doesn't exactly place them in a good light, does it?"

The priest shrugged. "Perhaps not. But, you must agree, the idea of an escaped slave returning as a figure of power to lead a slave rebellion sounds more like wishful thinking than reality. Such things happen only in stories."

Kathrael studied Hameen for a moment. "Tell me, Novice Hameen—were you a slave before you became a priest?"

"I was not," Hameen said after a short pause. "My parents purchased me a place as an acolyte when I first displayed unnatural urges for other boys as a youngster. Though I know, of course, that Ta'vesh was a slave before he was chosen for initiation."

"And I suppose your parents also paid for pain medicine and sleeping draughts for you during your novitiate? To ease your castration?" Kathrael asked pointedly.

"They did."

Her voice grew accusing. "Vesh had no such comfort or assistance."

Hameen looked pained. "I am aware. But slavery has been a reality in Rhyth for countless generations. It will take more than one shapeshifter to change it, however distasteful you or I might find the practice."

"So you won't help me?" Kathrael prodded.

The eunuch sighed. "I didn't say that. What, precisely, do you require of me?"

"Sandals," Kathrael said without hesitation. "A blanket. Traveling rations. Money, if possible."

"I cannot give you enough food and drink for such a long journey. Even if I could, you wouldn't be able to carry it all."

"But the rest?"

"I will find you a pair of sandals. And you may take my blanket—you have more need of it than I, whether you decide to attempt this journey or not. Stay here, and I will see if any coins have been deposited in the alms box that will not be missed." Hameen peered at her for a long moment. "I am doing this in Ta'vesh's memory, though he would probably not thank me for it. The pilgrimage you describe is fraught with danger, especially for a woman traveling alone."

"He's not here anymore to disapprove," Kathrael reminded him, "and you have my sincerest thanks."

Hameen stood. "I'll pray for you."

"I'm not certain anyone has ever done that for me before."

The novice shook his head. "No. Ta'vesh did, I feel sure. It wasn't the gods he was fleeing when he left the temple, it was the men."

Kathrael swallowed around the hard lump that rose in her throat, and nodded. "Perhaps so. Thank you again."

"Wait here. I'll return for you once I've gathered what I can." Hameen looked vaguely uncomfortable for a moment. "Afterward, I will take you to one of the back entrances to depart. You should not allow yourself to be seen if you can avoid it. The senior priests would not approve of what I am doing."

"I understand," she told him.

When he left, Kathrael ate the rest of the bread and stowed as many of the tart mayapples as she could fit into the pockets of her skirts. Before the sun had reached the top of the king's grand palace in the west, she was hurrying out of the temple through a small, little used door, laden with a sleeping roll and a bag of dried meat and cheese. A tiny ceremonial dagger nestled in the ragged sash tied around her waist—an unexpected addition.

Kathrael wondered if she would ever encounter Novice Hameen again. It seemed unlikely, as she fully expected to lose her life before she could successfully achieve her goals.

She hoped he would not be caught and punished for his unsanctioned generosity—her conscience was already heavy enough as it was.

There was no point in tarrying. Though it was already mid-afternoon, she might as well get underway. It wasn't as if she had anything holding her to the city, after all. And the sooner she was out of it, away from the crush of people, the safer she would be.

It was easier getting out than it had been getting in. She kept to the shadows and quiet side-roads, years of practice at remaining unnoticed holding her in good stead. She joined the crowd at the gate heading back to their homes outside of the walls after a day of commerce, and passed through unremarked. Not only were the guards more lenient about letting undesirables *out* of the city than letting them *in*, but also her bundle of possessions gave her an air of legitimacy despite her ragged clothing.

Once beyond the walls, she kept her head down and let the crowd carry her along until it started to thin. Her stomach was beginning to ache and gurgle unpleasantly, protesting the unexpected feast of fruit and bread after so long with almost nothing. Still, she was determined to get out into the rural areas north of the city. There, she could find a quiet patch of woods and hunker down for the night where no one would be likely to stumble across her while she slept.

The buildings and huts around her grew farther apart, separated by expanses of pasture and tilled land. These were the smallholdings, mostly owned by freefolk eking out an existence from the land. When Rhyth had been at the height of its power, there had been relatively few such holdings.

Now, opportunity inside the city was drying up along with the trade across the sea, and anyone who could was moving back to the countryside.

Kathrael had grown up working the fields, but not here. She had been a slave on one of the large plantations further from the city, owned by some fat, wealthy noble who only deigned to ride out and survey his lands once or twice a year. Those places still existed, and from what she had heard, they were worse than ever as the overseers tried to extract even more labor from the slaves to meet the ever-increasing quotas demanded by the owners. With the raw materials and ore from the north cut off, the rich turned to agriculture to support their outrageous lifestyles… and the grain they sold was grown on the backs of slaves.

It was probably ironic that she had spent years as a prostitute extracting money from the same sort of men who had once owned her. They had been happy enough to pay her to dance and entertain their posh friends at the endless, decadent parties — *orgies*, more accurately — that seemed to serve as a sort of status symbol in the wealthy parts of the city, near the palace. Yet it never would have occurred to them to pay her for her years of backbreaking labor in the fields.

Fuck them all — every last one. Kathrael was going to tear down everything in this world that had tried to destroy her. She would see the slave owners thrown out into the streets, stripped of everything they'd stolen from her people, or she would die in the attempt.

The last few smallholdings were finally behind her, and the sun was dipping toward the horizon. Every muscle and joint in her body ached, unused to covering such distance in the space of a day. Her feet were on fire despite the too-large sandals Hameen had given her. She looked around. Her surroundings were uncultivated, a mixture of trees and grass. She left the road and made her way down a gentle embankment, to a flat area surrounded by shagbark trees.

The nuts were still green at this time of year, though she would have probably braved the resulting stomachache and eaten them anyway had she not managed to acquire food at the temple. As it was, she made a careful inventory of her supplies before the light faded, and measured out a small portion to eat.

Even though her gut was still churning from her earlier meal, she slowly chewed and swallowed the modest handful of dried goat meat strips and hard cheese. She did not know exactly how far away Draebard lay, but it was a long, long way. She knew it took people on foot a week to walk from Rhyth to the mountains. She would not only have to do that—she would have to *cross* the mountains and then travel on even farther, into the barbarian lands.

It would need all of her strength, and that meant eating as much and as often as she could.

It was dark when she finished her pitiful repast, washing everything down with weak, watered wine from the skin Hameen had given her. The wine would not last long in the summer heat, though she could stretch it by continuing to water it down further for a few days. After that… well… there were plenty of rivers running through the southern lands. The water in some of them was safe to drink, and the water from others wasn't. She would have to make do.

There was no need for a fire in the warm, humid weather, and lighting one would have drawn attention to her presence that she did not want. With nothing left to do, she unrolled Hameen's blanket and laid it on the ground. It smelled of sandalwood, and with no one here to see her do it, she buried her nose in the rough wool and breathed in.

It took time for her exhaustion to overcome the pain of her blistered feet and aching muscles, but eventually, she slipped into a heavy sleep, feeling a sense of freedom and purpose that she hadn't known in months… if not years.

Sunlight filtering through the leaves woke her the following morning. A light breeze from the north brought relief from the humidity. Kathrael's thin, starvation-weakened body protested movement with sharp aches and stiff, popping joints when she stretched. A moment later, her feet chimed in, reminding her of the blisters that had risen over the course of the day yesterday, as the straps of her unfamiliar footwear rubbed against the skin.

She flopped onto her back, and stared up at the ever-changing mosaic of leaves above her. It would be so easy to stay here. To rest for a few days and work her way through the bounty of food she'd received from the temple until it was gone.

It was nice here. No one would bother her. It would be so much easier.

You were never a quitter, Kath.

The half-heard whisper sounded exactly like Vesh. Kathrael bolted upright and whipped her head around, filled with irrational hope that the movement at the edge of her vision would coalesce into the slender, dark-haired form she knew so well. But it was only the wind rustling the grass. Her racing heart slowed, mired back into the dull listlessness of grief.

"Go away, Vesh," she told the empty glade. "You're dead."

The whisper of leaves moving in the breeze sounded like distant laughter.

Kathrael gritted her teeth and forced her body into motion. There was little that needed to be done before she could start moving again. She rolled up the blanket, ate a bit of cheese, and relieved herself in the tall grass. It was less painful to go barefoot, so she let the sandals dangle from her fingers as she climbed back up the slope leading to the little-used track she'd been following. With a brief glance at the sun to make sure she hadn't gotten turned around, she headed north.

By midday, she was struggling badly. The obvious thing would have been to stop and rest, but innate stubbornness, combined with confusion due to heat and exhaustion, had Kathrael convinced that if she stopped, she would never be able to start again.

The stretch of road she was on ran through a bit of forest, winding this way and that around trees that were too large and numerous to be easily cut down to clear the area for pasture or cropland. At least it was cooler in the shade. After taking a long drink of watered wine—now unpleasantly warm—from her wineskin, her thoughts began to clear. Ahead, she could just make out the sound of voices. There were two, both male, talking and laughing raucously. And they were coming her way.

She froze, caught in a moment of indecision. Should she hide, or keep walking? But then it was too late. The pair rounded the bend in front of her and paused. Caught, she fumbled with her shawl, drawing it quickly forward to obscure her scars.

"Well, well," said the one on the right. "What have we here?"

They were young—not boys, but barely men. The one who had spoken was tall and broad. The other was a few inches shorter, but wiry. Both were well, but not ostentatiously, dressed. Overseers' sons, perhaps, or members of a merchant family traveling from one village to another. The sixth sense that had kept Kathrael safe for most of her life immediately started tingling, raising the fine hair at the back of her neck.

"What're you doing out here all alone, love?" asked the one on the left, as the pair started walking toward her once more.

Kathrael turned her head to further obscure the left side of her face, but glared at them with her good eye. "I'm traveling. What does it look like?"

The broad one laughed, and the sound grated like a rusted axle. "It looks like that dress you're wearing is more holes than cloth — *that's* what it looks like. Where did a little beggar girl like you get that nice blanket and satchel? Did you steal it?"

"Maybe we should take a look in her bag. See what's in there. It might be money."

"It's moldy cheese and a bit of dried goat. Let me pass." Kathrael's free hand went to her sash, seeking the reassuring form of the dagger nestled there. Never mind that there were two of them, each towering over her, and she was on the verge of collapse from exhaustion.

"Nah, I don't think we will," said the wiry one. "Not until you let us have the bag."

She pulled the dagger free. It suddenly seemed very small and inadequate.

The broad one laughed. "What's that you've got there? A knitting needle? If you had another one, maybe you could mend that shawl."

Inspiration struck in a flash. She grabbed the shawl and pulled it back, revealing her face. Both of the men flinched, and the broad one took a step back. She bared her teeth. "Go ahead," she snarled. "Come a little closer. Touch me. Touch my satchel. I'd *love* to see what the two of you look like after you've caught the face-melting plague. Maybe you'd both like a kiss?"

The wiry one was still frozen in place like a statue, but his friend grabbed him by the arm and dragged him back. "*Fuck!*" he cursed. "You stay back, you crazy bitch!"

Kathrael took a step toward them, and spat at the wiry one's boots. He danced back as if he feared the gob of saliva might eat through the leather and contaminate him somehow.

"Naloth's balls!" Her target started hustling his friend around her on the road, giving her a wide berth. "Go find a hole to climb into and finish dying, you vicious cunt!"

Kathrael glared after them. "Thanks, but no thanks. I've got some people I need to take with me when I go."

"Leave her," said the other. "Come on, let's get *out of here*."

Kathrael watched them hurry away, casting occasional glances over their shoulders at her as they kept to the side of the track, as if afraid to even walk on the same ground her bare feet had touched. She felt suddenly powerful, even as the familiar, crawling horror at what had happened to her face skittered through her stomach. Exhaustion momentarily banished, she turned her back on the rapidly disappearing figures and continued on.

By the time she collapsed onto Hameen's blanket, hours later, her exhaustion had returned tenfold. At least she'd managed to find a place to sleep near running water this time. After a night of restless sleep interrupted by bad dreams and throbbing pain, she spent a few minutes soaking her aching feet in the trickling brook. Some of the blisters had burst, and would no doubt infect. Her soles were bruised and scraped from walking miles barefoot the previous day.

She looked at her torn, threadbare underskirt for long moments before ripping strips from the bottom and using them to bind the worst of the damage. The sandals actually fit a bit better over the added bulk of the makeshift bandages, but even so, she could barely walk for the pain. Steeling herself to go on regardless, she shouldered her meager belongings and limped forward toward the line of mountains visible to the north, keeping her good eye focused on the distant goal.

By mid-morning, she was curled up by the side of the road, having broken her self-imposed vow not to stop, no matter what. Every step was agony. At some point she'd stumbled and, just as she had feared, once she'd gone down she couldn't find the strength to rise again. Now, the sun was beating down on her, making her head swim. Her wineskin was still more than half full after she'd filled it in the brook that morning, but she was afraid to drink it. Once it was gone, she had no way to get more if she couldn't even walk.

She thought that maybe she should want to cry, but all she could do was stare into the distance, blinking occasionally and feeling nothing.

She had no conception of time passing, but when her attention finally caught on distant movement in the direction from which she had come, the sun was high overhead. It was an emaciated donkey hauling a cart, with a figure walking alongside. Kathrael watched and waited, her shawl pulled up across her face, well aware that she couldn't get away even if she'd wanted to. A short time later, the cart pulled up next to her.

"Whoa, there!" said the drover. The donkey came to a stop and immediately cocked its hip to rest a hind foot, head drooping as if in sleep.

Looking up with her good eye, Kathrael tried to get a sense of the stranger. She was struck immediately by his face — his upper lip was split like a rabbit's. The strange gap in the flesh extended up to his nose, disappearing into one of his nostrils. She couldn't help staring; it was odd to see his gums and front teeth through the missing part of his lip, as if he was unfinished, somehow.

Upon seeing where her attention had landed, the man raised a hand, positioning loosely curled fingers in such a way that his disfigurement was hidden — obviously a habitual nervous gesture.

"Are you all right, miss?" he asked, the gap in his lip making some of the words come out oddly.

"No," Kathrael said honestly. "I need help. I have to get north, to the mountains, but I'm not used to traveling. My feet are blistered and bleeding, and I can't walk anymore."

"Oh," said the stranger, still hiding his lip and not meeting her gaze directly. His eyes flickered back to the cart, laden with melons. "Um, my employer would cane me if he found out I'd overloaded the donkey... but, well, you don't look like you weigh much. I could maybe take you to Penth, if you wanted? That's where I'm headed."

His nervous eyes skittered back to her, awaiting her answer. Instinct propelled her to shift her shawl back a bit, enough to give him a glimpse of her face. His breath caught.

"I'd like that very much," she said.

"What happened to your face?" he asked, completely guileless.

"I was burned," she said, rather than getting into the details. "What happened to your lip?"

"I was born this way. The midwife figured someone had put a curse on my mother."

Kathrael smiled up at him softly. "It must not have been a very good curse if she ended up with a son as kind as you."

Perhaps she should have felt guilt at manipulating such a simple soul, but she could find none as he smiled back, letting his hand fall away from his face. "You want to ride on the back?" he asked. "I can pile some of the melons higher to make space, but you'll have to make sure none of them fall out."

"I can do that," she said. "What's your name? I'm Kathrael."

"They call me Mouse, 'cause I look like a rodent," he replied, looking away again.

"What does your mother call you?" Kathrael asked.

"Livvy," he said. "My mother calls me Livvy."

"Well, Livvy, would you mind helping me up? I'm afraid I'm a proper invalid at the moment."

Her rescuer scrambled forward to help her to her feet, and gave her his arm to lean on as she hobbled to the cart. There was a rough board braced across the back of the thing, and Livvy rearranged the produce until he could take it off, giving her a place to sit with her feet dangling down off the edge. She eyed the rather precarious looking pile of melons and leaned back against it, using her arms to block the places where it seemed most in danger of collapsing once they set off. When she was situated, Livvy grinned at her and headed back to the front to get the donkey moving again.

Their progress was slow and bumpy, and Kathrael occasionally had to lunge after a stray melon attempting escape. Conversation was difficult in the rattling cart with Livvy out of her line of sight, walking beside the donkey. She gathered after a few shouted exchanges that he had been sent to Penth by his employer, who was also his uncle, when the man had heard that vendors in the village were paying high prices for produce after blight had destroyed the local crops.

It was a two-day trip, but Livvy's uncle still expected to turn a tidy profit even after giving his nephew enough coin to stay overnight at a town along the way.

"You could... uh... stay with me," he called over his shoulder, stumbling a bit over the words. "If—if you need a place to sleep tonight, I mean."

"In fact, I do. That's very generous of you, Livvy." Kathrael felt herself returning to firmer ground. She recognized that stammering male hopefulness of old. And she knew now that even with her disfigurement, she had the means to pay her debt to her unexpected benefactor using a form of coin that she had long assumed to be completely devalued.

⟜ ⚜ ⟊

Hours later, the cart rattled and juddered its way into a collection of ramshackle buildings clustered near the convergence of two rivers. To call the place a *town* was being somewhat generous, but this was apparently to be their destination for the night.

"We're here!" Livvy called back to her, as he guided the donkey to a falling-down barn near what Kathrael assumed was the way-house. A boy emerged from the sagging structure, all elbows and knees and sharp, jutting cheekbones. He and Livvy conversed in low voices as Kathrael set about the painful process of getting down from the back of the cart.

While it had been a relief not to have to walk, the jouncing, jarring ride had done little more than add a new set of aches to her existing ones. Her head pounded from the combination of exhaustion and the hot sun. Her back and shoulders were knotted with strain, and her feet still felt like they were on fire.

Nevertheless, she was determined to walk into the way-house under her own power, so she gritted her teeth and forced rebellious muscles into use. Her gait was hitching and stilted as she gimped along. Livvy noticed immediately, and hurried to offer her a supporting arm.

"Easy, there," he said. "You look like a stiff wind would fell you."

"I'll be all right," Kathrael said, trying not to lean on him too much. "It's just cramps from sitting in the wagon so long."

Her companion frowned, dubious. "Well, if you say so. I paid the boy to care for the donkey and watch over Uncle's produce tonight. Let me get us a room and you can rest while I see about dinner."

"And here I thought we'd be dining on melons," she joked weakly.

Livvy laughed, his free hand coming up to cover his harelip—a nervous tic. "Gods, no," he said. "At this time of year, even the thought of eating melon makes me ill."

The proprietor of the way-house was a sour-faced old man who eyed them with suspicion as they entered. Kathrael twitched her shawl forward a bit more over the side of her face and straightened away from Livvy's supporting arm as much as possible.

She let the men's voices wash over her and tried not to draw attention to herself as they haggled. How different things had once been, when drawing men's attention was her livelihood. And yet, she had drawn Livvy's attention easily enough today. She let him help her up a short flight of stairs that squeaked and flexed alarmingly under their weight, down an uneven hallway to a crooked doorway standing invitingly open.

The room could have been moldy and infested with fleas, and it still would have been the nicest place she'd slept in for weeks. Surprisingly, though, it was fairly well kept. The straw mattress sat on an actual bed frame rather than the floor—which had been swept recently. The small table nearby held two candles and a flint striker.

Livvy deposited her on the edge of the bed, and she had to stifle a moan of pleasure at the idea of sleeping on something softer than the ground.

"Why don't you lie down for a bit while I bring up some food?" he asked.

She smiled and nodded silently, though she had no intention of lying down. The gods knew when she'd be able to get up again, once she did.

Dinner was thick gruel and weak ale that smelled like horse piss. Kathrael wolfed it down without tasting it, manners forgotten in the face of hot, nourishing food. When the bowl was scraped clean and the flagon, emptied to the last dregs, she came back to herself enough to notice Livvy watching her while trying not to be obvious about it. A faint flush of embarrassment traveled up the unscarred side of her neck to color her face.

She willed it down. After tomorrow—assuming Livvy was still willing to take her all the way to Penth—she would never see him again. Let him stare his fill. At least he had helped her.

"You, um, you must be tired," he said when they had both finished the humble meal. "I can... take a couple of blankets and sleep on the floor, I guess."

She stilled. It was time to pay for her passage, aching body or no.

THREE

Kathrael loosened the frayed laces holding the front of her bodice together, and looked up at Livvy with her good eye. "Don't be silly," she said. "You should sleep on the bed with me."

Livvy caught his breath, and Kathrael could see his gaze darken in the candlelight. He started to speak, but the words caught in his throat. He had to swallow hard before he could reply. "I've never slept with a girl before. You know... because of my lip. Father always says no girl is likely to want me, and I should just get used to it."

"But that's not true. I want you, Livvy," Kathrael lied. She glanced down, a calculated move. "Unless you find my scars repulsive..."

It was a surprise how much the beat of silence affected her, as if her heart had suddenly decided that this awkward young man's opinion of her mattered, without bothering to consult her head. She looked up again to find him staring at her open-mouthed.

"No!" he said quickly. "No, I'm just surprised is all. I never expected—"

"Come here then, and sit next to me," Kathrael told him. He did, carefully not touching her. Nervous excitement rolled off of him in waves. She continued, "So, you've never even gone to the temple, then? Dallied with the novices?"

He shook his head and looked down. "Father said there wasn't any point. It would just make me want what I couldn't have."

Kathrael angled her body toward him, one hand coming to rest on his tense thigh as the old, familiar dance came back to her. "Well, that's simply not true. I'm sure you're not the only person in Rhyth with a harelip, Livvy. Perhaps you'll find a nice girl who looks like you do, and you'll fall in love with each other."

Several expressions chased each other across Livvy's open face as she watched, and slid her hand a little higher. "Or... maybe a girl with scars?" he asked, utterly artless.

The smile Kathrael pasted on felt like it would crack her damaged face. "Perhaps so," she managed. To forestall any further conversation, she cupped his cock through his loose trousers, drawing a groan from him.

He was large and hard, and when she knelt between his legs on sore, creaking knees to unlace his clothing and free him from his smallclothes, he grasped the edge of the mattress tightly with both hands. His prick reeked of stale sweat, and she had to battle nausea as she sucked him off. He was the first man she had serviced since her face was ruined, and the scars around the left side of her mouth pulled painfully as her lips stretched around him. Thankfully, his lack of experience had him coming down her throat in great spurts after mere moments.

Later, she lay back on the bed, making encouraging noises as he rutted into her. There was no oil-filled lamp in the room, nor was there any grease, or anything else she could use to ease the way into her dry passage. Despite the gob of spit that she'd managed to surreptitiously smear over him, the familiar push-pull between her legs went beyond the usual vague discomfort, spilling over into full-fledged pain as flesh that had lain untouched for months stretched to accommodate Livvy's large cock.

She had learned years ago to retreat inside her mind at such times, but something about letting another person this close to her scars and hurts brought a terrible sense of vulnerability to the fore. By the time Livvy finally cried out and shuddered through his second release, Kathrael's skin was crawling in a way it hadn't for years.

Afterward, she lay very still and quiet in his sweaty grip. When his loud snores filled the room, she wriggled free and pulled on her ruined dress with jerky, uncoordinated movements, covering herself. Then, she curled up on the rough wooden boards of the floor and fell into an exhausted sleep.

A hand on her shoulder woke her the following morning, and she was unable to suppress her flinch. Sleeping with someone nearby who wasn't Vesh was a terrifying prospect. She never would have let herself drift off had she not already been on the verge of collapse.

"Hey," Livvy said. "S-sorry. I didn't mean to startle you. Why are you on the floor?"

Kathrael's tongue felt thick and dry as she unstuck it from the roof of her mouth to reply.

"I was... too hot," she said eventually, after casting around for a reasonable sounding excuse. "I didn't want to wake you with my tossing and turning."

Livvy frowned, looking unhappy, but he only said, "Oh. I see."

"Is it time to leave?" Kathrael asked, hoping to distract him.

"Yeah," he said. "Did, uh, did you still want to come with me the rest of the way to Penth?"

What Kathrael *wanted* was to flee the room and never see him again, but that wouldn't get her any closer to Draebard. "If you're willing to take me, yes."

Livvy nodded. "All right. Well. You'll have to get out of the cart before we reach the edge of the village. If any of Uncle's contacts tell him I've been taking on passengers, I'll be in big trouble."

"That's fine," Kathrael said. "I appreciate you helping me, Livvy. You're a good person."

In fact, Livvy's plan sounded better than fine. If he dropped her off on the road somewhere, he wouldn't expect a repeat of last night before they parted. Which suited Kathrael right down to the ground.

Livvy blushed, embarrassed by the compliment. "It's nothing, really. I just like to help where I can, you know?" He cleared his throat. "If you, uh, want to wash, there's a ewer of water and a bowl in the hallway. I'll see if I can talk the innkeeper out of some bread or something, and then we should go."

"Of course." Kathrael forced another smile and hobbled into the hall to rinse off her face.

Livvy disappeared down the rickety stairs, and she looked around the now-deserted space to make sure she was truly alone. The other doors were closed and no sounds emerged from within, so she hiked up her torn skirts and ran the damp cloth between her legs. There was no blood, thankfully, though her flesh was raw and aching. The cool cloth went some way toward soothing it, but she was nearly as sore from last night's coupling as she had been after her first few painful times at the tender age of thirteen.

She sighed. It would get better in a couple of days, and it seemed unlikely that she would be called upon to repeat the performance anytime soon.

When Livvy returned with a couple of hunks of two-day-old brown bread, she was as ready to face the day as she could be, under the circumstances. She knew she would barely have made it half a league today if forced to walk on her own, but the food and drink combined with a few hours of sleep had at least revived her enough that she could manage sitting on the back of the melon wagon for a few more hours.

It was cooler than the previous day, and cloudy. At first, Livvy kept up an intermittent stream of banal small talk, shouted awkwardly back and forth between his place in front with the donkey and her perch on the back of the wagon. By late morning, it began to rain—a steady drizzle—and the talk dried up even as the parched dirt turned to mud. Kathrael let the chilly water drip down her hair and the back of her neck, shivering a bit as her wet clothing clung to her skin.

She was so thin these days that she had no defense against changes in temperature, and she dreaded the coming winter. Perhaps, she thought as another round of trembling took her, she would be dead by then. Perhaps that would be preferable — particularly if she was able to gain her revenge first.

Late in the afternoon, the cart rolled to a stop on the uneven road. The rain had finally ceased, and the returning sun steamed the moisture back out of the ground, making the air thick and humid. Livvy appeared at the rear of the wagon.

"Time for me to get off?" Kathrael asked, and the young man nodded reluctantly.

"Penth is in the valley, just over the crest of this hill," he said. "It's not far. I, uh, wish I could keep you with me..."

Livvy was a sweet, decent young man, for all that he was awkward and uncouth. Even so, something about the wording made Kathrael's stomach churn and a shiver travel up the length of her spine.

Keep you with me...

Like a possession. Like an object — something to be *owned*.

The pasted-on smile seemed harder to conjure each time she summoned it. "I have to keep heading north, Livvy. And you have to get back to your uncle. Remember what I said, though. I'm sure there's someone out there for you. You just have to find her."

Livvy's face twisted through a complicated mixture of hope and disappointment, before he darted forward and kissed her undamaged cheek. She forced herself not jerk away from the contact.

"You'll be all right, though?" he asked.

"Of course I will," she said airily, as if such a question was ridiculous. "Go on. Off with you, now. Thank you again for helping me."

Livvy caught his lower lip in his teeth and chewed on it before nodding and turning away. A moment later, the cart rattled forward, leaving Kathrael standing on the side of the road with her waterskin and satchel, sandals clasped in her hand. She looked past the slow-moving cart and the young man shooting occasional glances over his shoulder at her as he crested the hill leading down to Penth.

The mountains had been at her back as she traveled in the wagon, but they were noticeably closer now than they had been yesterday. A genuine smile flickered over her features for an instant as she looked at the rugged peaks. Her satchel still contained food and a few precious coins. The waterskin was heavy at her shoulder. Her feet ached, but not with the unbearable stabbing pain that had brought her to her knees the morning before. The blisters were already starting to scab over, protected by the bindings torn from her skirts.

She could keep going.

Kathrael started limping slowly toward the village of Penth.

⚬⚬⚬

The blight had obviously hit Penth hard. The fields outside the village were mostly wilted and yellow, with immature, wrinkled vegetables withering on the vine. The air smelled of rot. In the town itself, people in the street gave her wary glances, their eyes flicking up only briefly before returning to the ground in front of them. Gaunt cheeks and sunken eyes were everywhere. The scent of desperation clung to them.

Kathrael kept her head down and tried to blend in, aided in doing so by her own jutting, starvation-sharpened bones. Penth was a good-sized settlement, somewhat larger than she had assumed it would be. As she wandered the streets toward the center of town, she began to realize that she was once again trapped by circumstance.

She'd had vague thoughts of using her meager collection of coins to purchase supplies for the next leg of her journey — the mountain crossing. The sad collection of food she now carried might conceivably suffice to get her *to* the mountains, but it would come nowhere close to getting her *over* them.

Livvy's generosity had gained her two meals she hadn't needed to acquire for herself, but it had also landed her in a place where food was scarce and unbelievably costly. There was a crowd in the marketplace; its mood restless as townsfolk vied for meat and produce that simply wasn't there.

After only a few minutes of walking stall-to-stall, Kathrael learned that her handful of coppers would buy her precisely nothing of use in Penth. The ugly atmosphere soon drove her onto a side street, the fine hair at the back of her neck prickling with unease.

From ahead came the sound of another crowd, this one punctuated by cries of excitement and occasional laughter rather than angry muttering. Curious, Kathrael followed the noise until the narrow street opened out into a second open square, paved with flagstones and surrounded by two-story, whitewashed buildings.

At one corner of the square, a collection of wagons and people dominated the crowd's attention. She could see a large number of children clustered near the front, laughing and hopping up and down in an attempt to see over the shoulders of those in front of them. As was her habit, Kathrael kept to the shadows and skirted the edge of the crowd until she reached a set of steps leading up to a sheltered doorway. There, she was able to get a decent view of what was going on without attracting attention.

It was a band of traveling entertainers, as she had half-suspected. A well-fed man in flamboyant dress stood atop a small wooden platform, waving his hands and sweet-talking the crowd. With few other options open to her at the moment, she settled in to watch for a bit.

The troupe was a small one, but included some very strange — even shocking — individuals. An exceptionally tall, skeletally thin man danced with a tiny, misshapen women who would barely have come up to Kathrael's waist. At the end of the dance, the woman clambered up the spokes of the wagon wheel so the man could take her in his arms like a child. They kissed to the sound of raucous jeers from the children, and titters from the adults.

A lad with no arms sat at a wooden table near the raised platform, playing a game of dice using his toes. Occasionally, he would pause to grasp a flagon between the soles of his feet, contorting himself to lift it to his lips and take a drink.

Another man—normal looking, though his expansive stomach set him immediately apart from the skinny townsfolk—made his way through the crowd, a young boy with large, sad eyes balanced on his hip. A girl the same age trailed behind him, one small hand gripping the bottom edge of the man's intricately embroidered tunic. In his free hand, he carried an upturned hat.

Kathrael was not close enough to hear the conversation as he moved from person to person in the crowd, but after a few soft words from the unhappy boy-child, many of the audience members who had been singled out gasped in surprise and nodded, sometimes taking a step back in shock. More often than not, they or the people around them would flip coins into the hat immediately afterward. She wondered what caused the reaction, but did not dare get closer to find out.

One thing was certain, however. The performers were making money. Quite a bit of it, in fact.

Half-formed ideas and plans circled Kathrael's mind as she continued to watch the spectacle. She was in a strange town, where the people were already desperate and unlikely to have much sympathy for a beggar, especially a hideously scarred one. Before her stood men who had money—enough money that the upturned hat was already sagging under the weight of coins after only a few minutes. If she followed them to wherever they stayed for the night...

Well. They would need to go to sleep sometime.

She'd have to make it to a town beyond the reach of the blight, but the money in the hat would be enough to buy food, and sturdy boots, and new clothes for her journey. Movement from one of the wagons caught her attention, breaking her free of her thoughts. The back of the cart was enclosed by bars, like a cage or a cell. Within, a tawny, four-legged shape rose and stretched, jaws cracking in a wide yawn to reveal sharp fangs.

It was a lion—thin and covered in scars, but still one of the most beautiful things Kathrael had ever seen. She caught her breath, unable to look away. The animal swept its ears back, and green-flecked eyes locked on hers without warning, pinning her in place in the sheltered doorway. Her heart jolted and began to beat double-time.

She tore her gaze away with considerable difficulty when the man on the platform raised his voice again, addressing the crowd.

"Ladies and gentlemen! I give you the main attraction. The king of predators, tamed and reduced to the gentleness of a kitten by the indomitable power of my will!" He turned to his partner, still carrying the boy while the girl clung to him. "Laronzo, *release the lion!*"

There were several shouts of fear around the square as the second man stepped up to the wagon and unlatched the barred door. Mothers hurried forward to drag their children away from the front rows. The lion shook itself and jumped down from the back of the cart before padding over to the raised platform and leaping nimbly onto it to stand next to the leader of the company.

"Now, now," said the man. "There's no cause for alarm, I assure you. Your young ones are as safe as they would be with a baby lamb. Watch!"

His partner joined him on the dais with the two children, and plopped the boy in his arms unceremoniously onto the lion's back. The child immediately grabbed the animal's scruffy mane, completely without fear. A moment later, the little girl wrapped her arms around the lion's neck, and Kathrael was hit with a flash of memory so strong it nearly sent her to her knees.

The wolf growled, its hackles rising as it crouched in front of her, keeping the overseer with the whip at bay. Kathrael gaped up at the legend made flesh standing less than an arm's length away, hope surging in her young breast.

She righted herself from where she lay sprawled on the ground and crept forward, wrapping her arms around the wolf's bristling shoulders fearlessly.

"Lupi?" she asked, tears running unchecked down her cheeks. "The gods have finally sent you for us, after so long?"

Kathrael thrust a hand out to steady herself against the doorframe behind her, caught between the past and the present even as the audience looked on in amazement.

"As you see," the man continued, "this beast is completely under my control. Only the strongest of wills can overpower the spirit of a lion, and I am pleased to count myself among that number."

The lion wrapped a large paw around the little girl and swiped its broad tongue across her hip, drawing a giggle from her. The audience gasped, but she only clung harder and buried her face in its mane. Kathrael stared as if entranced as the man on the platform motioned for his partner to drag the children away, and then guided the animal through a series of tricks as one might do with a pampered lapdog.

He seemed totally unconcerned for his safety, supremely confident of his control over the beast. Kathrael wondered if she was imagining the sense that the lion was humoring its jailer, biding its time until... *what*?

At the end of the show, however, the beast leapt lightly back up into its cage. It flopped down next to the bars and yawned again, its eyes returning unerringly to Kathrael in her shadowed hiding place. She couldn't help the shiver of reaction that skittered up her spine.

That night, she sat huddled in a small hollow behind two scrubby bushes on the outskirts of Penth, waiting for the moon to rise. Exhaustion circled like a carrion bird, threatening to swoop in and carry her off to unintended sleep at any moment. She knew, though, that this might be her only chance to get the money she needed to continue her journey.

There was every possibility that the traveling entertainers would be heading off for greener pastures in the morning.

The group had chosen a campsite a little way outside of the town. Kathrael had been hard-pressed to keep up with them on her aching feet, even with the relatively slow pace of the heavily laden wagons.

Something rustled in the darkness and she blinked her eyes open with a jerk, unaware of having closed them. To her relief, she found the camp illuminated only by a faint silver glow of moonlight. The two men she took to be the owners had finally retired to their enclosed caravans, and the fire had burned down to embers.

Earlier, before night had fallen, she'd watched as the pair herded the others into various caravans with bars on the windows, and locked them inside. It made something inside her itch and prickle, but she told herself firmly that it wasn't why she was here. These people were not her responsibility.

And yet, a voice in her head taunted, *you vowed to Elarra that you would free all the slaves in the south. Does that not make them your responsibility?*

At least the little voice didn't sound like Vesh this time. Yes, she had vowed to her sister when they were children that she would lead an uprising against the slavers. But first, she *would* have her revenge. She deserved that much out of life, surely. And *revenge* meant getting across the mountains.

In the moonlight, the camp was completely quiet. Kathrael slipped on silent feet from her hiding place and into the circle of wagons. Someone had left a crust of bread and the dregs of a cup of wine next to the remains of the fire. Kathrael ate and drank without thought, finishing every drop, every crumb.

She was just looking around, trying to decide the best way to find where the money was stashed without waking anyone, when a soft noise pierced the silence.

"*Psst!*"

Her heart thudded in her ribcage and she froze, *caught*, but no cry of alarm followed that first quiet sound. She cast around in the near darkness, silently cursing her blind, useless left eye. Eventually, her gaze came to rest on the lion's cage. The animal was nowhere to be seen. Instead, a naked man crouched inside facing her, his arms resting casually through the bars as he watched her.

FOUR

Favian of Draebard took a deep breath and knocked on the door to the High Priest's private quarters in the back of the temple. He'd always known it would be a challenge to convince his mentor that he was truly ready to undergo his novitiate into the priesthood, but the situation was starting to become ridiculous. It was time to speak plainly, and finally hash out the argument once and for all.

There were low voices coming from within, though the conversation paused at the sound of his knocking. As it was fairly late in the evening, it came as no surprise to Favian that the High Priest was not alone in his rooms. And indeed, it was not Senovo, but Carivel — Draebard's Horse Mistress — who opened the door for him.

"Oh! Hello, Favian. Come on in," she said with a sheepish smile, rubbing a hand over the back of her neck as she stood back to let him pass. She was barefoot, dressed casually in a man's tunic and breeches — clearly not intending to leave anytime soon. "We were just discussing some village business. Have you eaten? There's a bit of roast left."

"Hi, Carivel. Thanks, but I ate earlier with the other acolytes. I just need to speak with Senovo, if he has time. You and Andoc as well, I guess, since you're here."

Carivel mouthed a silent "*ahh*" of understanding, and waved him into the room.

Chief Andoc looked up as he entered, a smile brightening his ruggedly handsome face. "Join us, Favian. What can we do for you tonight?"

Next to him, Senovo leaned back in his chair and lowered the goblet he'd been holding to the table before him. His black hair hung loose over his shoulders, freed from the tightly plaited queue favored by members of the priesthood. He raised a dark, finely sculpted eyebrow at his protégé, a question in his gold-green eyes.

Andoc and Carivel had been Favian's formal guardians since he lost his father several years ago. His mother had died giving birth to his sister, Frella, when he was still quite young. After his father was killed in an accident while traveling, Senovo had immediately taken both Favian and Frella under his wing, welcoming them into the temple and ensuring that their day-to-day needs were met. Soon afterward, Andoc and Carivel had used their positions of authority within the village to make a more permanent arrangement for the siblings. None of the three had ever attempted to replace his dead parents, but nonetheless, he and Frella had quickly come to rely on them as family.

Favian was more grateful to the eccentric trio seated before him than he could express. Now, though, he needed to make Senovo, in particular, understand that it was time for him to move on to the next stage in his life. He swallowed, and licked his dry lips to wet them.

"High Priest Senovo," he said, "I formally request that you either agree to let me undergo my novitiate and elevate me to the priesthood, or throw me out of the temple altogether."

Understanding flooded Senovo's features. "Favian—" he began, looking pained.

Favian didn't give him a chance to continue. "I have completed all of the requirements to join the priesthood, and expressed my desire to dedicate myself to the gods' service. *Several times,* in fact," he added dryly. "I can only assume that your continued resistance to my request means you do not consider me worthy of becoming a novice priest."

Senovo closed his eyes for a moment and sighed. "Of course it doesn't, Favian," he said, "as you know perfectly well. I merely wish to ensure that you truly understand what you will be undertaking, Little Brother. Once done, it can never be undone."

Favian relaxed his stiff stance enough to lean his hands on the table, meeting Senovo's gaze evenly across the expanse of wood. "I know you're only trying to protect me, Elder Brother," he replied, echoing the less formal term of address used between members of the temple, "but in the end, it's my life. *My* choice."

Andoc, along with Carivel, had been watching the confrontation silently. Now, the village chief looked at Senovo and rolled his eyes. "It's not as if you haven't tried every trick you could think of to talk him out of it already, *amadi,*" he pointed out, one hand resting on the back of Senovo's chair with casual familiarity. "He wants to be a priest, and he wants to be a eunuch. It's a completely different situation than the one you suffered as a young man."

Carivel ran a hand through her close-cropped hair, ruffling it. "There's nothing that says you have to do it personally, is there? The castration, I mean," she asked Senovo with a frown.

The High Priest pinched the bridge of his nose between his forefinger and thumb. He was silent for a long moment before speaking again. "No. No, there is not." He looked back up at Favian, pinning him with an intense gaze. "Very well, Favian. Give me your word that you are truly running *toward* the priesthood—not running *away* from your physical desires or inclinations... and I will agree to your request."

Favian forced himself to hold that too-knowing gaze and reply in an even voice, "You have my word."

It was the truth, now that Ithric was gone, seemingly for good—sneaking away from Draebard months ago in the middle of the night, without so much as an explanation or a goodbye.

Well... it was *mostly* the truth, at any rate, and Favian refused to feel guilty about the small deceit.

Senovo's eyes burned into his for another beat before he blinked and said, "In that case, I will speak to Healer Sagdea. She is the most qualified person in Draebard to perform the procedure, in any case. Brother Eiridan can assist her in my stead."

"Congratulations, Favian," Carivel said quietly. "I've always said you were going to be a terrific priest someday."

"We're all very proud of you, you know," Andoc put in. "It took courage to beard our stubborn High Priest in his den and state your case. Carivel's right—you'll make a great priest."

"Thank you," Favian said, the words meant for all three of them, but his attention still focused on Senovo.

Senovo huffed out a breath. "Don't thank me yet, Favian. You may assume that my reluctance to see you castrated stems merely from my own unfortunate initiation into the Priest's Guild, but there is also another matter to address."

Favian felt a moment's confusion before he realized what Senovo meant.

"Ah," he said. "Right. I'd almost forgotten about the dream."

Andoc's expression sharpened immediately, and Carivel drew in an audible breath.

"*The dream*?" Andoc echoed. "What dream are we discussing, here, and why is this the first I've heard about it?"

Favian opened his mouth to speak, but Senovo beat him to it. "Favian has many dreams, Andoc. He shared this one with me not long after the battle at Llanmeer, but it didn't seem relevant until his novitiate approached. It did, however, have many of the hallmarks of a true vision. Favian?"

Favian cleared his throat. "Yes, it felt like a seer's dream at the time. You have to understand, it's been years ago, now, so it's pretty hazy, I'm

afraid. But I was definitely lying in my room, recovering from the novitiation ceremony. I think it
was a few days afterward. And there was this
girl…"

Later, after his guardians had extracted every detail
from him that he could remember, Favian left them
to their discussion and went to find Limdya. She
had offered earlier to keep his sister Frella company while he spoke to Senovo, and she'd made
him promise to tell her everything once he returned.

   Limdya and her two sisters had been orphaned
in the Alyrion attack on Draebard, only a few
months before Favian's own father had died. She'd
been a huge help to both him and Frella as they
dealt with their grief and fear for the future. In return, Favian had assisted her wherever he could
with her job at the horse pens — she had been the
first girl ever accepted as an apprentice there. Well,
the first girl if you didn't count Carivel, who had
originally gained her position at the pens because
everyone thought she was a boy.

   At any rate, Limdya had never been allowed
near the horses when she was growing up, so she
was at a considerable disadvantage compared to
the other apprentices. Since Favian had worked at
the pens before becoming a temple acolyte, he was
happy to tutor her in horsemanship whenever he
was able. Though he was confident his decision to
leave the pens and join the temple had been the
right one, he still missed the horses, and it was

good to get out with them when his other duties allowed.

In the beginning of their friendship, it quickly became obvious that Limdya had something of a crush on him. Which was, well... *awkward*. Though Favian had always craved close relationships and emotional intimacy with females and males alike, he had only ever been sexually attracted to men. Unfortunately, such liaisons were strictly taboo in Eburosi society — to be caught with another man could result in exile at the very least.

Not that Favian thought Andoc would actually throw him out of the village, of course. Rumor had it that their fearless chieftain had entertained his share of male lovers in his own misspent youth. And there was also the fact that Andoc and Carivel were handfasted to a eunuch High Priest — though the controversial three-way relationship had brought its own measure of scandal when it first became public knowledge.

Still, a eunuch being with a man was *different*. Not encouraged, exactly. But... tolerated.

A few months after they had become close, Favian haltingly told Limdya all of this, terrified that she would pull away in disgust once she knew of his unnatural leanings. She sat very still and quiet for several long moments after his flood of words had finally dried up, before leaning forward and pulling him into a tight hug.

"It's not fair," she'd said, her voice full of sadness on his behalf. "It's no more fair than saying that women can't tend the animals or men can't be healers. It's just so... *stupid* — all of it!" She pulled back, wiping away tears. "Sorry, I'm being an idiot." She gave a wet laugh, obviously directed at herself. "Apparently, I have a type, when it comes to men. The *unavailable* type."

"You'll find someone, Limdya," he'd told her with complete certainty. He placed a kiss on her forehead, even as relief poured through him that she hadn't reacted with anger or hurt. "If it weren't for the sex thing, we could go get handfasted tomorrow as far as I'm concerned. I *do* love you. I just don't... *desire* you."

Her smile was watery. "That's a tempting offer," she said. "I want children, though. Lots of them. And I *do* want to be desired, Favian." Her eyes grew far away. "Maybe someday..." When she looked at him again, her usual playful good humor had returned. "I'm afraid you'll just have to put up with me as a friend."

He'd smiled back at her and made some light quip, but inside, he'd longed for someone in his life who was more than *just a friend*.

As it turned out, Limdya hadn't needed to wait long before love found her — in the form of Dalon, Carivel's assistant at the horse pens. He was a few years older than her, and their relative positions in the village made it awkward at first, but Favian was convinced that their feelings for each other were genuine. They had been together for almost two years, and were now discussing entering into a more permanent arrangement in the fall.

Still, Limdya had made good on her promise of continued friendship, and she was the one he went to whenever he needed support or a sympathetic ear from someone close to his own age. Now, she was waiting for him with Frella in the room he and his sister shared in the temple.

Frella must have heard his footsteps approaching, because she yanked open the door, eyes wide, and asked, "*Well*?"

"He said yes," Favian confirmed, and caught Frella when she squealed with excitement and threw herself into his arms.

Limdya appeared in the doorway, a smile making her round, soft features glow. "Congratulations, Favian. When is the ceremony?"

"Two days from now," he told her, flooded with a strange combination of relief and nervousness.

She nodded her understanding before turning sober. "What about the dream, though? You remember the one I mean? Did you tell them about the girl with the knife?"

"Yes, I did." Favian disentangled himself from his sister and crossed to sit down on his bed. "Senovo knew already, but I recounted everything I could remember about it to all three of them, which unfortunately wasn't as much as I'd have liked."

"It might not even happen, you know," said Limdya, though she sounded doubtful. "Not all of your dreams come true."

"Thank goodness," Frella put in, her face screwing up in disgust. "Remember that one you told us about where no one in the village could find any clothes, and everyone had to go around naked? *That* would have been a real nightmare."

Limdya laughed, clear and light. "It all depends on the person in question, sweetheart. Am I right, Favian?"

Favian blushed to the roots of his hair, remembering with perfect clarity how Ithric's body had looked in the odd dream—lean and perfect and covered with old scars. "No comment," he said.

"Eww," groaned Frella. "Why do you two have to say things like that?"

Limdya only laughed harder. "It'll all make sense someday, sweetheart—you'll see. And may the gods help the male population of Draebard when that day finally comes."

At the age of ten, Frella had already perfected the art of the offended flounce. She employed it now. "Ugh," she said over her shoulder in a tone of disgust. "You're *awful*, Limdya! I don't have to listen to this. I'm going to go and tell the others the news!"

"Don't mention the dream," Favian called after her. "I don't want it to turn into some great big deal!"

Ever since he had begun to exhibit signs of the second sight at the age of fourteen, Favian's gift had been a mixed blessing, at best. At first, he had only dreamed of catastrophic events—terrible things that left him wracked with guilt when they came to pass in reality. Later, he started to foresee stupid, meaningless things. People slipping and falling in the mud after a rainstorm, or spilling their drinks. Piglets escaping from the hog pens—that sort of thing.

Eventually, his dreams seemed to settle along a sort of middle ground, of things that were important, but not world ending. Possibly this was only because Draebard had been relatively quiet in recent years, since the war. Whatever the case, Favian wasn't about to complain. He didn't think he could have maintained his sanity with death and destruction playing out behind his closed eyelids at night.

"Here," said Limdya, drawing him back to his surroundings. "I brought some ale from the cookhouse. We'll celebrate with a toast."

"Thanks," Favian said, accepting a cup from her. Limdya's older sisters still ran their late mother's cookhouse, and even though Limdya no longer worked there, she always seemed able to get the best food and drink for any occasion.

"To Novice Favian," Limdya toasted with a smile, raising her own clay cup.

Favian could not contain his pleased grin as he touched his cup to hers. "It does have kind of a nice ring to it, doesn't it?"

"It does indeed, my friend," Limdya agreed. "So, are you going to have a last fling before the ceremony? See your balls off in style, so to speak?"

Favian choked on his mouthful of ale. "Limdya!" he said after he managed to clear his throat. "Be serious! Who exactly in Draebard am I going to fuck?"

Limdya sobered. "I *was* being serious. You could have a night with one of the novices, couldn't you? Or maybe even another acolyte. Even if people found out, I don't think they'd hold it against you. You're *almost* a eunuch now, after all."

He laughed, but it was a weak sound. "Oh, gods, no. I couldn't. It would be like bedding a family member." He shook his head and gave a little shudder, dismissing the frankly disturbing image. "Besides," he added, "I don't really go for eunuchs."

Limdya let out an unladylike snort of amusement, as Favian had intended. It seemed she wasn't ready to let it pass so easily, though. "I just think it's sad that you'll never get a chance to really experience it. As a man, I mean. I know eunuchs still *do* have sex, of course—some of them, at least. But it must be really different for them, right?" She paused, frowning. "Don't you want to at least know what it's like?"

Favian looked down, studying his ale. "I do know what it's like," he said quietly.

Limdya was silent for a long moment, before blurting, "Oh, my gods. You don't mean... you and Ithric—?"

"Once," Favian confirmed, and added in a voice laced heavily with irony, "right before he left, in fact."

"But I thought you two could barely stand each other!" Limdya said.

"That's because Ithric is an infuriating ass," Favian muttered.

Limdya made a dismissive noise. "*Dalon* is an infuriating ass, but that doesn't mean I'm not in love with him." Favian could practically see her rearranging things inside her head to accommodate this new information. "Merciful Utarr. Everything makes *so* much more sense now. He broke your heart, didn't he?"

Favian scoffed to hide the way his chest ached. "Don't be ridiculous. I'm fine. It could never have worked between us anyway. What would a novice priest want with a scruffy, itinerant shape-shifter?"

What, indeed?

Limdya opened her mouth to say something else that Favian was fairly sure he didn't want to hear. Fortunately, approaching footsteps and a ragged cheer from the hallway interrupted her. Moments later, several of Favian's fellow acolytes and novices poured into the too-small room, armed with flagons of wine liberated from the refectory.

Reston grabbed Favian in a one-armed hug and ruffled his hair. "Congratulations, Little Brother. Frella just told us the good news. Think the gods will forgive us in the morning if we get you thoroughly plastered tonight to celebrate?"

Favian took a deep breath and gave his melancholy thoughts a firm shove to one side. "I think there's only one way to find out. Pour me a cup?"

FIVE

Kathrael approached the lion cage without realizing she was doing it, getting close enough to confirm that the animal really wasn't inside.

"You were at the performance this evening," said the young man, his voice pitched low. "What are you doing here?"

His features were angular — pleasing to the eye in the faint illumination, though with a heavy northern cast to the brow and chin. His nose had been broken at some point. Whoever set it had done a better job than Hameen had done with Vesh's nose, but there was still a decided lump about a third of the way down its length. His tangled mane of wavy hair was dark in the moonlight, but not black. Brown, perhaps. His lean, sinewy body was covered in a patchwork of scars, visible as thin silver lines against his darker skin.

His eyes were piercing and strangely intense.

"Where is the lion?" Kathrael blurted.

"It's around," the stranger said, still seeming strangely relaxed for someone crouched naked in a dangerous animal's cage and talking to an intruder in the middle of the night.

With a sudden flash of mortification, Kathrael realized that her shawl had fallen to her shoulders, leaving her face uncovered. The man hadn't even reacted.

"Why are you here?" he asked again, still watching her with those strange, faintly glowing eyes.

Once again, words came out of Kathrael's mouth before she consciously decided to speak them. "I'm going to steal money from the men who own you."

The young man's eyes widened, his expression caught between amusement and offense. "They don't *own* me!"

"You're naked and locked in a cage," Kathrael pointed out, though it seemed highly unlikely he could have missed those two facts.

The stranger's smile was sharp, dangerous, and short-lived. "Locking me in a cage helps them sleep better at night. Anyway, I can't leave this place quite yet." His gaze turned assessing. "You could do something for me, though."

Kathrael's own expression turned wary. "You're not going to raise the alarm?"

"Not now, certainly. Maybe in a bit."

By rights, Kathrael should have run at that point. Instead, she glared at him through her good eye.

He ignored her sour look and continued, "You won't be able to get anywhere near Turvick's money stash, you know. He keeps it under his mattress... and he's a light sleeper."

"Then I'll knock him out first," Kathrael said.

"You could try that, I guess," the man agreed. "Of course, then you'd still have to deal with Laronzo. They sleep in the same caravan."

A bush rustled nearby. Kathrael jumped, but it was only some small night creature, probably looking for scraps. Her heart began to sink as she cast around for ways to get a bag of money away from two men twice her size within the enclosed space of a caravan… and came up empty.

"So, will you help me?" the stranger asked.

"You want me to let you out? Why should I help you?"

He looked at her oddly. "No, I told you, I can't leave just yet. And, well, to be more accurate, it wouldn't actually be *me* you'd be helping. You'd be helping the twins. They need to get away from here — the sooner, the better."

Kathrael had no idea why she was still standing around talking. And yet… "What twins?"

"You saw them earlier. The two children. This place isn't good for them."

She remembered the very young boy and girl who had clung fearlessly to the lion. Remembered their huge, sad eyes. "What can I do for a couple of children barely off the breast?" she asked sharply. "I can't even keep *myself* fed and clothed!"

The man didn't react to her sudden anger. "The boy reads minds," he said in a quiet voice. "Thoughts, emotions, intentions. Turvick and Laronzo are cold-hearted thugs, driven by greed. The others here are frightened. Trapped. Humiliated at being forced to display their differences for people's entertainment, day in and day out; locked up like animals at night."

Instinctive, superstitious wonder flooded Kathrael, followed closely by nausea at the idea of someone so young constantly having such ugliness forced into his mind.

The stranger continued. "Laronzo drags the boy through the crowd during performances, telling the rubes what they're thinking. It hurts Dex to be surrounded by strangers like that, but if he resists, they separate him from his sister." His eyes grew hard and dangerous. "I don't know the nature of her gift. I don't know if anyone does. She never speaks—not that I've heard, at least. But if she and her brother are forcibly parted by more than a few dozen paces, they scream in agony as though they're both being burned by flames."

Kathrael choked on a gasp, and swallowed it down harshly. "What are you asking of me? I told you, I'm barely keeping my own body and spirit together."

"I'm asking you to rescue them and take them back to their family. Turvick stole them from the village of Darveen a little over a week ago. It's east of here—only two days' walk from Penth."

She was silent for a long moment, listening to the tiny night noises around the camp. "I don't have enough food left for a two-day journey with children," she said eventually.

The stranger raised a sardonic eyebrow, his expression turning wry. "The money stash is well-guarded, but the provision wagon—not so much." He jerked his chin toward a cart off to their left. "It's right over there. It's not locked. Help yourself, just leave enough for the rest of us for a day or two. Food's scarce around Penth."

Kathrael's eyes widened and she hurried over to the wagon. As promised, it was laden with wooden boxes—none of them secured. Her stomach growled, and she immediately set about stuffing as much food as she could carry into her leather satchel. When it was full, she slung a second wineskin over her shoulder, and rearranged everything as best she could in the boxes to hide the pilferage.

"The twins are in the caravan behind you," came the quiet voice from the lion's cage.

She stilled. There was nothing to stop her leaving with the food and never looking back. It was madness to try to take children with her through the wilderness to Darveen. The twins were, what? Three, perhaps four years of age?

She thought of frantic toddlers screaming as they were ripped away from mothers, from siblings—families torn from each other and dragged onto the auction block. Sold and shipped across the land like cattle. Her heart thudded painfully in her chest and she had to stand still for a long moment and just breathe.

It was madness, yes. But Kathrael had been mad for some time now. She opened her eyes and went to examine the twins' caravan. It was not nearly as sturdy-looking as most of the other wagons, or the lion cage. There were bars on the small windows and a lock on the door, true, but the wood around the lock was cracked with age and riddled with woodworm. She supposed that it didn't take much to keep a couple of small, frightened children from escaping during the night.

After exploring the warded locking mecha-
nism with her fingers, she returned to the lion cage
and its mysterious occupant. "I'll have to break the
lock," she said. "It will make noise."

The sharp smile returned. "You'll need a distraction, in that case. I've got just the thing." He
sobered. "Do you know how to get to Darveen?"

"Go east?" she offered dryly.

"The main road from Penth splits beyond the
bridge over the river. You'll need to take the south
fork, and then turn east again at the crossroads beyond the forest."

"All right," she said. "But what about you?"

"Turvick is heading north to the towns along
the west coast, on the other side of the mountains.
He thinks it will be safer to exhibit his show there,
and he's probably right," said the man. "I need to
head north anyway—might as well get free food
and transportation for the journey. He's suppos-
edly got a ship booked for our passage in a few
days."

With the hysteria in Rhyth and the surrounding lands over people who showed evidence of
magic, Turvick was smart to run. Sooner or later,
someone would start the wrong kind of talk about
his human exhibits, and a mob would show up,
baying for blood. In fact, that probably explained
why they were camped away from town.

"I'm heading north as well," Kathrael said, ap-
ropos of nothing. She couldn't explain her odd
fascination with the strange young man. He
seemed a little bent in the head, to be perfectly
honest, and yet she couldn't stop herself from

drawing out the conversation. Perhaps it was merely a case of like calling to like, she thought wryly.

He smiled again, and there was less of a manic edge to it this time. "Perhaps I'll see you there, in that case. Now, though, you'd better get a move on. Try to break the lock. If Turvick or Laronzo wake up, I'll make sure their focus stays on me while you get the twins away."

"How?" she asked, still not liking the element of risk involved in such a half-baked plan.

"Easy," he said, the sharp grin returning. "Safe journey, Little Cat."

With that, he stretched and shook himself, and suddenly there was a skinny lion with a scruffy mane lounging against the bars of the cage where a lean, crazy-eyed man had crouched a moment before.

Kathrael staggered back in shock, nearly falling to the ground as she tripped over her own feet. A moment later, though, she was creeping back up to the bars as if drawn by an invisible cord.

Of course.

Even though she was dizzy with reaction, she could barely hold back the harsh laughter that wanted to rise up. *How many people could say they'd met not one shape-shifter, but two?* She only hoped this meeting would not herald the same kind of turmoil that had turned her life upside down six years ago.

The lion blinked glowing eyes at her. She lifted a hand, reaching through the bars to cradle the animal's jaw. It rubbed its head against her palm like an overgrown mouser in the granary, its eyes never leaving hers.

"Well, lion-boy," she said. "Aren't you just full of surprises?"

The beast shoved her hand playfully with its blocky head, a low rumble that might have been amusement—or encouragement for her to get a move-on—rising from its chest.

"Yes, yes—fine," she groused. "I'm going. You should know, though, that the last person I met who was like you ruined my life. If your crazy plan ends up with me locked in a caravan and being exhibited to gawping crowds as the *Wax-faced Girl* or some such, I'm going to take it *very personally*."

At least you'd have food, said the voice that sounded like Vesh. *And you could learn more about the lion-boy.*

And I'd be a slave again, in all but name, she thought, before shaking herself free of the argument.

"Right," she said decisively. After a final scratch of the lion's soft cheek, she pivoted and moved toward the burned-out remains of the campfire with steady deliberation. One of the stones from the fire ring would do nicely to break the half-rotted wood around the lock. She selected a rounded stone that fit easily in her hand. It was still warm from the earlier fire, and the deep heat against her palm was soothing.

The lion tracked her movement as she crept over to the twins' caravan. "Dex?" she called in a quiet voice, hoping it would be enough to wake the children. "Dex, wake up. You don't know me, but

I've come to take you and your sister back to Darveen. To your home. I'm going to break the lock on your door, and then we have to sneak away very quietly. Do you understand?"

There was only silence from within. Kathrael sighed.

"Well, stay back from the door if you can hear me." With a final glance back at the lion, who was still watching with interest, she hauled off and slammed the heavy stone into the soft wood around the lock. There was a loud cracking noise as it hit, and she held her breath. There was no time to worry, though, so she hit the lock a second time, and a third, her sore joints and aching muscles already protesting the effort.

Eventually, the aged wood gave way, and the splintered door creaked open on abused hinges. By this time, there was a commotion coming from the largest and finest of the caravans, as the owners awoke and scrambled out to see what was causing the noise. Desperate not to be seen, Kathrael clambered into the twins' wagon and pulled the ruined door shut behind her as best she could.

It was dark inside except for a square of moonlight coming through the bars of the small, east-facing window. However, she could sense two small bodies nearby, huddled together in a corner.

"Shh," she whispered. "It's all right. I won't hurt you. We need to hide for a minute. The lion-boy said he would cause a distraction. Then we can run."

The nature of the distraction became clear an instant later, when a deafening roar came from the direction of the lion's cage, followed by the rattle of wood and metal as a heavy body slammed against the bars repeatedly. Kathrael risked a glance through the window. Across the camp, the owners were hurrying toward the animal's cage, half-dressed in sleeping robes and carrying wooden staves, shouting to each other in confusion.

"What's wrong with him?"

"He's gone crazy—he'll break out! Stop him!"

She caught her breath in a gasp as the men started flailing their staves at the lion through the bars, trying to beat it off before it damaged the sturdy cage with its apparent escape attempt. The lion only fought harder, ignoring the blows.

A small hand closed around Kathrael's forearm, startling her, and then she was looking into Dex's large sad eyes, his face pale in the square of moonlight.

"They won't kill him," said the child. "They need him. For the show."

She swallowed, unwilling to acknowledge the depth of her worry for the crazy lion-boy she'd only just met. "We should go," she said instead. "Will you come with me back to Darveen?"

Dex's sister crawled forward to join her brother. The tiny girl stared at Kathrael's face for a long moment. Then, she and her brother shared a quick look, and she nodded.

"We can go home?" Dex asked.

"I'll do my best to get you there," Kathrael replied, unwilling to promise what she wasn't at all sure she could deliver. "Quick—get anything you need. We have to leave now."

"We only have our clothes," Dex said. "Well, our clothes, and Fish."

The little girl nodded, and clutched a lump of stuffed burlap to her chest that might, at a stretch, be described as fish-shaped.

"Come along, then. Quiet as you can." She eased the battered door open just enough to help the two children down from the wagon and follow them out before shutting it as best she could with the doorframe bent. With one of their hands in each of hers, she guided them back so that the bulk of the caravan was between them and the lion's cage. She was unable to control her flinch at the sound of wood hitting flesh, followed by a yowl of pain.

"Hurry," she hissed urgently, and led the twins away from the camp and into the brush where she had been hiding earlier. They struggled to keep up on their short legs.

With luck, the pair would not be missed until morning. *Luck* had not been a friend to Kathrael over the years, however, so she kept the children moving. When they began to flag, she carried them, ignoring the protests of her own abused body. She had toiled under sacks of grain as a girl working in the fields, so the weight — and the pain of an aching back as she bore it — was no stranger to her.

Now, though, she was barely recovered from her collapse on the road north of Rhyth. When she could go no further, she found the first sheltered spot among the trees and bushes that seemed to offer a temporary haven, and sank to the ground gratefully.

She had been following the rising moon, but with the moon now overhead, it would be too easy to lose her sense of direction. Better to lie low until sunrise started to paint the east. It was hard to see details in the shadow of the rustling leaves above them, but the two siblings both seemed very quiet and pale.

"Are you hungry?" she asked, rummaging in her pack for something to give them.

The girl nodded, and reached for the unleavened bread Kathrael handed her.

"I'm thirsty," said the boy.

"Here." She handed him the heavy waterskin and helped him hold it so he could drink his fill. "Better?"

He nodded.

"So," she said, addressing the girl. "I know your brother is called Dex. What's your name? I'm Kathrael."

The girl only shook her head and looked away. Kathrael wondered if she truly could not speak, or if she merely chose not to as the result of some trauma or fear.

"She pretends she doesn't have a name," said Dex. "But she does. She just doesn't like it."

Kathrael gave her an assessing look. "Well, then... what would you *like* to be called?"

"She wants to be called Petra," Dex said, leaving the mystery of Petra's speaking ability — or lack thereof — unsolved.

"Is that right, Petra?" Kathrael asked. The girl nodded, still silent.

"All right, you two," she continued. "We're staying here tonight. I have a blanket if you're cold. Do you think you can sleep while I keep watch?"

"I don't know," said Dex.

"Try," Kathrael said in a dry voice. "Tomorrow will be a very long day."

Petra took the blanket when she offered it. Kathrael felt around until she found a hollow at the base of a tree where she could lean back to listen to the night sounds around them. She was fairly confident that the twins would fall asleep within moments of lying down, even in such unfamiliar surroundings. They had to be exhausted — she certainly was.

An edge of surprise cut through the gray fog of weariness shrouding her mind when Petra crawled half into her lap and curled up to sleep there, rather than lying down nearby. Dex snuggled up against them a moment later, and as she had suspected, their breathing evened out into sleep within minutes.

She sat still as a statue, unwilling to risk waking them. The little girl's warm, trusting weight in her arms was a stark *might-have-been* that made her heart ache.

When Kathrael jerked awake some time later, it was light. She had not intended to sleep, although that had probably been unrealistic. Their hiding place hadn't been discovered — not that there was truly much risk of it without a fire or anything else to mark their presence.

Petra was watching her with large, liquid eyes.

Kathrael stared back, realizing with a sudden jolt that she had not given her scars a single thought since last night when she'd been talking to the lion-boy. Neither he nor the twins had reacted to her disfigurement in any way. She would have put it down to the nighttime darkness and the stressful situation, but even now in the dappled morning sunlight, Petra was watching her without a hint of fear or repulsion.

"They don't matter," Dex said from where he was sitting nearby, tousle-haired, and with a smudge of dirt on his cheek.

He reads thoughts, she reminded herself, feeling a wash of superstitious unease.

"'M sorry," he muttered. "I can't help it. It's all right, though. You're a good person. It doesn't hurt."

"I'm really not, you know," Kathrael said, the words slipping out without conscious thought.

"Petra needs to pee," Dex said, in the disconnected way that young children often seemed to converse. Petra nodded agreement, still staring at Kathrael's face from inches away.

Kathrael blinked, and forced her mind back to the practical. "Right. I imagine we all do. Then we'll eat something and be on our way. The sooner we start, the sooner you two can get home."

And the sooner I can get moving in the right direction again.

The three of them prepared for the day as best they could with their limited resources. Kathrael had to fight the urge to gorge on the food she had stolen from the provisions cart, knowing that not only would they need it for the rest of the trip, but also that it would probably make her sick. She ate a reasonable portion and tried her best to ignore the way her hands itched to grab more and stuff it into her face like some kind of savage.

After making sure that the children's needs were seen to as far as was possible, Kathrael readied them to set off.

"I need one of you to walk while I carry the other one," she said. "When you get tired, let me know and we'll switch."

"I can walk," said Dex.

"Very well. Tell me if I'm going too fast, though."

Dex nodded, and followed her as she hitched Petra against her hip and settled the satchel, skins, and blanket over her shoulders.

The day seemed to creep by, and Kathrael had the constant feeling that they were barely making progress. It didn't help that she was keeping them away from the road as much as possible, unwilling to risk being seen while they were still so close to Penth. When the river appeared through gaps between the trees with the fork in the road visible beyond, it was a relief. At least they were following the correct route, if nothing else.

Kathrael took a chance and quickly crossed the bridge before returning to the cover of the trees and brush. It was too dangerous to risk ruining the food if the river turned out to be deeper than expected, and she probably would have had to take the twins across one at a time.

She cursed silently when a farmer saw them from a distance, but the odds of the brief sighting coming to anything were negligible. No doubt the farmer had more important things to attend to than immediately running to Penth and gossiping about a woman in a tattered dress with two small children. He was almost certainly too far away to see her scars.

As the day wore on, they had to stop more and more frequently to rest. Even carrying one of the youngsters, such travel was too much to ask of children so young. She tried carrying both of them again for a while, but her own strength was simply not up to the task. When Kathrael finally admitted defeat for the day, they still had not reached the crossroads.

That night, she tried once more to keep watch, and once more fell asleep. A nightmare woke her, accompanied by the sound of stifled sobs from the blanket next to her. It took a few moments to get her bearings and remember where she was, but then she was leaning over to check Petra, who was still crying.

"You dreamed," Dex said, making the simple words sound like an accusation. His own voice was a little quivery around the edges.

"Oh, gods," Kathrael said softly. They could see into her mind. Feel what she felt. They were so *young*. " —I'm sorry."

"You can't stop dreams," the boy said.

She ground her teeth together. "Oh, yes, I can. Go back to sleep. It won't happen again tonight, I promise."

Dex gave her a skeptical look, but went back to soothing his sister. Before too long had passed, they were both asleep once more. Kathrael leaned her back against a rough patch of bark, determined not to sleep any more before morning.

At first, she thought about the lion-boy. She hoped he was all right after being beaten by his captors. She still couldn't explain her fascination with him. By rights, she should be wary of shifters, to say the least. They certainly seemed to have a knack for thrusting her into dangerous circumstances with little thought for the consequences to her life.

As the dawn slowly lightened the east to reveal a sky heavy with slate-gray clouds, her thoughts naturally turned to the Wolf Patron, and what she had planned for him. Sometimes it seemed that her desire for revenge was all that kept her from collapsing in a heap by the side of the road somewhere and never getting up again. The idea of a slave rebellion was too big — too *distant* — to truly seem real. For all that she had vowed to make such a rebellion happen, there were so many obstacles to overcome, she fully expected to be dead before it ever came to be.

There was only one obstacle between her and Senovo of Draebard, though — the mountains. And people crossed the mountains all the time. The sharp little ceremonial dagger still nestled in Kathrael's sash, and all it would take was a single thrust.

What would it feel like to kill a man?

Would the blade slide in easily, or would she have to force it with all her strength? Where would be the best place to strike? He would probably be facing her. The heart? Would his ribs get in the way, though? Maybe the stomach? Or a slashing cut to the throat? She pictured the way the blood would spray out, coating her as he clutched at his neck and collapsed to the ground.

Though she had kept her promise not to sleep and dream, her eyes had still fallen shut as she sat thinking. So it came as a shock when a small, soft hand cradled her unscarred cheek. She opened her eyes with a gasp to find Petra looking at her from barely a hands' width away.

"Don't," said the little girl, very distinctly. She sounded unutterably sad.

Kathrael quashed the small stab of guilt that threatened to pierce her righteous indignation over the Wolf Patron's actions all those long years ago.

"So you *do* speak, then," she said instead.

Petra just looked at her with brown eyes that seemed far too old for her young face.

~~~ 🐚 ~~~

Their final day of travel grew terribly hot and humid as the morning wore on. They came upon the crossroads fairly early on. Dex perked up as they looked out from a copse of trees nearby. He pointed one chubby finger toward a monument stone sitting like a sentinel at the corner where the two tracks met.

"I've been here before!" he said with some excitement.

"Home is that way," Kathrael told them, indicating the road that disappeared into the woods in the direction of the mid-morning sun.

Dex tugged at her hand, the familiar landmark lending him new energy. "Let's go!"

Kathrael hitched Petra higher onto her hip and surveyed their surroundings. There was a cart pulled by oxen approaching from the west, and a man carrying a large sheaf of grain on his back to the south, though he was moving away from them. Neither had much reason to pay attention to them, and they were quite some distance from Penth by now.

Judging it was worth the risk, she let go of Dex's hand long enough to pull her shawl over the scarred side of her face. When she was certain that she was well covered, she led the way onto the road and headed east. They were able to make good progress for perhaps half an hour before the road grew busier and she took them back into the trees.

Shortly after midday, the skies opened. There was no shelter even in the woods, and all she could do was take the blanket from her back and tell the twins to hold it over their heads as they walked. The ground grew muddy and treacherous, so she took them back onto the road, confident that few other people would be out and about in the storm.

The rain continued into the afternoon, until all three of them were soaked to the bone. Though unpleasant, it was at least still fairly warm. Only when the skies cleared did a brisk breeze from the north begin to cool things off and make her shiver.

They walked on, and Kathrael was starting to worry that she would deliver the children to Darveen only for them to succumb to the coughing sickness, when the village appeared in the distance.

"Home!" Dex cried, and shoved at her until she let him down from her arms. He grabbed Petra's hand and they ran forward, their weariness and discomfort forgotten.

"It's still quite a distance," Kathrael called to them, but their childish excitement was too great for such practicalities to move them. Instead, she let them wear themselves out, and caught up when they had covered perhaps a third of the remaining distance.

The sun was slanting toward evening and their clothing was finally beginning to dry on their bodies when the bedraggled trio got close enough to the modest village to attract attention.

"Dex? Lalla?" said a middle-aged woman standing in front of a hut at the edge of the settlement. "Gods above! Is that really you?" The basket she was carrying sagged in her grip as her attention turned to Kathrael. "Who are you, girl? What are you doing with these children? And why are you hiding your face?" Without giving Kathrael a chance to answer, she turned back toward the hut and yelled, "Boys! Come here! I've caught the girl who kidnapped Shayla's twins! *Hurry!*"

SIX

Ithric stayed in the form of the lion for nearly two days after the twins' escape. In many ways, it was easier to bear the pain of his newly acquired bruises and aches that way. The lion lived only in the moment, nursing its hurts with slow swipes of its tongue, but with no concerns about what was happening outside of the confines of the camp and its immediate surroundings. No worries about the twins, or the girl who had helped them.

The troupe was still traveling toward the coast, and Ithric could smell the distant tang of salt in the air. They were far away from Penth now, traveling in the opposite direction from where he'd sent the twins and their unlikely rescuer. After a few fruitless hours spent riding around on two of the draft horses, searching for the children the morning after Ithric's distraction, Turvick and Laronzo had apparently given up on recapturing them.

It was time to put the second part of his admittedly hare-brained scheme into play.

He waited until his two captors were puttering around the fire, getting things in the camp ready for evening, before shifting back to human form with a piteous groan.

"*Ahh,*" he cried, rolling over onto his side in the dirty straw and clutching his ribs. "It hurts!

Turvick, is that you? Laronzo? Why did you beat me?"

Both men had looked up at his words, and Turvick approached the cage with cautious steps. "Finally decided to shift back, boy?" he asked. "You're lucky I didn't cut my losses in Penth and put a spear through your heart. What the hell possessed you? Did you help the twins escape somehow?"

Ithric glared at him through the bars, still cradling his bruised torso. "How could I have helped *anyone* do *anything* when I'm stuck in this cage? I was trying to warn you, you morons!"

"Mind your tongue, boy!" Turvick snapped.

"If you wanted to warn us of something, why didn't you just change back to human and tell us?" Laronzo asked, still hanging back a few paces as if he expected Ithric to shift back to animal form and attack at any moment.

"Because of the witch, of course!" Ithric said, as if it was obvious.

"Because of the *what*?" Laronzo said, taken aback.

Ithric stared at him as if he was an idiot—no great feat of acting.

"The *crone*. The old woman who snuck into camp and spirited the children away! I asked her what she was doing and she put a curse on me. I shifted into animal form and couldn't shift back— I've been stuck as the lion for nearly two days now! She must have been a witch. The gods only know what she wanted with those poor children." He shuddered theatrically and touched his fingers to his forehead and heart in a superstitious gesture. "I tried to get your attention so you could stop her, but then you started hitting me for no reason!"

Laronzo looked at Turvick. "I guess that sort of makes sense, doesn't it?" he said in an uncertain tone. "He seems all right now, at any rate…"

"Shut up, Laronzo," said the other man, before turning his attention back to Ithric. "What did this supposed *witch* look like, boy? How did she break the lock?"

Ithric met Turvick's gaze with wide, innocent eyes. "She was tall and stooped, with long hair that was nearly white. I'm not sure I've ever seen anyone that old before. She pointed at the lock and muttered something, and it just kind of exploded. That was when I started making noise, trying to wake you."

Turvick glared at him for long moments, as if hoping to make him look away. When Ithric did not flinch or look down, he eventually growled, "Fine. There's nothing to be done about it now — not if we want to reach the ship on time for our passage north."

Ithric shrugged his agreement.

"The witch stole a bunch of our food, though," Laronzo said. "We've barely got enough now to make it to the coast."

"I know," said Ithric. "I saw. It's not like I could do anything to stop her, though, was it?"

Turvick regarded him with a sneer. "Maybe not, but I'm still inclined to take it out of your rations, not ours. Lions don't need to eat all that often anyway, right?"

As he had not been given any food since the night of the twins' escape, this came as no great surprise—even though the mere talk of food was making his stomach rumble and growl audibly.

"Fuck you, Turvick," he said in a tired voice. "You're a real bastard sometimes, you know that? Isn't he a real bastard sometimes, Laronzo?"

Laronzo looked startled, like he hadn't expected to be drawn into the conversation in such a way. His mouth opened, but no words came out. Ithric hid a smirk at the sight, taking his amusement wherever he could find it these days.

"Think you're funny, boy?" Turvick asked, unperturbed. "Just you remember—if the lion takes a step wrong, it won't be your flea-bitten hide I take it out on, it'll be the others. And if you shift into human form where the rubes can see you, your fellow freaks will be the ones to suffer for it. Clear?"

"Very," Ithric said. "Unlike some people here, I'm not mentally deficient."

Turvick stared at him like one might stare at a smear of manure on one's boot sole. "You think? Makes you wonder why you're the one in the cage, then, doesn't it?"

"Not really," Ithric replied, and gave his captors the too-wide smile that Favian had once told him people found deeply disconcerting.

Turvick only made a noise of disgust and stalked away, gesturing sharply for Laronzo to follow him.

When they were gone, Ithric slumped back against the bars and gave in to the ache of an empty belly, the throb of slow-healing bruises, and the carefully hidden pang of worry for his fellow captives... for the escaped twins... for the angry, desperate girl who had risked herself to rescue them on the strength of a complete stranger's request.

Despite his bravado, he was finally beginning to realize just how far in over his head he'd ended up. Ithric sighed. He'd always hated swimming.

SEVEN

"Wait, no—" Kathrael said, taken by surprise as the woman shouted for help. Stupidly, she had not thought much beyond the act of physically getting the children back to Darveen. *Of course* her ragged clothing and disfigured face would make her appear some sort of miscreant and raise the villagers' suspicions.

She thought about running, but knew it was hopeless. She had been traveling on aching, blistered feet, carrying a child and a heavy pack for two days. Her skirts were still heavy with rainwater, and she wouldn't get fifty steps before she was caught. Besides, running would only make her seem guilty of something.

Three young men ranging from adolescence to perhaps twenty-five were jogging toward them—the woman's sons, she suspected.

"Put that little girl down and back away!" barked the oldest, his voice like a whip-crack.

Petra clung to Kathrael, seeming frozen in place, while Dex grabbed a fistful of her skirt and held tightly. *They can feel the fear and anger around them*, she remembered, and made a conscious effort to stay calm.

"You're scaring them," she said as evenly as she could, "I'm just trying to get them back to their family."

One of the men grabbed her by the arm, and the woman darted in to pull Petra from her grasp.

"Tell it to the village council," said her captor, only to flinch back a moment later as he peered under her shawl. "What the — ! What's wrong with your *face*?"

"They're just burn scars," she said through gritted teeth, unable to quell the unwelcome pitch and roll of her stomach at his tone of disgust.

He relaxed a bit, renewing his grip on her arm as he blew out a noisy breath. "Utarr's tits, I'm surprised you could get within five paces of a child, looking like that."

Dex had pulled away from Kathrael to follow his sister as the woman carried her a safe distance away, but he spoke up at that. "She helped us!"

"Come away, child," said the woman. "Let the adults deal with this. Poor things — you're soaked! We must get you back to your parents so you can dry off and warm up..."

Kathrael's spirits sank as the twins were led away, throwing worried glances over their shoulders as they headed into the village.

"Come on, you," said the oldest of the three brothers, as he grasped her other arm and tugged her forward. "Perron, go find someone from the council and tell them what happened. We'll take the girl to the square in front of the meeting hall."

Kathrael let them tug her forward, and wondered if she was about to be strung up or burned at the stake, courtesy of another shape-shifter. *Serves me right*, she thought, anger at the injustice of it all flooding her and banishing her exhaustion from the demanding journey.

They arrived in front of the modest building a short time later, just as the youngest brother came hurrying back with a white-haired elder in tow.

"What's this?" demanded the old man, peering at Kathrael through rheumy eyes as he approached. "Good grief! What's the matter with this girl? Does she have some kind of disease?"

"She says they're just burns," said one of the pair holding her.

"I have a tongue!" Kathrael flared. "I can speak for myself!" She jerked against her captors' hold, but the movement was weak and ineffectual—her lack of strength only made her angrier.

The old man raised an eyebrow. "Then perhaps you'd care to explain what you were doing with Shayla's children, girl. Darveen has no mercy for kidnappers."

She glared through her good eye, a lifetime of anger threatening to rise up and swallow her whole. "Am I an idiot? Why would I bring kidnapped children back to the place where they would be recognized after—what? A week? Two? Does the village council of Darveen intend to execute me for rescuing them and returning them home?"

Two more elders joined them from inside the meeting hall, drawn by the ruckus and shouting.

"Calm yourself, girl," said the taller one, a great hulking man with an iron gray beard and a bald, shiny head. "We are not barbarians. You will be given a chance to state your case, and if the council deems you guilty, you will be branded on the cheek as a criminal and expelled from the village."

Branded. On the cheek. Kathrael had to fight completely inappropriate, hysterical laughter. Of course. Of *course* they would want to burn her face.

"*Stop!*" cried a man from across the village square. Kathrael twisted in her captor's grip and saw a plain-faced man running toward them, holding Petra securely against his hip. A pale woman hurried along a few steps behind, holding Dex as she tried to keep up. Kathrael nearly sagged in relief.

The newcomer slid to a stop, panting for breath. "Stop," he said again, quieter this time. "Let her go."

The man on Kathrael's left looked to the little knot of elders for guidance, and the bald man nodded cautiously. She snatched her arms back the instant her guards' grips loosened, and rubbed resentfully at the bruises they'd left.

"You have something to say, Melko? Shayla?" the first elder asked, squinting at the couple with his weak eyes.

"Yes, I have something to say!" said the twins' father. "This woman is innocent. My son says he and his sister were kidnapped by the two men who came through the village a couple of weeks ago with the traveling show. She rescued them and brought them home."

Melko and Shayla approached her. Both looked startled when they got a good look at her face, but Dex laid a hand on his mother's cheek and said, "Don't be scared, Mama. Look deeper."

Shayla blinked and stepped forward to stand face to face with Kathrael. "Forgive me for staring. Rudeness is a poor way to greet the woman who saved my family. You've returned my heart and soul to me, stranger. *Thank you*."

To Kathrael's surprise, the woman reached out and drew her into a one-armed embrace. Unless you counted Livvy's sweaty, post-coital clutch, no one had embraced her since before Vesh died. Her breath caught, instincts torn between the need for human contact and the desire to flee and hold herself safe from the dangers presented by such vulnerability.

Shayla must have felt her stiffen, because she pulled away with a final light squeeze of Kathrael's shoulder. Her husband turned to address the small knot of elders.

"I accept this woman into my home and consider her under my family's protection," he said. "Does the council take issue with this?"

Kathrael turned to see what the response would be. The bald man shook his head. "Of course not, Melko. If you are satisfied with the girl's innocence then the council has no reason to intervene." His attention turned to Kathrael, though he looked uncomfortable as he took in the ruin of her face. "You'll have to forgive us, young woman. The village of Darveen is very protective of its children, and the twins are... special."

"The village of Darveen wasn't protective *enough*, apparently," Kathrael said in a bitter tone.

"Since you let them be taken from under your noses."

"Believe me," Shayla said quietly. "I've been blaming myself since the moment I came back from hanging the washing and found them gone."

"The important thing is that they're back now," said Melko, holding Petra a little tighter. The little girl smiled in utter contentment and burrowed her face into her father's neck. "Thanks to you," he continued. "Please, allow us to make you welcome in our home, and accept our deepest apologies for the misunderstanding. We can never repay you, but we can at least provide you with food and a clean bed."

All at once, reaction to the journey and the ugly confrontation washed over her, leaving her dizzy and weak. She nodded, lost for both words, and the strength to speak them.

"She doesn't feel well," Dex said from his perch against his mother's hip.

Shayla put the boy down and he immediately reached up to take Kathrael's hand. A moment later, Shayla put a gentle arm around her shoulders, steadying her. "Come, please. It's not far. Let me help you."

Kathrael nodded and let herself be led, the buzzing in her ears drowning out the sound of conversation behind her as Melko exchanged some final words with the elders. She was dimly aware of entering a modest house and being guided to a neat, comfortable looking bed. Gentle hands helped her pull off the tattered remains of her wet dress, and replace it with a soft linen shift. Her head hit a down-filled pillow that felt like resting on a summer cloud, and the world went black.

>━━ ⚜ ━━<

She awoke later to the sound of cheerful humming and the scent of cooking meat. She lay very still for several moments, disoriented, with absolutely no idea where she was. A warm weight against her side drew her attention to where Petra lay curled in the space between her arm and body, watching her, and everything came flooding back. She craned around to look on her other side and found Dex laid out on his stomach like a starfish in the generous bed, his hair sticking out in every direction as he blinked into wakefulness.

"Mama, she's awake," he slurred, still sounding mostly asleep himself.

Light footsteps approached and Kathrael tensed, but it was only Shayla. "Hello, there," she said, wiping her hands on her apron. "I was starting to think you'd sleep straight through the day and into the night."

"How long—?" Kathrael rasped, her throat feeling like sand.

"It's late afternoon," said Shayla, reaching out a hand to help her extricate herself from the little girl and sit up. "You arrived early yesterday evening."

"Oh," she said, her mind still mired in sleep. She looked down at herself, noticing the borrowed shift properly for the first time. A jolt of fear hit her squarely in the chest—*where was the satchel with her food? Where was her blanket? Her dagger?*

"They won't steal your things," Dex said, answering the unspoken thought. "It's all right by the bed."

"Yes," Shayla said, evidently well practiced at following Dex's one-sided conversations. "It's all right there. Well, except your dress. I had thought to mend it for you while you rested, but I'm afraid it's a bit beyond my ability."

"A bit beyond help, you mean," Kathrael said, relaxing as she realized that she was safe here.

Shayla smiled. "I imagine that old dress has some stories to tell. Have you traveled up from Rhyth, then? I thought I recognized the style. It must have been beautiful when it was new."

Kathrael hadn't owned it when it was new, of course, but there was no point in saying so. "Yes," she said instead. "I'm traveling north, over the mountains. I was in Penth when one of the other people stuck in that awful traveling show asked me to help Dex and Petra."

Shayla looked surprised for a moment. "She told you her name was Petra?"

Kathrael shook her head. "Not exactly. Dex said she preferred it. She only spoke to me once, and only a single word."

Shayla looked at her daughter, eyebrows furrowed. "You really are set on that name, aren't you, sweet one?"

"Yes," Petra said, meeting her mother's eyes with her wide, brown ones.

"Perhaps we'll speak with the elders about a name changing ceremony."

Petra's face lit up, and Dex muttered, "About time," under his breath. When Kathrael looked at him, he shrugged. "She goes on about it *constantly*," he explained. Kathrael shook her head in wonder and amusement, trying to imagine what it must be like for the two siblings to be connected in such a way.

"Why *Petra*, though?" she asked, curious.

It was Shayla who answered. "That was my grandmother's name. She had the same gift as the twins. Sometimes looking into their eyes is like seeing her alive again."

Kathrael digested that for a moment. "I'd never even heard of such a gift before."

Shayla's expression turned pensive. "It's a dangerous time to be gifted. I worry for the future, but I suppose it's in the gods' hands."

Though she maintained a healthy skepticism when it came to putting things in the gods' hands, Kathrael was loathe to say so aloud in the presence of the small family. She was saved from having to come up with anything else to say by the sound of the door.

"I'm back," called a male voice—Melko. "Is she awake yet?"

"She is!" Shayla called back. She patted Kathrael's shoulder. "There's clothing of mine for you to wear folded over the back of the chair. I'll keep Melko out of your hair while you get dressed, and then we'd love you to join us for dinner."

"Thank you," Kathrael said, momentarily overwhelmed by the sudden free availability of food, clothing, and shelter.

"Come on, you two." Shayla herded the children off of the bed and out of the room. "Let's leave your friend in peace for a few minutes."

The door closed, leaving Kathrael in silence that seemed to echo after the friendly presence of Shayla and the twins. She looked around. The house was a pleasant, well-furnished space that confirmed her muddled impression from last night of a family that was comfortably well off. The smart thing to do would be to grab everything of value that she could carry and disappear through the window as soon as darkness fell.

And yet... what kind of person would that make her?

She picked up the dress hanging over the chair and held it against her body. It was a plain piece of clothing — the dress of a tradesman's wife, cut from sturdy material and without ornamentation. It would hang on her bony frame. It would also be the nicest clothing she'd worn in months. She shrugged out of the shift and pulled it on, cinching up the belt to hold it in at the waist so the bodice didn't gape too badly. When she was decent, she padded out into the main room on bare feet.

Melko greeted her with a broad grin. "There's our hero!" he said, and she felt a flush of surprise. As far as she knew, Kathrael had never been anyone's hero before. It was a very odd feeling, to say the least. "Are you feeling better after some rest, I hope?" Melko continued.

"Yes, thank you," Kathrael said hesitantly, still wrong-footed at being treated like a normal person deserving of care and attention.

"Well, I hope you're hungry," he said. "It looks like Shayla has made us enough stew to feed the entire village."

Kathrael's stomach cramped with hunger at the words.

"She's *starving*, Papa," Dex said solemnly from his perch on a stool near the table. His tone made it clear he was using the word in its literal meaning, and Melko's smile faltered and fell away.

"Not anymore. Not while you're under my roof," he told her, his voice going quiet. "Come. Sit. Please. Can I get you wine?"

Kathrael blushed and nodded, still unprepared for the depth of Melko and Shayla's gratitude, and the hospitality they offered her so freely. "Yes. Wine would be... very nice. Thank you."

When they had all seated themselves and partaken of the hearty stew, Melko sat back in his chair and regarded her. Kathrael was still working her way slowly through a third bowl, sopping up the rich broth with chunks of freshly baked flatbread, but she looked up when she became aware of the others' eyes on her.

"Shayla said you were planning on crossing the mountains," he said. "I've been thinking about what you'll need for the journey."

Kathrael blinked at him, uncomprehending.

"It gets cold up there, even in the summer," he continued, "and the terrain is rugged and rocky. You'll need decent boots, and a tent hide to use for shelter. Clothes for traveling. Dried rations, so you can carry enough food with you to get across."

"I'll manage," she said cautiously, wondering why he seemed so intent on pointing out all the things she lacked.

"I have no doubt that you'd find a way," he agreed, "but I think we can help you with those things."

"It's the least we can do," added Shayla.

She stared at them.

"I don't understand," she said.

"Our oldest son died last year," Shayla said, adding to Kathrael's confusion with the apparent *non sequitur*. "He was about your size, I think. His things… I couldn't…" She trailed off.

"We still have his boots and clothing," Melko explained.

"And I could take in one of my dresses to fit you. Our neighbors borrowed our traveling tent last year and never gave it back. We don't ever use it. But they still have it, and we'd like to give it to you, along with some of our food stores. We don't need as much now with Persy gone, and it was a good harvest last year."

Kathrael continued to stare, her spoon dipping slowly in her hand, forgotten, until it slipped out of her fingers and clattered in the bowl. "I don't know what to say."

"Say *thank you*," Dex advised.

"Thank you," she said in a weak voice.

The world ran on commerce, she knew — at least it did when neither party was strong enough to take what they wanted by force. Kathrael's whole life had been commerce. She'd been born as a commodity, to be sold or traded. After escaping slavery — or, at least, trading one form of slavery for another — she had bartered her body for what she had needed.

When that had no longer been an option, Vesh had made a foolish trade, wasting resources to keep her alive when she could no longer keep up her end of the bargain. There were intangible resources involved in commerce sometimes, she knew. Vesh had acted on sentiment, not self-interest.

There were few sentiments as strong as those between family members — parent and child, brother and sister. Kathrael had returned Melko and Shayla's children to them. Perhaps it was not so surprising after all that they would wish to pay her somehow for her actions. Food and clothing were commodities they could afford, and so they would give these things to her in return for Dex and Petra's safe recovery.

"If there's anything else we can do?" Shayla offered.

"No," Kathrael replied, feeling more certain of the situation now. "Clothing and supplies would be immensely helpful, thank you."

>━ ⚜ ━<

At the couple's insistence, Kathrael stayed two more days with them, resting and regaining her strength. True to their word, Melko and Shayla assembled a practical traveling outfit for her, composed of Persy's thick-soled boots and breeches, with a modified split skirt to wear over them and a fitted bodice that could be worn with or without a linen shift underneath.

Her worn blanket from Novice Hameen was joined by a light tent hide. The tent could be draped over a branch or propped over a short central pole that doubled as a walking stick for rough terrain. Not only was her belly full from three days of Shayla's excellent cooking, but her leather satchel was filled to bursting with dried meat, fruit, and rendered tallow for the journey. She also carried a single wineskin. Melko had advised her to ration it until she got into the mountains, where there were numerous small springs and brooks with clean, safe water to drink.

Finally, on the morning of the fourth day, she readied herself to depart. Shayla met her at the door with a swath of lightweight woven fabric in her hands, dyed a striking shade of purple.

"I have one more thing for you," she said. "I noticed that your shawl was in a similar state to your old dress. I'd like you to take this to use instead, assuming you want it. It was my mother's. I never wear it, and it's too fine a shawl to sit unused, waiting for the moths to destroy it."

Kathrael reached out a hand to take the delicately woven cloth, feeling the silky strands slide across her fingers. "It's beautiful," she said. "Are you sure—?"

"I'm sure," replied Shayla without hesitation. "Here. Put it on."

Kathrael set down the satchel and tent roll so she could remove her old, worn shawl and slip the new one over her head and shoulders. It seemed to weigh nothing and settled easily in place, a fold falling across the left side of her face to hide her scars.

"It suits you," Shayla said.

They were joined by Melko, holding each of the twins' hands in his. "Go with the gods, Kathrael of Rhyth. Should you ever pass this way again, you will always have friends in Darveen."

"Thank you, Melko. Shayla. You've both been very kind," she said, before crouching down to the twins' level. "And you two—be good, and stay away from strange men, all right?"

Dex nodded. "We will. Remember, you're a good person," he told her solemnly.

Petra darted forward to hug her. "Bye," she said.

"Goodbye," she replied, trying not to give into sentiment as she straightened away.

Shayla and Melko had been immeasurably kind to her, but their debt to her was surely repaid by now. As tempting as it might be to stay in this welcoming, generous place, that generosity would not extend indefinitely. It would be far too painful to watch their gratitude fade into resentment as she became more and more of a burden to them. Better to leave while they still felt they owed her. She had what she needed from them. That should be enough, shouldn't it?

With that thought firmly in mind, she set off from the comfortable little house and did not look back. Ahead lay the mountains, and beyond— Draebard.

EIGHT

The morning of Favian's novitiate dawned muggy and overcast. He had been up for hours already, ever since Senovo's light grip on his shoulder woke him from a strange dream full of half-remembered voices and a feeling of vague regret.

The High Priest's eyes shone in the flickering light of the single candle he'd brought with him. "Come, Favian. It's time to purify yourself before the ceremony. I won't insult you by asking if you're still certain you wish to proceed."

In fact, nervousness had slammed into Favian's stomach with all the subtlety of a runaway wagon the moment he'd realized that *it was today, it was time, this was really going to happen now.* Nervousness was different than uncertainty, however, so he mustered a wan smile for the man who had cared for him and his little sister these last several years.

"Thank you for that, Elder Brother," he said, managing to project dry humor rather than stark terror, fortunately. "Are you sure Frella will be all right?"

One of the strictures surrounding the novitiation was the ban on contact with anyone outside of the Priests' Guild or the Healers until after the ceremony was complete. Limdya had shared a meal with Favian yesterday, while Andoc and Carivel had wished him well last night and taken Frella to stay with them for the duration.

"Your sister will be fine," Senovo reassured. "She is worried for you, but that's only natural. She is happy for you as well, and she has many friends to keep her company until she can see you again."

Favian nodded and tried to compose himself, aware that he was only worrying about Frella as a distraction from worrying about himself.

"Up with you, now, Little Brother," Senovo said. "We will bathe in the river before you perform your devotions to the gods. The Healer will arrive soon after sunup."

The entire temple had woken early in a show of solidarity, priests and acolytes emerging into the darkness of predawn, shedding robes and wading into the slow-moving waters of the river at the sheltered bend behind the sprawling structure of stone and wood. They were largely silent as befitted their peaceful, deserted surroundings.

Priest Eiridan—a pleasant-faced man with intelligent eyes and a noticeable pot belly who had come to Draebard's temple from the village of Meren a number of years before—guided Favian to a calm pool near the edge of the river and helped him lather himself from head to foot with herb-scented lye soap. When he was satisfied, Eiridan took him back out into the current and urged him down to rinse. Favian held his breath, feeling the water tug at him as it flowed past the negligible obstruction caused by his submerged body.

How easy to let oneself float away under the on-slaught, he thought as the rushing river filled his senses. *How much more difficult to stand against the torrent and move upstream.*

Eiridan guided him up to the surface with a gentle touch under his chin. Favian emerged into the cool morning air, his eyes and nose stinging as he shook the water from his face. He staggered a bit as his balance shifted in the current, but a firm grip on his shoulder steadied him. He looked to his right to find that Senovo had joined them, his own black hair hanging in a wet mass between his shoulder blades.

"There is one final thing to address," his mentor said, "if you would allow me the honor."

Favian nodded, wide-eyed, and let Senovo lead him up the pebbled beach and into the bathing room at the back of the temple. A sturdy chair had been placed next to a table holding a ewer of water, a basin, and several candles; an oil lamp hung nearby. Favian sat, tipping his head back at Senovo's direction. The High Priest picked up the wickedly sharp blade that lay next to the basin, glinting in the yellow lamplight.

Favian closed his eyes trustingly, his heart beating a complicated rhythm as the razor slid over the front half of his scalp, shaving the hair away as was customary for a proper priest's queue.

Gods above. I'm going to be a priest, he thought with something like awe. *I'm finally going to be what I was born to be.*

Senovo shaved the blond hair away with the greatest of care, leaving the back half of his skull untouched. Perhaps it was the emotion of the day making Favian maudlin, but the love in that careful touch made tears prickle at the back of his eyes. How difficult must it be for Senovo to see *any* of his acolytes undergo castration after what had been done to him as a young man? Much less *Favian*, who was as close to a son to him as any eunuch could ever have.

When Senovo was finished, he carefully brushed the stray hairs from Favian's forehead and straightened. Favian reached out a hand and closed it around Senovo's wrist before he could step away. The High Priest froze, the wicked blade still held in his sure grip.

"Thank you," Favian said, craning around to meet his mentor's green-flecked eyes with his blue ones.

The mask of *High Priest* slipped for a moment, revealing the vulnerable man beneath. "You are most welcome, Little Brother. The look of the priesthood suits you."

Favian smiled up at him, helplessly fond, feeling his earlier nervousness slip away. "I had an excellent role model," he said, serenity settling in place across his shoulders like a comfortable cloak.

"I'll be sure to tell Brother Eiridan you said so," Senovo replied with a flash of his customary self-deprecating humor, a small smile quirking one side of his own lips in response. "Now, though, you should visit the altar and prepare yourself for the ceremony. The sun is almost up."

"Yes, Elder Brother," he said. "And... don't worry. Everything will be fine."

"I believe that's supposed to be my line," said Senovo, raising an eyebrow. "Go, Favian. I will see you after the ceremony." His voice turned wry. "Though you may not be in any condition to remember it. Nevertheless, we will watch over you."

The altar room was almost completely dark, illuminated by a single candle on the large stone slab dedicated to Naloth and his goddess, Utarr. Favian knelt in the small circle of light, hands folded and resting on the warm stone, head bowed.

I know that we humans don't truly understand all that you have attempted to tell us, he thought. *I'm trying to do the right thing. I swear that I will dedicate myself to your service. I will help all of your children who have need of me, to the best of my ability. Only... I cannot give up on the idea that there's someone out there, waiting for me. Surely you wouldn't have given Carivel and Andoc to High Priest Senovo if it were truly wrong for a priest to desire such a thing?*

I don't know why you made me the way I am. These urges for men — they're so strong. So overpowering. I hate *the loss of control that they make me feel. It will be a relief to finally be free of them. Perhaps that's what the gods intended all along. Perhaps I was given these... inclinations... so that I would be drawn to the priesthood to escape them.*

I hope that's the case, anyway. I just want to do what's right. But... I also hope... that I won't always have to do it alone. Perhaps you'll show me a dream to point the way. Perhaps —

Eiridan's low voice interrupted his prayer. "Brother Favian. The Healer is here. It is time." Favian looked up, and the priest handed him a cup of brown liquid, earthy-smelling and laced with the sharp hint of herbs. "Drink now, and I will help you back to your room."

Favian took a deep breath and let it out. While he'd knelt in front of the altar, the gray light of a cloudy morning had crept in around the edges of his awareness. He closed his eyes and tipped the cup back, letting the contents slide over his tongue. The liquid was rich and complex, with a hint of bitterness. He swallowed until nothing was left but a few dregs, and handed it back to Eiridan.

The older priest helped him to his feet and kept a hand cupped under his elbow as they made their way through the quiet hallways, to the familiar room that Senovo had set up for him and Frella after their father's death. He swayed a bit as they rounded the final corner, the sleeping draught beginning to hit him at the same moment he saw the other temple denizens arrayed along the final stretch of hall like an honor guard.

Reston and Crenelo, who had survived the temple massacre during the Alyrion attack all those years ago... Brother Feldes, who prepared their food every night, channeling his nurturing tendencies into providing the temple with nourishment... slender Mithral, the youngest acolyte, his hazel eyes seeming huge in his thin face... all of the others, meeting his eyes one by one, standing silent and proud as he walked past.

Again, Favian felt tears rise. Perhaps his inability to hold them back this time was a side effect of the sleeping draught. Eiridan guided him through the door of the room, where Healer Sagdea waited for them with her long white hair bound up in braids. A clean apron covered her simple gray robes.

"Help him lie down," she said, her voice softened somewhat from its usual brusque tone. "I can see that the draught is already taking effect."

Hands helped Favian down to lie on the bed, and his vision swam at the change in elevation.

"'S all right," he slurred. "'M all right. Tell S'novo not to worry..."

"We'll tell him, lad," Sagdea said, as if humoring him. "Now, just close your eyes for a few minutes, and everything will be fine."

Favian snickered, suddenly overcome with amusement at the way everyone seemed to feel the need to reassure everyone else about his castration. He opened his mouth to explain the joke, but before he could make the words come out, colors exploded behind his closed eyelids and his awareness floated away through the rafters above him, disappearing into the darkness like mist.

The mountains were nothing like Kathrael had pictured them. She'd thought they must be stately. Peaceful. An oasis of nature, largely free from the touch of men. Instead, they were a terrible, haunted place. Wind whistled through the rocks and trees, leaching the moisture from her skin and making her lips crack and bleed.

It was cold at night, as Melko had warned—unnaturally so, for summertime. In the daytime, the sun baked her, reddening any exposed skin until it peeled. Something about the air near the top had a strange effect on her body and mind. Her heart labored, beating hard and fast even when she stopped to rest. She was light-headed. Dizzy. Her muscles ached constantly from the steady climb, keeping her awake at night.

One might have assumed that things would get better once she crested the top of the trail and started down the northern slope. However, almost six years after what had become known as the Massacre at the Western Pass, the northern slope was still a strange wasteland of rocks, scrub, and the creaking skeletons of burned trees.

And, of course, where was she going, madwoman that she was? She was heading to Draebard to confront one of the men who had turned the mountain forest into a raging inferno, trapping and burning to death hundreds of Alyrion soldiers as they marched toward the northern villages.

With no leaves or branches overhead to dampen it, the wind was even worse on this side of the range. It keened and shrieked at night, threatening to blow her sad little tent down around her. Worse, as her journey wore on, it started to sound like voices. Or rather, it started to sound like one very specific voice.

"*Help me, Kath,*" Vesh whispered in her ear as she lay in pitch darkness, exhausted and trying to sleep. "*Help me, please!*"

Kathrael pressed her palms to her ears as hard as she could and screwed her eyes shut. "You're dead, Vesh. I may be losing my mind, but you're *still dead*, damn you! I *can't* help you!"

"*Don't leave me,*" Vesh said in the same strange, attenuated voice. "*don't leave me alone...*"

Tears squeezed between the tightly closed lids of her good eye, cold on her cheek as the wind whipped around her through gaps in the tent. "Fine!" she nearly screamed. "Fine! You can stay, only *please* shut *up*!"

Vesh didn't shut up. On the contrary, his voice was joined by others as the hours passed. Her mother. Her sister. The baby that had perished in her womb, years ago. Kathrael curled up in a tight ball and hid her head in her arms, trying to hold on until morning.

When she finally emerged from the foothills days later, everything inside her had been scoured away except for the overwhelming need to reach Draebard and find the Wolf Patron... to *end* things, one way or another. Unseen presences still hovered around her, harrying her forward toward her goal. In moments of clarity, she knew with utter certainty that without the supplies that Shayla and Melko had given her, her body would have perished somewhere on the mountain pass, along with her wits.

As it was, the sole of one of her boots was coming loose, and her food was almost gone — which would have been more alarming if she hadn't become too disoriented to remember to eat and drink most of the time. All that mattered now was putting one foot in front of the other. So she walked, and she walked, and she walked.

Even with her face covered, other travelers gave her a wide berth, something in her bearing proclaiming the dangerous madness that threatened to swallow her whole. Whenever she reached a crossroads, she would wait for the next person to pass and waylay them, hissing, *"Which way to Draebard?"* Inevitably, they would blanch and stammer directions, at which point Kathrael headed whichever way they were pointing until she became lost again and had to accost the next unlucky person.

When she rounded a bend in the logging road she was following and came upon a large village in the valley below, surprise momentarily snapped her out of her fugue. This had to be it. This had to be the place. The last people who had directed her made it sound close by. Kathrael's heart sped up. There, in front of her in the distance, was the temple—the sprawling single-story building unmistakable with its enclosed courtyard and beaten metal icons adorning the walls.

He was there. The Wolf Patron had to be *right there.*

She looked around at her surrounding. Her vision swam in and out of focus. Voices still whispered in her mind, making it hard to think, and she clutched at her temples angrily, releasing a cry of frustration.

A plan. She needed a plan. She would hide until nightfall and sneak inside. If she couldn't find the Wolf Patron, she would use her knife to capture the first wide-eyed acolyte she found and demand to be taken to him. And then... and then... she would run forward and sink her dagger into him again and again until he stopped haunting her dreams.

And it would all be over. Either they would catch her and execute her for killing their High Priest, or else she would escape and make her way back to Rhyth to help the slaves.

"*You know better, Kath,*" Vesh whispered, his breath tickling her ear. "*It will never be over. Not ever.*"

Kathrael let out a ragged sob and stumbled into the forest, hunching up at the base of a tree to wait for evening.

Favian tossed and turned, his head moving restlessly from side to side. His mind spun in lazy, drugged circles that were only partially effective as a distraction from the deep ache between his legs where his balls had previously hung.

Healer Sagdea had done the deed neatly and efficiently with the assistance of Priest Eiridan, while Favian snored and drooled under the influence of the powerful sleeping draught. Or so Reston and Crenelo had informed him afterward in cheerful tones, during one of the woozy stretches when he could actually stay awake and aware enough to understand speech.

Gods, his sac *really hurt*. He stared up at the rafters, trying to focus on the way the heavy beams moved in slow, surreal waves when he was fairly sure they were supposed to stay still and support the thatched roof. Why had he woken up in the first place? Things had been fine when he was asleep. Maybe it was Frella who had disturbed him? But that couldn't be right. His guardians had taken his little sister away to stay in their quarters while Favian recovered. So if it hadn't been Frella, then what had awakened him?

Oh, yes.

The girl. That was it. He looked back to the doorway to see if he'd imagined her. Which, apparently, he hadn't. Or at least, if so, he hadn't *stopped* imagining her yet, because she was definitely still there.

He didn't think she was supposed to be in his room, hovering inside the door like a ghost while he lay naked under the light woven blanket, drugged out of his mind and barely able to string together a coherent sentence.

"Wha—?" he asked, his tongue feeling thick and dry.

He stared at her profile as she peered into the hallway—dark-haired, golden-skinned, fine-boned. Pretty, if one happened to be interested in such things. Which Favian wasn't, particularly. At the sound of his voice, she whirled to look at him, and a tendril of shock wormed its way past the fluffy layer of wool stuffed inside his head.

The other half of her face was horribly scarred, the flesh looking nearly melted in places. Her eye on that side was wide open and milky.

"Shh!" she said sharply.

The world went gray at the edges for a moment. When it came back, she was standing next to the bed, and there was a wicked little blade pressed

under Favian's chin. He snapped his jaw shut re-
flexively.

It had been sheer luck finding a sick, defenseless
novice alone in his room in the quiet hallway of the
temple barracks. Candles illuminated the modest
space, which contained cots for two people. The
young man lay on his back, looking up at her with
hazy blue eyes. He was strikingly attractive in that
exotic northern way, she noted distantly, with fine
features and a chiseled jaw. His hair was a shade of
pale gold that she had never seen before, and his
eyes were the color of the sky just after dawn. The
combination lent him an almost unearthly air of
beauty.

She pressed the blade a little more firmly into
the skin of his neck.

"This is Draebard, yes?" she asked, just to be
sure. He started to nod, only to stop short as the
knife jabbed into the flesh of his neck. She took the
aborted gesture for assent, and her racing heart
beat even faster. "Good. Now, priest-boy, unless
you want me to open up your guts like a fish, take
me to the shape-shifter called Senovo. I have unfinished business with him."

The novice stared at her blearily as if trying to
make sense of her words. She was just gathering
herself to try to drag him to his feet by force when
they were interrupted by a voice from the doorway.

"That will not be necessary. I am here."

"Step away from the bed," said a second voice, deep and commanding. "*Now*."

Kathrael whirled in shock, the sudden movement making her dizzy. *No, wait, he couldn't be here yet. She wasn't ready to face him now —*

But there he was, standing just inside the doorway. Clad in the white robes of a High Priest, with his tightly plaited black hair and dark southern complexion, it could be no one else. He was flanked on one side by a powerful man with a withered leg who leaned on a stout walking stick, and on the other, by a slender, androgynous boy with close-cropped hair and a soft, beardless chin, who sighted down the shaft of a small bow and arrow pointed at her.

"You heard him," said the boy, drawing the bowstring back another fraction. "Step *away*."

This wasn't how it was supposed to happen. She'd meant to take him by surprise, but now there were three of them, and she couldn't —

Kathrael raised the dagger in front of her defensively — an instinctive movement. Before she could even blink, the lame man's walking stick flashed out and her hand exploded in pain, the little knife flying from her grip to skitter along the flagstones and come to rest next to the wall. She cried out and lunged after it, only to be intercepted by a gray shape that slammed into her, rolling her onto her back and knocking the breath from her lungs.

The large wolf pinned her beneath its body, its rank breath puffing in her face. A snarl curled its lips, revealing sharp canines as Kathrael stared at the beast, transfixed.

How appropriate that you should be the one to finally take my life, she thought. *How terribly, pathetically apt.*

She had failed. She had failed at *everything*. Kathrael looked up, meeting gold eyes ringed with green, trying to draw breath into her lungs and failing. The buzzing in her ears grew until it threatened to drown out everything else. Suddenly, the wolf stiffened above her, its snarl subsiding as it leaned down to snuffle at her face and neck. A moment later, the body pinning her in place twisted impossibly, and a slender eunuch with piercing green-gold eyes gripped her shoulders, staring down at her in shock.

"*You*?" he said, as if the word had been punched from him. "I *remember* you. Merciful gods. You're... *alive*?"

Kathrael tried desperately to suck air into lungs that did not want to work properly, and couldn't manage more than a wheeze. Gray fog flowed in from the edges of her vision and smothered her until she finally slipped down into darkness.

NINE

"There's only one punishment for thieving, you little bitch!"

In her dreams, Kathrael would always be a skinny thirteen-year-old girl, powerless against the forces that controlled her life. Vesh's spirit had been right—she would never escape this. *Never.* Perhaps this was to be her punishment in death, to relive the dream again and again for all eternity.

The overseer's whip whistled down and laid a line of fire across her back as she cowered, holding in the screams that wanted to escape. Once... twice... and, then—

"Stop right there!" shouted a female voice with a heavy, unfamiliar accent. Kathrael gaped up in amazement as a barbarian woman galloped up from nowhere and reined her horse to a halt. The woman was dressed in leather and fur, with feathers braided in her hair— wild and beautiful. She nocked an arrow into her bow and steadied her mount with her knees as she trained the weapon on Kathrael's tormenter.

More barbarians followed. A powerful man swung down from his saddle and handed his horse off to a boy who was still mounted. The man's sword scraped ominously as he drew it from his belt and stalked toward the overseer, careful to keep out of the female warrior's line of fire.

"Back away from the girl," he ordered, and, oh, wait, she knew that voice now. It was the same voice that had ordered her to back away from the sick novice's bed.

In her dream, the overseer lowered his whip and took a single step back. Another of the newcomers dismounted — a slender eunuch in white robes.

"What is the meaning of this?" the overseer demanded. "What business of yours is this? A barbarian, a woman, a priest, and a beardless boy?"

"I might be a barbarian," said the powerful man, "but if you think I'm going to let you whip a little girl bloody, you're even stupider than you look."

Kathrael cringed. Everyone knew that angering an overseer just made things worse. And indeed, the man's face grew red with outrage as he puffed himself up.

"How dare you! These slaves are the property of Master Iaden of the Five Lakes! Set yourself against me, and you set yourself against him."

The woman drew the arrow back another fraction and sighted down it. "Wow. That would probably sound really impressive if we had any idea whatsoever who this Master Iaden was," she said in a dry voice, her aim never faltering.

Kathrael tried to crawl away from the confrontation, toward the other slaves, desperate to put more distance between herself and the whip. With a cry of rage, the overseer lifted the weapon to strike her again. Before it could fall, however, an angry wolf appeared between them as if from thin air, ears flat back against its head and lips curled in a dangerous snarl.

Confusion erupted around Kathrael, as the slaves began to point and cry, "Lupiandas! Lupiandas!"

Kathrael fell backwards onto the ground in surprise, her mouth open as she stared at the large animal standing protectively in front of her. Could it be? Could the prophecy have finally come to pass? She righted herself and crawled forward, wrapping her arms around the wolf's bristling shoulders, fearless.

"Lupi?" she asked, hope flooding her breast even as her back throbbed with fire. "The gods have finally sent you for us, after so long?" Tears spilled over and trailed down her cheeks, unchecked.

The wolf allowed the embrace, continuing to hold the overseer at bay with bared teeth and a sinister growl. In the distance, hoof beats thundered, heralding the approach of more riders. Elarra darted forward and snatched Kathrael away from wolf. Taken by surprise, she gasped and tried to break free — to return to the Wolf Patron's side — but her older sister's grip was strong and sure.

"Hurry!" Elarra cried, and ran after several of the other slaves as they darted toward the tall grain and the woods beyond.

Kathrael found herself dragged along with them, even as she cried, "No, no — wait!" and tried to look back over her shoulder to where the powerful barbarian man was holding the wolf back, keeping it from tearing out the overseer's throat by virtue of a hand on the back of its neck. "What are you doing, Elarra?" she wailed. "The Wolf Patron is here! He has come for us — he will lead us to freedom!"

"He did lead us to freedom, little sister," Elarra said between gasping breaths as they ran. "We are free! Now, run!"

Kathrael clamped her jaw shut and ran.

He will come for us, she thought, as they hid in a sheltered hollow that night, hungry and sore.

He will return and lead us to a better life, she thought, as they stole food from a farmhouse, then used a sharp piece of flint to try to saw through the stiff leather collars sewn onto their necks.

He will help us rise up against the Masters and free all the slaves, she thought, as Elarra kissed her forehead and headed off into the city with two of the other women, to try to procure food and money for them by selling their bodies.

Oh, gods. He's not coming back. He's left us all to die, she thought, when Elarra failed to return. *I'm alone. I'm all alone now, and I don't know what to do. What do I do?*

Kathrael gasped, jerking awake. Her hand throbbed, and her chest ached, and her spirit was empty, filled with dust and cobwebs. Someone had laid her on a straw mattress somewhere, maybe still in Draebard's temple. Not that it mattered. She was alone.

No, that was wrong. There was someone seated by the closed door. The chair was tipped back on two legs, its occupant resting one booted foot casually on the footboard of the simple bed. It was the boy with the bow and arrow from earlier. He sat slouched in the precariously balanced chair, arms folded across his chest. His face seemed too old to be so young, with fine creases around his eyes and lips despite the lack of stubble on his soft chin.

Upon noticing that she had awoken, he let the chair settle back on to four legs and leaned forward to look at her. "You're the slave girl from the field outside of Rhyth." His voice was a low contralto. "The one we saved from being whipped."

Kathrael sneered and turned on her side to put her back to him.

"When you ran," the boy continued, "Senovo was certain you would be recaptured and killed. He wept for you, you know."

And what good did his tears do me, or anyone else, she wanted to ask, but even those simple words seemed like too much effort. She huddled in on herself, relieved when her captor didn't try to talk to her anymore. Eventually, sleep overcame the hunger pangs in her belly and the pain in her hand, and she slid back down into dreams.

⤙ 𝒲 ⤚

The next time she woke, it was a slow emergence into the realms of consciousness rather than an abrupt transition. Two voices were speaking in low tones nearby. The sense of their words emerged in fits and starts.

"… have to figure out what we're going to do with her sooner or later, *amadi*…"

"… while she's unconscious…"

"Perhaps not, but…"

Her sudden realization that the voices belonged to the Wolf Patron and the man with the withered leg, and that they were talking about her, caught at her awareness and dragged her more fully awake. She kept her eyes closed and her breathing even, not wishing to give herself away.

"She had a dagger pressed to Favian's neck, Senovo." There was controlled anger in the powerful man's tone. "I won't let her stay here in Draebard. She'll have to be expelled from the village, at the very least."

"No. I forbid it."

"It was you she was coming after. I'd think you of all people would understand the danger she represents."

"I have extended her the amnesty of the temple, as is my right as High Priest. Do not oppose me on this, Andoc. She is under my protection, as she should have been under my protection years ago."

The powerful man — *Andoc* — blew out a frustrated breath. "And you think Chief Volya would have let us drag a little girl along with us to the meetings in Rhyth, just because we felt bad for her? Should we have freed all of the slaves we came across on the journey and brought them with us as well?"

There was a stretch of silence. "Perhaps we should have. Whatever the case, it's immaterial. She is here now, and I will not see her harmed further."

"I'm more concerned about whether she would see you harmed further, given the chance."

"She is unarmed, half-starved, and has barely regained consciousness in the last day and a half. Save your concern for whether she will recover from whatever has befallen her in the years since we last saw her."

Another stretch of silence. "Yes. All right, *amadi*, your point is taken. Those scars…"

"Indeed."

"Just be careful. And if you can't manage that on your own behalf, do it for Favian. He's the one who was in danger of having his throat slit."

"Of course."

"How is he today, anyway?"

"The Healer is letting him spend more time awake without pain draughts. She says that the incision is closing well and he should be up and about for short periods within the next couple of days."

"That's good to hear. Does he remember—?"

"He does, and I've already had to bar him from coming here to sit with her. I doubt I'll be able to stop him once Sagdea clears him to leave his bed."

A sigh. "You've been a terrible influence on that boy. Or possibly a wonderful one. I haven't decided yet."

"I've been no more of an influence on him than you and Carivel."

The Chief snorted. "Right. Sure you haven't. Keep telling yourself that, *amadi*." There was the sound of rustling clothing—someone standing up. "Come on. We both need to meet with the elders about the ore production from the eastern mines. And, of course, about the… other matter."

"I'll be there momentarily."

The door opened and closed, the sound of a wooden walking stick tapping rhythmically against flagstones announcing the Chief's departure. Some sixth sense told Kathrael that the Wolf Patron had remained behind, watching her silently. The knowledge should have elicited some sort of reaction within her—anger, fear, her long-banked desire for revenge—but Kathrael couldn't muster anything. Only the desire to sleep again, and hopefully never wake up.

There was nothing left for her in this world. If the gods were just, she would have died on the mountain, or under the fangs of a slavering wolf. But when had the gods ever been just?

Eventually, the door opened and closed a second time, as the Wolf Patron exited on silent feet. Some time later, darkness claimed her again.

"Wake up," said an unfamiliar voice. "You've slept enough. I've brought a Healer to see you. You need to eat and drink something, and no one here wants to have to force it down your throat."

Kathrael blinked gritty eyes open almost against her will. It was daytime, and she was still in the same plain room, lying on the same straw mattress. The sick novice with the golden hair and blue eyes was gazing down at her, looking just about as awful as Kathrael felt. He was terribly pale, with dark circles under his eyes and lines of pain bracketing his full lips.

"Sit *down*, Favian," said a cranky female voice from nearby. "Preferably before you fall down."

"Well, I would—only it hurts to sit, Healer," said her would-be hostage. "Probably on account of you cutting my balls off last week."

"Don't be cheeky," said the Healer. "Remember who brought you into this world. I'll remind you that you were the one who insisted on coming here with me. For that matter, you were the one who insisted on becoming a priest. It's a little late to start complaining about it now."

"Who's complaining?" the golden-haired boy asked rhetorically. Kathrael watched with a dull expression as his attention returned to her, his blue gaze taking in the ruin of her face. "Now, come on, you—sit up a bit. You can lean against the headboard."

Kathrael opened her mouth to tell him where he could take his brisk demeanor and sympathetic glances, but a dry croak emerged instead. She descended into helpless coughing.

The novice held out a metal goblet and waggled it back and forth invitingly. "It'll be easier to tell me to go fuck myself if you have a drink first."

Kathrael gritted her teeth and struggled into a sitting position, using muscles that felt as weak as a newborn kitten's. She grabbed the goblet with an angry movement, sloshing watered wine over the rim. Once she had drained it, she shoved it back at the novice's chest.

"Go fuck yourself," she rasped.

He fumbled the cup for a moment before steadying it, and grinned. "Can't," he said cheerfully, and indicated his lower body with a brief sweep of his free hand. "Eunuch."

Kathrael continued to glare at him. "Get creative. You can use a rusty javelin point for all I care."

His expression morphed into one of mock hurt, and he placed his hand over his heart as if struck. "That's not a terribly nice thing to say to the person who brought you food and wine, now is it? And I thought we were getting along so well."

Completely against her will, Kathrael's stomach rumbled audibly at the mention of food. Again, she cursed her traitorous body that seemed so intent on *surviving* when there was nothing left to survive *for*.

The cranky, white-haired Healer stepped back into Kathrael's line of sight.

"Let's have a look at you," she said, and reached out toward Kathrael's face with one gnarled hand.

She shrank back instinctively, drawing in a sharp breath.

"*Wait*," said the novice. "Healer, this woman is a former slave."

Kathrael held her breath, looking back and forth between the two of them mistrustfully — unsure what the novice was getting at.

The Healer eyed the novice with irritation. "And? Don't be ridiculous, Favian. It's not as though I'm going to hurt her."

The young man — Favian — nodded. "I know that, Healer. Only — " He met Kathrael's gaze with a searching one of his own. "Being examined can be a bit unpleasant. A bit intrusive. But if you want Healer Sagdea to stop doing something, you can tell her and she will. It's your body. I just... thought you should know that." The words trailed off, sounding a bit sheepish.

Kathrael stared at him as if he'd grown a second head, complicated feelings warring in her chest, filling the space that had been empty since she'd woken on the plain bed in this small room.

The Healer huffed as if she found the whole thing terribly tiresome. "Well, of course it's your body, young woman. And if you'd like it to recover, I would strongly suggest that you let me examine you. Preferably before I perish of old age."

Kathrael clenched her jaw against the unwelcome tangle of emotion and tried to return to the empty place where she didn't have to feel anything. "Do what you will. I won't stop you." *Or help you*, she added silently.

"How very accommodating of you," the old woman said in a dry voice.

"Do you want me to stay, or go?" asked the novice.

Kathrael mustered enough energy to glare at him. "I want you to go find that rusty javelin."

He shrugged. "Sorry to disappoint you, but the warriors in Draebard aren't big on javelins. I think they're more of a southern thing, actually. I'll just be outside in the hallway."

The Healer pointed an imperious finger at him. "Take that chair with you and *sit down*." Her voice dropped to a mutter. "I should have kept you confined to your room for another day, stubborn boy." When the door closed behind the novice, her attention returned to Kathrael, who merely continued to glare. "Right, then. Let me take a look at you."

The examination was as unpleasant and personal as the novice had warned it would be.

Kathrael submitted to being poked and prodded, disappearing inside herself as she had been prone to do whenever someone else was touching her body. She answered all of the Healer's questions and mumbled commentary with stony silence. Only when the woman explored her scarred cheek with gentle fingers did she suck in a surprised breath and jerk away.

"Don't—" she gasped, the word torn from her against her will.

The Healer only raised an eyebrow. "Does it pain you?"

Kathrael pressed her lips together and looked away, determined not to let herself be engaged in further pointless conversation.

"Fine," said the old woman. "If you don't want to talk, I will. You are chronically undernourished, and you have a heavy infestation of intestinal parasites. I'll wager that your joints ache, and you suffer from frequent muscle cramps. Your stools are irregular and your stomach pains you frequently. Your scars are about six months old. They are well healed given the obvious severity of the burns that caused them. Not from a fire, I don't think. The pattern is wrong. Boiling water or hot oil, maybe. It matters little at this point. The conjunctiva around your blind eye are inflamed. I suspect the capacity to produce tears in that eye was damaged. You might consider wearing a patch to protect it from debris and further injury."

Every word was true, but Kathrael remained stubbornly silent regardless.

"Let me call Favian back in," the old woman said with a sigh. "No doubt he'll insist on helping with your treatment. You're lucky you picked such a kind-hearted young idiot to threaten with a knife, my dear. Most would be clamoring to the village elders for your punishment and expulsion after such a thing."

"More fool him," Kathrael growled, despite herself.

The Healer only shook her head and went to retrieve Favian, who was looking, if anything, even more ghastly than before.

She retrieved the chair as well, and plunked it down next to the bed, shoving the novice into it without ceremony.

"*Ow*," he complained, shooting her a sullen look that sat poorly on his finely drawn features. "I did mention the part about how it hurts to sit, yes?"

"My heart bleeds for you," retorted the Healer. "Now, there are two problems with our young guest that need to be addressed most urgently. First, I'm prescribing a mixture of honey, raw garlic, and roasted winter squash seeds four times a day for the next week, to get the intestinal worms under control."

Kathrael closed her eyes, convinced that she could feel worms wriggling in her belly now that the Healer had described the problem.

"She should take the mixture on an empty stomach, between meals," the old woman continued. "The parasites will make it difficult for her to gain weight even with sufficient food, but start her out with frequent small meals anyway. Moisten everything with rich broth and cook it well so that it's easy to chew and digest. Avoid bread and sweet fruit for now; they will feed the parasites more than they feed her."

Now hunger was warring with the roiling nausea.

"The second issue is more your area than mine, Favian," said the Healer. "I am concerned that this young woman is suffering from a derangement of the mind as well as the body. Not surprising, perhaps, given what she must have experienced."

Kathrael's eyes flew open, a sudden rage burning through her and sweeping away her earlier determination not to be drawn into any discussion.

"*Derangement of the mind*?" she mimicked. "You speak of madness? Yes, I am mad! I have been *mad* for some time now! So, what will you do with this dangerous madwoman in your midst? Perhaps you'd like to brand what's left of my face, like they threatened to do in the last village where I stopped! Or lock me away in a cage, like the boy I met outside of Penth!"

Favian leaned forward, looking at her intently, but without either fear or pity. "Neither of those things are going to happen," he said matter-of-factly. He wove his fingers together and rested his chin on his joined hands. "Most mad people don't have the drive and focus to plan and execute a difficult journey with almost no resources at their disposal. So tell me what makes you think you're mad."

The rage was replaced in an instant by fear and exhaustion so strong that she shook with it, shivering like a child lost in a blizzard. Out of nowhere, tears pressed at the back of her good eye, burning like vitriol.

"I am haunted by spirits," she said in a tiny, lost voice, the words jerked free from her chest on by one. She hated that voice instantly. *Hated* the weak, helpless person that she had become. That she had always been? And yet, the words continued to come, pulled from her even as she tried to stem the flood. "Ghosts. So many ghosts. They torment me constantly. I don't know how to make them stop!"

Her hands were shaking, clenched in the blanket covering her. The novice stretched forward and covered the nearest with one of his own, steadying it. "Tell me about these spirits," he said, sounding genuinely interested.

Kathrael swallowed convulsively, and began to talk.

She told Favian and the Healer about Vesh — about who he'd been in life and who he was in death. She told them about her sister, who'd dragged her to freedom and then disappeared without a trace, leaving Kathrael alone in a world that cared nothing for her. About her mother, whose spirit had died long before she'd borne two daughters for the masters who owned her, body and soul.

Whenever her voice grew hoarse, Favian stopped her and urged her to drink more watered wine and eat a bit of the stew he'd brought earlier.

By the time she finally trailed off, unable to speak of the way her dead, unborn infant daughter cried inconsolably in the depths of night, the bowl was empty and the cup had been refilled twice.

She blinked, looking blankly around the small room, overcome by a wave of surrealism. *This is all just another dream,* she thought. *It cannot possibly be anything else.* Dizziness assailed her, but a gnarled hand steadied her shoulder and guided her back down to lie prone on the bed.

"That was a lot to get out," said the Healer. "Now that you've eaten and had something to drink, you should sleep some more, young woman."

"Someone will be nearby when you wake," said the novice. "And for what it's worth, I don't know if your spirits live inside your head or outside of it. But whatever the case, I think it's clear that they care about you a great deal, to hover so near."

Kathrael's face twisted in pain at the words. She hid it in the bedding, curling away from the young man and the old woman. "Go away," she croaked. "Go away and leave me alone, *please.*"

"Of course, if that's what you wish," Favian said kindly. "But remember—you are in the temple now, where you will gain the help you need."

She gripped the bedding tighter, and steeled herself not to respond.

TEN

The belly of the lumbering cargo ship was dark, damp, and fetid. The lion hated it, and would have hated it even if Turvick hadn't insisted on shackling him with an iron collar chained to the wall.

The smell of briny water was thick in the air. Timbers creaked as the waves buffeted them. It made him nervous. Lions *could* swim, if there was a good reason to do so, but they would also avoid it if there were any other option. And here, shackled to a wall in this strange den of floating logs, the lion's instincts were screaming that if the water started coming in, it would mean certain death.

He paced restlessly, irritated by the way the damp, filthy straw stuck to his footpads, but not wishing to lie down on it, either. It was night. Faint slivers of starlight crept in through gaps in the boards above, and a larger chink came down through the open hatch leading to the outside world above. It was more than sufficient for him to see his surroundings, though it would have seemed like near-complete darkness in his human form.

The others were all asleep in their moldering cloth hammocks. No. Wait. There was movement from the corner. The short, stunted female was climbing carefully out of her sleeping place and tiptoeing across the distance separating them. The lion ceased its pacing and focused its attention on the other humans, who slept on, oblivious.

"Ithric?" she whispered, when she was close enough to reach out and touch him. There were damp trails running down her cheeks, and her voice sounded wet. Congested. "Can I talk to you?"

There was a mental shift as his human alter ego stirred. The lion allowed the change to happen, settling into the background as his flesh rippled and twisted. Ithric blinked and steadied himself against the dirty floor for a moment, briefly disoriented in the darkness after spending several days in animal form. The heavy metal collar settled uncomfortably around his bare throat and he raised a hand to ease it.

After a moment of holding his breath and listening, it seemed clear that they had not awoken the others. "What is it, Rona?" he asked, the low whisper made hoarse by thirst. "Has something happened? You're crying…"

Rona's voice trembled when she replied, "I'm scared, Ithric. I don't know what to do. I-" She swallowed hard. "I think I'm pregnant. I've missed my moon bleeding twice now."

Ithric blinked in surprise and took a moment to digest that. "And you think the father is—"

"It's Nimbral's. It has to be. There hasn't been anyone else."

Ithric blew out a silent breath. Nimbral was the skinny giant that Turvick and Laronzo had paired with Rona as a bizarre couple for the purposes of the traveling show. He'd known they cared for each other, but he hadn't realized they'd actually, well, *coupled*. He stared for a beat, trying to wrap his brain around the logistics involved before shaking his head and deliberately letting it go.

"I never thought I might get pregnant. But… but I did, and now I'm afraid this baby is going to kill me. Nimbral is so big, Ithric, and I'm so small. What if—"

"We need to get you out of here, Rona. We need to get you to a Healer," Ithric interrupted, unease growing in the pit of his stomach. For weeks now, he'd been contenting himself with the vague hint of a plan. Get north, where he had friends who would help, assuming he could get word to them somehow. Take any chance that presented itself to get the others away from Turvick. It had worked with the twins—at least, he hoped it had. But how often would such circumstances arise, in reality? Rona needed help *now*. Or at least, *soon*.

"Turvick won't let me go. Even if he would, I'm not leaving without Nimbral!" Rona's voice was shaking again, growing louder as she grew more emotional.

"Well," said a voice from across the hold, "isn't that touching."

Turvick. Ithric tensed, a sense of deep foreboding sweeping over him. Sparks flew in the corner where Turvick lay, as he struck a flint. A candle flared into life.

"Pouring your heart out to the beast-man, love?" Turvick asked, the candle illuminating his sneer as he rose and moved closer to them. Rona scurried backward, trying to keep distance between them.

"We were just talking," Ithric said, in an attempt to draw the man's attention onto himself.

Turvick stopped a couple of paces beyond the length of chain attaching Ithric to the wall. "Yes. You were *talking*. I heard. And I seem to recall warning you what would happen if you stepped out of line. Do you remember, I wonder?"

Ithric paled. "You said I wasn't to change form in front of the rubes. You never said anything about talking to Rona and the others!"

"I said *if you take a step wrong*, boy." Turvick's face in the candlelight was twisted in anger. Around them, the others were waking at the commotion. "Laronzo! Get my whip."

"What's going on?" Laronzo asked, barely awake.

"Nothing that concerns you," Turvick snapped. "Now stop asking stupid questions and do as I say!"

Ithric leaned forward until the collar bit into his neck, anger rising from the pit of his stomach. "You wouldn't dare whip a defenseless woman," he said in a low, dangerous voice.

"You have no idea what I would or wouldn't dare," Turvick said. "But as it happens, I have no intention of whipping your little friend. Watch and learn, boy. And think twice the next time you want to have a nice little chat with one of your fellow freaks."

Laronzo handed him the whip and took the candle when Turvick thrust it into his hand. Their captor stalked over to the hammock where Nimbral was cowering and grabbed the huge man by the shoulder, toppling him out onto the floor.

"No!" Rona screamed. She scrambled over and grabbed Turvick's leg, only to go flying when he kicked her carelessly away.

Nimbral was still sprawled on the floor, trying to get his feet under himself. He was immensely tall, but Ithric knew he was not very strong. In fact, his joints pained him terribly most of the time, and he tended toward clumsiness. Now, Turvick easily shoved him onto his hands and knees, ignoring his startled cry. The whip rose and fell, and the cries became screams.

Nausea flooded Ithric's gut and his heart pounded against the cage of his ribs like a drum. The lion rose up without his conscious realization and took over, lunging against the metal collar and subsiding back in frustration when the heavy chain did not give way. A deafening roar of anger echoed around the hold, joining the shrieks of pain and fear.

⊱ ⚜ ⊰

Kathrael tossed and turned. It was the dream again. The same fucking dream. For days now, she had submitted meekly to Favian and the Healers' care. She let them feed her. She swallowed the rank mixture that made the worms die and pass out of her body — a process so foul and nauseating that she heartily wished for death on more than one occasion.

Otherwise, she was blank and distant.

Silent.

Broken.

After the surge of anguish buried inside her had briefly spilled over into words, she found her spirit once again empty but for the whisper of haunting voices... and, of course, dreams.

She was thirteen again, skinny and knock-kneed. Elarra had left days ago to try to sell her body in the city. In the dream, she was caught endlessly in that moment of horror when the realization that her sister wasn't coming back finally penetrated her mind and stuck fast. No one was coming for her. When Elarra and the other women failed to return on the morning after they'd left, the other slaves who had run away with them had gone off to try to find work or something to steal.

One of the boys urged her to come with them, but she had refused — foolishly believing that Elarra would return soon with a bag full of money and an entertaining story about why she was so late. Perhaps she would even have the Wolf Patron in tow, ready to lead them in a glorious uprising against the Masters.

But of course, Elarra didn't return. And neither did he.

She was alone on the outskirts of an unfamiliar city — an abandoned child with no food, no water, no money, and no friends. She was going to starve. She was going to die, alone and afraid. She was —

Something cold and wet nudged her arm, jerking her free of the old, familiar wash of panic. She bolted upright with a startled cry, awareness of her surroundings filtering in as her heartbeat began to slow from its staccato rhythm. She was in Draebard, in the temple. In the room where she had been ever since she failed in her quest for revenge.

The soft light from a single oil lamp illuminated her surroundings.

The wolf was looking up at her.

It was seated on the floor next to the bed, resting its head flat on the edge of the straw mattress and watching her with a quizzical expression—as unthreatening as a wolf could possibly be. When her breathing evened out from its panicked tempo, the animal placed a paw on the mattress and half-crept, half-wriggled onto it until it could nuzzle at her face and neck, as if in reassurance.

Kathrael froze, every muscle strung tight. Air caught fast in her throat and stuck there painfully, only to erupt without warning into an ugly sob. Every terrible thing she had experienced seemed to rise up at once from her chest, trying to choke her on its way out, escaping as painful, wracking tears. She crumpled forward, catching herself against the slender wolf's unexpected strength—grabbing handfuls of thick fur and hanging on for dear life. The animal took her weight without complaint and continued to lick at whatever part of her it could reach.

Merciful gods.

The Wolf Patron had finally come to rescue her from the nightmare of her life… six years too late. She closed her eyes tightly, and cried harder.

Favian woke from a restless doze to the muffled sound of weeping. He looked across at Frella, still sound asleep in her bed on the other side of the room. The noise was further away, coming from down the hall somewhere. Realization struck, and he rolled upright, getting silently to his feet with teeth gritted against the slowly fading ache between his legs.

The room and the hallways beyond were as familiar to him as his own hand, even in the dark. As he had suspected, the sound of sobbing grew louder as he approached the room where the nameless girl who had threatened him with a knife was recuperating. The door was open a few inches, light from the lamp he'd left burning for her escaping into the hallway to form an irregular wedge of weak illumination.

He knew he should go and alert one of the more experienced priests to come help her — as a brand new novice, he was hardly qualified to offer counsel to someone in as much pain as their reluctant guest obviously was. But for some reason, the thought of leaving her like this for even that short time was unbearable — he had to at least let her know that she wasn't alone, that people here would help her. That *he* would help her.

When he pushed the door open another few inches and looked inside, Favian was more than a little shocked to find the wolf with her. Senovo had been avoiding her to a noticeable degree, ostensibly because he thought his presence would only upset her more, but also, Favian knew, because he blamed himself for not somehow saving her as a young girl when they had briefly met outside of Rhyth, years earlier.

Now, though, she was clinging to him with the desperation of a drowning woman, weeping as if she would die. The sight pierced his chest like an arrow, even though he knew, intellectually, that weeping was a definite step forward from the frightening apathy she'd exhibited for the last few days.

"Hey," he said softly from the doorway, alerting the pair to his presence. She tensed, but did not release her death grip on the wolf's fur. "It's all right. You're all right. You're not alone any more. I'm just going to go get Senovo a robe for when he changes back, and I'll come sit with you. You're fine — you're safe here."

He hurried back to his room and grabbed a spare set of dun robes from the chest. When he returned, Senovo had shifted into human form and was holding the girl against his chest. Her lank hair hung in a dark curtain across her face, obscuring it. Something about the sight made Favian want to weep himself — perhaps it was the stricken look on his mentor's face, or the girl's air of utter vulnerability now that her stony anger had finally dissolved into grief.

"Here," he said in a quiet voice, and draped the simple garment over Senovo's shoulders. Senovo thanked him with a look. Favian sat down on the other side of the bed and waited to see what their guest needed.

She cried for a long time — the exhausted weeping of a child who had lost everything. Favian was more familiar with that kind of weeping than he cared to dwell on, though even after his father died, he had never been nearly as alone as the broken girl in front of him. He'd had Frella, who loved him and needed him to be strong for her. He'd had Senovo and Carivel. Andoc. A village full of people who'd known him his entire life.

But even then, he'd wanted to curl up and die. He couldn't imagine what the young woman shuddering in Senovo's arms was going through. Something about her called to him, for all that their first real meeting had taken place with a dagger pressed to his throat. Maybe it was the fact that he'd dreamed her, years ago. Or maybe it was the courage she'd shown, crossing the mountains alone — borne along on the crest of her anger despite a failing, half-starved body.

Now, she sucked in a wet, noisy breath and shoved at Senovo with all of her remaining strength. He let her go immediately and vacated the bed, donning the robe Favian had brought him properly and doing up the fastenings.

"I wanted you dead," she grated, her voice roughened by tears and mucus. She still kept her face down, hiding behind the curtain of dirty hair.

Senovo folded himself into the chair near the bed. "I'm not surprised."

"Maybe I still do," she added.

Senovo only nodded, though she could not see the movement. "Though it will admittedly sound self-serving, I can tell you with some certainty that bloody revenge against those who have wronged you does not, in the end, make things better."

He was talking, Favian knew, about the priests that the wolf had killed during his escape from the southern temple. Even now — against all reason — he still blamed himself for their deaths. However, an injured wolf's moment of madness was a far different thing than traveling half the length of Eburos for the sole purpose of killing a man, though Favian kept that opinion to himself under the circumstances.

The girl ignored his words and continued. "The idea of revenge has been all that kept me from curling up by the side of the road to die, these past weeks. I would wake in the morning, and think *today I will get closer to Draebard. I will take my revenge on the Wolf Patron, and then –* " She cut herself off, still not looking at either of them. "But now I have failed. What am I without that anger to keep me going? An escaped slave with a disfigured face, alone in a strange land? There is nothing left for me. What do I *do* now?"

Senovo closed his eyes. "What you can. We all do what we can. It is, in the end, the only choice we have."

"*You left us.* You came in and upended our world, and then you disappeared without a trace." She finally looked up, glaring at Senovo with her good eye. "*Why didn't you come back?*"

Senovo's shoulders fell for a bare instant before he squared them and met her accusing gaze. "I was a terrified boy who ran away from my masters, and didn't stop running until Rhyth was just a strange, distant place that people spoke of as if it was a completely different world. When our traveling party came across you, on the way to the talks at the southern palace six years ago, I'd never even heard of the prophecy of the Wolf Patron. I am not who you think me to be — and for that, I am sorry."

The girl continued to glare. "You are still the Wolf Patron, whether you want to be or not."

"Perhaps so," Senovo allowed, sounding suddenly very tired. "But I cannot be the savior you want me to be."

"And so the southern slaves will continue to suffer under the Masters' yoke while you hide here in your temple, wearing your white High Priest's robes."

Favian could see the barb strike home, but Senovo merely said, "I wish it could be different. Perhaps salvation will still come for those suffering in the south, just from a different source."

The girl scoffed. "There is no one else. Now, leave me. Both of you. Get out of my sight. It makes me sick to look at you."

Senovo nodded, and rose to go without comment. Favian followed his lead, but paused by the bed.

"We're going now," he said. "But I'll be back in the morning."

Kathrael didn't think she'd ever cried as much in her life as she did over the course of that dark, endless night. She also couldn't remember ever feeling worse physically than she did when the sun finally hoisted itself over the horizon by slow degrees, spilling gray light through the room's small window. As bad, perhaps—but not worse.

Her head pounded, and her throat burned, and her stomach ached, and her eyes felt like someone had tried to set fire to them—even the one that could no longer make proper tears. Not for the first time in recent days, she lay there looking at the blurry rafters above her and fervently wished to die.

What she got instead was Favian, poking his head through the door a scant few moments after warning her of his approach with a maddeningly cheerful flurry of knocks. She stared at him with swollen eyes in a puffy red face and silently dared him to offer some comforting remark about it.

"I made you some willow bark tea," he said. "Drink it and come with me. You look awful, and frankly, you smell worse. I've drawn a warm bath for you, which I hope you appreciate, since hauling heavy buckets around with a half-healed scrotum is not the most fun I've ever had in my life."

"Then you shouldn't have bothered," Kathrael rasped, not moving.

"I did mention the part about you stinking like ten-day-old fish, yes?"

"Maybe I'm actually dead and just haven't re-alized it yet."

Favian pinched her upper arm without warning and she yelped, jerking upright in surprise. "Nope," he said. "Still alive, notwithstanding the smell. Now drink your tea before it gets cold. It'll help with your headache. That was always my least favorite part about crying my eyes out, personally."

He more or less shoved the tea into her hands, and she took it as a self-defensive measure to keep it from spilling over her lap. The curls of steam rising from the clay cup were undeniably soothing. At this point, she was desperate enough for the pain in her head to stop that she drank the bitter brew. When she was done, she shoved the empty cup back at him with as little care as he had shown. The small flash of satisfaction when he fumbled it and barely rescued it from shattering on the floor took her by surprise.

He shot her a look and set the cup aside. "Come on. Up. Bath. You'll feel much better afterward, I assure you."

"No."

He raised an eyebrow. "Come with me and I'll answer one question on any subject completely truthfully. No second thoughts, no backing down."

Despite herself, she eyed him with a speculative expression, a wisp of curiosity curling through the fog of misery that shrouded her. "Fine," she said, and tried to get up—only for her knees to buckle.

Favian grabbed her arm without comment and steadied her as she rose on shaky feet. Shockingly, the same legs that had carried her over the mountains had seemingly forgotten how to work at all, after days spent bedridden. To her surprise, though, the novice's touch did not repel her. Quite the opposite—something about it reminded her sharply of nights spent curled up with Vesh, safe in arms that demanded nothing of her but quiet affection. Tears threatened to rise again, though she would have sworn she'd cried herself dry last night. She swallowed them back, angry at the weakness.

Favian was looking down at her oddly. When she frowned at him, he seemed to shake himself free of his reverie. "Sorry," he said. "It's just—I thought you'd be taller."

She ignored the strange observation. "Are we going to stand here all day? I thought you were the one who was offended by my stench."

A smile pulled at his full lips before he hid it. "Just so. Let's go, then."

Their progress through the halls of the village temple was depressingly slow. They passed a handful of acolytes going about their business, all of whom nodded to Favian and kept their eyes carefully averted from her disfigured face. The bathing room was at the back of the structure. Kathrael could hear a river flowing nearby through the open doors and windows in the large room. The place was humid and smelled faintly of mildew.

She thought back to the spectacular bathhouses in the wealthy quarter of Rhyth, with their intricate mosaics and tiled pools fed by hot springs. When she had been younger and beautiful, in demand by wealthy fools with too much money, she had been part of the entertainment at such places on numerous occasions. There, the air had smelled of sulfur and cedar smoke. She had adored the bathhouses.

The simple bathing room in the temple of Draebard was a poor substitute, but it had a deep copper tub filled with steaming water, and a cloth hanging next to a container of soft lye soap. Now that she was here, Kathrael couldn't deny the appeal of finally being clean. Aside from a rag and a bowl of water in the village where Livvy had stopped on the way to Penth, and, later, at the twins' home in Darveen, she had not washed properly in weeks.

"You're still pretty shaky," Favian observed as he helped her to the bath and let her lean against the rim to balance. "Would you like me to stay and help you?"

She unlaced the neck opening of the shift they'd dressed her in and let it fall free of her shoulders to puddle on the ground. Her gaze met his, challenging.

"Stay if you want, priest-boy. I was a whore for *years*, you know. A good one, too. You're freshly cut, you say?" She looked down the length of his body and back up at his face, hit by the sudden desire to do something that would shock him and finally put the disgust she expected to see into his expression. "Probably wondering if your prick still works, right? I'll get it up for you if you'd like."

Favian didn't reply, but helped her step out of the circle of linen around her ankles and into the tub, where she sank down into the blood-warm water with an undeniable sigh of pleasure. When she was settled, he pulled a chair up to the head of the tub and sat down.

"Well?" she insisted, looking up at him.

"It still works," he said quietly, lathering up the rag and handing it to her. "To an extent, at least. I gather it takes a few weeks for all of the changes to happen."

"So whip it out. I'll make you feel good — pay you back for nursing me like a sick babe this last week." She raised an eyebrow, still looking him square in the eye and daring him to back down. "I've never sucked off a fresh-cut eunuch before."

A faint blush did rise to his cheeks, but his expression remained open and unguarded. "I'm afraid you're not really my type, in that regard."

Understanding dawned. "Oh. Queer?" she asked.

"Sort of," he said, still blushing. "I could only ever get hard for men, though I had my share of romantic crushes on girls and boys both, growing up. I guess you could say that makes me queer. Thankfully, before long, I won't be that way anymore — instead, I'll be nothing at all."

She stared at him, surprised by his candor. "And you *wanted* that?"

His brow furrowed. "Draebard isn't Rhyth. No one here is forced into the Priests' Guild." His voice had gone hard on the last sentence but it softened again, growing reflective. "To answer your question, yes, I wanted it. Sex and lust have brought me nothing but heartache. I'm happy to be done with them."

The memory of tearing agony as a fat old man forced his way into her thirteen-year-old body for first time flickered across her mind's eye, followed by the flash of a glass vial filled with vitriol. She sank back in the bath, abandoning her attempt to goad him. "I know the feeling," she said on a breath. "You're right. You're better off without it, and so am I."

He shrugged. "Well. Don't get me wrong. There can be a beauty to it sometimes. I'm coming to appreciate that, now that it's no longer something I have to worry about personally. Brother Eiridan has started letting me sit in on some of the intimate counseling now that I'm a castrate, and I can understand the appeal from a purely aesthetic perspective."

Kathrael scoffed and ran the soapy rag over her body, scrubbing at the travel grime. "Pah! Don't be fooled," she said, not even trying to hold back the bitterness. "Sex is a transaction, nothing more. It's what women give men so they'll stay in a handfasting, and what prostitutes give men for money."

Favian looked troubled, but he said nothing.

Kathrael dunked her head back to wet her greasy hair. She worked soap into the tangles, enjoying the feel of the lather against her scalp. "So," she said. "You promised me the answer to a question."

That got his attention again. "You've already asked several very personal questions, you do realize."

She waved his words away. "Those didn't count."

Amusement flitted across his features. "If you say so. What's your question?"

She looked at him, her good eye burning into his. "Who is the Wolf Patron to you?"

Favian answered without hesitation. "He's my High Priest. My mentor."

"No. Not good enough." A little rivulet of soapy water dribbled down her cheek, but she ignored it.

"I—" The young priest blinked, taken aback. "Well... he's the man who accepted me into the priesthood with open arms when I thought that I would never find a place in life where I could fit in. He's the one who ignored the rules and brought my sister to live at the temple when we were orphaned less than a year later. He was like a parent to her... to both of us, really. I love him deeply."

"In the south," Kathrael said, "he is known as a powerful mage who was prophesied to save us all from the overseers' yoke... and didn't."

"Prophesied by whom?" Favian asked. "He's a shape-shifter, yes. But believe me when I tell you, shifters are only people—no better or worse than anyone else." He shook his head before continuing. "How was he even supposed to be aware of this *prophecy*? There was a war coming in the north, and we all knew it. A terrible, unwinnable war. Is it such a surprise that he would focus his efforts on helping the land that had taken him in and given him a life, rather than running back to the place that had enslaved and mutilated him?"

"The war was years ago," she said stubbornly. "And I've heard the stories about the Battle of Llanmeer, where he led an army of wolves to defeat the Alyrions. He *is* powerful. He could have come."

Favian was silent for a moment. "I'm... not sure an army of wolves would help the slaves in Rhyth," he said. "Who would they attack? Slavery is not a battle in a war."

She scowled. "You know nothing about it."

Favian lowered his gaze. "No. I suppose you're right about that." He looked up at her again. "But you still can't expect one man to walk in — on four legs or two — and magically fix things, just because someone said it was going to happen. Prophesy is a tricky business, and I say that with more authority on the subject than most."

She shrugged, dismissing his words angrily. "Tell it to the child who has just been pulled from his mother's breast and sold to the highest bidder."

He chewed his lip for a moment before speaking. "I'm sorry," he said with every indication of sincerity. "I wish I had a better answer."

Kathrael made a noise of disgust and went back to washing, suddenly aware that she'd been arguing passionately with him, her spirit filled with the familiar fire that had deserted her after her failed attempt at revenge. In addition, the steaming bath and the willow bark tea had cleared her aching head. She was clean and fed, her belly free of parasites. For the first time since before Vesh was murdered, she felt like a human being again... and she had no idea what to do with the realization.

Favian helped her rinse and oil her hair. He was silent as he steadied her while she dried off, and he hovered nearby as she walked back to her room unaided. Someone had aired the bed and put fresh blankets on it while they'd been gone, but she found, unexpectedly, that the idea of lying down in it did not appeal.

"I'm sick of the sight of this bed," she said.

Favian looked surprised, but pleased. "Then come to the refectory and have a meal. You can meet some of the others."

A faint sense of trepidation washed over her as she began to think about what her actions must have looked like to these people whose High Priest she had tried to attack. A dangerous madwoman with a scarred face, intent on murder and wielding a knife. It was an uncomfortable realization.

Sometimes madness isn't permanent, whispered a familiar voice, tickling her ear.

She must have gone still and silent for too long, because Favian was watching her carefully. "What is it? Are you all right?"

She shook her head. "It was only Vesh, talking to me. I'm all right now."

He nodded, accepting the words with an ease that made something inside her chest relax and unknot after weeks of tension.

"You know," he said, "it seems strange that I know the names of the spirits that surround you, but not yours."

She was quiet for a long moment, remembering what it was like to be somewhere that people cared enough to want to know what you were called. "Kathrael," she said. "My name is Kathrael."

ELEVEN

Kathrael did, in fact, accompany Favian to eat in the temple's communal dining area, where several of the priests and acolytes were gathered for a meal after their morning devotions. Some of the younger boys at the heavy trestle table had difficulty looking at her directly, and she caught one brown-haired lad staring fixedly at her scars with an expression of sick fascination on his face.

She suddenly wished for the fine woven shawl that Shayla had gifted her — she had been so ill and distraught that it had only now occurred to her to wonder where her meager belongings were.

The High Priest was notably absent, though the others appeared to defer to an oddly matched pair of senior priests. One — an immensely fat eunuch with heavy jowls and sandy brown hair — was ladling bowls of fragrant cooked cereals from a large cauldron. Despite the ready access to food she'd enjoyed over the last few days, Kathrael's stomach rumbled at the smell. The second priest was seated at the table, but rose as she and Favian entered. He was younger and thinner, though still with the noticeable pot belly that many eunuchs seemed to acquire as they aged. His eyes drew her attention — they were the kind of eyes that saw deeply, and kept secrets.

"Greetings," he said, in an accent notably different than Favian's. "It's good to see you up and about, honored guest. I am Brother Eiridan, and this is Brother Feldes." He indicated the fat priest, who dipped his head in a small bow. "Please, join us for breakfast. The High Priest has instructed that we serve you as best we are able during your stay here. Would you care for a bowl of spiced barley meal?"

Kathrael stood frozen inside the doorway, looking at the nervous acolytes fiddling with their spoons and trying to remember how to be around people. Priest Eiridan's intelligent eyes followed her gaze, and he cleared his throat softly.

"You'll have to forgive some of our number for their discomfort regarding your facial scars," he said, his tone unconcerned and forthright. "It is a natural human reaction to empathize with the pain that must have been involved, and then immediately think about what it would be like to have such a thing happen to oneself. They do not intend disrespect, and the reaction will fade as they have a chance to interact with you for a few minutes."

His blunt speech was refreshing, and she decided that she liked him. "I'm used to it... or should be, at least," she said hesitantly. "Thank you. I would like a bowl of barley; it smells delicious."

The fat priest—Feldes—smiled and puffed up as if she'd complimented him personally. "Of course, my dear," he said in the same strange accent. "Have as much as you like. It's one of my favorite recipes. My grandmother used to make it for breakfast on festival days when I was a child, back in Meren."

"Thank you," she said again, and took the bowl he handed her. Favian gestured her to a seat at the end of the table. He sat next to her on the hard wooden bench—somewhat gingerly, she noted—and she wondered if he was purposely using his presence at her side to insulate her from the group of strangers further down the table.

She focused on her bowl and the delicious contents. Chunks of fruit had been stewed in with the barley, and autumn spices had been added with a liberal hand. Around her, the conversation turned back to other things, and she relaxed a bit.

Apparently there was, in fact, a festival planned for that evening. Eiridan and Feldes were explaining to the younger acolytes what would be required of them as the townsfolk celebrated. In Rhyth, the festivals devoted to the Old Gods had long ago devolved into excuses for the wealthy to flaunt their wealth, the drunkards to drink more wine than usual, and the corrupt to revel in their corruption. That said, it was also a good opportunity to make money as a prostitute, particularly if one also had a talent for dancing or playing a musical instrument.

In Draebard, festivals sounded like much simpler affairs. Plentiful, rich food, games, storytelling, mind-altering substances, and lots of people having sex in public. Though perhaps, she thought wryly, they were not so different from the celebrations in Rhyth after all.

"You're welcome to attend, of course, if you'd like to get out of the temple for a night," Favian said quietly, startling her.

She looked at him, her brows drawing together in a frown. "I'm not likely to get stoned or branded as a criminal if I set foot outside, then?"

He looked at her in consternation. "No. I would hardly have suggested it if that were the case. Aside from you and me, the only people who know the details about the night of your arrival are Senovo, Andoc, and Carivel. Well... and Healer Sagdea, I suppose. But it's not like any of them are going to go spreading rumors around."

"They're not rumors when they're true," Kathrael muttered.

"Even so..." Favian shrugged. "The High Priest of Draebard has offered you sanctuary, and everyone in the village will respect that. You are free to go, wherever and whenever you choose." His voice lowered further, for her ears alone. "I've been on the wrong end of your knife, Kathrael and I don't think you really would have pressed the point into my throat. Am I wrong?"

A bubble of dizziness made her head spin for a moment, as she pictured scarlet blooming from Favian's neck, trickling down to soak the linen of his robes.

"No," she whispered, the stewed cereal she'd eaten suddenly settling in her belly like lead. "You're not wrong." She pushed the bowl away and swallowed hard.

The corner of Favian's lip quirked up in a brief, sad smile. "Yeah—I didn't think so."

"... Favian?" She and Favian both looked up somewhat guiltily as Brother Feldes called Favian's name, obviously not for the first time.

"I'm sorry, Elder Brother," Favian said. "Could you repeat that?"

"I asked if you were recovered enough to assist at the festival tonight, Favian," said the priest with a faint huff.

The novice flushed. "Oh... yes. Of course. Though I might need to sit down and rest occasionally."

"Certainly, Little Brother," said Eiridan. "Do only what you are able. Now, if everyone is finished, there is much to prepare."

"I do believe that was a hint," Favian said in a whispered aside. "Are you all right on your own now?"

"Yes," she said, her mind still whirling. "Go and do priest things, priest-boy. I'll be fine."

In fact, she was completely exhausted after the small amount she had done this morning. She supposed it would take time to recover her strength, such as it was. And there was also the fact that she had been awake for most of the night weeping like a babe. Even now, her face felt puffy and hot. She wished again for her shawl, and shot a hand out to stop Favian as he was leaving.

"Where are my things?" she asked. "My clothes and satchel?"

"They're in the chest at the foot of the bed," he said. "Everything except your dagger, that is. I'll see if I can get that back for you later today."

She frowned. "You would give me back my knife, after what I did to you?"

"As long as you're not still intending to use it on Senovo, or anyone else in Draebard—why wouldn't I?"

Kathrael looked at him closely, trying to understand him. "I can't make sense of you," she said eventually.

He shrugged. "For what it's worth, I can't make sense of a lot of things in life," he replied. "Sometimes you just have to accept what's around you and move on. Try to get some more rest, all right? I'll see you later."

Kathrael shook her head lightly and let him go. She was still a bit shaky as she made her way back to the room where she'd spent the last week, but walking was growing easier the more she did it. The comfortable bed seemed to call to her, the clean blankets warm and sweet smelling. Within moments of her head hitting the pillow, she was fast asleep, deep in blessedly dreamless slumber.

⟶ ⚜ ⟵

Hours later, a knock at the door woke her. She expected Favian to appear, but instead it was the deep-eyed priest with the forthright manner, Eiridan.

"Forgive me for waking you," he said, hovering just inside the doorway. "Favian said you were thinking about attending the festival, and it will be getting underway shortly."

She glanced at the window, surprised to find that darkness was rapidly falling and she had slept the day away. "Oh," she said. "Thank you. I didn't realize it was getting so late."

Eiridan smiled, then sobered. "I daresay you still need the rest. If I may, I'd like to ask you something while I'm here. Young Favian has been quite worried about you these last days. I have been tasked with assisting his education in the arts of counseling those in need, and he shared with me that you are beset by spirits who speak and interact with you."

Kathrael drew the blanket up around her, suddenly defensive. "What of it?"

"The spirit world is a particular interest of mine, as it happens. I was merely wondering if you would be willing to speak with me about the matter in more detail at some future time."

She relaxed marginally. "Oh. I… suppose that would be all right. You know about such things, then?"

"I've studied it as much as I'm able to, but it's not a well-understood phenomenon. That's why I'd be fascinated to hear about your experiences. Also, if you're not averse, I'd like to have Favian sit in on the discussion. He still has much to learn about the world beyond the visible."

Strangely, the idea of having her self-appointed nursemaid present was a rather comforting one. Perhaps this priest with the disconcerting eyes could help her quiet the voices somehow — especially her inconsolable baby.

"Very well. I'll talk to you both," she said, "as long as you promise not to have me caged up as a madwoman after you hear what I have to say."

"You don't seem mad to me," Eiridan said, "for what it's worth."

"Maybe not now," she said, the words coming out without her intending them, "but I think I might have been, before."

Eiridan tipped his head, considering her words. "It's possible, certainly. Sometimes madness is only temporary."

She couldn't help her startled huff of laughter. Eiridan looked at her questioningly.

"Sorry, it's nothing. Only... one of the spirits said very nearly the same thing to me earlier today."

His features lit with understanding, then amusement. "So, a *wise* spirit, no less. Fascinating. I look forward to hearing more. Now, though, I'll leave you to ready yourself for the evening. Is there anything you need?"

"No, I'm fine," she said.

"Enjoy Draebard's hospitality, in that case. May the gods' blessings be upon you."

Eiridan tipped his head respectfully and withdrew, leaving her to ponder the turn her fortunes had taken. She rose on stiff legs and dressed, carefully arranging the shawl over her face to cover her scars. Outside, night had fallen, and the town was illuminated by torchlight. Bonfires dotted the village green, the smell of roasting meat permeating the air.

Feeling suddenly uncertain, Kathrael kept to the shadows and did not join in the revelry. Around her, people were drinking and laughing, helping themselves to the plentiful food as they talked and joked. The aroma of burning herbs wafted to her hiding place, heady and complex. Drums beat a primal rhythm in the open area at the center of the village, and several men and women were dancing, eyes closed, lost in their own worlds.

Once, she would have prowled through the crowd like a tigress, drawing the eyes of every man who saw her. Now, she was a wraith, haunting the edges of the feast—a timid woodland creature hoping for scraps, but terrified of discovery.

Perhaps she should have stayed in the temple. But she was here now, and it made sense to familiarize herself more with the village and its people. To that end, she continued her slow circuit, moving from shadowed building to shadowed building without drawing attention to herself.

At one point, she saw Favian wandering through the crowd with a wineskin slung over his shoulder, stopping to greet passersby and refill their cups or goblets. She watched him, momentarily torn between gaining his attention and staying hidden. He moved to speak with a young couple who smiled and called a friendly greeting at his approach. The rosy-cheeked woman got up from her perch on the man's lap to kiss Favian on the cheek and embrace him. When she released him, she took his hand and tugged him over to sit with them. Favian followed willingly, a smile lighting his attractive features.

Kathrael left him to it and moved on, not acknowledging a small pang at seeing him so comfortable among his close friends.

Away from the central green, things were quieter. Trees grew at the edge of the village, a series of trails and small clearings also lit by the ubiquitous torches. Here, Kathrael wandered at the edges of the circles of light, enjoying the peaceful, pleasant night. As the evening wore on, couples began to filter into the forest — giggling women and the low voices of men intent on bedding them.

Such things held no interest for her, and she wandered deeper into the woods, following the string of flickering torches through the winding maze of trails. At the farthest extent of the illuminated area, more voices filtered through the leaves — *familiar* voices.

The Draebardi chieftain, Andoc. The smooth-faced boy who had been guarding her room when she first woke up after her thwarted attack.

The Wolf Patron.

The High Priest's low voice cut off with a gasp, followed by a soft moan. She crept closer, as if drawn by an invisible cord.

The three of them were in the last clearing lit by torchlight, with only darkness beyond. They were naked, and Kathrael was surprised to see that the slender boy had breasts — not a boy at all, then, but rather a coltish, angular woman with narrow hips and the sort of rangy muscles that were only gained through hard use.

A leather harness buckled snugly around her pelvis. Kathrael recognized the type from her days around Rhyth's brothels — rich men at orgies would sometimes pay to watch one woman fucking another with such a device, which held a fake cock of wood or leather in place over a girl's cunt.

Somewhat to her shock, the boyish woman was using it to fuck Senovo with slow, rolling thrusts of her hips as he lay sprawled back against Andoc's broad chest. Andoc had settled himself against a convenient tree trunk and was cupping Senovo's face in his hands, kissing his lips like one drinking from a chalice.

She watched, unable to look away, as the woman changed her angle of attack and thrust in deeper. Senovo bucked under her and cried out into the kiss. She remembered that Vesh used to claim he could still get some pleasure from being fucked under certain circumstances. Kathrael had been skeptical at the time, but despite being a eunuch, Senovo's small prick bobbed out, stiff and ready, and he writhed on the fake cock with every indication of enjoyment.

The odd, androgynous woman reached down and wrapped a fist around his modest shaft, pumping in time with her thrusts. Before long, he trembled through a release as strong as any Kathrael had seen from an uncut man—his moans swallowed by the Draebardi chief's demanding kiss.

After he went limp and pliant between them, the pair manhandled the spent eunuch onto his front. The woman pressed his leg out of her way and thrust into him again, his body yielding to the assault with a new shudder. His head was resting on Andoc's thigh now, and he rubbed his cheek against the man's hard cock like a cat. Andoc hissed out a breath, and Senovo braced himself on shaky arms so he could wrap his lips around the hard length. He bobbed up and down in slow movements, matching his tempo to the woman's thrusts.

Andoc's hand came up to rest on the back of his head, fingers tangling in the long black plait of hair. "So good, *amadi*," he breathed, his voice impossibly tender. "Love you both so much…"

The words twisted something inside Kathrael's chest painfully. She clenched her jaw. *Men will say all sorts of things during sex*, she reminded herself. *It doesn't mean anything.* In the clearing, Senovo moaned around the cock he was sucking, and let the hand on his head press him smoothly down to take it to the root.

"I will never, ever get enough of this," said the woman in a low, shaky voice, her hand sliding up the relaxed curve of Senovo's spine. "I love you two so much it hurts."

Kathrael had absolutely no idea what the strange, boyish woman was getting out of her playacting. Still, she was smart to play the man's role as long as the others allowed it. Better to be the taker than the taken.

A rustle behind her hiding place in the shadows made Kathrael jump. But it was only Favian, approaching quietly along the illuminated trail. He must have seen her movement, because he came over to her immediately, greeting her with a smile.

"There you are," he said quietly, in deference to the various lovers scattered around the woods. "I thought I saw you head back here earlier. Everything all right? What are you doing hiding back here all alone?"

She saw the moment his attention moved past her, to the clearing beyond. His face twisted into an expression of amused horror — with the emphasis on the horror.

"Aaand there's a mental image I really could have done without, thanks *so* much," he muttered under his breath. "Could we, er, go someplace else? *Now*?"

She allowed him to lead her back the way they'd both come, unable to let his obvious discomfiture pass unremarked. "Problem, priest-boy? I thought it was a pretty passable performance, myself. Your mentor's cock-sucking technique seems quite... *practiced*..."

"Right. Just stop talking. Seriously."

Amusement bubbled up inside her and she laughed at him; she couldn't help it. How long had it been since she *laughed*?

"It's *not funny*," Favian said, the words belied by twist in his lips as he tried to keep his expression suitably severe. His face was still beet red.

"It is a *bit* funny," she retorted. "You're going to make a sorry excuse for a priest if seeing people having sex makes you blush like a virgin. I can picture you now at your first handfasting, stammering over the vows with your cheeks glowing like a pair of hot coals."

"Don't insult the person who drew you a hot bath this morning." Favian glared at her, not terribly convincingly. "It's not the sex, it's the *people who raised* me having sex. Which they do. All. The.

Fucking. Time. It's almost a running joke at this point." He gave up his attempt at severity and ran a hand over his face, a snort of appalled laughter escaping from behind it. "They probably thought they were safe, way back here in the woods."

"Who's the woman?" Kathrael asked, finally having pity on him. "I thought she was a man."

"Oh, that's Carivel. Draebard's Horse Mistress. We all thought she was a boy for years, after she first moved here. Turns out she's sort of... both. The way she explains it, she was born with a male spirit in a female body." He shrugged. "She's just Carivel, really. You sort of have to take her as she is."

"Actually, from where I was standing, it looked like she was the one doing the taking."

Favian emitted a sort of choked noise.

Kathrael laughed again, but then she sobered. She had known of a young male prostitute in Rhyth who had dressed and acted like a woman. She'd only spoken to him briefly on a couple of occasions, but he'd been one of the first to be targeted by the cult members. He hadn't survived long.

"Who is she to the Wolf Patron, and your Chief?" she asked, bringing herself back to the present. "They say in the south that Senovo and Andoc are lovers. I guess that part was true, at least."

"They're bondmates."

She frowned. "Andoc and Carivel, you mean?"

"No, all three of them. They were handfasted six years ago, before the Alyrion invasion."

"Three people can't enter into a handfasting together," Kathrael said. "And Senovo is a eunuch."

"Well, obviously they *can* enter into a handfasting, since they did exactly that," Favian replied. "To be fair, though, I think it's the first time it's happened. The High Priest in Meren has second sight. He foresaw their union in a vision, and performed the ceremony himself."

"Oh, so it was a *prophecy*?" she goaded, feeling her good mood begin to sour. "How interesting."

"It was a vision," Favian reiterated, "and it was something that all three of them desired to do. So they did, at which point it turned out to be a *true* vision. Second sight can be a tricky business."

"Words, priest boy. Just words."

Favian shrugged. "It's the truth. Prophecies are meaningless unless they come to pass. I can say that the sun is destined to disappear from the sky and leave the world in darkness, but unless it happens, I'm just flapping my lips."

"The sun disappeared from the sky a couple of hours ago," Kathrael pointed out in a dry tone. "And it's dark right now."

He shot her a look. "You know what I mean."

She blew out a sharp breath of irritation through her nose and let the argument lie.

"Have you eaten?" Favian asked, changing the subject as they emerged from the woods and headed back into the village.

"No," she said, not adding that she'd been afraid to come forward and interact with anyone long enough to get food. Now, though, the smell of succulent pork and beef was making her stomach rumble.

"Well, come with me, in that case. I'll introduce you to some people. There are definite benefits to being friends with a member of the family who run the village cookhouse."

Kathrael screwed up her courage and gestured ahead of them. "All right — if you're sure. Lead on, then."

➤ ⚜ ⬤

When the festival had finally run its course, with the last drunken holdouts stumbling back to their own huts or someone else's, the temple denizens made their way back to collapse into their own beds for a few hours. Several of the older acolytes — and some of the younger priests who still took pleasure in such things — were looking decidedly well fucked, if Favian was any judge. He marveled for the thousandth time how anyone could use sex in such a casual way, taking fleeting pleasure and then just moving on as if nothing of import had happened.

Once again, he felt a quiet surge of relief that he would soon be beyond such things.

Now, though, he was bone-tired. Everything had gone smoothly in the village — no brawls had marred the celebration of the gods' bounty, and it appeared that everyone had enjoyed themselves. Even Kathrael had relaxed a bit after he'd introduced her to Limdya and Dalon, unbending enough to wish him a good night as she left for her own room.

The elders who no longer had much interest in attending such festivals had taken the village children out to the summer horse pastures to camp under the stars. This meant, of course, that their parents would have the evening to relax without worrying. Frella was out with them, so Favian had their room to himself tonight. With a sigh of relief, he fell into bed, and was soon fast asleep.

Some time later, he dreamed.

The lion growled low in its throat, stalking toward the man in the gaudy tunic and breeches with dangerous intent. Around Favian, the crowd was muttering nervously, milling around. The big cat roared in anger, and someone at the front screamed. A moment later, people were running... scrambling to get out of the village square... blocking his view.

He cast around for somewhere higher, where he could climb up and try to get the beast's attention. Terrified people shoved past him, threatening to send him to the ground. Favian was yelling something, trying to move against the tide — his words lost in the noise and meaningless to his own ears. Soon, he was left at the edge of the ever-expanding clear space left behind as the crowd fled. The lion surged forward, tackling its victim to the ground even as he turned to run.

Without warning, the beast's head jerked up, its attention drawn from its prey to Favian. A moment later, there was a twisting change*, and Ithric crouched over the downed man, looking frantically at Favian with wide, shocked eyes. The man on the ground scrabbled for something at his belt, and a shiny knife appeared in his hand.*

Favian cried out a warning. The knife jabbed up, towards Ithric's unprotected side —

"No!" The strangled cry echoed around the empty room. Favian clawed his way upright among the tangled blankets, dizzy and nauseous. He lunged for the edge of the bed, barely making it before the contents of his stomach burned their way up his throat and splattered onto the flagstone floor below as he heaved.

⤞⟍ ☙ ⟋⤝

Kathrael lay in bed, staring up into the darkness. Her thoughts circled endlessly, keeping her from slumber — her own fault for sleeping the day away, she knew. A noise drew her attention, and she sat up. If she hadn't already been wide awake, she would never have heard the strange, choked cry, muffled nearly to nothing by the walls separating her from whoever had called out.

She froze for a moment, unsure what — if anything — to do.

Go, Vesh whispered. *You want to go and help, so go and help.*

No one should be all alone in the dark of night, Elarra added.

"You left me alone in the night," she reminded both of them.

Yes, but they *didn't*, said Vesh.

It was true. The Wolf Patron — damn his hide — had come to her and roused her from her nightmares. Minutes later, Favian had followed the sound of her weeping to sit with her while she grieved. She sighed and rolled to her feet, glad that the world no longer tilted and swayed when she did so. Perhaps she was finally regaining her health under the priests' care.

She lit a candle, then padded over to the door and opened it, listening. Faint sounds of distress were coming from her right, and as she got closer they resolved into the unmistakable sound of vomiting.

It could have been as innocuous as an acolyte who had overindulged during the festival earlier... but members of the temple were discouraged from such things when they had public duties to perform. And there had been a cry a few moments ago —

Another noise of pain emerged from behind the closed door, and Kathrael reached up to knock. When there was no answer, she opened the door with a tentative push, unsure what she was likely to find. The flickering light from the candle she was carrying illuminated Favian, clutching the bedpost with one hand and his stomach with the other as he heaved another thin stream of bile onto the floor.

"Favian!" she exclaimed, hurrying forward and setting the candlestick on the table by the bed.

Favian gasped in a breath as if drowning and clutched at her arm. "Kathrael," he croaked, "I have — I have to — "

"Do you need to throw up again?" she asked, more than a little frightened by his demeanor. "Should I get someone? The Healer?"

He shook his head, still clinging to her arm. "I have to see Senovo. Please! *Please* help me get to him."

"I'm not sure you should try to get up," she said dubiously, but she braced herself as he used his grip on her arm to pull himself upright, barely keeping his feet clear of the mess on the floor.

"Wait," she said, and picked up the candle again. She slung his arm across her shoulders, but he was reeling. The candle guttered dangerously as they wavered, threatening to plunge them into darkness. "Favian, you're scaring me!"

"I'm sorry," he said. "I can't—" He managed to get his feet under him a bit more squarely. "I *have* to talk to Senovo *right now. Please*, Kathrael!"

If nothing else, perhaps Senovo would know what to do to help him, she thought. Assuming they could get there without Favian collapsing in a heap first.

"All right, I'll take you," she said finally. "You'll have to direct me, though. I don't know where we're going."

He gave a tight nod and stumbled toward the door, leaning on her heavily. They staggered through the hallways into a part of the temple where she hadn't been before, away from the public spaces. Eventually, they fetched up against an unassuming wooden door. Favian knocked frantically and burst into the room beyond without waiting for an answer.

Inside, the space was illuminated by an oil lamp. It was spacious and well furnished, with an open doorway leading to a second room beyond.

"Who's there?" called a startled voice, and a rumpled, half-dressed figure entered the circle of light. It was the woman Kathrael had taken for a man—Carivel. Her eyes widened in alarm. "Favian?" she said, and hurried forward, giving Kathrael a wary glance as she took Favian's arm and steadied him. "What is it? What's wrong?"

"I had a dream," Favian said, sounding very young and frightened. "Carivel, I have to tell Senovo, I have to—"

"Right," Carivel said, sounding inexplicably grim. "Just breathe for a minute, Favian—you look like you're about to pass out." She twisted to call over her shoulder. "Senovo!"

"I'm here." The Wolf Patron emerged from the other room, his eyes sliding over Kathrael and cataloguing her presence at Favian's side for an instant before his attention settled firmly on his protégé. He took the arm that Carivel had been holding and urged Favian to a chair. "Sit, Little Brother. Andoc is awake and will be here momentarily. Do you want to wait for him?"

Favian shook his head. "Ithric is in danger," he said, all in a rush.

Kathrael had remained stubbornly at Favian's side, for all that she was bewildered by his strange behavior. Why would a grown man—albeit a young one—go running to his guardians after a nightmare? And why would those guardians seem so worried about a mere bad dream? Without understanding exactly why, she moved to stand behind Favian's chair and put a protective hand on his shoulder. Again, the Wolf Patron's sharp, amber-green eyes took note of the gesture, and she stared at him, daring him to make something of it.

He was more concerned about Favian, though, and crouched down in front of him at eye level. "You had a dream about Ithric?"

Favian nodded, tension cording the muscles under Kathrael's hand. At that moment, Andoc limped in from the other room where the three had apparently been sharing a bed, bare-chested, bleary-eyed, and bracing his bad leg with the same walking stick he'd used to disarm Kathrael on the night of her arrival, when she'd threatened Favian with her dagger.

Andoc pulled up a second chair and sat in it. "Favian? You had a vision? Tell us."

Kathrael blinked. A *vision*? Did he mean—

Favian took a deep breath as if steeling himself. "I was in a strange village. I didn't recognize it. Ithric was threatening a man—an oddly dressed man. His clothes were very bright and elaborate. There was a crowd, but they were frightened. They started screaming and running away." He broke off in a hoarse cough, and swallowed hard. Carivel moved to the table and poured him a cup of wine, which he sipped before continuing.

"I couldn't see past the people trying to get away. I was pushing against the crowd, yelling something to Ithric, and trying to get closer. He—"

Favian cut himself off and curled forward as if he would be sick again. Senovo took him by the arms and steadied him, even as Kathrael tightened her grip on his shoulder.

"He... saw me. He looked right at me, and changed. But the man had a knife. He... lifted it to plunge it into Ithric's side, and—" Favian breathed deeply for a moment. "I woke up."

Andoc sat back heavily in his chair, lifting a hand to rub over the lower half of his face. He appeared suddenly pale in the lamplight... almost as pale as Favian. Senovo glanced over his shoulder, and the two exchanged a look.

"He's alive, then," Andoc said.

"So it would appear," Senovo replied softly.

Favian looked between them, confusion twisting his features. "What do you mean, *he's alive*? Someone's going to kill him! We have to find him somehow!"

There was an awkward silence, as Andoc seemed poised to speak, but didn't.

"Tell him," Carivel said, sounding angry. "He deserves to know. Andoc, you should never have agreed to keep it a secret from him. And Senovo and I should never have gone along with it."

TWELVE

"What secret, what are you talking about?" Favian was shaking now, under Kathrael's grip.

Andoc closed his eyes for a brief moment, then met Favian's gaze squarely. "A few months ago, Ithric came to me and asked to be one of my spies in the south. I warned him that it was dangerous, but he said he was tired of wintering in the north, and that there was nothing holding him here. He was going south anyway, and I might as well make use of him—his words, not mine, Favian."

Favian's trembling turned to full-blown shuddering. "And you *agreed* to this?" The words were very nearly a shout.

Andoc was still pale, but he didn't back down from Favian's anger. "I figured that at least if I was paying him to spy for me, he'd be in regular contact. And he'd also have money to live on. Things were fine for a while. We were getting regular updates via the messengers that run back and forth through the port at Llanmeer."

The Chief paused again. "But... a few weeks ago, I stopped getting any news from him at all. The last report had been normal, and then, just... nothing. I was honestly afraid that he was dead, but... well, it seemed needlessly cruel to tell you, when I didn't have any solid information to offer."

Favian shook off her hand and surged to his feet. "You sent a *shape-shifter* to be a spy in *Rhyth*? They *burn* shape-shifters in Rhyth!"

Kathrael froze, her breath catching in her throat.

Andoc got to his feet as well, as did Senovo. "I didn't send him anywhere, Favian. He was going, and he asked, and I agreed. I'm sorry—I know you two had been... whatever you were to each other. But I also know you were barely on speaking terms when he left. He specifically asked me not to tell you where he was headed."

Favian drew breath to say something, but Kathrael beat him to it.

"This *Ithric*—you say he is a shape-shifter?"

Suddenly, she was the center of attention. She felt a flush rise up her neck, and swallowed. "Does he, by chance, take the form of a lion?"

Favian whirled on her. "How do you know that?"

Her heart was pounding in her ribcage at the sudden revelation. "I met a boy who could change into a lion outside of Penth. He was part of a traveling show. They were keeping him in a cage."

"They were *what*?" Favian breathed.

"The two owners were exhibiting him as a tame lion. They also had several other people in the show who were... different, I suppose you'd say. A very short woman and a very tall man. A boy with no arms. They were all virtual prisoners of the two men named Turvick and Laronzo. Your friend, Ithric—he talked me into rescuing a pair of young children who could read minds, and returning them to the village where they'd been kidnapped."

Favian collapsed back into the chair from which he'd risen only moments before. "Ow," he said blankly, presumably when the impact jarred the half-healed scars from his recent castration.

"Well, *shit*," Carivel said. "There can't be that many lion-shifters running around in the south, can there? Did he tell you his name?"

"No," Kathrael said. "He looked like a northerner, though. Shaggy hair, skinny, lots of scars. A bit bent in the head."

"Definitely Ithric, then," Favian said in a heavy tone. He looked back at Andoc. "We have to go rescue him. You *can't* leave him stuck in a cage somewhere in the south, especially now that you know his life is in danger."

"He's not in the south any more," Kathrael interrupted, remembering something else the lion-boy had said.

"He's not?" Favian asked. "How could you know?"

She shook her head. "The men who ran the traveling show were planning on going north by sea, to one of the western ports. They thought it would be safer than staying in the south, and they were probably right."

"Perhaps there is method to Ithric's madness," Senovo murmured.

Andoc looked at him sharply. "You think he's trying to get back to Draebard?"

"He did say that he needed to get north. He wouldn't let me help him escape when I freed the children," said Kathrael.

"We have to find him. Rescue him," Favian said, addressing Andoc again. "We know where he is. The place I saw in my dream—it, well, it might have been a western port village. We could ask around. People would remember a traveling show like that!"

"Favian," Andoc said, his voice regretful. "I can't send an armed party into unaffiliated villages and start demanding things. The tribes in the west want nothing to do with Draebard and its allies these days. If we go rattling our swords within their territories, they're likely to start uniting against us, and that's the last thing the north needs right now."

"Then don't send an armed party! Send—I don't know—send a group from the temple!" Favian was leaning forward now, his voice growing increasingly desperate.

Senovo crossed his arms. "And would you count yourself among such a group, Favian? You do realize, if your dream is a true vision, then Ithric isn't in danger *until you see him*. Your own presence is part of the very sequence of events you wish to thwart."

Favian sank back, covering his face with one hand as he tried to regain his composure. "It will be different this time. This time, I know exactly what's coming. I know exactly what to *avoid*."

Kathrael could keep silent no longer. "Wait. You're a *seer*, Favian? You... dream the future?"

Favian let out a noise that could almost have been laughter, were it not so laced with bitterness. "I dreamed *you*, the night you snuck into my room with a knife and demanded to see Senovo. I dreamed you *years* ago."

Kathrael could barely take in this new disclosure, so close on the heels of the revelation about the lion-boy she'd met near Penth.

Favian shrugged. "I did tell you that I spoke with more authority than most people on the subject of prophesy," he said, the same bitterness still heavy in his words.

"I suppose you did, at that," she said faintly.

Andoc shifted, drawing their attention. "Favian, we'll have to speak with the elders about your dream, and what, if anything, is to be done about it. Senovo's right, though. The fact the he was whole and safe when you saw him in the dream means that we have time to decide what to do."

"You don't know that," Favian shot back. "We have no idea what's happening to him!"

"Nevertheless, I won't act rashly on this," Andoc said, and it was clear from his tone that he considered the matter closed. "Not even for Ithric, Favian. Give me a day or two. Now, are you all right? You looked ready to collapse when you came in here earlier."

"I'm fine now," Favian said in a tight voice. "It's not me you should be worrying about."

With that, he rose to his feet again, shaking off Kathrael's hand when she moved to help him.

"Favian—" Carivel said, but he was already opening the door and stalking out.

With nothing else to do, Kathrael followed him, throwing a nervous glance over her shoulder at his three guardians. Carivel was frowning. Andoc was scrubbing his hand over his face. But the Wolf Patron met her look with one of his own, and Kathrael knew he was urging her to stay with Favian and keep an eye on him.

She turned and hurried from the room.

Unfortunately, she had been paying more attention to keeping Favian upright than memorizing their route on the wavering journey from his room to his mentor's. It took a couple of wrong turnings before she was able to successfully retrace their steps. When she caught up with Favian back at his room, it was to find him scrubbing away at the puddle of sick next to his bed. He dipped a rag in a bucket of water and rubbed it back and forth over the flagstones with short, angry movements, not looking up at her arrival.

"Is the Chief wrong about your friend being safe?" she asked, leaning a shoulder against the heavy wood of the doorframe and crossing her arms over her chest.

"He's not my friend," Favian said, biting off each word like it had personally offended him.

Kathrael raised a skeptical eyebrow, but he couldn't see it from where he was crouched, cleaning up his mess. "That doesn't really answer my question."

Favian threw the rag in the bucket with a sharp flick of his wrist. "I don't *know*, all right? Just because he was alive and not obviously injured in the dream doesn't mean that they aren't starving him, or torturing him, or — "

With a pang, she remembered the sound of wood hitting flesh as the lion distracted its captors so Kathrael and the twins could get away unnoticed. There was no point in relating that to Favian, though — not now. "They weren't doing any of those things when I spoke with him," she said, which was technically true.

Favian flopped down on a clean part of the floor, leaning his head back against the edge of the bed and staring up at the rafters.

"If he's not your friend, who is Ithric to you?" she asked.

"No one. He's no one to me." Favian was still burning holes in the ceiling with his gaze. "He's an infuriating prat without an ounce of good sense or self-preservation."

"Then I imagine he'll still be an infuriating prat in a day or two, when your Chief Andoc has had a chance to speak to the village elders. Can you get back to sleep?"

Favian shrugged and rolled his head upright. "No point," he said with a sigh. "It's almost dawn. I should finish cleaning up this mess, and then maybe I'll go start chopping up vegetables for Brother Feldes. I imagine everyone else will be dragging this morning after the festival last night."

"All right," she said, and gestured imperiously for a clean rag. "I'll help you, in that case."

>━ 〰 ━<

The following day had a vaguely dreamlike quality. At mid-morning, the children and their chaperones trooped back into the village. Other than that, Draebard was quiet, with everyone who could do so sleeping off their hangovers. Kathrael was tired, but she was also determined not to sleep another day away and end up lying awake at night.

She helped Favian for a while, and met his sister Frella when she returned. The young girl was bold and intelligent for her age. She stared at Kathrael fearlessly for a moment, and it seemed she was on the cusp of asking about her scarred face. Instead, though, her searching gaze turned to her brother.

"Something happened to you," she said. "Did you dream?"

"Yes," Favian said.

"Bad?" Frella asked.

"Bad for Ithric," her brother replied.

Her face twisted into a frown. "Oh. You're going to try to stop it, aren't you?"

"Maybe."

Frella looked at him for a long time, and nodded as if resigned.

After witnessing the odd, abbreviated conversation between the siblings, Kathrael went out to wash her clothes in the river. Favian, meanwhile, was called away to attend to the morning devotions. At midday, he reappeared and took her to the horse pens, of all places. Kathrael had never so much as touched a horse before. She was a bit shocked to find that the northerners let girls as well as boys care for the animals.

"Carivel's doing, mostly," Favian explained. "She'd already inherited the position of Horse Master while everyone still thought she was a man. When her secret came out, she just sort of... stayed there. Though there are other tribes where women do men's jobs. The Mereni even have a female Chief and a female First Warrior. Meren is only a couple of days east of here, and our tribes are close allies."

"Your tribe is strange, priest-boy," she said, looking around at the powerful animals with equal amounts of admiration and trepidation. "But... I think I like it."

Favian smiled, though he was still pale and distracted. "Here. Let me introduce you to the last colt I ever trained before I left the horse pens to become an acolyte in the temple. I still like to come out here and visit him when I need to clear my mind."

Unlike the rest of the village, the horse pens were bustling with people. "The animals need to be fed and cared for, whether there was a festival or not," Favian explained.

A girl who had been shoveling manure in one of the corrals looked up as they passed and waved; Kathrael recognized Limdya, and gave a tentative wave in return. Ahead, a smaller pen held a handful of horses kept for use during the day, while the others were turned out to graze on the rolling pastures north and west of the village. Her attention was caught by two creamy white animals standing nose to tail in one corner, contentedly swishing flies from each other's faces.

Favian whistled, soft and low. The shorter of the two horses immediately pricked his ears toward the sound and gave a low nicker.

"That's Ozias and Audris," Favian said. "They're brothers. The shorter one was born the morning after Alyrion soldiers attacked the village during the night and massacred the priests in the temple. One bright spot in a terribly dark day, I suppose you could say."

The horse had wandered over to meet them at the fence as Favian spoke. He nudged the young priest with his nose before turning to sniff at Kathrael, who took a nervous step back.

"He's so big," she said.

"He's far from the largest horse in the herd," Favian told her. "Don't yield your personal space to him like that. Horses are prey animals. It's easy enough to get them to move away." He made a small waving motion with his hand to demonstrate, and the white horse moved back obligingly. "Come here and stretch out your hand, palm down. Let him sniff it and greet you like he would another horse."

Kathrael stepped back up to the fence and reached over it. The horse arched his neck and snuffled at the backs of her fingers. Its breath tickled warm and damp over her skin as she watched in fascination.

"He's beautiful," she breathed. The other white horse joined them to see what its brother found so interesting. "They both are."

"Cream-colored horses are rare. These belonged to the old chief, Volya, but they passed to

Andoc after he died. They're trained for battle as a chariot team, though you can also ride them, obviously."

"Maybe *you* can ride them," Kathrael said as the second horse took its turn sniffing her hand. "The closest I've ever come to riding is sitting on the back of a melon cart pulled by an ancient donkey."

Favian smiled. "I'll teach you someday, if you like. Or Carivel will. She's far better than I am, in any case."

Before she could protest that Carivel probably had no interest in teaching her anything after she'd threatened both Favian and Senovo with a knife, a small disturbance in the herd drew her attention. A short black and white horse with a barrel-shaped body and a ridiculously extravagant mane came trotting toward the white horses, shaking its head and pinning its ears flat against its blocky skull.

The creamy animals whirled and fled the scene as if their tails were on fire, retreating to the far side of the pen. The conqueror tossed his head up and down once in victory and stretched it over the top rail of the fence, only to let out a terrific sneeze that sent a fine mist of snot over both Favian and Kathrael.

Favian sighed. "Hello to you, too, trouble-maker. Kathrael, meet Kekenu — Carivel's horse."

Kathrael looked from the little horse, to Favian's long-suffering expression, and back again, before bursting out into peals of laughter.

That evening, Favian was called away to the village meeting house, where Kathrael expected he was being questioned by the elders about the details of his dream. The deep-eyed priest, Eiridan, had invited her earlier to dine with him and continue their discussion from the previous evening. Favian had originally intended to join them, but she decided there was no reason not to go on her own, since he was needed elsewhere.

Brother Eiridan met her in the large hall housing the altar to Utarr and Naloth. He ushered her into a cozy room just off the annex, where bowls of soup and plates of flatbread awaited them. Kathrael wasn't sure she would ever get used to the ready supply of hearty, delicious food. Despite the fact that she had eaten three meals already today, her stomach gurgled and growled in anticipation. She had to force herself not to fall on the food like a scavenger attacking a fresh carcass.

Eiridan merely poured her a goblet of wine, and offered a simple blessing before devoting himself to his own meal. Kathrael waited until he had taken the first mouthful and followed suit, trying not to slurp her soup.

Perhaps in deference to her obvious single-mindedness around food, the priest did not attempt to keep up a conversation as they ate. She was surprised to find that the silence was surprisingly comfortable. When she was finished, her stomach full to bursting and a feeling of warm drowsiness sliding over her like a warm blanket, Eiridan sat back in his chair and laced his fingers together over his round belly.

"Well, I believe Brother Feldes has outdone himself tonight. That was a truly excellent meal," he said in his mild, oddly accented voice.

Kathrael gave him a hesitant smile. "Yes. I still have to pinch myself whenever someone just offers me food like that. I've never eaten as well as I have since I arrived here."

Eiridan nodded. "I gather food was difficult to come by when you were in Rhyth, and on your journey over the mountains."

The smile twisted bitterly, and Kathrael looked down. "I used to make money by selling my body, but I'm afraid there wasn't much demand for a prostitute with a ruined face. Times were hard. My friend Vesh did what he could to feed both of us, but in the end, desperation made him careless and he lost his life for it."

"That is a true tragedy," the priest said sadly. "Your friend Vesh is one of the spirits who speaks to you, I take it?"

"Yes. He was the first, though he is not the loudest." A faint cry, as if from a restless babe, pricked at the edge of Kathrael's hearing.

She looked up again to find Eiridan still regarding her solemnly. "Please feel free to ignore any of my questions that you find too painful or intrusive," he said, "but I confess, I find your situation very interesting. The gods teach us that the human spirit returns to the sky from whence it came on the smoke of the funeral pyre, even as the body returns to the earth as ashes. Can I assume... that your noble friend did not receive a proper funeral after his death?"

The piercing stab in her chest took Kathrael by surprise, and she had to pause for a moment to breathe. "No," she said, once the pain had subsided to the more familiar dull ache. "He was stoned to death by a mob from the cult of Deimok. They... paraded his corpse through the streets. I don't know what they did to him... to *it*... afterward. I was too afraid to follow them back into the heart of the city."

"Understandably so," Eiridan said, his tone grave, but devoid of either pity or censure. "One wonders if his spirit fled to you for safe haven after it parted from his body. He must have great trust in you to give you that most vital part of himself, if that is the case."

The ache grew deeper. "If so, it was misplaced trust. It was looking after me that got him killed in the first place."

"I can't help disagreeing with your assessment," said Eiridan, leaning forward now to regard her. "Have you not safeguarded his spirit in the weeks since his death? Did you not undertake a journey of great difficulty to come to a place where we might be able to help him find peace?"

"I didn't come here because of Vesh," she said, only to catch her breath as the rest of Eiridan's words settled in her awareness. "Wait. You think you can free my spirits and help them find peace? Really?"

"I don't know. I'm afraid such a situation has never arisen before within my experience. However, the members of the temple of Draebard will try to help you in any way we can. And if we fail, there are other more experienced priests in neighboring villages with whom we can speak. Now, tell me, do the other spirits share the same circumstances? Violent death? Lack of a funeral?"

Kathrael steeled herself to think about the others. "Some do," she said in a faint tone. "Some I'm not sure about. My mother. My sister — she disappeared. I don't know what happened to either of them. But... the worst is — " Her voice cracked, and she broke off, not having intended to speak of it in the first place.

Eiridan frowned. "Go on, please — if you can. I wish only to understand, and to help."

"My baby," she whispered after a long moment of indecision.

The priest breathed out slowly. "The spirits of lost children always haunt their parents, Kathrael. *Always*."

Tears rose up without warning and burned their way down her unscarred cheek. She curled into herself, chest hitching silently in time with the plaintive cries of an infant that only she could hear. Soft fingers pressed a clean cloth into her hand, and Eiridan perched himself on the edge of the table nearby. Not touching. Just sitting with her quietly as she cried.

Eventually, she regained enough control of herself to speak. "I'm not a parent. I was thirteen when I first sold my body to a man. Barely fourteen when I fell pregnant. I was small. Thin, even then. My belly was just beginning to swell when I woke up one morning with blood soaking my thighs. One of the other women had some experience as a midwife. I think she felt sorry for me—she cared for me and kept me alive, but my..." She swallowed hard. "... my baby girl was dead. The miscarriage damaged me inside, the woman told me afterward, and I guess she was right. I never became pregnant again."

"Fourteen is very young to fall pregnant. You were still a child yourself."

She made a dismissive noise, and wiped at her face with the cloth in disgust. "I hadn't been a child for years."

"Perhaps not in spirit," Eiridan allowed. "But in body, you were."

She shrugged a shoulder angrily, and he let the silence stretch.

"She cries at night sometimes," Kathrael whispered after the pause grew too heavy. "Inconsolably."

"And nothing is more painful to a mother than her child's cries," Eiridan offered in a quiet voice.

Tears threatened again, but she swallowed them back. "I told you, I'm not a mother!"

"I think, in your heart, that you are." Eiridan stood and returned to his chair on the other side of the low table, giving her space. "I wonder, Kathrael... does your unborn child cling to you, or do you cling to her?"

She glared at him. "Why would I cling to this pain?"

"Why, indeed?" he replied unhelpfully.

"You said you'd help me," she reminded him. "You said you'd help my spirits find peace."

"Yes," Eiridan replied. "And to that end, I would like to consult with the other priests on the matter, but I will need your permission to do so."

Her heart froze for a moment. "Not the Wolf Patron."

A furrow appeared between Eiridan's brows, but then his expression smoothed and he nodded. "The others, though?"

She hesitated, and nodded her assent.

Eiridan dipped his chin in acknowledgement. "Thank you. For now, I will offer a thought of my own. From what I have been able to learn about cases like yours, physical weakness and illness lower the veil between this world and the spirit realm. As the body grows closer to death, it becomes easier to communicate with the other side. It is very possible that as you regain your strength and health, that veil will rise again on its own. Tell me, have the voices changed at all or grown less frequent since you've started to recover physically?"

Kathrael thought back carefully over the last few days. "Except for my baby, they aren't as angry or frightened as they were when I was traveling. In the mountains, it was as if my desperation was feeding theirs, and vice versa. But since I started feeling stronger, I suppose it's true that I don't hear them as often, and that they are calmer."

"That is encouraging," said Eiridan. "I'll speak to the others and see if they have any further ideas to offer. In the mean time, don't hesitate to come to either Favian or myself if you need anything."

She nodded, but didn't rise. He took his leave and closed the door behind him to give her privacy. She sat there for a very long time, staring at the beaten metal sculpture hanging on the far wall, and thinking.

Favian left the meeting that night as frustrated as when he'd arrived. The elders listened carefully to his recounting of the dream, asked several pertinent questions about it, and then dismissed him without another word. He knew they'd be up until the small hours, debating things seemingly for the sole purpose of listening to the sound of their own voices. He *knew* they'd *hem* and *haw* and end up doing absolutely nothing, because the gods forbid they should ever just *act* without first dissecting every single aspect of the situation until they managed to convince themselves that action was unnecessary.

Unsure what else to do to distract himself, Favian poked his head into his room just long enough to confirm that Frella was there, and peacefully asleep. Then, he went further down the hall to check on Kathrael.

The door was open, and a candle burned inside. Unlike his sister, Kathrael was awake, seated on the bed with her knees curled up to her chest and her arms wrapped around them. She had been staring at the candle flame as if attempting to find meaning within it, but she looked up as Favian lifted a hand to rest against the rough wood of the doorframe.

"How did your meeting go?" she asked.

"About like I expected it would," Favian said, knowing his voice sounded tired and bitter. "How did *your* meeting go?"

She lifted her shoulders in a shrug and let them drop, her gaze turning back to the candle.

Favian sighed. "Did Brother Eiridan do that thing where he assures you he just wants to discuss something with you because he finds it such an interesting subject, and then twenty minutes later you realize that you're telling him about your deepest, darkest secrets while blubbering like an infant? Because I've always hated that trick."

Kathrael's expression twisted in pain, and a sob jerked its way free of her chest as she hid her face against her knees.

Favian's brows drew together in sympathy. "I guess that's a *yes*, then."

Something about her demeanor had changed in the last day or two. Favian couldn't have put his finger on it, exactly, but he knew what to do now, nonetheless. Without a word, he climbed onto the bed, crossing to sit on the side closest to the wall with his back leaning against the headboard, so she could move away from him easily if she needed to.

She was still crying. He put an arm around her shoulders and eased her out of her tightly curled ball to rest next to him. She flinched in surprise at his touch, and froze for a moment. Just as he once would have done with a frightened horse, Favian stayed still and unthreatening, letting her decide what to do. He wasn't surprised, however, when she gave in with a shudder of trembling muscles and let him settle her against his side.

In many ways, Favian knew he had been lucky. Though his life had included more than its fair share of tragedy, he had never lacked for people to love and comfort him when he was in need. He could barely imagine facing such things with no one there to help.

"I'm here," he said. "You're not alone with your spirits anymore, Kathrael."

She shuddered again and dragged her breathing under control, still not looking at him. "We talked about my baby," she said in a voice so low it was barely audible.

"You had a child?" Favian asked.

"No. No, I didn't. I *almost* had a child. But I didn't, and now I can never have children again."

He nodded his understanding. "My mother died giving birth to Frella. I never understood why the gods seem bent on making what should be a happy occurrence into a tragedy so often."

"I wouldn't have been able to support her even if she'd lived," Kathrael said in a tone of defeat. "She just would have died a bit later, is all."

A terrible thought hit him. "Is she one of the voices that haunt you?"

Kathrael nodded against his shoulder. "She... cries sometimes. At night. She's always hungry, or scared, and I can't do anything to fix it, because she's dead."

Favian made a small noise of pain and tightened his arm. "Oh, Kathrael."

"I think I could live with the others," she continued. "But when she wakes me in the middle of the night, sometimes I just want to die."

Favian swallowed the lump of emotion that tried to clog his throat. He reached up with his free hand to tip Kathrael's chin toward him — to make her meet his eyes — and was a bit surprised when she let him.

"When that happens, you come and get someone, you understand?" he said, willing her to accept the words. "You wake me, or Eiridan, or anyone else in the temple for that matter. Kathrael — promise me. Don't face that pain alone. Not here. Not now, when there are people to help."

"Help how?" she asked. "What can you or anyone else do to quiet my dead baby?"

"I don't know. Maybe there's something, or maybe there's nothing. But we can at least be there, with you."

She was silent, digesting this.

"Do you promise?" he asked again.

She paused and spoke slowly, as if feeling the words out. "If... I think your presence will help, I will come and wake you, Favian."

It wasn't exactly a heartfelt vow, and he noticed she didn't say anything about seeking help from the others. That might become a problem in the next few days, but he suspected it was about the best he could hope for from her right now.

He nodded his understanding. "Good."

They sat silently for a long time, lost in their own thoughts. Favian couldn't help wondering about the feeling of rightness as he held her against his side. She fit in a way he would never have expected—filled a gap he hadn't realized was there. How had a woman who greeted him with a knife against his jugular and a threat against the man he loved like a father become so important to him in the space of two short weeks?

He was still pondering the question when exhaustion from the dream last night and the emotion of the day dragged him down into sleep.

Kathrael jerked awake to the sound of a small throat being cleared. It was light outside—after a fashion, at least. The sort of murky gray light that heralded a cloudy dawn in the offing. Her neck ached—the result, apparently, of having slept sitting up for the entire night. Of having slept—the entire night—while leaning against Favian's side.

Favian's sister was regarding her steadily from beside the bed. Kathrael flushed without knowing exactly why, and nudged Favian's ribs with her elbow. He snorted awake and groaned, his hand flying to his own neck.

"Ugh," he said. "What... what time is it?"

"A little bit before Feldes or one of the others comes looking for you, I imagine," Frella said, and Kathrael couldn't help being impressed by her ready command of irony at such a young age.

"Oh," Favian said, and wiped a hand over his face. Kathrael sheepishly sat up and let him have his arm back. He shook it out to get the blood flowing and gave her a wan smile in return.

Frella was still watching the two of them with her arms crossed in front of her—a tiny princess with rumpled bed-hair. "What did the elders say last night, Favian? Are you going to go and rescue Ithric?"

"They didn't say anything," he replied, sounding tired. "And... maybe."

"Can I come with you, if you do?"

"*No*," Favian said immediately.

She frowned. "You're *not* going alone." It wasn't a question.

"No one's going anywhere, alone or otherwise, until the elders make their decision," said Favian.

Frella's piercing gaze flicked back to Kathrael. "*You*. You'll help make sure he doesn't do anything stupid, yes?"

"*Frella*." Favian said reproachfully, before Kathrael could fashion a response with her groggy wits. "Stop being rude. I'll be along in a minute, all right?"

The girl looked rebellious, but she did leave to give them a moment of privacy.

"Sorry about that," Favian said.

Kathrael stretched, feeling her spine crack and pop. "Don't be. She's your sister. She's just worried about you. About the lion-boy, too, it sounds like."

For some reason, that last part brought a faint flush to Favian's cheeks. "Yes, well," he said, not sounding thrilled. "She always did like him. Kindred spirits, I suppose."

A moment later, the quiet rustling of robes heralded a second visitor. Kathrael looked up to find the Wolf Patron darkening her door, though his attention seemed to be for Favian alone.

"Favian," he said. "Andoc wishes to speak with you."

Kathrael felt Favian tense beside her.

"Of course," he said, and clambered somewhat awkwardly off the bed. Before he left, he gave her a searching look. "Will you be all right?"

She nodded. "Go on, priest-boy. Don't leave your Chief waiting. I hope you receive the news you seek."

"Thanks," he said. "Don't stay cooped up in here by yourself today, Kathrael. I'll see you when I can."

"*Go*," she prodded. "Don't worry about me, I'll be fine." With a faint jolt, she realized that she actually meant the words. Favian was already leaving, but when she looked to the doorway, the Wolf Patron was once again regarding her with that odd, speaking look. He held her gaze for a moment before turning to follow Favian. As before, the silent exchange left her off-balance and restless in her own skin.

He sees *you*, Vesh whispered unhelpfully. *They all do, here.*

She shook off the strange feeling and swung her feet off the bed. There was nothing stopping her from curling up to sleep some more, but the prospect was not as appealing as she might have expected. She was, in fact, surprisingly rested after the night spent leaning on Favian's shoulder. No dreams or voices had disturbed her—it had been as if she'd closed her eyes, and opened them a mere moment later, but the whole night had passed peacefully.

After a bit of thought, she rose and washed with the bowl of water on the bedside table. Perhaps Priest Feldes would appreciate an additional pair of hands in the kitchens again this morning.

>⟶ ⚜ ⟵<

The fat, fussy priest welcomed Kathrael with enthusiasm and set her to stirring batter for the brown, fruit-filled cakes he was planning on serving that morning.

"Brother Eiridan spoke with me about your unseen voices," he said casually, once the preparations for breakfast were in hand.

Her expression must have soured on hearing Eiridan's name, because Feldes immediately looked sympathetic. "Ah. I can see you have been a victim of our esteemed brother's belief that wounds of the spirit must be lanced in a similar manner to wounds of the body, in order to prevent festering. He did mention that you'd become rather upset during your discussion."

"He shouldn't have tricked me into talking to him," she muttered, anger warring with embarrassment.

"I fear you do him a disservice, my dear. That's the thing, you see—he truly is interested. Fascinated, in fact. You should have heard him going on about the metaphysical implications of lost spirits clinging to a loved one. I could barely shut him up long enough to get a word in edgewise."

She glanced up, curious despite herself. "And did you come up with a way to quiet them?" she asked.

"I'm afraid not, child. That said, Brother Eiridan is planning a journey back to our old village to speak with the High Priest there. I gather you do not wish to include our own High Priest in your confidence, which is certainly your right. While Senovo is undeniably a powerful man, at the end of the day, he is also a young one. High Priest Jyrrel is more experienced, and has seen much in his life. He may well have fresh wisdom to offer us."

Her irritation with Priest Eiridan faded considerably upon hearing how much trouble he was putting himself to on her behalf. "I'm... not used to people going to such effort for me," she said. "Or any effort at all, to be perfectly honest."

Feldes only smiled. "I told you—he's interested. He can also become a bit, shall we say, *singleminded* about things on occasion. Ask him sometime about his studies into the written symbols the Alyrions and Rhytheeri use to communicate information without a messenger. Or don't, unless you want to be treated to an hour's lecture on the subject."

"I've seen those symbols," she said in mild surprise. "I only learned a handful of them, though."

"Good gracious. In that case, I'd definitely advise you to steer clear of the subject unless you have a spare week or two to devote to answering Eiridan's questions."

204

Suddenly and without warning, the emptiness that was her life now nearly overwhelmed her. She no longer had any goals to achieve. No mountains to cross, no fantasies of bloody revenge to give her strength when her body threatened to fail. Who *was* she now? And… who had she been before?

Some of this must have showed on her face, because Feldes frowned. "Are you all right, my dear?"

"Yes," she said on a faint quaver. "Sorry. It just occurred to me that should Priest Eiridan wish to question me for two weeks about Rhytheeri symbols, I… really have nothing more pressing to do with my time."

Feldes nodded his understanding. "I see. Well, for what it's worth, you are free now to make whatever new goals and plans you choose. And I would suggest doing so promptly, if only so you *will* have a good excuse to avoid his questions on the subject. Right now, however, you can help me divide up this batter and get it in the ovens."

It was evening before Kathrael saw Favian again. She'd spent the day finding odds and ends to keep herself busy, even screwing up her courage to take the leftover fruit cakes out to the apprentices at the horse pens. Limdya greeted her cheerfully and helped her distribute them, and Dalon gave her a friendly nod from across the yard where he was instructing a young boy about something involving a mass of tangled leather harness straps.

To her surprise, the boyish Horse Mistress herself stopped Kathrael as she was preparing to leave and return to the temple. She tensed, well aware that Carivel was still less than pleased with Kathrael's grief-fueled plan to get revenge on High Priest Senovo—not to mention her willingness to go through Favian to do so.

As it turned out, it was the latter person that Carivel was interested in.

"Have you seen Favian?" she asked, and up close, Kathrael could see that the crease in her brow stemmed not from anger, but from worry.

"Not since this morning," Kathrael said warily. "Why?"

"I need to talk to him, and he's been avoiding me. He is—unfortunately—quite skilled in avoidance when he wants to be." The worried frown grew deeper.

"Did the Chief have bad news for him this morning, then?" Kathrael asked.

Carivel seemed unsurprised that she knew of Favian's meeting with Andoc. Perhaps the Wolf Patron had told her of finding Favian in Kathrael's room. "He had news that Favian didn't want to hear, certainly."

She felt a twinge of anger on Favian's behalf warm her belly. "The elders will not act to help his friend?"

"They aren't friends. But, no, the elders won't sanction anything that might ruffle feathers in the west." Carivel took a deep breath and let it out. "They plan to wait and see if Ithric can get free on his own, or if this traveling show you described

206

will come within the territory of Draebard and its allies."

"Favian didn't take it well," Kathrael guessed.

"To put it mildly, yeah." She ran a hand through her close-cropped hair. "So if you see him, tell him I need to speak with him, all right?"

"I'll tell him."

"Thanks," Carivel said, her lips twisting into something that tried to be a smile, and failed.

But Favian was conspicuously absent that afternoon, and when she finally did see him, it was because he found her, not the other way around. She was taking a bucket of scraps from the evening meal outside to the feed the chickens when Favian appeared from the shadows.

"I need you to relay a message to Frella for me," he said without preamble.

"What kind of message?" she asked.

"Tell her I had to leave, and that I'll be back as soon as I can. But don't tell her until tomorrow."

"You're going after him." She didn't bother to phrase it as a question.

"I don't have a *choice*. No one else will do anything!" Favian pressed his hands under his armpits, visibly reining in his need to *act*. "Will you give Frella the message?"

Something clicked inside of Kathrael's mind, settling into place with a heavy sense of utter rightness. "Sorry, priest-boy. I'm afraid I can't."

He looked surprised. Hurt, even. "Why not?"

"Because," Kathrael said, "I'm going with you."

THIRTEEN

Favian's expression of betrayal morphed back into one of surprise. "It... might be dangerous," he said after a momentary pause. "I probably shouldn't let you come. And for that matter... why would you even offer? You don't owe me any-thing."

She raised an eyebrow and drew herself up to her admittedly not-very-impressive height. "First, priest-boy, let's get something straight. You don't *let* me come along. I choose to come with you, and then I do it. End of story. Second, you helped me when you had every reason not to. And the lion-boy helped children he barely knew get to freedom, when he could have asked for his own freedom in-stead. Why should I *not* try to help you both in return?"

"It will be a difficult journey," said Favian, still obviously off-balance. The look she gave him took only a few seconds to penetrate, and he blushed. "Right. Sorry. That was a bit stupid, wasn't it."

"A bit," she allowed dryly, thinking of hunger and thirst and blisters bleeding on her feet. "You're forgiven, though. Now, tell me you at least have a plan?"

He nodded. "I have most of what we'll need gathered together and hidden in the woods behind the temple. You should see about getting some more food from the kitchens, though—I only packed for one. I'll, um, I'll see if my friend Lundis will relay the message to Frella in the morning, so she knows what's happening."

"She would figure it out, regardless, you know. She's smart, your sister."

"Yes, well. I'd feel better leaving her the message anyway." Favian took a deep breath and let it out. A faint puff of steam formed in front of his face and dissipated almost immediately—the first hint of autumn had cooled the evening air to a slight nip. "Beyond that," he continued, "we just need to wait until she's asleep and sneak out to the horse pens. There's usually a guard posted at night, but they all know me. I'll tell them neither of us could sleep and we wanted to come out and calm our minds for a few minutes."

"You want me to ride a horse?" Kathrael asked, a feeling of trepidation creeping over her for the first time.

"Well… I'd planned to take two horses, so Ithric could ride back," Favian said. "That's probably still the best plan—you can ride double with me since you don't have any experience. The horses can handle it—you barely weigh anything."

Kathrael was still nervous about this aspect of the scheme, but she could hardly back out now. Besides, there *was* something rather appealing about the idea of sitting on top of one of the great beasts' backs. Especially if someone else was controlling it.

"All right," she allowed. "I suppose I can manage that." A new thought came to her. "What about your—" she gestured toward his crotch. "You know. Won't riding be painful?"

"Probably," Favian said with a grimace. "Walking will take too long, though, and a wagon would be just as uncomfortable—assuming I could even sneak a wagon out of town successfully, which is doubtful."

She shrugged. "If you say so. You'll come and get me when it's time, then?"

"If you're still certain you want to do this, yes."

"I'm certain." She suddenly remembered her visit to the horse pens earlier in the day. "Oh! I almost forgot. The Horse Mistress was looking for you. She wanted to talk to you."

Favian's expression snapped closed. "Yeah. Not happening."

"Your decision, priest-boy," she said. "I'm just relaying the message."

"If she wanted to say something, it would have been more useful for her to say it during the meeting with the elders," he said tightly, before visibly forcing himself to relax. "Frella can pass on my message to the others—including Carivel—in the morning."

"Fine," Kathrael said. "I'll get us some more food and wait for you in my room. Don't worry, we'll find your lost shape-shifter, Favian."

He tried for a smile, though it didn't reach his eyes. "Thank you, Kathrael. I'll see you later tonight. Be ready."

It was very late when Favian finally crept into Kathrael's room. She was propped up in bed, half-dozing while she waited for him. Nevertheless, the instant she heard the swish of his robes, she was completely alert. The prospect of having a *purpose* again was intoxicating — surprisingly so.

The whispers of half-heard voices that had floated around the dark recesses of the room as she napped dissipated like mist in the sunlight, and she swung her feet down to rest on the floor. She was dressed in the traveling clothes Shayla had found for her. Someone at the temple had repaired the sole of her left boot. Her satchel was full of food; her dagger nestled at her waist.

She was ready.

"Sorry to be so long," Favian said in a low voice. "Frella got it into her head to stay up and *make sure I didn't do anything foolish*, as she put it. It took forever for her to finally drift off."

"She's going to be furious with you," Kathrael observed.

"Yes," Favian agreed. "She is. Fortunately, she's my sister, so she's pretty much obligated to forgive me. Especially when we bring Ithric back with us."

Kathrael was unavoidably reminded of her own sister heading off to the city with promises of bringing food and money back when she returned.

Do you forgive me, little sister? Elarra whispered from the shadows.

I don't know, she thought. Aloud, she held her peace.

They snuck out through a back entrance, thereby avoiding the sleepy acolyte posted at the main door to help anyone who had need of the priests during the night. The air was crisp and chill, a prelude of things to come. The waning moon played hide and seek in the clouds, intermittently illuminating their surroundings with pale silver light. Even so, Kathrael kept a hand on Favian's arm to help guide her steps. Having a blind eye had reduced her night vision considerably, whereas Favian was so familiar with the village that he moved with as much confidence as if it had been daylight.

The sound and smell of many large animals gathered in one place heralded their arrival at the horse pens.

Favian paused, looking around. "There's no guard tonight. That's strange."

Kathrael felt a prickle of unease, but shrugged it off. "Maybe he just went off for a piss or something."

"Maybe," Favian said, sounding unconvinced. "Well, I guess we'd better take advantage of it, whatever the case. Come on. We'll need saddles and bridles from the tack shed."

He led her to a large structure with a simple shed-roof, situated not far from the corrals where the horses milled about restlessly in the dark. The door creaked on iron hinges as he pulled it open, and they both froze when a familiar voice from inside said, "It's about bloody time. I expected you hours ago, you know."

Sparks flew as the unseen speaker struck a flint, and a moment later, a hanging lamp flared to life, revealing Carivel. She and Favian stared at each other for a long moment.

"Well, shit," Favian said, breaking the awkward silence.

"Does Senovo know you still curse like that, *Novice Favian*?" Carivel asked in a dry tone, before her attention caught and held on Kathrael.

"Probably." Favian sounded tired. "He knows most things, in my experience."

"Are you here to stop us, Horse Mistress?" Kathrael asked, tilting her chin up to level a glare at Carivel. "Everyone has gone to great lengths to assure me that I'm not a prisoner here. I assume the same can be said of Favian."

The twitch of Carivel's lips suggested an emotion somewhere between irritation and amusement. Her attention turned to Favian, and it was to him that she directed her reply. "If I were here to stop you, I probably wouldn't have sent away the guard. I also wouldn't have gone to the trouble of saddling Kekenu, Audris, and Ozias while I waited."

"You... what?" Favian asked, looking lost.

Carivel huffed in annoyance. "I was planning on coming with you, you clod. It's not as if we were going to let you go off alone."

"*We*?" Favian echoed, still very obviously lagging several steps behind in the conversation.

Carivel rolled her eyes and made a low noise of disgust. "Yes, *we*. You think the others didn't know to expect this?" Her gaze flicked back to

Kathrael, who was watching her warily. "I'll admit, however, that we didn't take *you* into account. Why are you here, Kathrael?"

In general, Kathrael appreciated the northerners' frankness, but for some reason the question still rankled. "I'm going with him, of course. The lion-boy deserves better than your village elders' abandonment."

Carivel's expression softened incrementally. "Yes. Yes, he does. That said, no one wants to see this thing turn into a diplomatic incident that spawns some messy intertribal conflict."

"Which is why you shouldn't go, Carivel," Favian said, having evidently caught up with the two of them once more. "You're known. I'm not."

"I am actually capable of pretending to be someone else for a week or two, Favian," Carivel pointed out.

"After riding in on a loudly colored black and white pinto, with Andoc's two white stallions in tow?" Favian shot back. He frowned suddenly. "Why did you choose them, anyway? I was going to borrow a couple of nondescript bays or chestnuts."

"Because they would make it much easier for Andoc and Senovo to find us if something went wrong," Carivel said.

"Favian's right about one thing, though," Kathrael interrupted. "If you are known to these other tribes, and you're so worried about provoking a *diplomatic incident*, then you shouldn't come. He isn't going alone. I'll be with him. Nobody in the north knows me. I'm not anyone special."

Carivel's eyes burned into her for a long, uncomfortable moment.

"You came all the way here from Rhyth on foot, is that right? By yourself?" she asked eventually.

"I rode for one day and part of another on the back of a donkey cart. Other than that, yes."

"And you managed to complete that kind of a journey without proper supplies?"

"When I started out, I didn't even have shoes."

The Horse Mistress's gaze drilled into her for another few heartbeats. "And why should I trust you alone with Favian after what you tried to do to him?"

Kathrael willed down the flush that was threatening to rise to her face. "Because *he* does. And you trust *him*."

"Let the two of us go, Carivel," Favian said earnestly. "We'll find Ithric and bring him back."

Carivel let out a slow breath through her teeth. "Favian… I understand why you have to go. I know you *have* to see the contents of your dream in the waking world, or else you couldn't have *Seen* it in the first place. But… after what you saw in your vision, how can you be so confident of bringing Ithric back safely?"

Kathrael had wondered that as well, though she could hardly claim to be an expert in such things. Her experience with *prophecy* to date had been a singularly painful and unfulfilling one.

"This is different," Favian replied earnestly. "Before, there was never any good way for me to influence what I saw. But I know what to do this time."

She saw the moment Carivel made her decision—saw it in the dip of her chin and the faint slump of her shoulders. "All right, Favian. Though I hope to the gods I'm not making a mistake."

"If so," he said, "it's not your mistake to make, Carivel. It's mine."

She shook her head, a tiny movement. "At least tell me you've gathered supplies for yourselves."

"They're hidden at the edge of town," he told her.

She frowned, and rummaged under her jerkin. "Well, then. Here. You'd better have this," she said, pulling out a cloth purse tied with a drawstring. She tossed it to Favian, who fumbled it one-handed before rescuing it from falling. It looked heavy; the contents clinked and jingled.

"That… is a lot of money," Favian said, sounding distinctly taken aback.

For her part, Kathrael couldn't help the way her eyes widened in awe. It was… quite possibly the most money she'd ever seen gathered together in one place. Carivel only shrugged.

"Andoc's contribution. You might need it," she said. "You being a priest now will probably help, but even so—mind that you keep a lookout for bandits."

"We will," said Favian, and moved forward to embrace her. "Thank you."

Carivel closed her eyes and squeezed back. "You can thank me by coming back safe. Preferably with Ithric in tow." She stepped back and turned to regard Kathrael. "That goes for you, too. Don't do anything to make me lose faith in Favian's judgment, all right?"

Kathrael did flush that time, but Carivel only stuck out a hand. After a moment, Kathrael gripped it forearm to forearm, an unspoken pact.

Carivel led them out into the darkness, where she had left the three horses tied to the fence. They were laden with saddles, bridles, saddlebags, loops of extra rope and various other sundries for traveling. She efficiently transferred some of the supplies from the splotchy black and white horse to the two white ones. The animals' coats reflected the moonlight, making them appear almost luminous in the murky night.

When everything was arranged to her satisfaction, she clapped Favian on the shoulder. "Off with you, then. Ithric is waiting. May the gods smile on your endeavors and return you safe and whole."

"Goodbye, Carivel," Favian said. "Tell the others we promise to be careful. We'll see you again soon."

With that, he took up the horses' reins. "Come on, Kathrael. We'll have to circle around and pick up the supplies at the western edge of the village. I want to get a bit of distance behind us tonight before we stop to rest."

"Lead on," she said, and followed along next to the shorter horse's shoulder when Favian headed off toward his hiding place.

An hour later, they were cantering along the western road at a steady pace. Favian had padded the seat of the saddle with a thick fur folded into a square and tied into place with twine, but he still found it more comfortable to balance his weight in the stirrups, gripping with his knees and letting his seat hover an inch or two above the saddle.

It would have been unpleasantly chilly with the wind in his face on the unexpectedly brisk night, but Kathrael was a warm weight pressed along his back. At first, her arms had clamped around his stomach almost hard enough to squeeze the breath out of him, and he could feel her pounding heartbeat even through their clothes. It hadn't taken long for her to get the feel of the horse's motion, though, and now she balanced more easily behind him while keeping a light grip around his waist.

They were riding Ozias, the colt who had been born the day after the Alyrion attack. He was the shorter of the two horses by about half a hand, and his gait was smoother than his brother's. Audris cantered next to them, his head even with his sibling's shoulder. Favian held the second stallion's lead rope looped once around the pommel and gathered in his right hand along with Ozias' reins.

"Doing all right?" he called back to Kathrael. He felt her nod in response, her cheek pressed against his left shoulder blade.

"It's not like I expected it to be," she replied, raising her voice over the wind. "I thought it would be bouncier!"

"That's because we're not trotting," Favian said in a wry tone. "And we won't be, if I can possibly help it."

Truth be told, it was probably foolish to undertake such a journey by horseback so soon after being castrated. He was no longer used to spending hours in the saddle every day, as he had been when he was Carivel's apprentice at the horse pens. For now, it was true that he could ride comfortably enough in the half-seat people used for crossing rugged terrain and jumping obstacles, but his thigh muscles would surely pay the price tomorrow, and all the days that followed.

"Do we have a plan, beyond showing up in a village and interrogating people about a traveling show that may or may not have passed through?" Kathrael asked, distracting Favian from his fretting.

"I thought we could claim that Ithric is your brother and your sole means of support, and that I'm helping you look for him after he was kidnapped," Favian said.

"My sole means of support? Because of my face, you mean," Kathrael said.

Though she maintained her grip around Favian's middle, he could feel something in her closing off. Favian had been so focused on cobbling together a plan that might help them find Ithric, he'd only realized at that very moment how it might sound to Kathrael.

"Would that... be all right?" he asked. "Sorry—it was more than a little presumptuous of me."

"No," she said. "It makes sense. He should be my bondmate, though, not my brother. He looks too northern, and I look too southern. No one would believe we're related."

"In that case," Favian said, trying for levity but unable to keep the bitterness from creeping into his voice, "my condolences on your unfortunate hand-fasting match."

There was silence behind him, though Favian felt Kathrael relax again after her earlier tension.

"I don't understand you, priest-boy," she said eventually. "One would almost think you hated this person you're going to such lengths to save."

It was Favian's turn to lapse into silence, as the horses' hooves ate up the road beneath them.

"I don't hate him," he said, several minutes later. "Things would actually be quite a bit simpler if I did."

Kathrael digested that as they rode on, her arms tightening around him.

They stopped a few hours later, when Favian could no longer keep his eyes from drifting shut every few minutes. It was still dark, but he thought he could detect a faint tinge of lighter sky behind them, in the east.

"We should get some rest," he said, and stifled the yawn that tried to come out with the words. "If we head back into the trees a bit, I don't think any-one will bother us."

Kathrael had progressively sagged against him as the night wore on, but she roused herself at his words. "Did you know I once scared off a pair of men who wanted to rob me on the road north of Rhyth?"

"No," Favian replied, "but I can't say I'm all that shocked, really. What did you do?"

"I uncovered my scars and threatened to give them the *face-melting plague*. They couldn't get away fast enough."

Favian was caught between amusement at the mental image, admiration at her utter fearlessness, respect for her formidable resourcefulness, and a surprisingly strong surge of protectiveness at the idea of thieves threatening her.

"We'll keep that particular defense in reserve for emergencies, I think," he said, not sure what else would be appropriate to say.

She snorted, sleepy and self-deprecating. "I believe that may be the only time I've ever been grateful for having this ruin of a face. There was something strangely satisfying about watching them scamper off in terror."

"I guess there would be, at that," he agreed, and linked elbows with her to help her slide down from Ozias' back. Her knees wobbled, and he kept a grip on her forearm until she steadied herself. "It takes a minute to get your land legs back sometimes," he told her. "Especially the first few times."

"So I see," she agreed wryly, taking a few tentative steps to get the muscles working again.

Favian could already feel the burn in his own legs from riding in a half-seat for so long. He dismounted cautiously, not wanting to make a fool of himself by folding into a crumpled heap on the ground, but fortunately his legs held his weight with only a moderate protest.

"There was a creek running alongside the road earlier—I could hear it," he said. "Let's see if we can find it, and maybe a clearing with enough grass so the horses can graze while we sleep."

He couldn't make out her expression in the dark, but the frown was audible in her voice. "Won't they run off?"

"We'll hobble them so they don't wander far," he explained. "I'll show you how it's done in the morning, when there's light to see."

They cautiously followed a wide, well-traveled animal track deeper into the trees. The horses heard the trickle of water before they did, and perked up, pressing forward with new energy. Before long, the woods opened up into a pleasant glade, with a babbling creek running along one edge.

"Perfect," said Kathrael. "Look, there's a big tree that fell down over here. There's space under the trunk where we can shelter out of the wind."

While it was not dangerously cold by any means, it was bordering on uncomfortable even without the added breeze caused by the horses' speed as they had traveled. And Favian hadn't missed the way Kathrael's chilly hands had burrowed into the folds at the front of his robes as they rode. She was not quite the same skeletal figure who had snuck into his sickroom that first night, but she still had barely an ounce of fat on her body. She was also a southern girl, born and bred.

"Are you cold?" he asked. "I can make a fire."

"As long as it won't draw the wrong sort of attention," she said cautiously.

"No reason why it should. We're back quite a way from the road, and the only other sign of people we've seen were campfires back near the crossroads we passed an hour ago." Favian tied up the horses as he spoke and began to unpack bedrolls and saddlebags. "Are you hungry?"

"I'm always hungry these days, it seems. Here, give me the tent hide."

They worked with an easy rapport, getting things set up for a few hours' rest and settling the horses to drink and graze. Kathrael gathered wood, and Favian started the fire with a pinch of the highly flammable powder that the priests used for effect during ceremonies. They heated bowls of water from the stream to boiling and used it to rehydrate some of the dried meat and root vegetables they carried with them.

Despite his earlier exhaustion, once he'd bedded down, Favian couldn't seem to quiet his mind enough to fall asleep. He tried to keep his tossing and turning to a minimum, painfully aware of Kathrael curled up in her blanket next to him. Some time later, it became apparent that his efforts to be still had been for nothing.

"Can't sleep?" Kathrael asked.

"No," he answered with a sigh. "Sorry. Am I keeping you awake?"

She scooted up to sit, leaning against the heavy bole that they were using as the main support for the tent. "No. The spirits are restless tonight.

Maybe they're remembering the last time we traveled."

She shivered a bit, whether from cold or disquiet, he didn't know. Following an instinct, he wrapped an arm around her back and drew her against him, blanket and all.

"Your baby?" he asked, and she shrugged a shoulder under his grip.

"All of them," she said.

He frowned. "Is there anything I can do?"

"I don't need your sympathy, Favian," she said. "Distraction would be good, though. What is it that keeps *your* mind from rest after such a long day?"

He blew out a breath. "Just worry. Worry about the journey, worry about finding Ithric, worry about what happens if we *do* find him. Stupid, really... worry won't help with any of it. It'll just make me exhausted tomorrow."

"You're as tense as a rabbit staring down a pack of hunting dogs," she observed. "Here. Budge up a bit."

She ducked out from under his arm and shoved him around until she could sit behind him, her legs on either side of his and her skirts bunched up at the small of his back.

"What are you—" He broke off with a grunt as strong fingers dug into the muscles of his shoulders. "Agh! Wait—I don't think—"

"Shut up, priest-boy," Kathrael said, her words tickling his ear. "If I were trying to seduce you, you'd know it. Trust me."

"*Nngh,*" he said, as agony where her vicious fingers were stabbing into him melted into pleasure. "Kathrael... you don't have to—"

"Didn't I tell you to shut up? I remember that part distinctly."

Another terribly undignified, choked-off moan of pleasure-pain slipped past Favian's control, after which he clamped his lips together and did as he was told. It was not unlike being trampled by a herd of very small horses... if the horses knew exactly how to trample him in such a way that their hooves hit *every. Single. Knot. In. His. Back.*

When she was finally satisfied with her efforts at torture, he would have been shaking like a newborn calf, had doing so not seemed like far too much work when his body was this relaxed.

Somehow, he'd ended up flat on his stomach during the process, with his right cheek mashed into the blanket. "Ow," he said into the rough wool. "I think."

"Can you sleep now?" Kathrael asked.

Favian thought about it for a moment, his mind moving like thick treacle.

"... maybe?" he hazarded. She was still leaning against his left hip, and he felt her shiver. "You're still cold," he said, and rolled onto his side with some considerable effort. "Come here. It'll be warmer together."

She came without protest, somewhat to his surprise. He arranged her in front of him, so she was between the fire and his body. When the blankets were wrapped around them and the warmth from both sides had begun to penetrate her chill, he felt her relax into his embrace with a silent sigh of relief.

Again, Favian was struck by how *right* it felt to have her there. Some considerable time must have passed as he lay there soaking up the feeling and trying to quantify it, because she stirred in his arms and asked, "Still awake?" in a sleepy voice.

"Sorry," he apologized again, vowing to stay camped here in the morning until she, at least, had gotten some decent rest.

"Don't apologize," she said, still in that soft-edged, middle-of-the-night voice. "I'm the queen of restless nights. No room to say a word, me."

Perhaps it was the late hour, darkness poised to give way to dawn. Or perhaps it was his own unusually relaxed state, coupled with lack of sleep and distraction over Ithric. Whatever the case, his thoughts moved straight to his mouth and out past his lips without any pause for censure.

"Do you ever think that it would be nice to have this kind of closeness without the complication of sex getting in the way?"

She shrugged in his arms, and yawned. "There's no *would be*. It *is* nice." She snuggled back against him. "I haven't had anything like this since Vesh died. I missed it. You remind me of him sometimes, you know."

Favian's heart ached for her—a sharp pang. "I take that as a very high compliment," he said.

"You do realize," she said around another yawn, "that if this was all you wanted out of life, you didn't need to get your balls cut off. Women would have lined up to get their claws into you."

"It's not *all* I wanted. I do have other reasons for choosing to become a priest," he clarified. "Though I must say, in my experience, women aren't usually terribly interested in a man who can't get it up for them."

She made a dismissive noise. "The only thing women get out of sex is children, and the illusion of security." She paused before adding, "Or, if they're smart, money."

Favian frowned at the tart tone of her reply, and tamped down his knee-jerk inclination to dispute it. This was not the time to have an in-depth discussion about a subject that obviously cut Kathrael close to the bone, but he filed it away to pursue later. Was it merely the bitterness of a woman who had been forced into a life of prostitution, or had Kathrael truly never found any pleasure in the gifts of the body?

For all that Favian was happy to see the back of his own lustful desires, it certainly wasn't because he'd found them un-pleasurable. In fact, it was a bit too much the opposite problem. Lust had led him into what was perhaps the worst decision he'd ever made in his life. And, because the gods' sense of humor was often more than a little sick... here he was, months later, riding pell-mell toward that very same bad decision.

Time passed, and Kathrael made a soft snuffling noise, sliding into sleep within the circle of his arms. A few minutes later, the warm, slumbering weight of her paired with the quiet rasp of her breathing pulled Favian down into darkness as well.

The sun was well up in the sky when the two of them woke, hours later. The fire had burned to ashes, but late summer was already wresting control back from autumn, driving the temperature and humidity up to something more seasonable.

Favian was still nursing that trampled-by-tiny-but-vicious-horses feeling, though to be fair, the tension that had gripped his neck and shoulders for days was all but gone. His legs, on the other hand, were every bit as stiff and sore as he'd expected they would be, and he knew he was going to have to grit his teeth and sit his ass down in the saddle for much of the day today, painful as it would certainly be.

Kathrael wasn't moving much better after her first experience riding double.

"I thought this was supposed to be easier than walking?" she observed as she gingerly climbed back up behind Favian, the two of them riding Audris this time.

"Faster, anyway," Favian replied as he fussed around with the fur pad on the seat of his saddle, trying to keep as much pressure as possible off of his newly healed scar. If he rounded his lower back and rocked back on his seat bones, it was just about tolerable. Though that probably wouldn't be the case a few hours from now. "Maybe we'll start off at a walk for a bit, to warm up our muscles."

"My muscles are on fire already, thanks," came the sarcastic reply.

They headed off, rejoining the road and continuing their westward trek.

"Where exactly are we going?" Kathrael asked. "Do you know the villages in the west?"

"To an extent," Favian said. "My father was born in Teth, so I figured we'd start there since I have blood ties with them. I thought about starting at the southernmost port town, but I'm sure they would have been there already and moved on. We'd end up chasing them. I think it'll be more efficient to start further north. If they've been to Teth already, we'll still need to head north to catch up, but we'll be much closer to them. And if they haven't been there, we'll know to head south until we come across them. Or at least, until we come across word of them."

"That makes sense, I suppose."

"It's a big area to search," Favian admitted. "But the good news is, there are only a handful of large villages and towns scattered through the region."

"People will be talking about a show like that for weeks, I'm sure," Kathrael said. "It should be easy enough to gain word of it."

"That's what I'm counting on. I just hope the Chief of whatever village we end up in will be sympathetic to us, and not to the men running the show. He should be, I think, after we tell them Ithric's a shape-shifter."

Kathrael was silent for a moment. "In the south, you definitely wouldn't want to tell them that."

Favian frowned. "This isn't the south, thank the gods. People still revere shape-shifters here.

Though the fact that Ithric isn't in the priesthood is going to raise some eyebrows."

"I take it the lion-boy is a bit more attached to his balls than you were to yours?"

"To put it mildly." Favian shook his head, thinking of the blazing rows they'd had on the subject over the years. "He has rather strong feelings on the matter, in fact."

"Well, maybe he's a special case, since he has to take care of his poor, disfigured bondmate." Kathrael's voice oozed honey.

Favian snorted. "Believe me, the highlight of this entire thing is going to be seeing his face when he finds out that he's *married*. He's... er... not really the type to settle down."

"That's all right," said Kathrael philosophically. "Neither am I."

FOURTEEN

Over the following hours of travel, Favian assured Kathrael that they were making good progress toward Teth, though riding became increasingly miserable as the day wore on. Kathrael could feel Favian alternately lifting himself to hover over the saddle, and settling down in an uncomfortable looking slouch. Neither seemed to give him much relief.

For her part, the muscles of her back and legs were burning with overuse, every rhythmic, rocking stride making them ache a little more. They slowed often to let the horses blow, and stopped at the occasional stream to water them. By mutual agreement, however, they did not dismount to eat or drink themselves. It would be far too hard to get back on and keep going afterward. Instead, they slowed to a walk and ate dried fruit and cheese straight from the saddlebags, washing it down with watered wine from one of the wineskins.

It was only the memory of her journey over the mountains and the hardship she had endured that kept Kathrael from begging Favian to stop early so they could rest. Her back might be aching, and her thighs might be starting to chafe — but things could be so much worse. They had food and drink. They had shelter and adequate clothing. They even had fast transportation — and, in fact, Favian assured her that they would reach Teth sometime the following day.

She could bear her discomfort for the space of a day, as Favian was bearing his.

Even so, it was a relief when the sun touched the western horizon, throwing long shadows behind them.

"No need to ride through the night tonight," Favian said. "I think we can both use a full night's rest."

"You'll get no argument from me," she replied.

The pair found another suitable spot for camping and dismounted with matching groans of discomfort. The terrain had changed over the course of the day, patchy forests giving way to open grasslands. They had seen a few fellow travelers as they rode, and Kathrael kept her face carefully covered with her shawl. While a couple of people had stared in interest at the unusual white horses, none had shown any further interest in them beyond an occasional muttered, "Good day, Brother," to Favian in his dun-colored priest's robes.

The two of them repeated the same steps they'd gone through the previous night to set up camp, the process made considerably easier this time by the slowly fading light of dusk. Favian showed Kathrael how to help unsaddle the horses and rub them down. She was still a little nervous around the animals when she was on the ground, but at the same time there was something both thrilling and delightfully *forbidden* about working with them.

She — a slave girl, a prostitute, the lowest of the low — was caring for a tribal chieftain's prized white horses. And they were as docile under her touch as they would be for any seasoned Horse Master. All her life, she had been taught that a woman's spirit was too weak to control the spirits of animals.

Who's the weak one now? she thought as Ozias nuzzled a tidbit of dried mayapple from her palm.

Never you, Kath, Vesh whispered, the noise fading into the rustle of tall grass around her.

When the horses were settled and the campfire was merrily crackling away in the warm twilight, they cooked a simple meal. Kathrael ate with ravenous single-mindedness, though she noticed Favian only picked at his food.

"You should eat," she said around a mouthful of bread and cheese. "Keep your strength up."

Favian's smile was wan; his face, pale. "Maybe after I stop aching quite so much. It's making me a bit queasy right now."

She swallowed and looked more closely at him. "You need to figure out something different for riding tomorrow. It can't be good for you when you're still not completely healed. Maybe we could alternate riding and walking?"

"The wound is closed and scarred over," he assured her quickly. "I guess it's just the inside that still needs more time. Whatever the case, I'd rather not walk. As it is, we'll make Teth late tomorrow afternoon if we don't run into any delays. But if we walk part of the way, we might have to camp for a third night."

"Well, it's your choice," she said. "I'd offer to work on it for you like I did last night with your back…"

He blushed and laughed, as she had intended. "Kind of you to offer, but I *really* don't think that would help the situation, unfortunately."

"Just trying to be helpful, priest-boy," she said, all innocence.

He snorted. "Of course you are. Nothing at all to do with the fact that you think it's funny when you can make me blush." He sobered. "How about you let me return the favor, instead? You were moving earlier like your back hurt."

Kathrael paused with the half-eaten slab of bread held poised, halfway to her mouth. She was strangely taken aback. It was one thing to offer some of the skills she'd picked up as a whore—she'd truly enjoyed massaging the tension from Favian's muscles until he melted into relaxation beneath her touch. But to have someone offer the same to her?

She had remained frozen for too long. Favian was looking at her carefully.

"Did I say something wrong, Kathrael?" he asked.

She blinked, breaking free of her paralysis. "No," she said slowly. "You didn't say anything wrong. I just… didn't expect you to offer, is all."

Favian settled further against the saddle he was using as a backrest and regarded her with his pale blue eyes. "Oh? Why wouldn't I, though? It only seems fair."

She did him the courtesy of thinking about the question for a few moments before answering.

"It's just that… women do things for men, to make them feel better and give them pleasure. Not the other way around. Men… *take*."

For some reason, that made him look sad.

"Haven't you ever been with a man who wasn't paying for your services? A man *you* chose to be with?" he asked.

Her temper flared. "I *chose* to be with all of them!"

He didn't rise to her anger. Nor did he back down. "But only for money, is that right? Never because you wanted it for yourself?"

"Please! Am I a fool, to give my body away for free?" She was still angry. Defensive. "It was bad enough when I was getting paid for it."

Favian let out a breath through his teeth. "It's true then, what you hinted at last night. You've never felt physical pleasure from any of your liaisons?"

She made a derisive noise. "Women don't get pleasure from being fucked. Some of them pretend to, but it's just a lie."

He was still looking at her in a way that made her want to squirm. "I assure you," he said, with evident sincerity, "it's not a lie. Have you never even touched yourself for pleasure? Sex with a man can produce those same feelings, and more."

"Why would I want to touch myself?" she asked, genuinely confused. Occasionally, men would ask a whore to touch herself while they watched, and the more experienced women had advised Kathrael to writhe around and moan while she was doing it because it made the man more excited.

But her cunt had always been swollen and uncomfortable when she was working regularly, and rubbing it mostly just chafed unless she could sneak some oil onto her fingers first. She'd never once found it pleasant.

Favian continued to stare at her as if he suspected her of having him on, but when she only looked back in confusion, he eventually said, "Many woman — *most* women, I would have thought — touch themselves to feel good and provoke a sexual release. Just as most men do."

She stared at him. "I think these women have been telling you fairy stories, Favian. Like I said, some women pretend to enjoy it because men like that sort of thing. Some men do, anyway — in my experience, most don't actually care one way or the other."

Her companion seemed lost for words, confirmed a moment later when he said, "I'm not sure how to even begin to respond to that."

"Why are you so surprised?" she asked. "I thought you didn't like sex anyway?"

"No, I *loved* sex," Favian replied. "I thought about it all the time, or at least it felt like I did. Sex with men, that is to say. It was almost obsessive... and *that* was the part I didn't like."

"So you went and got your balls cut off?" She was deflecting, she knew — trying to move him away from the uncomfortable topic by pissing him off, but she couldn't seem to stop herself.

He still wasn't rising to the bait, though, leaning back against his saddle in such a relaxed and thoroughly unthreatening manner that it made her want to shake him until his teeth rattled.

"I got castrated because I wanted to be a priest, for a variety of reasons that we can discuss in more detail if you're interested. But a happy side effect has been that, yes, I'm no longer obsessed by the idea of sex. I don't hate the idea. I don't love the idea. It's just a thing that people do with each other to feel good. When it's used to give mutual pleasure and express love, it's quite beautiful, really. When it's used as a weapon to hurt someone, it's very, very ugly. When it's used as a cold transaction with no meaning behind it—" Favian paused, searching for the words he wanted. "—it's... rather sad, I suppose."

"Spoken like a man," she managed to spit, not liking the way his words prodded at something deep inside her chest.

He shrugged. "Like a eunuch, at any rate. Now, since we're apparently going to have to agree to disagree on that subject for the moment, *would* you like me to work on your back? I assure you, I'm only interested in repaying the favor from last night, and making it a little easier for you to ride tomorrow." He paused. "Well. There might also be the aspect of distracting myself from the ache between my legs for a bit, too. But don't tell anyone."

The air escaped Kathrael's lungs in a slow sigh that took most of her defensive anger with it. Favian was a eunuch, and a hopelessly naive one, at that. He was offering. She would be a fool to pass up that offer when her back was tied up in painful knots.

"Fine," she said, trying to say it a sharp enough tone to convey that she still thought him a fool. She wasn't at all sure it worked.

She finished her bowl of reconstituted meat and parched grains, wiping up the last traces with a chunk of coarse bread. Favian still hadn't managed more than a few mouthfuls of his own food, so he poured the remains into a covered container by the fire for the morning meal.

After everything was cleaned up and packed away for a quick start the next day, Favian went off to check the horses one last time while she laid out the bedrolls. Since the night was fair and there were no convenient trees around, she decided to forego the tent.

"The horses seem happy," Favian observed upon his return. "Though why wouldn't they be? They're surrounded by a sea of grass."

"Simple pleasures," she said, accepting the peace offering implicit in the change of subject. "I can appreciate the appeal of a full belly and a warm, dry night."

"I'm sure you can, more than most people," Favian replied. "Now, let's see if we can give you the chance to appreciate a back that isn't tied up in knots." He indicated the buckskin leather bodice that Kathrael was wearing over her linen underblouse. "Do you want to take that off first?"

It was odd to have a man—or a eunuch, rather—ask her to disrobe for some reason other than sex. She shrugged, and loosened the laces on the bodice enough that she could shimmy out of it. In the muggy, late summer warmth and the privacy of their campsite, she untied the heavy split skirts she wore over her breeches, and stepped out of those as well. Finally, she toed off the worn pair of boots Shayla had given her, and settled herself on the ground cloth she'd put down at the edge of the firelight, where they would sleep tonight.

Favian knelt behind her, his knees bracketing her hips. "Where does it hurt?"

"All over," she said tartly.

"Hmm, you're *ever* so helpful, you know," Favian teased, and his large hands closed over her shoulders, warm and heavy.

It was a bizarre feeling. Vesh would occasionally sling an arm around her shoulders as they sat together, or pat her on the back, or hold her when she was upset—but he had never pressed strong fingers into her muscles and kneaded away the tension there.

Kathrael knew she had been a little bit cruel with Favian last night, digging into his rigid back without mercy to get at the knots as quickly and efficiently as possible. By contrast, Favian started with slow, firm movements to warm and relax her muscles. She was admittedly tense in the unfamiliar situation, for all that she'd trusted Favian enough to sleep peacefully in his arms on two separate occasions now.

This seemed... different somehow, perhaps because it was completely new territory for her.

"All right?" Favian asked, gathering her heavy length of dark hair and draping it over her shoulder so he could get at the back of her neck.

She grunted in reply as his thumbs dragged along taut tendons.

"This wasn't exactly the best introduction to horseback riding," he apologized. "Though I suppose it's something of a trial by fire. You'll probably develop a decent seat by the time we get back to Draebard, purely out of self defense."

A small noise slipped past her control as his palms slid down the strained muscles framing her spine, fresh blood flow tingling in their wake.

"Tell me more about this plan you have for rescuing our lion-shifter," she said, mostly as a way to distract herself from the dark magic Favian's hands were working on her abused back. "You said that this time would be *different* from your other visions — that you knew what to do. What did you mean by that?"

Favian's fingers stilled for a moment before continuing their delicious torture. Kathrael squirmed and hissed out a sharp breath as the heel of one hand pressed into a knot, rocking back and forth until the tension melted away.

"In the past, either I wasn't closely enough involved in the events I was seeing to have much of a direct impact on them, or else the event in question was already happening when I saw it, so nothing I did would make a difference. Assuming I *wanted* to make a difference in the first place, which wasn't always the case."

Kathrael frowned, thinking about it. "But if you saw Ithric get stabbed..."

"I saw the knife flash up toward his body," Favian clarified, "as I was standing at the edge of the crowd, yelling something to get his attention."

"Same thing, surely?" Kathrael asked, the pitch of her voice rising abruptly on the last word as Favian's fingers hit another knot. She cleared her throat. "I still don't understand what you think you can do to stop it."

"Simple," Favian said. "I know he could hear me — he looked straight at me. So I'm going to yell, 'Watch out, he has a knife,' as loud as I possibly can."

Kathrael blinked. "Well, as plans go, that's... direct, I suppose."

She felt Favian shrug behind her, and draw in a slow breath. "I've been over it a hundred times in my mind, and it's what I can do. I have to believe that by not showing me the moment when the knife struck home, the gods are telling me I can save him."

There was a heartbreaking air of vulnerability behind the words. Favian's hands had worked back up the length of her back as he spoke, and now rested on her shoulders again. She reached up to cover one of them with her own. "I hope you're right."

"Me, too," he whispered.

Without thinking, she twisted around until she was half-facing him, and brushed her lips against his in a chaste kiss. "You're a good friend, Favian of Draebard," she said. "Or perhaps a good enemy.

I still don't claim to understand what you and the lion-boy are to each other."

"Then you're in excellent company," Favian said into the small gap between them.

Suddenly remembering herself, she sat back, giving him space. "Sorry," she said. "I know women aren't your type, but I really wasn't trying to make you blush that time."

Favian smiled, the faintest quirk of his lips. "I told you before, Kathrael—I've had feelings for both men and women... but I could only ever get it up for men." His amusement grew more visible. "However, since it's unlikely I'll be able to get it up for anyone in the future, I suppose that's rather leveled the field." The smile faded into thoughtfulness. "Though I'm surprised, I'll admit. You haven't had a single good thing to say about physical affection between men and women."

Kathrael looked down and to the side. "I never kissed them," she muttered.

When Favian frowned in confusion and ducked his head to regain eye contact, she swallowed and continued in a more normal tone. "Kissing isn't sex. I never used to kiss the men I was servicing." She glanced away again, honesty compelling her to add, "Not... voluntarily, anyway."

Favian breathed out softly, and she clenched her jaw. Those forced kisses had always been far worse than any other perverse degradation she'd participated in for money. Sweaty hands wrapped in her hair or gripping the back of her neck... foul breath suffocating her as a slimy tongue forced its way into her mouth. It always sent her awareness scurrying into the hidden places in her mind within seconds. Sometimes she lost entire hours that way, only a blank space in her memory and a sense of rage left behind when she came back to herself.

Favian's forehead came to rest gently against her own. "Oh, Kath..." he said, as if she'd just told him the saddest story he'd ever heard. The tips of his fingers came up to brush against the left side of her face, trailing over the twists of scar tissue with a pressure so light she could barely feel it through the damaged flesh, for all that the gesture brought the burn of tears to her good eye.

He tipped up her chin with the barest suggestion of a touch, and she followed, stretching forward until her lips brushed his a second time. He met her with a sweetness that threatened to shatter her heart into a thousand diamond-edged shards. His lips were dry, a bit chapped... his hand came up to cup her scarred cheek as if it were precious rather than ugly. Her chest did hitch then, but she had cried enough tears to last a lifetime these past days. Instead, she poured the feelings into the press of their lips.

Whereas another man might have tried to take control of the kiss and deepen it, Favian seemed utterly content to continue with light, butterfly touches, undemanding of more. Eventually, when she was warm and heavy with the slowly settling weight of pent-up emotion, he stroked his thumb over her cheek and eased away. Her eyes had closed at some point; she blinked them open until he came into focus, pale-skinned and golden-haired in the flickering firelight. His blue eyes were as bottomless as the ocean.

"I won't see anyone else take from you what you do not freely give," he said, and a hint of his earlier sadness still lingered behind the words. "Never again, Kath. *Not ever.*"

"Are you going to be my protector, Favian?" she asked, knowing that such ideas were the province of youthful foolishness and naivety. Wishing, in this moment, that they were not.

"I think," Favian said after a beat, "that you are perfectly capable of being your own protector. But I fully intend to be the person who proves to you that you are deserving of protection."

She stared at him in silence, trying to wrap her mind around his words and failing. After a while, he had pity on her and kissed her forehead, breaking the moment.

"Come on," he said, urging her to turn around again. "You must be tired. I know I am. Lie on your stomach, and I'll try to get those last few knots in your back. Then we'll sleep."

Relieved by the offer of distraction, she did as she was instructed and stretched out on the blankets, pillowing her head on her arms. Her thoughts still circled restlessly, but the long day combined with the slow kneading of Favian's fingers along the length of her spine soon had her drowsing. She was only vaguely aware when he finished with a final slow stroke down her back, and lay down next to her. He pulled a blanket over them both, and she rolled over without conscious thought to

244

fit herself against his side. She fell asleep soon after, to the sounds of night insects chirping in the grass.

~~~ ☙ ~~~

The nightmare jerked her awake hours later. She sat up with a pounding heart, clammy sweat beading on her face and chest.

Help me, daughter, her mother begged. *Why did you abandon me?* Kathrael could vividly see her lifeless eyes, staring in blank hopelessness as her sister Elarra pulled Kathrael away and ran from the overseer. Ran from the Wolf Patron. She and Elarra had abandoned the old woman when they left. Had *abandoned their mother*.

The squalling cry of a hungry baby echoed strangely at the edge of Kathrael's hearing, and she moaned in denial, clapping her hands over her ears. It did nothing to muffle the noise, and she moved to pull at her hair instead, trying to distract herself with pain.

"No..." she whispered, as the cries grew in pitch and volume. "I can't help you—you're dead. You're all *dead*—"

She gasped and flinched in surprise when a hand touched her arm.

"Kathrael?" a voice asked, dragging her into a slightly greater awareness of her surroundings.

Favian. It was Favian, and what a fool she'd been to hope that just because she'd spent two peaceful nights in his arms, somehow that meant he could magically keep the ghosts away while she slept.

"Kath?" he asked again. "Talk to me, please. Did you have a nightmare?"

She nodded, not sure if the movement was visible in the faint glow of burning embers from the fire, but unable to offer more as the baby's cries grew still louder, nearly drowning out his concerned voice.

"Is it the spirits?" he asked, his firm grip on her shoulder grounding her as she shook. He paused, and continued, "Is it your baby?"

She made a noise of pain and clutched at her head again. "Yes," she said, barely recognizing her own voice. "She's starving. She's *scared*. I—I can't..."

Favian clasped her other shoulder as well, squeezing until she looked at him with a wild expression.

"Kathrael," he said in a firmer voice, "she's not starving. She's in the spirit world. She didn't starve. She just... died. Quietly, inside you. I don't know why she cries at night, but I have a feeling that when you get upset it only makes it worse. Can you take a few deep breaths for me? Try to focus on me, and on your surroundings."

Kathrael stared at him and tried to breathe. Gradually, her heart rate slowed, though the cries continued to tug painfully at her heart. For the first time in many days, the old, familiar feeling of wanting to die washed over her, leaving her shaky and nauseous.

"I can't do this..." she said. "I can't keep *doing* this! *Why won't they leave me alone?*"

Favian looked nearly as upset as she was, and there was pain in his voice when he said, "I'm so sorry, Kath. I wish I knew what to do."

"I don't need your pity!" she flared. "It doesn't help! It only makes me feel worse!"

He swallowed and forced his expression into something more neutral. "What, then? What did you do before, when you were alone?"

She thought back, to *before*. It was surprisingly difficult to do so. "I... moved. I got up and started walking again. I... don't honestly know if I would have made it over the mountains at all, if not for the spirits harrying me along." She paused, and swallowed. "Can we just go? Right now?"

Favian looked taken aback for only a moment, before he nodded. "Of course. I doubt either of us would be able to sleep any more tonight, anyway. Let me stir up the fire so we can see what we're doing to pack up the camp. You roll up the blankets, and I'll get the horses ready."

Her relief was a palpable thing. "Thank you," she breathed, and rose on unsteady feet to start putting their belongings to rights.

Favian built up the fire and retrieved the horses, saddling them with the efficiency of long practice. Kathrael helped him fasten the saddlebags and bedrolls in place, trying to focus on her task rather than the plaintive cries of distress whispering through the windblown grass.

When they were ready, Favian said, "I want to try something different today. I've thought of a way I might be able to ride more comfortably, but you won't be able to ride behind me safely while

I'm doing it. I'd like you to ride Audris by yourself, while I ride Ozias."

That caught her attention, dragging it forcibly back to her companion. "What? I don't know how to control him. All I know how to do is hang on and not fall off!"

"I'll still be leading you by a rope attached to his halter," Favian replied quickly. "You won't have to steer him. The only difference is that you'll have to hang onto the saddle for balance instead of hanging onto me."

She thought about this for a moment and decided it would actually provide a useful distraction. "All right. I can do that, I think. Can we go now?"

"Yes, we're going." Favian brought Audris over and showed her how to step up onto his bent knee and into the saddle. He fussed with the stirrups until they were the right length and arranged her feet in them. Once he'd demonstrated how to hold the reins, he stepped back and gave her a critical once-over.

"If something happens and he gets loose, sit up straight in the saddle, plant your seat, pull back on both reins smoothly, and say *whoa*. If I catch you pulling on the reins otherwise, I'll channel my inner Carivel and give you a verbal reaming you won't forget. Those reins are attached to a hunk of metal in your horse's mouth and several people — myself included — put a lot of effort into training him to trust his rider not to hurt him with the bit."

"Yes, *sir*," Kathrael said, laying the irony on thick, even though his distraction really *was* helping. "Such an authoritative streak you've been hiding all these weeks, priest-boy. I had no idea."

His mouth quirked as if he was hiding a smile. "Well," he pointed out, "I *was* raised by a village chieftain, a High Priest, and a Horse Mistress. You'd expect some of it to have rubbed off on me at some point."

Still holding both horses' ropes, he gave a final look around the fire-lit campsite to make sure they hadn't forgotten anything. Apparently satisfied, he kicked dirt over the campfire until it was thoroughly smothered, plunging them into darkness. The white horse Kathrael was riding snorted at the sudden change and the smell of smoke, but barely shifted beneath her. She gathered the reins in one hand as Favian had shown her, and hooked her fingers under the pommel of the saddle so she wouldn't accidentally tug on them.

There was the sound of movement in the darkness next to her as Favian mounted and got himself settled. It was after moonset, and only a handful of stars peeking between patchy clouds lent any sort of illumination. She could make out the white blur beneath her and another one to the side, but that was all.

"Let's see if this will work," Favian muttered, to the accompaniment of more shifting and rustling. "Huh. That's not so bad. A little precarious, maybe. Let's just hope we don't run into any unexpected excitement along the way. Ready?"

"Yes, please," she said, impatient to be going.

"All right, then—off we go. Hold onto the saddle, and try not to grip with your legs—that's the cue to make him go faster."

Favian clucked softly to the horses, which moved off at an easy walk. They headed back toward the road and started the trek westward toward Teth. She held on and tried to sway with the horse's movements, as the sound of a crying babe rose and fell around her.

Kathrael gritted her teeth and focused on staying atop Audris as he ambled along next to his sibling. She was only vaguely aware of time passing, of the sky gradually growing lighter at their backs. As if it was some sort of signal, at the first rays of light from the rising sun, the ghostly cries of distress faded into silence.

She sagged in relief, her free hand coming to rest on the firm shoulder of the animal beneath her.

The movement caught Favian's attention. "Better now?" he asked, peering at her closely in the uncertain morning light.

"I can't hear her any more," Kathrael said, "or any of the others."

"Good," he replied. "You were so quiet—I was worried."

There was nothing to say to that, so she only shrugged, already exhausted though the day had scarcely started.

"If you're ready, we can let the horses lope for a while," he continued. "Do you think you're steady enough up there?"

"I think so," she assured him, aware that any additional speed they could manage would get them to Teth more quickly.

She looked at Favian properly for the first time since they'd left their camp, and realized that he was riding half-sideways, with his right leg hooked over the pommel of his saddle and his weight resting cockeyed on his right hip.

"Is that safe?" she asked.

He only grinned. "Oh, yes — as long as absolutely nothing unexpected happens."

"I'm not sure that's particularly reassuring," she said. He *was*, after all, the one controlling her horse, as well as his own.

"That's why I rode Ozias and gave you Audris, even though Audris is a bit harder to sit." Favian reached down to rub his horse's withers. "Ozias will look after me. He's known me his whole life."

"So it's helping with your... problem, then? Because, and I'm sorry to be the one to say this, but you do look a bit ridiculous."

He rolled his eyes at her. "Yes, it's much more comfortable, thank you. I can even switch sides if my muscles start to get cramped. But perhaps I'll swing my leg back over before we ride in to my father's old village. I wouldn't want to embarrass you."

"Ha," she said, though she was painfully aware that it was more likely that his own reputation would suffer among his clansmen for being associated with someone as disfigured as she was. Still, his plan to use her scars to their advantage was a clever one. And, somewhat oddly, it did make her feel a bit better about what they were likely to encounter in their search for the traveling show.

"Sit up straight and hold on," Favian warned her. "We're going to speed up now."

Kathrael sat back and renewed her grip on the saddle as Audris surged into a rolling canter, his hooves skimming over the road in a steady, three-beat rhythm.

FIFTEEN

Teth was a bustling little village surrounded by lush pastureland and inhabited, it seemed, by far more cattle than people.

"Draebard has its horses," Favian said when he saw her staring at the large herds of black and red cattle. "Teth has its cattle. Definitely try the cheese while we're here. It's excellent."

As he had promised, Favian slung his leg back over the saddle to ride normally as they approached the edge of town. Kathrael nervously tugged her shawl forward, struck anew by how odd it had been not to have to worry much about the reaction to her face while she was staying in the temple in Draebard.

"Hullo!" Favian called as they rode up to the cluster of buildings and huts. "It's Favian — Renthro's son. Is Sula around? Or Vineet?"

Several people looked up from what they'd been doing, and a man with light brown hair called back, "Favian? Well now, it's *Novice* Favian, I see! Welcome back. Your aunt and uncle are probably out with the cattle." He paused upon noticing Kathrael. "Uh, hello, miss. Welcome to Teth."

Kathrael only nodded, keeping her face hidden.

"Thank you," Favian said, drawing the man's attention back to him. "It's Kesin, isn't it?"

The man grinned. "You remember! I wasn't sure you would—you were just a boy when we last met. I must say, I'm surprised to see you in those robes. Thought you were horse-crazy. Apprenticed to Draebard's Horse Master, weren't you?"

"It's a very long story, I'm afraid," Favian said.

Kesin nodded. "I bet it is. Well, I won't keep you from your kin. You remember where their grazing lots are?"

"I think so," Favian said. "It was a pleasure to see you again, Kesin. May the gods' blessings be on you and yours."

"Thank you, Brother," Kesin said with another smile. "It's good to see you doing so well. Good-bye, miss."

"Goodbye," Kathrael said softly, averting her face from the man's curious gaze.

Favian led them further into the village, greeting people who recognized him and others who merely recognized his position as a visiting priest. Eventually, they came to a smallholding at the northern edge of the settlement. Favian rode past the house with its thatched roof and window boxes of fragrant herbs. Behind the humble structure was a larger one, apparently for livestock. Cattle were penned nearby, mooing occasionally.

"Aunt Sula?" Favian called. "Uncle Vineet?"

A moment later, the door to the barn flew open and a middle-aged woman with hair the same pale gold as Favian's rushed out.

"Favian?" she said in disbelief. "Favian! Merciful Utarr, it really is you!"

Favian dismounted in time to meet his aunt as she threw her arms around him and hugged tight. He hugged back, and Kathrael could see the crooked smile that curled his lips at the bittersweet reunion with his dead father's kin.

"It's really me," he confirmed.

"What's all this ruckus?" a new voice asked. A powerful man with bushy eyebrows and hair just beginning to turn gray approached from the direction of the pens.

"Vineet!" Sula said. "Favian has come for a visit!"

"Is that so?" Vineet said, striding up to Favian with a grin. "Let's have a look at you, then!" He gave Favian a critical once-over before pulling him into a back-slapping embrace. "The temple life suits you, boy. Still living in Draebard with that Wolf Priest?"

"I am," Favian replied once they parted. "It's good to see you, Uncle. Good to see both of you."

"And who's this?" Sula asked politely, smiling up at Kathrael where she still sat on Audris' back, her shawl hiding her face.

"Ah—forgive my poor manners," Favian said, returning to the horses so he could help her down. "This is Kathrael. She's actually the reason for my visit. We're looking for her bondmate, who was recently abducted. Kathrael, this is Sula, my father's sister, and her husband, Vineet."

"Hello," Kathrael said, still not looking at them directly.

"Oh, my goodness!" Sula said in sympathy. "You poor dear—abducted, you say?"

Vineet was peering curiously at her, trying to see under her shawl.

"Are you unwell, young woman?" he asked, a note of caution seeping into his voice.

"Kathrael was burned rather badly some months ago," Favian said smoothly. "She suffered scarring that made it impossible for her to continue in her chosen trade. Since then, she's been completely reliant on her bondmate for their livelihood. We have reason to believe that his abductors are heading north, following the towns near the coastline. When she appealed at the temple for assistance, I offered to help her search for him."

Kathrael reluctantly lifted her head, giving them a glimpse of what lay behind the shadow of her shawl. Sula gasped, and Vineet took an involuntary step back. Kathrael told herself firmly that she didn't care, and met Vineet's look of horror with a challenging one of her own.

"Gods above," Vineet said. "Yes... I suppose you couldn't manage much for yourself, looking like that."

"*Vineet*," Sula hissed.

Kathrael glanced at Favian, and saw a tendon tighten in his jaw. "You'd be surprised," he said, even though it contradicted the story he himself had concocted for them. He gave himself a slight shake, and continued, "At any rate, you can understand how important it is that we find Ithric and return him home safely."

"Of course," Sula said. "But how can we help?"

"Not sure how you expect to find this man with so little to go on," Vineet added gruffly. "He could be anywhere, assuming he's even still alive."

Apparently, tact was not a trait that Favian's uncle possessed in excess, but Favian merely replied, "He's alive. He's being held prisoner by the owners of a traveling show that exhibits people and animals as curiosities.'

"The show with the freaks, you mean?" Vineet blurted. "I saw that one! Gods above, her husband isn't the one with no arms, is he?"

Kathrael's heart pounded, half in excitement and half in outrage at the man's callousness. Beside her, Favian sucked in a sharp breath.

"They were here in Teth?" he asked, straining forward like one of the overseer's hounds scenting prey. "*When*?"

"Yes. About a week ago," Vineet said. "Something like that, anyway."

"No," Sula put in. "It was nine days ago that they left. I remember because Janna's baby boy was sick that day."

"How long were they here?" Favian asked sharply. "Did they say where they were going next?"

"Calm down, lad," Vineet said. "Goodness — anyone would think it was your own bondmate you were tracking. Let me see, now... I think they were only here for three days or so — "

"Yes, that's right," Sula confirmed.

"No idea where they were headed, though," Favian's uncle added.

"Did they socialize with anyone when they were staying here?" Kathrael asked.

Vineet avoided looking at her as he answered. "Well, the freaks pretty much kept to themselves—"

Of course they did, you fool, Kathrael thought. *They're prisoners.*

"—but the two who seemed to be in charge spent a fair amount of coin in the tavern, of an evening," he finished, still directing his words to his nephew rather than to her. "You might go and have a word with old Clarry, Favian."

"Thank you, I will," Favian said, throwing her a brief, apologetic look. "I don't suppose we could prevail on you to provide beds for the night? We'll have to head out first thing in the morning."

"Of course—" Sula began, but Vineet cut her off and spoke over her.

"I dunno, lad," he said, "we're a bit hard up for space. And your cousin is feeling poorly right now. I, uh, wouldn't want to give her a shock with, well, you know…"

He gestured a bit awkwardly toward Kathrael, who continued to stare at him with a level gaze. Beside her, Favian stiffened.

"Vineet!" Sula chided again. "He's family!"

"Hush, Sula," he said, a bit harshly. "Look, Favian, I just think it would be best if your friend stayed elsewhere. You know what they say about bringing bad luck into a house. This family has already had more than its share of ill fortune."

Kathrael had never before seen Favian go as cold as he did at Vineet's words.

"Of course, Uncle," he said, all traces of his earlier affection vanished. "We wouldn't dream of imposing. Thank you for your help—we'll stay at the temple instead. Give my love to Cousin Trina and tell her I hope she feels better soon."

"Favian—" Sula said, sounding terribly sad.

Favian dredged a smile for her and gave her another embrace. "It's all right, Aunt Sula. Being a priest has its advantages. We won't lack for hospitality tonight."

"Tell Frella hello for me," Sula said. "I've still never gotten to meet her."

"We'll have to remedy that one day," said Favian, giving her a final squeeze and releasing her. "Goodbye. It was good to see you."

"Goodbye, Favian," she replied. "Be careful, please. I couldn't bear to lose another family member senselessly."

"Father's death wasn't senseless," Favian said without hesitation. "He died doing what he could to protect Eburos from invasion by the Empire. Mother's wasn't either. She died bringing Frella into the world. But nevertheless, we'll be careful—don't worry."

"Goodbye, lad," Vineet said stiffly. "Take care of yourself, eh?"

"Of course," Favian said evenly. "You do the same, Uncle."

With that, he helped Kathrael climb up onto her horse's back and followed a moment later, taking the reins and leading her away. Except for the occasional greeting to passersby, Favian was silent during the journey to the temple, and Kathrael let him stew until they approached the large building.

"You could have sent me to stay at the temple while you spent more time with your kin," she said finally.

Favian shook his head. "Just because someone is family doesn't automatically make their actions acceptable. I feel bad that Sula was caught in the middle, but for me to argue with her husband would have put an unnecessary strain on their relationship, while sending you away would have made me as bad as Vineet."

"You're very calculating sometimes," Kathrael observed. "That always surprises me about you."

Favian looked at her. "All priests are calculating, to some degree. Part of the training for the priesthood is to place ourselves outside of a situation rather than becoming embroiled in it. I've always struggled with that, but I guess the lesson finally stuck in the end."

Kathrael thought of Favian stumbling frantically to his mentor's rooms in the aftermath of his prophetic dream about Ithric. She thought of his obsessive quest to change the future against all odds.

"Of course it did," she murmured.

After securing a couple of rooms in the temple and enjoying a meal of cold meats and onion soup, Favian left Kathrael to rest while he went to speak with the tavern owner. He ignored the small stir caused by a priest in a drinking establishment and strode up to the filthy wooden counter, trying his best not to limp on legs that still felt sore and shaky from far too much time perched awkwardly in the saddle over the past few days.

Old Clarry was a grizzled, stoop-shouldered man with one ear missing. "Evening, Brother," he said, somewhat warily. "Not used to seeing your type in here. Not local, are you? Can't say as I rightly recognize you.'

"I'm Renthro's son, as it happens," Favian said, already grown tired of repeating it. "Just visiting relatives on my way to find the owners of a traveling show that came through recently."

Clarry made a considering noise. "Heard he passed away a few years back, is that right? Renthro, I mean."

"That's right," Favian said in a flat tone. "He was traveling in winter and his horse fell into a crevasse."

"Huh," said the tavern keeper. "Pity, that."

Favian silently recited a short stanza from the religious histories about the importance of tolerance, feeling his temper fraying at the continual reminders of the tragedy that had torn his and Frella's lives apart when they were younger.

"Yes," he said in an even tone. "It was a terrible loss. Now, about that traveling show…"

"Y'mean the freaks?" Clarry asked, pausing to swipe out a dirty tankard with an equally dirty rag.

Favian mentally repeated the words of the stanza a second time and took a deep breath. "That's the one. I gather the owners drank here when they were in town? I don't suppose they mentioned where they were headed next? It's vital that I speak with them."

Clarry frowned. "Vital, eh? What would a priest need to talk about with the likes of them? Queer bunch, if you ask me."

Favian gritted his teeth, giving up on the stanza and trying to channel Senovo's endless patience, instead. "We have... a mutual acquaintance."

Clarry shrugged. "Huh. If you say so. It's true the big one liked to flap his lips when he came in. Tarvick, his name was—or something like that. Said they was heading up to Gebrall, and then on to Woodhaerst. Planning to go right along the length of the coast, they were, and spend the winter up north somewhere. Crazy, if you ask me. Shoulda headed east to the big towns like Venzor and Llanmeer, instead."

"Hmm," Favian said, noncommittal, trying to ignore the fast tripping of his pulse. "Well, thank you—that's exactly what I needed. I'll stop disconcerting your customers now, and get out of your way."

"Aye. That's prob'ly for the best," Clarry agreed with a philosophical tilt of the head, and went back to transferring dirt from one goblet to another with the grungy old rag.

Kathrael looked up as Favian burst into the tiny sleeping cell she had been allocated in Teth's temple. He was bristling with energy, pacing back and forth in the cramped, inadequate space.

"They're in Woodhaerst," Favian said, his arms crossed tightly in front of his chest. "Or they will be in the next day or two. If we're fast enough, we can catch them before they leave."

"You got the information you needed, then? That's wonderful, Favian."

He nodded, a jerky movement, his eyes far away in the light of the flickering candle. She reached out and grabbed his arm, pulling him to sit on the edge of the bed, where he fidgeted.

"What's wrong?" she asked. "You're pulled tighter than a bowstring."

He took a deep breath and let it out. "Nothing. Everything. Sorry — it's strange, being here. I want to get going, now that we have what we need."

"In the morning," she said firmly. "You're exhausted. We both are."

"I know. I know. Not that I could sleep right now." His knee was jiggling up and down, a nervous movement that put her teeth on edge.

"Can you get a sleeping draught from one of the priests here?" she asked.

He groaned. "Ugh. I guess so, but I practically lived on those things for more than a week after my novitiate. I think they've started to lose effectiveness."

"Then maybe you should go... pray, or something?" She stared at him critically, and he had the good grace to look abashed.

"Yes, sorry. Maybe I should. Don't mind me — try to get some rest. We haven't had all that much the past two nights."

To Kathrael's surprise, he leaned forward and kissed her forehead—a warm, lingering press of lips—before leaving her to her rest. She was not terribly surprised, however, when hours later, a familiar body slid into the narrow bed behind her and slung an arm over her waist, spooning around her back. Only half awake, she snuggled into the welcoming warmth and drifted off again.

Eighteen leagues north of Teth, a lion paced restlessly in its cage, eyes glowing in the darkness. Ithric's ribs and hipbones stood out starkly against his scruffy late-summer pelt. It suited Turvick to starve him these days. The man saw it as a way to weaken his captive, physically and mentally. He seemed not to realize how this new cruelty was affecting Ithric's animal mind—the lion was ready to lose control at the slightest additional provocation.

Ithric's human sensibilities had grown increasingly confused over the weeks since Rona had confessed her pregnancy to him in the darkness of the ship's hold. After brutally whipping Nimbral—the baby's unlikely father—as punishment, Turvick had threatened the same for Rona if Ithric dared to shift into human form again.

At the time, Ithric had vowed to get Rona away to safety and find a healer to help her with the dangerous pregnancy, but as the days and weeks passed without an opportunity to make good on his promise, his grip on control in animal form was slipping, His mind increasingly descended into thoughts of tooth and claw and bloody revenge.

Not that Turvick was taking any chances with him. In addition to feeding him just enough to keep him alive and able to perform at the shows, Turvick had started making Laronzo hold a knife to Rona's stomach whenever Ithric was out of his cage. The human part of him was terrified that his control would snap, and the lion would savage one or both of the bastards — getting Rona and her unborn child killed in the process.

Ever since the embarrassing fiasco with Favian months ago in Draebard, Ithric had told himself over and over that he didn't need anyone. Being a spy in Rhyth had been challenging, while also providing the occasional excitement he craved. The whole place was a tinderbox waiting for the right spark, and the darker part of him had reveled in the atmosphere of imminent havoc — the prospect of seeing everything torn down and burned. It was a part of himself of which he wasn't particularly proud, and one he could now admit came to the fore when he was left on his own for too long.

Ithric's decision to reveal himself as a shapeshifter to Turvick and Laronzo had been spur-of-the-moment. Favian would doubtless describe it as another example of his willful self-destructiveness, but he'd be wrong. When he'd seen the way the others were being maltreated and kept prisoner by Turvick and his partner, he'd decided on the spot to do something about it.

Since people as strange and unique as Rona, Nimbral, and Arnav would be in as much — if not more—danger on their own in the south, he'd done the only thing he could think of at the time. He'd offered to join Turvick's show, claiming that he was terrified of being discovered and burned at the stake for his shape-shifting ability. Turvick had been easy enough to convince. His eyes had immediately grown wide, shining with avarice at the thought of possessing a tame lion that would follow his every command.

Laronzo, on the other hand, had rightly been wary—worried that if Ithric was discovered, they'd be dragged down with him by the followers of Deimok. Ithric saw the potential in this immediately, and casually planted the idea of going north in Turvick's mind. It was safer there, he'd mentioned, making sure his voice sounded suitably wistful.

At first, he'd been rather proud of the plan. Get north, get everyone free from Turvick's clutches, and take them somewhere he knew people… Venzor, for preference, or perhaps Meren. Even Draebard, in a pinch, though he tamped down the stab of pain and longing which came hard on the heels of that particular thought.

But Turvick hadn't been satisfied with his existing troupe of human oddities. When he'd kidnapped the young twins in Darveen, Ithric blamed himself. If not for his plan to get north, they would never have been anywhere near Darveen. For the first time, he realized that he'd been pulled in deeper than expected. Only the lucky and completely unforeseen appearance of the beautiful, bitter girl with the scarred face had allowed him—

hopefully — to undo the mistake that had nearly cost the twins their family and their freedom.

Even now, he had no way to confirm that his angry visitor had kept her word and returned the children safely... but something about her made him feel confident that she had.

Now, it was Rona in danger. Every week that passed increased the risk that the dangerous pregnancy would damage her tiny body, perhaps fatally. And Ithric had no idea what to do. His original plan to subtly guide Turvick east, toward the places where people might know him, had relied too heavily on Turvick's continued trust. That was a complete joke now. Turvick didn't trust him a finger's width after the twins' disappearance and the scene with Rona on the ship.

He was stuck, and while it frightened him — the *human* part of him — it only made the lion angrier. Without the chance to take human form occasionally, he was slowly losing his will to the animal's. Once again, just as he had when he was spying in Rhyth, Ithric was overwhelmed by a sense of tumbling faster and faster toward calamity. This time, however, it was a far more personal sort of calamity. He might have started this journey with the intention of saving the others, but now it seemed far more likely that he would bring them all to blood and ruin.

Tomorrow they would arrive in Woodhaerst and start performing again. Turvick would attempt to control Ithric by threatening Rona, and Ithric would attempt to control his inner animal and not rip Turvick's throat out regardless. Everything was spiraling out of control, and he had no idea how to stop it.

The lion growled low in its chest and continued pacing obsessively, back and forth along the short length of the filthy cage.

Kathrael would never have imagined being able to cover such a long distance in such a short span of time. Now that Favian had a firm goal in mind, he was relentless, pushing Kathrael, their two horses, and himself to the limit.

She continued to ride on the second horse as a means of spreading the load more evenly between them, with Favian still controlling both animals. Her seat and legs felt like they were one big, aching bruise from the days of riding, but she said nothing—well aware that Favian had his own issues stemming from long hours in the saddle. Besides, as they closed in on their quarry, Kathrael found his single-mindedness catching. What had begun as *Favian's quest to save Ithric* had somehow become *their quest to save Ithric*.

She only hoped that the lion-boy would have the good grace not to get himself killed after all the trouble they'd gone to in trying to rescue him.

They rode late into the night and snatched a few hours' sleep, only to rise before the sun and begin again. As they cantered along the rutted and pockmarked road that paralleled the coastline, Favian gave her little pointers and let her practice controlling the stallion she rode while he kept slack in the rope connecting them. Even during these lessons, though, she could tell that Favian's spirit was straining toward Woodhaerst, his mind only partly on the here and now.

Her own spirits were restless — especially Vesh, who whispered doubts and misgivings in her ear.

If your golden-haired priest fails in this endeavor, it will surely break him.

What if the lion-boy's death is only the first?

There was a panicked mob in his vision... what if they turn on him, like they turned on me? What if they turn on you?

"Shut up, Vesh," she muttered through gritted teeth. "You're not helping."

Favian glanced at her. "What was that? Sorry, I couldn't hear."

"Nothing," she said more loudly.

The town of Gebrall came and went; they didn't stop. They barely slowed, in fact. She wondered what the townsfolk made of the priest and the woman with the veiled face riding through the village green on a pair of white horses, shouting questions about which day the traveling show had left their town. Favian seemed satisfied with the answers provided by the confused residents, and the two of them immediately traveled on.

Kathrael was desperately tired, and she knew Favian was, too. When she found herself nodding off in the saddle, her body slipping sideways for a heart-stopping instant before she grabbed her horse's thick mane and righted herself, she turned to her companion in the dim light of the crescent moon.

"Favian, we have to stop! The horses are exhausted. I'm exhausted. You're exhausted. One of us is going to get hurt, and then where will we be?"

Even though she couldn't see the muscle ticking at the corner of Favian's jaw, she could imagine it easily enough in the stubborn silence that followed.

"We're almost there," he said after a lengthy pause.

"Then we'll still be almost there in a few hours," she said, and carefully gathered up the reins to slow her mount to a walk as he had showed her. Favian was forced to follow suit or risk being jerked from his precarious sideways position by the rope he was holding. She continued, "Look, I know you're in a hurry to get there, but I fell asleep and nearly slid right out of the saddle just now. We're stopping."

The horses were eager for the rest, too, their low snorts echoing rhythmically as they huffed and blew.

Favian seemed to come back to himself. "I'm sorry, Kath. Of course we'll stop."

"It smells like rain, as well. We should put up the tent," she pointed out.

He groaned, but veered them off the road in search of a suitable site to camp. "Rain is all we need."

Kathrael shrugged, though he probably couldn't see it. "The weather is the weather. There's nothing to be done about it. Besides, rain will slow heavy caravans more than it slows us."

"Yes... I suppose you're right," Favian said in resignation.

They reached a small copse of trees, and he dismounted. She followed, hitting the ground on shaky legs. It was difficult to stay awake as she helped him unsaddle the horses and set up the tent in the near dark, but the alternative was to get soaked when the rain moved in. To save time, they didn't bother with a campfire. As it was, heavy clouds swallowed the sliver of moon just as they were moving the bedrolls inside the makeshift shelter.

Kathrael fell asleep shortly thereafter to the sound of raindrops hitting the thick hide stretched above them.

Gray light was peeking through the tent flap when she woke. Favian was already outside, heedless of the steady drizzle as he packed the saddlebags.

"Did you sleep?" she called, worrying that he'd stayed up fretting all night.

"Some," he replied. "You were out like a snuffed candle, though. Sorry I pushed so hard yesterday."

"It's all right. I want to get to him, too. Is there food?"

Favian gestured to a pair of saddlebags next to the tent. "Nothing hot, I'm afraid. A fire seemed like too much of a challenge in this weather."

She nodded and rummaged for some bread and dried meat, washing down the simple repast with watered wine. They finished packing the tent and saddled the horses, who seemed cranky and unenthusiastic about the prospect of being rained on all day. Donning cloaks, they clambered onto the animals' backs with stiff movements and made their way up to the road, which was already growing slick and muddy.

"Almost there," Favian said under his breath, as if reminding himself. "Not much longer now."

SIXTEEN

It was the morning of the troupe's final day in Woodhaerst, and the lion flicked its ears back in displeasure as a gust of wind blew another spattering of cold raindrops through the bars of the cage. Laronzo had thrown Ithric a joint of rotten meat the night before, after days of nothing but stale water. He'd fallen on the stinking haunch without a second thought, but now his belly churned and gurgled, adding to the day's general misery.

Perhaps the rain would prevent Turvick from putting on the show that afternoon, and Ithric wouldn't be forced to fight the primal and increasingly overpowering urge to sink his teeth into the man's neck and taste human blood spurting over his muzzle.

We mustn't do it. We mustn't do it. We can't. Remember Rona. Remember the baby, he thought like a chant. The lion's lip curled, its rasping tongue swiping out as if to savor the imagined gore.

The sun was almost directly overhead when the rain finally stopped and the clouds parted. Kathrael threw back the hood of her wet cloak, aware of Favian doing the same thing beside her.

"Look," he said, pointing into the valley ahead of them as they crested a small hill. "There it is."

Kathrael couldn't hold back a sigh of relief. Even though they only had Favian's vague calculations of travel times for a group of slow-moving caravans to go on, she could *feel* that they were close to their target.

"He's here," she said. "I know he is."

Favian nodded, and she thought he felt it, too. They were close. "Come on," he said. "Let's go get him."

They cantered down the gentle slope leading to the outskirts of town. The place was a tiny speck compared to Rhyth, but it was still much larger than Teth and most of the other villages she'd seen in the north, Draebard included. It would not be as simple as riding in and finding the village green; they would have to search for their quarry.

"Were they in the central square when you saw them before, in Penth?" Favian asked, lifting his voice over the wind so he could be heard.

Kathrael thought back to the blighted southern town, surprised at how distant the memories seemed. Even though it had been mere weeks, nearly every single aspect of her life had changed since then.

"No," she said, "they were set up in another plaza a few blocks away. Penth was a bit bigger than this, though. Does Woodhaerst even have more than one square?"

Favian shook his head in frustration. "I've never been here before, so I have no idea. We'll have to ask." He chewed his lower lip for a moment. "The temple should be easy to find. Someone there will almost certainly know, and we can tell them the owners are imprisoning a shape-shifter. That way we'll have some support if things get ugly."

Kathrael didn't bother to point out that Favian's vision pretty well guaranteed things *would* get ugly. Instead, she merely nodded agreement. "Good idea. Do all of the temples in the north wield as much political power as the Wolf Patron's? Can the priests here force Woodhaerst's chief and elders to free the other people that the owners are keeping prisoner?"

"I don't know," Favian said. "My understanding is that the temples in the west don't hold as much sway as they do in places like Draebard and Meren, but they'll still be more likely to take us seriously than the council would — assuming the council would even agree to see us in the first place."

"The temple it is, then."

They were at the edge of the town now, and as they rode further in, the roads grew narrow and twisting. The ground was still muddy from the morning's rain, and the familiar stench of many people living in a small area — food and waste and piss and sweat — assailed Kathrael's nose, making her realize that she had barely noticed the smell in the smaller villages like Draebard and Teth. The twisted tangle of homesickness and dread the scents evoked took her by surprise.

It didn't take long to get directions to the temple from a merchant selling ceramic cups at the side of the road. The large building was adorned with the now-familiar northern style of artwork in stone, wood, and beaten metal. It seemed to be dedicated to the goddess of war and flame, Deresta. Kathrael, who had always identified strongly with She-Who-Burns, felt herself relax a bit at the idea that the goddess was somehow standing behind them at the culmination of their quest.

They tied the horses nearby and approached the main doors, where a pudgy acolyte with reddish hair greeted them. He bowed to Favian and looked quickly away from Kathrael after catching a glimpse of her face.

"Welcome to the temple, Honored Guests," he said, recovering smoothly. "How may I assist you?"

Favian stood straight, his hands clasped inside the sleeves of his dun robes. "I am Favian of Draebard, novice to Senovo, the Wolf Priest. I must speak to your High Priest on a matter of great urgency."

Kathrael was a bit taken aback to hear Favian name his famous mentor so casually, especially after Chief Andoc had made it clear that he would not countenance any action among the western tribes that might be seen as interference by Draebard. Nonetheless, the strategy was effective — the acolyte's eyes widened, and he stammered, "Of... of course, Elder Brother. I will go immediately and see if he is available. Come with me, please, and I will take you to a room where you may wait and refresh yourselves."

They were brought to a small room off the main annex, where wine and fruit awaited them on a low table. Kathrael ate and drank while Favian paced. Eventually, she glared up at him and said, "Sit *down*, Favian. Do you want to greet the High Priest looking like a madman?"

Favian growled, but compromised by standing still against the far wall. He faced the door, staring at it with an intensity that made his blue eyes burn and his already chiseled features harden into marble. Kathrael couldn't help staring in turn, struck oddly and unexpectedly by his beauty. Something inside her flared into warmth at the sight, but she was distracted from regarding him when Woodhaerst's High Priest swept in.

"Greetings, my children," he said in a raspy voice, and the salutation might have been insulting were it not for the man's obviously advanced age. "What brings you to my temple after such a long journey?"

Favian bowed deeply. "Greetings, Respected Elder. I am Novice Favian of Draebard, and my companion's name is Kathrael. We have reason to believe that a shape-shifter is being held captive within the town of Woodhaerst." The old man had been looking curiously at Kathrael's face, but now his eyes shot back to Favian as he continued, "Tell me, please—is there a traveling show in town right now, exhibiting people as oddities?"

"There is," the High Priest replied cautiously. "In fact, there has been much talk of it the past two days. I understand that this rather distasteful show has another unusual exhibit as well—"

"A tame lion?" Favian suggested, his voice grim.

The priest let out a slow breath between his lips. "Indeed. You claim this beast is actually a shape-shifter's animal form? That is a very serious allegation, Novice Favian."

"I don't claim it. I know it," Favian said evenly.

"Not only that," Kathrael added. "The owners are keeping all of their exhibits as prisoners."

Favian drew the old man's attention again before he could ask how Kathrael could know such a thing.

"The shifter in question is Kathrael's bondmate. He was abducted several weeks ago. She sought assistance at the temple, and we have been chasing them ever since," he explained.

"Your bondmate?" the High Priest asked in surprise. "This shape-shifter is not a member of the priesthood?"

"They were already handfasted when his ability first manifested itself," Favian said, a bit too quickly.

Kathrael drew her shawl back, exposing herself to the priest's gaze. "Ever since I was burned, Ithric has been my sole means of support," she said, throwing herself into the role. "I cannot earn a living now. Without him, I would be destitute. He refused to cut the handfasting thongs and abandon me for a life in the temple."

The old man regarded her with a mixture of pity and thoughtfulness. "It is an unusual situation, certainly. Though it is highly irregular for a shape-shifter to remain outside the purview of the temple, I suppose this young man's motives were noble enough. What precisely are you asking of me, Novice Favian? Are you here on the Wolf Priest's behalf?"

"I am here on Kathrael's behalf, to see her husband freed, along with the other people being held captive by these men for their own profit. Nothing more, nothing less." Favian's voice had gone as hard as his features, and Kathrael held her breath, waiting to see how the High Priest would respond.

He frowned, contemplating Favian's words for long moments before nodding thoughtfully. "I will speak to Chief Ezrol about the situation and see if he is willing to take action. You must understand that I hold very little sway with the council, but the fact that this young man is a shape-shifter brings the situation within the scope of the temple to some degree."

"Thank you, Elder Brother," Favian said, still looking tense. "Time is of the essence. Based on what we've learned of these men, it is likely that this will be their last day in Woodhaerst before they move north again. Do you know where this show is being held?"

The priest shook his head. "I fear I have no taste for such things. A moment, please. Young Peltres may know the answer."

He stuck his head out the door and called for Peltres. The red-haired acolyte who had greeted them hurried in a moment later. "Yes, Elder Brother?" he asked in a nervous voice, his eyes still skating away from Kathrael's scars.

"Do you know where the men exhibiting the lion are going to be this afternoon?" the High Priest asked.

"I believe they are set up in the square behind the meeting hall, High Priest," the boy said. "Though, of course, I would not attend such a thing myself."

"Of course not, Little Brother. Don't worry, you are not in trouble," The old man assured. "In fact, go to the meeting hall right now, and ask the Chief if he would consent to meet with me on a matter of some urgency. I will follow behind in a few minutes."

"Yes, Elder Brother," said the boy, and hurried off after a final wide-eyed look at Favian and Kathrael.

"Is the meeting hall within walking distance, then?" Favian asked.

"It is," the High Priest confirmed.

"In that case, we will follow your acolyte and find the men we're looking for." The hard look had returned to Favian's eyes.

The High Priest frowned. "It would be better if you waited until I can speak with the town's leaders."

"No," Favian retorted. "It really wouldn't. Good day to you, Elder Brother, and thank you for your assistance."

He gestured Kathrael to precede him out of the room, and they left the High Priest frowning in confusion behind them.

"Are you sure we shouldn't wait for help?" she asked, as they hurried toward the entrance to catch up to the red-haired acolyte.

"I'm sure. I've already seen what will happen. There were no guardsmen or other priests around, which isn't a surprise since I know how long it can take to get a council of elders to take action on *any-thing*." Favian cupped her elbow and pointed ahead to where Peltres was speaking to another boy in the entryway. "Come on."

Kathrael hid her face as they followed the aco-lyte along the twisting roads and alleys. She was honestly grateful for the excuse to stretch her legs after so much time riding. The town of Woodhaerst seemed to be a relatively prosperous settlement, if a somewhat chaotic one. Just the sort of place that would appeal to men with a controversial traveling show, actually. She wondered how much money they'd made here, on the backs of the people they were mistreating.

"This is the meeting hall, Novice Favian," Peltres said nervously, indicating the long building they were approaching. "The square is behind it, one street over."

Favian was already looking in that direction as if he could see straight through the walls separat-ing him from their destination. "Thank you. We'll be fine from here."

"Yes, thank you," Kathrael echoed, even though the boy still seemed terribly awkward around her. "Go and deliver your message. We'll need some help before things are done and dusted, I suspect."

The acolyte nodded and hurried toward the entrance of the hall. Favian was fairly vibrating with nervous energy, and she took his hand when he extended it. The two of them headed with single-minded purpose toward the next street, and whatever awaited them there.

As they approached, Kathrael could hear the same kind of crowd noise that had drawn her to the show in Penth—people laughing, talking, the occasional shout of excitement. Her heart beat faster, and Favian's hand tightened around hers. They emerged, moments later, into the southern edge of the square, which was absolutely packed with people—*hundreds* of them.

"They must be at the other end," Kathrael said, over the noise of rowdy spectators. "I can't see a thing!"

Favian was craning his head, trying to see over the wall of people. Kathrael was much shorter, and all she could make out was the row of shoulders in front of her. A ragged cheer of excitement filtered back to them from the front of the crowd, adding to their frustration at not being able to see what was happening.

"This is no good," Kathrael shouted in Favian's ear, standing on tiptoe to do so. "You try to get closer. I'm going to skirt around and see if I can find a vantage point off to the side."

He nodded, his attention focused on what he could not see. They were still at the very back of the crowd, so Kathrael slipped away, retracing their steps and hurrying down the road until she came to an alley which presumably backed along one of the sides of the square. She could still hear the crowd clearly, even with a row of close-set buildings separating her from the mass of people.

When she judged she was behind the area where the caravans were set up, she started looking for a way to get back to the plaza. Eventually, she was forced to climb over a rickety section of wooden fence between two narrow houses, but once she'd managed it, she was rewarded with a relatively clear view of the show from behind.

The lion cage was on the far side of one of the other wagons, half hidden from her line of sight, but she could see tawny haunches and a tail lashing back and forth angrily. A jolt of mingled excitement and worry hit her upon seeing Ithric, alive and in the flesh. Though the gods had never done much for her up to this point, she couldn't help sending up a quick prayer that the lion-boy would survive whatever was to come next.

With difficulty, she tore her gaze away from that lashing tail and took in the rest of the scene. It was very much as before, only without the presence of the twins. She couldn't help the surge of satisfaction she felt over her role in that. The boy with no arms was seated at his table, feeding himself with a spoon held in his toes. Nearby, the tall man danced with the short woman.

This time, she was close enough to take in their haggard countenances as they capered and performed for the crowd. She wondered what these people had endured since she saw them last, and vowed that whatever else happened today, she *would* see them safe at the end of things... even if they were unable to save Ithric from his prophesied fate.

Kathrael looked around herself, seeking a path that would get her closer and perhaps give her a better view of the cage. The strange couple's dance ended to a round of whoops and bawdy catcalls. As it did, the man in charge—Turvick, she recalled—stepped up on his platform to gain the crowd's attention and begin his spiel about the tame lion.

Her attention was caught, however, when the shorter, fatter man—Turvick's partner, who had dragged the twins around the crowd during the show in Penth—moved quietly to grab the tiny woman's arm. She *cringed* at his touch, and tried half-heartedly to struggle away as he dragged her behind the shelter of the caravans. Kathrael's jaw clenched, her hand gripping the edge of the fence she was standing next to until the knuckles turned white.

Something was deeply wrong with the scene, and every instinct she possessed screamed at her to act. But act how?

She looked around again. The unnaturally tall man who had been dancing with the small woman stood empty-armed now, his face pale as milk. Turvick's partner had positioned himself in such a way that he and his tiny captive were not obvious to the crowd, but could still be seen by anyone standing to the side or behind them, as Kathrael currently was. A moment later, the man drew a wicked looking knife and pressed the tip to the woman's belly. Kathrael caught her breath, her own stomach clenching in empathy.

Just then, the woman's captor turned his head and looked straight toward the lion's cage. Kathrael followed his gaze and found the lion, fully visible now, staring fixedly back at him with glowing eyes. Suddenly, everything fell into place. They were using the small woman as a hostage against Ithric's good behavior while he was in the form of a lion.

Indeed, Turvick was stepping up at that very moment to open the lion's cage, his face twisted in a sneer now that he was facing away from the crowd. There was a familiar litany of fearful cries from the crowd as the animal jumped down from its enclosure, and Turvick immediately started giving his reassurances about the animal's docility.

To Kathrael's eye, Ithric looked anything but docile at that moment. His lithe body was fairly vibrating with anger. Halfway to the raised platform, the lion froze. As it had in Penth, its head turned slowly until it was looking straight at her. This time, instead of being afraid, Kathrael let her features twist into a sharp, predatory smile. The lion's lip curled, and a low, rumbling snarl rolled across the space separating them. The crowd muttered nervously in the background.

Suddenly, glaringly cognizant of what she needed to do, Kathrael straightened from her hiding place and stalked directly toward the man holding the knife.

>~~ ⚜ ~~<

Favian shoved his way through the claustrophobic press of people, trying to get to the front. Already, the sick feeling that always overcame him when reality started to synchronize with one of his visions was washing over him, made worse by the stench of unwashed bodies and rotting garbage around him.

He elbowed his way between two burly men. One of them growled and grasped his sleeve, only to let it drop an instant later when his partially shaven head and priest's robes penetrated the man's awareness.

"Let me pass," Favian said, barely recognizing his own voice. Some combination of his tone and the man's innate respect for the priesthood caused him to squeeze back against his companion for an instant so Favian could slip through.

Ahead of him, gasps and cries of fear erupted from the crowd. His heart pounded triple time as he pressed forward against the wall of people once more, this time catching a sharp—though probably accidental—elbow to the sternum for his troubles. He staggered a bit as the crowd heaved, pushing back from whatever had alarmed the people at the front.

As if I can't guess, he thought, somewhat desperately, trying to stand his ground and not be swept backward by the people jostling around him.

Favian gritted his teeth and jammed a shoulder between the next two people in front of him, attempting to widen the space enough to force his way through.

The man holding the knife to the tiny woman's belly must have seen Kathrael move toward him from the corner of his eye, because his head whipped around from where he'd been craning to watch Turvick force the lion to perform for the crowd.

"Who are you?" he demanded angrily. "You can't be back here!"

Kathrael, still flooded with righteous anger, ignored him and addressed his terrified captive instead. "Don't be scared," she said. "When he drops the knife, run."

The woman stared at her with wide, frightened eyes, even as the man frowned and said, "What—?"

Kathrael pulled her shawl down and twisted her face into a snarl, cutting off his indignant question. The man's face paled and he took an unconscious step backward, the knife slipping from his limp grip to clatter on the flagstones lining the plaza. The short woman stamped on his toes with one tiny boot and darted away, running for the tall man she'd been dancing with earlier. He crouched and met her with open arms, holding her close.

With a final sneer at Turvick's dumbstruck partner, Kathrael turned her attention to the lion. The animal looked from the mismatched couple embracing each other tightly, to the shocked man in front of Kathrael—unarmed now as he backed slowly away from her. Its glowing gold-flecked eyes tracked slowly back to Turvick, whose body jolted as if he'd been struck. Suddenly, all of the sneering bravado he'd displayed earlier around the dangerous animal drained away in a moment, and he stumbled back a step. The lion prowled forward on silent paws, pacing him with clear intent.

Favian shoved his way between two women, finally close enough to the action to see over the shoulders of those still remaining in front of him. His heart seized as his eyes caught and held on Ithric, his imposing animal form now bony and scarred from whatever had been done to him over the months since he'd left Draebard. As Favian watched in horror, the lion faced off with a portly man in a gaudy tunic and breeches, who backed away in obvious fear… just as he had foreseen.

The beast growled low in its throat, stalking its victim with dangerous intent. Around Favian, the crowd was muttering nervously, milling around. The big cat roared in anger, and someone in the front row screamed. A moment later, people were running… scrambling to get out of the packed village square… buffeting him as they pushed past… blocking his view.

He cast around for any kind of high ground — a wagon, or a barrel, or *anything* where he could climb up and try to get the beast's attention, but there was nothing. Terrified people continued to shove at him, threatening to send him to the ground.

Favian yelled at the top of his lungs, trying to get the lion's attention. "Ithric! *Ithric!*"

A moment later he was standing — battered and bruised — at the edge of the ever-expanding clear space left behind as the crowd fled. The lion surged forward, tackling its prey to the ground even as the gaudily dressed man turned to run.

"Ithric!" Favian cried again. "Be careful, you idiot! *He's got a knife!*"

Without warning, the beast's head jerked up, its attention drawn from its prey to Favian. A moment later, there was a twisting *change*, and Ithric crouched over the downed man in human form, looking frantically at Favian with wide, shocked eyes. The man on the ground scrabbled at his belt, and a shiny dagger appeared in his hand.

Favian shouted in dismay. The knife jabbed up even as Ithric tried to twist away, and blood sprayed from Ithric's unprotected side as it hit home.

SEVENTEEN

Ithric cried out as his side erupted in agony, cutting through the remnants of the bloodlust that had turned his feline vision red and made his mouth water with the need to tear into Turvick's flesh. The dual shocks of the knife wound, along with the unexpected change of form, threatened to send him reeling—but his earlier anger gave him the strength to knock the knife from his tormentor's hand.

The pair rolled over, grappling, and the pain in Ithric's side spiked as Turvick's weight settled on top of him. Ithric roared in the man's face, his voice barely human, and kneed him as hard as he could between the legs. Turvick grunted and tried to curl up, giving Ithric the chance he needed to roll them over again. Wheezing, he straddled the fucking bastard who had terrorized his fellow captives for so long, and smashed his fist into the man's ugly face, over and over until he stopped moving.

The world was narrowing down to a tunnel, his vision going gray and the noises around him sounding oddly attenuated. For this reason, he didn't see the owners of the hands that closed around his upper arms and pulled him away from the unconscious man lying underneath him.

"I'll kill him," he gasped, struggling weakly to get back to the body on the ground. "Lemme—"

"Let's leave something for the others, yes?" said a low, musical female voice. "Guards should be here before long to sort things out, and hopefully someone from the council, or at least from the temple."

Ithric craned to look at the woman's scarred face, blinking as his fuzzy mind made the connection. "Little Cat? I was right, then — thought it was you. Told you we'd meet again…"

"Now who's predicting the future?" said a second painfully familiar voice, sounding grim.

Ithric rolled his head to the other side, confirming that, first, he hadn't been hallucinating Favian's presence earlier and, second, that he was really growing *very* dizzy now.

"Oh. It's you," he said. "What in the gods' names are *you* doing here?"

Even with his wavering vision, Ithric could see the tendons working at the corners of Favian's jaw.

"Good to see you, too, you cock-sucking son of a bitch," Favian said, his tone deceptively mild. "Now shut up, and I swear by all that's holy that if you die on me after all this, Ithric, I will fucking kill you."

"Language," Ithric chided in an annoying singsong voice, and promptly passed out in their arms.

>⚜◇

Favian swallowed hard, holding panic at bay by a mere thread as Ithric went limp against them. His eyes sought Kathrael's face. She was pulling Ithric's left arm out of the way so she could get a clear view of the bloody gash in his side.

"Is he — ?" Favian asked, the words pulled from him almost against his will.

"He's still breathing," Kathrael said, hitching herself around so she could tear a strip of cloth from the hem of her skirts. "I think he just fainted."

Favian placed a hand flat over Ithric's naked chest, feeling the slow rise and fall for himself, along with the thrum of a still-beating heart. He took a deep breath and dragged his eyes away to scan the nearly deserted square.

"We need a healer," he said.

"We *need* you to keep your head on straight in case that crowd we just panicked turns into a mob and comes back for us," Kathrael retorted, wadding up the strip of cloth and pressing it hard to the gory knife wound. "Favian, you're the only person here with any kind of authority whatsoever. The rest of us are freaks in their eyes. We might as well have targets painted on our backs if those frightened people decide to come after us with torches and pitchforks."

Favian looked around again, truly taking in the scene. Turvick's other three captives had closed in around his now weaponless partner, trapping the man against the side of one of the caravans. Despite the fact that one of the three people surrounding him only came up to his stomach and another had no arms, he looked utterly terrified — the expression of someone who knew exactly what he deserved for his crimes, and was staring his comeuppance in the eye.

A short distance away, Turvick himself lay in a heap on the muddy cobbles, still out cold, his breath coming in wet wheezes. Favian looked down again, at Ithric's pale, slack face, and made himself move. He eased Ithric down to lie with his head in Kathrael's lap. She steadied his limp body and continued to press the wad of cloth hard to his wound, looking up long enough to give Favian a reassuring nod.

He glanced down at himself. There was mud and blood staining his robes, but he straightened them into a semblance of order and dragged his tattered composure together.

"Wait. Don't harm him," he called to the three strange people arrayed in a hostile half-circle around Turvick's partner. "Guards will be coming any minute, and they mustn't find you doing anything threatening."

The tiny woman looked up at him uncertainly as he came closer. "Who are you? What business of yours is this?"

"Kathrael and I are friends of Ithric," he said, which was much simpler than explaining that he'd been in love with the shape-shifter and gotten his heart trampled into the mud for his troubles. For good measure, he added, "Kathrael is also the one who rescued the twins and took them back to their family."

The armless boy looked at him sharply with dark, flashing eyes. "The children are safe? She took them back to Darveen?"

"She did. They were reunited with their mother and father, safe and sound."

"Is Ithric dead?" the woman asked, her face still gray with fear and anger.

"No!" Favian said, too loudly. He forced himself to modulate his voice to something approaching normality. "No. He's wounded, though. I don't know how badly. He needs a healer. Guards will be here soon. I'll call for one then."

"Rona needs a healer, too," said the unnaturally tall man. Of the three, he looked the most likely to lose control and tear the cowering man in front of him limb from limb.

Favian looked at the small woman again. "Are you hurt?"

She shook her head, two spots of color rising in her pale cheeks. "Pregnant." Her eyes moved of their own volition to the tall man, and Favian blinked, putting the pieces together with some surprise.

She continued, "I'm afraid the child will kill me if it's too big. Ithric promised to get me away to a healer, but Turvick overheard us talking. That's when things started to get really bad." She wrapped her arms around herself. "He whipped Nimbral. Started withholding food from Ithric, and forbade him to change into human form. He made Laronzo threaten me with a knife whenever the lion was out of his cage, because he was afraid Ithric would kill him otherwise." Her gaze swept over to the man Ithric had beaten unconscious. "Did he?"

"No," Favian said. "Just punched him in the face a few times before we pulled him away."

"Pity," Rona said with a dark look.

A noise drew their attention. Guards were jogging across the square toward them, weapons drawn.

"Please. Stay where you are, all three of you." Favian told them. "Don't make any threatening moves. I'll talk to them."

"Why should we trust you?" the tall man asked, still sounding combative.

Favian gestured around. "Because you have no one else to trust."

He turned away and walked forward with raised hands to meet the guards before they could get too close. The man in front came to a halt a few steps away from him and scanned the plaza, gesturing for his compatriots to stop as well.

"I am Priest Favian of Draebard," Favian said, the title still not coming naturally to him. "Thank you for coming—there are people injured and we are in urgent need of assistance."

The guards' leader regarded him with wary eyes. His sword was still drawn, but he held it lowered at his side. "Brother Favian," he acknowledged cautiously. "There were reports of an escaped lion attacking people; part of this traveling show that's been camped in town for the last few days."

"No lions here now, as you can see," Favian said, gesturing around the largely deserted space. "Just two cruel and greedy men preying on those weaker than themselves for their own gain."

He was playing for time, more than anything—hoping that the High Priest had spoken with the chief and the elders, and that help would arrive from that quarter.

"There *was* a lion in the show," the guard said, still looking as though he was as likely to detain them all as to send for a healer to attend the injured. "The cage is empty now."

"That wasn't a lion," Favian said, playing his only available card. "It was a shape-shifter held captive, beaten and starved into submission. He's right over there, and he's wounded. He *needs* a *healer*."

The man appeared surprised, and followed Favian's pointing finger to where Ithric lay limp in Kathrael's hold. Kathrael had already replaced her shawl, covering her face, so she looked like any passerby might, who had stopped to help.

"Miss?" the guard asked. "Did you see any of this?"

Kathrael nodded, still not lifting her head. "I did. I was right up front." She pointed at Turvick's partner, careful to keep her face angled away. "That man was in the back, threatening the small woman with a knife. He didn't think anyone in the crowd could see him, but I was off to the side. The lion changed into this boy and tried to help her, but the owner over there grabbed him and tried to stop him.

"They fought, and the owner stabbed him before the shape-shifter knocked him unconscious. The others got the small woman away from the man who was threatening her. This priest saw what was happening and came to help."

It was a masterful performance, and Favian dove in to play his part. "That's right. I've been chasing these men for some time. There were reports that they had kidnapped a shape-shifter, and were holding other people against their will as well. Apparently it was all true."

From behind him, Turvick's partner finally managed to find his tongue. "No! Don't listen to them—they're lying! These freaks turned on us for no reason! Look what they did to Turvick!" He pointed at his crumpled partner with a shaking finger.

The guards looked somewhat bewildered by the deluge of conflicting information, and their leader appeared to be fighting the beginnings of a headache.

"Look," he said. "I've got a frightened mob outside the square, multiple reports of a dangerous wild animal attacking people, and a collection of freaks who look intent on murder. What are you suggesting I do? Pat everyone on the head and send them on their way?"

Favian's temper surged, making his fists clench inside the sleeves of his robes. "I'm *suggesting* you send someone for a healer before the injured shape-shifter currently bleeding all over the cobblestones ends up a *dead* shape-shifter!"

"Do as the priest says," came a new voice, and Favian's head whipped around to see a powerful man with close-cropped brown hair approach. The elderly High Priest flanked him, following a step behind.

The guard's demeanor immediately changed. He stepped back and gave a short half-bow. "Of course, sir. Right away," he said, and gestured one of his men to go in search of help.

The new arrival surveyed the motley group of injured and uninjured with an impatient sigh. "Had a bad feeling about this lot when they pulled into town three days ago," he muttered. "Should've paid more attention to my gut, obviously." He jerked his chin toward Ithric's naked form. "This your shape-shifter?"

Not mine. Never mine, Favian thought bitterly, but aloud, he only said, "Yes, that's him." He had to fight the urge to step in front of Ithric and Kathrael protectively as the newcomer walked over and reached down, lifting Kathrael's shawl enough to peer underneath. She said nothing in response to the man's presumption, but Favian could sense her covering a flinch. His fists clenched harder.

"Huh," the man said. "That's a real mess, all right. Guess you weren't exaggerating about her, Oslud."

The High Priest nodded. "Their story had the ring of truth to it, Chief Ezrol. The fact that the young man in question is not a member of the temple *is* rather irregular, but nonetheless, holding a shape-shifter against his will is a serious offense against the gods."

"We weren't holding him against his will!" Turvick's partner cried, evidently sensing the tide turning against him. "He joined us voluntarily — practically begged us to let him in!"

"Lies!" Kathrael replied indignantly, changing course effortlessly to play the part of Ithric's wife. "Did he beg you to starve him, or put these scars on his body? He's skin and bones! You kidnapped him from our home village!"

The Chief shook his head impatiently. "Maybe he was kidnapped, or maybe he was looking for an easy way out of an unhappy handfasting to a disfigured woman. Whatever the case, it's clear that he's been mistreated, and I won't have folks saying that I allowed such treatment of a shape-shifter in my town. Guards, take that man and his partner away and lock them up while the council decides what to do with 'em. As for the rest of these... people..."

He looked uncertainly at Rona, her tall, thin mate, and the boy with no arms.

Favian stepped in quickly. "Perhaps they could stay at the temple until more permanent plans can be made. They are welcome to come back to Draebard with us when we leave. High Priest?"

The old man jerked as if startled. "What? Oh, yes... that would probably be for the best."

One of the guards had grabbed a bucket of water from the well at the corner of the plaza while they were talking. He dumped it unceremoniously over Turvick's head, making the man splutter and gasp as he was dragged roughly back to consciousness. More guards pulled him to unsteady feet, while others edged warily past the three still holding his partner at bay.

When the pair were escorted away with their hands tied behind them — Turvick staggering drunkenly between two of the large men — Favian felt a modicum of his tension ease. When a dark-haired, middle-aged healer arrived, clutching a satchel of herbs and bandages, it eased a bit more.

After a brief double take at the collection of strange individuals standing around, she fussed over Ithric's wound and peeled his eyelids back to check his pupils. "I'll need a stretcher, and some-place clean and quiet to work," she snapped.

The High Priest finally seemed to shake him-self free of his stupor, and gestured toward the southern edge of the square. "Come. Everyone, back to the temple. It would be best for you to keep out of the public eye after the panic earlier."

The healer's sharp gaze flicked over the others, landing for a moment on Favian's bloodstained robes. "Is anyone else hurt, aside from the one who was dragged out of here a few minutes ago?"

The tall man, Nimbral, stepped forward. "Rona needs help," he said, and gestured at the tiny woman.

The healer looked at her pale countenance. "Are you ill, then?"

The short woman shook her head. "I'm preg-nant. It's his."

Rona nodded up at Nimbral. The healer blinked in surprise, echoing Favian's earlier re-sponse, and blew out a large breath. "Right. Well. First things first. Let's get your friend seen to, and then we'll talk." She glanced around at the remain-ing guards. "Now, where's that stretcher?"

"Will he live?" Favian asked some time later, his arms wrapped tightly around himself.

Kathrael was relieved to be back in the quiet solitude of the temple after the tense scene in the plaza, but she, too, looked to the sharp-featured healer in concern. The blood pouring from Ithric's wound had slowed to a trickle after the stretch of time she'd spent keeping pressure on it, but he showed no signs of waking even after all the jostling and prodding.

"Hmm," said the woman in a non-committal tone, sounding eerily like Favian's friend in Draebard, Healer Sagdea. Perhaps all healers in the north were crotchety by nature.

"The knife left a ragged tear, but it didn't look as deep as it could have been," Kathrael offered to fill the silence. It was true — she'd seen more knife wounds than she cared to admit among her fellow prostitutes over the years. This one — while messy — was not as bad as some she'd seen.

"I've had worse…" came a slurred voice from the bed.

"Ah, that's what I was waiting for," said the healer, even as Favian hurried forward to hover at her shoulder. "How do you feel, young man?"

Ithric pried sticky eyelids open and tried to wet his mouth with his tongue. "Like I've been starved, kept in a cage for weeks, and then knifed," he said eventually. "Why? How do I look?"

Kathrael raised an eyebrow. "Like you've been starved, kept in a cage for weeks, and then knifed," she confirmed, and turned away to pour him a cup of the medicinal tea the healer had prepared earlier.

Ithric frowned suddenly. "The others? Are they—"

"Your friends are safe. They're here in the temple," the healer told him.

Ithric relaxed back, and let Kathrael support his head so he could sip at the warm liquid. When he had swallowed a few sips, he coughed and winced as the movement pulled at the wound. "Rona needs a healer. She's pregnant," he rasped.

"I am aware," said the woman. "Though I'd've thought you'd be more worried about your own condition."

Ithric only lifted a shoulder and let it drop. His eyes skated around Favian and came to rest on neutral territory, staring at the rafters above. "Just another scar," he mumbled. "'S worth it if it means the others are safe."

Favian had stepped back from the bed after it became obvious that Ithric was awake and more-or-less aware. Now, he inhaled sharply as if about to say something, but no words followed. Kathrael looked between the two of them with interest, trying to decipher them.

The healer made a noise of disapproval. "You're very lucky, as it happens. The blade slid along one of your lower ribs rather than piercing deeper, into your organs. As long as the wound does not putrefy, it should heal well enough."

"Not to worry, in that case," Ithric said, sounding weary. "I have the constitution of a lion."

The woman regarded him with interest. "It's true, then? You are a shape-shifter?"

"It's true," Ithric said, still in the same flat tone. "Why? Do you want a demonstration?"

The healer chewed her lip as if strongly considering it, before her professional ethics stopped her. "No, no," she said. "You shouldn't tax yourself. I've just never met one before, that's all. Well... I should go speak to the dwarf, I suppose. Get some rest, now, and have your friends bring you some light broth to drink in a few hours. Keep the bandages clean, and I'll look in on you later this evening."

Ithric nodded carelessly and let his eyes slip closed. Favian was standing against the wall now, his arms still tightly crossed, face pale even though Kathrael would have expected him to be relieved that Ithric was awake and seemed to have his wits about him.

Since it seemed no one else was going to respond, she said, "Thank you, Healer. Your help is much appreciated."

The woman merely nodded and waved a hand in acknowledgement, before gathering her things together and bustling out of the room. Favian was still staring silently at Ithric's sleeping form from his place against the wall. There was a chair next to the bed, so Kathrael sat. She brushed back a lock of Ithric's tousled auburn mane of hair and hooked it behind his ear before looking up.

"You did it, Favian," she said in a quiet voice. "You saved him. Aren't you happy?"

"Yes," he whispered, his face pale and his expression closed off. A moment later, he turned abruptly and strode from the room, not looking back.

Kathrael stared after him for the span of several breaths before returning her attention to the injured shape-shifter on the bed. "What's your story, lion-boy?" she asked. "How did you hurt each other so badly, without managing to cut the cord that draws you together?"

Ithric slept on, oblivious.

When Favian had still not returned hours later, Kathrael made a brief, unsuccessful search for him. Unwilling to leave Ithric too long on his own, and confident—or at least, *mostly* confident—that Favian would not actually take the horses and leave, she returned to the borrowed sick room.

When she entered, it was to find her charge awake again, regarding her with clear hazel eyes.

"What happened to the twins?" he said.

She smiled, remembering the task with which he'd challenged her, and the little family's joy when they had been reunited. Looking back, she thought that his request might have been the only thing that kept her spirit from sliding into complete ruin during those dark and hopeless days. Somehow, he had seen good in her. The *children* had seen good in her, as well—and *they* had the power to see straight into her thoughts.

What might she have become, if not for that small reminder of love and light?

"They're safe at home with their mother and father," she said, a hint of pride slipping into her tone. "Why? Did you doubt me?"

"Never for a minute," Ithric said.

Kathrael suddenly remembered their cover story. "Oh, I almost forgot. You should know that we've been telling everyone you and I are handfasted. You didn't join the priesthood because you've had to provide for me ever since my face was ruined. Apparently, I'd be lost without you."

Ithric looked at her oddly. "And people buy that story after meeting you?"

She couldn't hold in the unladylike snort. "Please. Why wouldn't they?" She drew her shawl forward and ducked her head bashfully, falling into the persona of the helpless damsel. "I'm *ever* so demure, you know. And I've been so *terribly* worried about you since you were kidnapped from our village..."

Ithric smirked despite his weakness, clearly amused. "Oh, dear. You poor little thing—my heart bleeds, just thinking about it." He shook his head slowly and looked her up and down. "So. We're handfasted, eh? In that case, you'd probably better tell me your name. Might raise a few eyebrows otherwise."

"It's Kathrael," she said, and offered him a drink of the pale broth sitting in a cup next to the bed.

He made a noise of surprise around the mouthful of liquid and swallowed it. "So I was right! You really are a Little *Kat*."

She mock-glared at him. "Who are you calling *little*, lion-boy?"

He laughed, only to pull up short, one hand flying to the rusty stain seeping through his bandages. "*Ow.* All right. No laughing, apparently. Why don't you tell me how you met our Most Holy and Exalted Brother Favian, instead? That should sober me right up."

"She held a knife to my throat and tried to use me as a hostage to get to Senovo," said Favian from the doorway. "We've been great friends ever since."

Kathrael blushed a bit, but Ithric apparently had other things on his mind as he stared at Favian with a complicated expression, taking in his appearance with a slow, head-to-toe sweep of his eyes.

"Huh," he said. "Looks like I missed a few things since I left. Nice new robes you've got there. Love the hair. So, how are the balls?"

Favian's blue eyes were as cold as a glacier in the mountains. "Absent," he said with sharp, precise elocution. "*Finally.* What about you? You've managed not to get burned at the stake yet, I gather?"

Ithric grinned, showing teeth. It was not a nice expression. "Not yet. Sorry to disappoint you."

Kathrael looked from Ithric to Favian and back again. "The healer said you were to drink that broth, lion-boy," she said. "Perhaps you two can wait to eviscerate each other until after it's finished?"

"Happily," Ithric said. His stomach rumbled a moment later. Kathrael handed him the cup, pleased to see that his hands were steady as he lifted it.

"Yes, by all means," Favian added. "I'm well acquainted with how much Ithric appreciates the hospitality of the temple."

"One cage is much the same as another," Ithric said pleasantly, and slurped the broth.

Favian's face clouded in anger, and he stalked out of the room without another word. Kathrael watched him go, and turned back to regard Ithric. "You shouldn't wield your claws so thoughtlessly, you know. He's been a wreck ever since he had a vision of you being stabbed. Perhaps you both ought to go a little easier on each other, whatever happened between you in the past."

Ithric looked surprised for a moment, the cup held frozen an inch from his lips. Then he finished the movement and took another thoughtful mouthful. "A vision? I suppose that answers the question of what he's even doing here," he said after he'd swallowed. "If he had a dream about it I guess he'd have to come. Otherwise he couldn't have seen it in the first place."

Kathrael attempted to wrap her mind around that, and failed. "Prophecy gives me a headache," she decided. "It's ridiculous."

"As ridiculous as a person turning into a lion?" Ithric said lightly, and Kathrael got the impression he was relieved to have a distraction from his earlier thoughts about Favian.

"As ridiculous as children who can see other people's thoughts," she agreed. "Seriously, though—I'm swearing off prophecy from now on. It's exhausting."

Ithric let out a breath of laughter and flinched again as pain from the wound flared. "You might need to rethink the company you're keeping, in that case." He set the empty cup aside. "Now—I hate to be an ingrate, but I don't suppose there's anything more substantial than broth to be had? I would *murder* for some roast mutton right now."

EIGHTEEN

For the next several days, Favian was a ghost. On those rare occasions Kathrael saw him, he was always deeply involved in conversation with Ithric's fellow captives. Once, she stayed for a bit to see what they were discussing. Apparently, Favian was attempting to talk them into coming back to Draebard, with mixed success.

Rona and Nimbral were at least somewhat open to the idea, mainly because the healer here in Woodhaerst had given Rona an answer she did not want to hear.

"She said I should kill the baby," the small woman said, and stroked a hand over her belly. "She even offered to make the tea for me that would do it. I don't *want* to kill it. It's *ours*."

There was a stubborn lilt to her voice, and the giant next to her put a large hand around her shoulder.

"Sagdea is one of the most respected healers in the north," Favian said. "Maybe she will know of some other way."

"I just want to go home," said Arnav, the armless boy. "I don't want to live in the north."

"Will your family take you back?" Kathrael asked bluntly.

"Why wouldn't they?" he shot back, sounding angry. "It's not my fault I was born like this!"

"Where are you from, Arnav?" Favian asked.

"Rhyth," he muttered, sullen.

"Rhyth is tearing itself apart," Kathrael pointed out. "No one is safe there—certainly no one… *different*. I should know."

"It's still where I belong," said the boy, glaring daggers at her.

Kathrael felt a surprising flush of homesickness, and wondered at it. It would be madness to leave the safe haven she'd found in Draebard and return to a place that wanted her dead. So why did thoughts of the humid nights and the chaos of city life make her heart ache? She could only shake her head, suddenly unable to answer Arnav with words.

Since Favian seemed more likely to do Ithric further bodily injury than to nurse him, Kathrael spent most of her time in the shape-shifter's sick room. It was no hardship. The fascination she'd had for him ever since their first brief meeting showed no signs of waning. Quite the opposite. Ithric was quick-witted and self-deprecating, full of humorous quips and completely unselfconscious in her company.

He looked at her as no one else had since before her injury. Even Vesh had gazed at her with regret afterward, as though he felt he should have protected her somehow. As though her scars were his personal failing. Livvy, of the harelip and the guileless mind, had looked at her as one looks at a mirror—fascinated by her *because* of her scars, rather than *despite* them. Favian and the twins

looked past the ugly injury, to what lay underneath.

But Ithric... Ithric simply did not appear to see
the scars. He looked at her as any man might look
at a beautiful woman. Drinking her in. Appreciat-
ing her. It touched something inside of her that she
had not realized was broken — a place that longed
to be *wanted*, for exactly what she was.

It was ridiculous.

Why would anyone want damaged goods,
when the world was full of buxom beauties with
soft, unblemished skin and clear, twinkling eyes?
Shape-shifters were still revered in the north — that
was obvious enough. Though Ithric's refusal to join
the priesthood made him something of an oddity,
Kathrael had no doubt that women would still
fight each other for a single moment of his time,
hoping to gain status from the association. Hoping
that the gods' gift of animal transformation would
somehow rub off on them and bring luck to their
own lives.

And yet, Ithric still watched her with eyes that
seemed to caress her.

Ridiculous.

Dusk was leeching the last of the day's light
from the windows when she nudged the door open
with her foot and backed into his room, holding a
heavy tray and a pitcher. It was the fifth evening
since their arrival, and Ithric's subsequent injury.
He was already up and around, though he could
not go far and he still tired easily.

"It took the better part of a week, but I finally came through with the mutton," Kathrael said without looking at the bed. "I hope you're suitably appreciative."

She pushed the door closed with her hip and turned around, only to find a lion sprawled among the blankets, regarding her with lazy eyes. Kathrael froze, staring at the animal in fascination. The beast had a puckered, half-healed gash along its ribcage, and a pile of damp, chewed-up bandages trailed over the edge of the straw-stuffed mattress and onto the floor below.

Before she could do more than stand there, gaping in wonder, the figure twisted unnaturally. Her gaze slid away from the odd wrinkle in reality as if unable to gain purchase on it. When she focused again, Ithric lay naked in the bed, looking sheepish.

"Sorry about that," he said, and threw a corner of the blanket carelessly over his lap. "When Turvick wouldn't let me change into human form, I thought I'd go mad with it... yet here I am, only a few days later, and already the lion is growing restless. Hope I didn't scare you."

Kathrael broke free from her paralysis and walked toward him to place the tray on the small table next to the bed. "You didn't scare me. Just gawping, for which I apologize. It's an impressive form."

"D'you think so?" he asked, looking oddly shy. "I've always felt a bit scrawny and flea-bitten. Still, I suppose I should count myself lucky that I don't transform into a field mouse or something." He chuckled. "I met some bears up north who told stories about a man who changed into a turtle. No idea if they were being serious or not."

Kathrael poured some wine for them and handed him a cup. "There are other shape-shifters in the north, then?" she asked, intrigued.

Ithric took a deep swallow and nodded. "Oh, yes. There are the bears—almost a dozen of them, though they mostly keep to themselves. And Senovo, of course. Also, there's an old woman down south who lives as a vixen—if she's still alive, that is. I haven't seen her since before the invasion." He frowned. "I imagine there would be more if the priests didn't try to castrate or sequester anyone who shows the ability. That's why the bears stay way up in the wastelands, away from people."

It had the sound of old resentment. Kathrael gained a sudden flash of insight into at least part of the conflict between Ithric—the shape-shifter who refused to be castrated—and Favian, the seer who'd *wanted* to be castrated.

"How did you avoid being drawn into the Priests' Guild, anyway?" she asked, curious.

Ithric gave a little self-deprecating snort. "Simple. I ran away and hid. Spent most of my time in animal form, because it was warmer, but I also nearly starved to death before Senovo found me and took me under his patronage. I was an adolescent lion with no pride to support me, and no experience hunting. I ate a lot of stringy rabbits and carrion that winter, let me tell you."

Kathrael smirked, and handed him a plate. "Well, I guess you'd better enjoy the mutton while you have the chance, in that case."

Ithric grinned in return, but there was a glint in his eye as he said, "Oh, I've gotten considerably more skilled since then, believe me."

"Not much help when you're locked in a cage, though," Kathrael pointed out, gesturing toward his body, which didn't have a trace of fat on it.

Ithric sobered. "Yeah. That was admittedly not my finest hour. Thought I could help the others by playing along with Turvick and his crony. But I just ended up making things worse."

His sullen tone surprised her. "Oh, come now. It all worked out in the end, didn't it?" she said.

With a sour expression, Ithric replied, "*Sure* it did. Because what I really need more than anything else is to be indebted to someone who holds me in utter contempt. The perfect ending to a complete fiasco."

"What? You mean *Favian*?" she asked in surprise, wondering how two otherwise intelligent people could possibly have gotten so twisted up. "Did the healer give you some funny herbs when I wasn't looking?" She shook her head and went back to sopping up gravy with a hunk of bread. "I really can't figure you two out."

Ithric mirrored her, returning his attention to his food. "There's nothing to figure out. He wasn't who I thought he was, and I wasn't who he thought *I* was. End of story."

And you're both mad as a box of frogs, Kathrael thought, but didn't say. It was increasingly appar-

314

ent that someone needed to bang their fool heads together, and she was coming to the uncomfortable realization that she was the only candidate for the job.

She had once witnessed a fire at a storage building in Rhyth's dockyards. The place had been full of barrels of creosote. She had a nasty feeling that this confrontation would be just as explosive.

⤛⚜⤜

Her opportunity for head banging came sooner than expected. The following evening, Favian overcame his reluctance to enter Ithric's presence and knocked on the door as she and Ithric were eating a meal of fish and mixed greens.

Ithric looked up warily, but Kathrael said, "Favian! Come join us. I've barely seen you in the past two days."

Favian entered, his leery expression matching Ithric's perfectly. "I've already eaten, thanks. Sorry I disappeared on you, though. The council has been hearing the complaint against Turvick and Laronzo. I've been wrapped up in that." He stood just inside the doorway, looking uncomfortable. Someone had finally gotten the bloodstains out of his robes, and the front of his skull was freshly shaved, making him look every inch the respectable young priest.

"Nice of you to let me know about the hearing ahead of time," Ithric said in a deceptively conversational tone.

Favian's eyes narrowed. "I offered at the beginning to bring you in to give testimony, but the elders declined. I think they're a bit in awe of you. The gods alone know why."

"Probably worried that he'll bring a curse down on the town if they offend him somehow," Kathrael said, and Ithric made a noise of disgust.

"Anyway, your presence—or lack thereof—was a moot point, as it turned out," Favian continued. "Turvick and Laronzo will be branded as kidnappers and taken back to Gebrall , where they'll be put on the first boat heading back to one of the southern ports."

"Good," said Ithric. "Anything else?"

"Yes," Favian said stiffly. "We need to either send a message back to Draebard, or head back there ourselves. Otherwise, we're likely to have people out searching for us before long, which is exactly the kind of thing Andoc and the elders wanted to avoid."

"So leave for Draebard, in that case," Ithric said easily. "What's stopping you?"

Kathrael looked back and forth between them, and decided that it was a good time to start poking the hornets' nest with a pointy stick. "He wants to know if you're well enough to leave *with* us, lion-boy. Don't be dense."

As casually as she could, she set her half-eaten plate aside and rose, wandering over to stand next to Favian. If that action *happened* to place her in front of the room's only exit, and if she *happened* to lean back against the closed door so that that the only way to leave would be to go through her bodily... well. Running away wasn't the answer for these two. It had obviously done them no favors in the past.

"And why would I want to come with you?" Ithric asked in a tired, flat voice.

"Don't you need to report back to your spymaster?" Favian said pointedly, and Ithric couldn't hide a brief flash of surprise. Kathrael settled back, prepared for the tinderbox to burst into flame.

"I have no idea what you're talking about," Ithric said after a beat, displaying impressive sincerity given that he was blatantly lying through his teeth.

"You might as well save your storytelling ability for something else, you ass. Andoc spilled everything," Favian shot back. "Including the part where you specifically asked him not to tell me where you'd gone."

Ithric huffed in disgust and crossed his arms defensively. "I guess it's a good thing I'm the spy, and not him. So much for honor among thieves."

"Says the man who snuck away from Draebard in the middle of the night."

"What? Can you think of a *better* time for sneaking?" Ithric retorted.

A stony silence descended as the two of them glared at each other across the width of the room. Kathrael pursed her lips, waiting for the tension to break and wondering if she could come up with any additional fuel to throw on the smoldering embers.

"Gods," Ithric spat eventually, running his hand through his hair with an angry movement. He rose and paced, still keeping most of the room between himself and Favian. "I need to get out of this place. It's driving me mad."

Kathrael frowned. "Out of Woodhaerst?"

"Out of the temple," he clarified, letting his eyes pin Favian for a bare instant before returning to Kathrael. "It makes the lion restless. As I said before, one cage is very like another."

"So what's stopping you?" Favian said, echoing Ithric's earlier snide remark. "I'm sure you could find a bed to warm elsewhere in town."

The mocking bitterness of his tone hid hurt beneath. Kathrael frowned, an idea forming—one that could either get right to the heart of the matter, or backfire quite spectacularly on her.

"If you're looking to relieve your restlessness, lion-boy, I'd be happy to help you out. I was a prostitute in Rhyth for years, you know," she said in an arch tone. "For you, it'd be on the house. I like you—and we *are* supposed to be bondmates, you know."

Favian turned to her, agape—his face a picture of shock and... betrayal? Ithric just looked surprised.

She steeled herself to ignore the pang she felt at hurting Favian, and pressed on. "You've been locked away for weeks with no company, after all. You must be about ready to burst by now. So, how about it? Favian has already turned me down—no accounting for taste." She paused, as if considering. "Though, to be fair to him, he is a *bloody* good kisser. Maybe he'd like to stay and watch us."

Ithric was definitely on the back foot, staring at her like she'd grown a second head. He blinked once, slowly, and regarded her like some sort of unfamiliar puzzle.

"Tempting offer, Little Cat," he said a moment later, recovering himself, "but I make a point of only taking lovers who are in heat for me. And, though you might like me well enough, you are decidedly *not* in heat right now."

"Oh... so, you mean lovers like Favian, then?" she asked in an innocent tone, and felt Favian freeze beside her. She didn't think he was even breathing.

Ithric's face grew hard, and he let out an unpleasant bark of laughter. "Favian chose to mutilate himself rather than feel desire. You shouldn't take his rejection personally, Kathrael. He won't be in heat for you, me, or anyone else... not ever again."

Kathrael gave them both pitying looks. "For a lion, Ithric, you sure don't see what's right in front of you very clearly. And for someone with the second sight, Favian, you are surprisingly blind."

Favian and Ithric stared at her for a handful of heartbeats before turning back to each other in perfect unison. Favian's fists clenched, and he leaned forward as if bracing for a physical attack.

"What is there to see? He *left*," he accused, his armor finally shattering to reveal the depth of hurt underneath. He glared at Ithric with anguished eyes. "You took everything I had to give, and talked about a future together, and then you *left* me without a single fucking word!"

Kathrael leaned against the door again, and hoped that things wouldn't actually descend into fisticuffs.

Ithric's fingers were digging into the back of the wooden chair so hard the knuckles turned white as the pair stared each other down. It was like watching a hungry lion square off with an angry bull aurochs, Kathrael thought. Or at least, it would have been… if the aurochs secretly *wanted* to be devoured.

"I talked about a future," Ithric said, his voice grating like stone on stone. "And you threw it back in my face."

"What?" Favian said, confusion touching his features. "I didn't—"

He straightened, and Ithric shoved the chair aside and took three steps forward, raising a hand to point in Favian's face. "You made it absolutely clear that you found the idea of having your balls cut off more appealing than the idea of *being with me*! Of *course* I left! What the hell else was I supposed to do?" He grimaced and clutched at his side, the growing force and volume of his words paining his half-healed wound.

Favian reeled back a step as if struck. He was breathing hard, his face flushed with righteous anger. "But… that *was* our future, Ithric! Once I became a priest, we could have been together without censure. No one could have stopped us, or made us outcasts! When you got angry and tried to talk me out of it, I didn't know what to think. I've wanted to be a priest since I was thirteen and realized that the world wasn't going to magically change and welcome my kind. The temple was the only place I had ever found acceptance. I was looking forward to sharing that future with you, until you pulled out a knife and hacked that dream to pieces."

His voice went quiet at the end, sounding terribly sad, and Kathrael held her breath.

Ithric made an inarticulate noise of pain and stumbled forward, grabbing Favian's shoulders and shoving him against the wall with a thump, Favian's hands came up to grip Ithric's arms as if he would try to throw off his hold — or perhaps drag him closer.

"You shouldn't have to mutilate yourself to be with another person," Ithric said. His voice was pained; pleading, though anger still colored his tone as well.

They clutched at each other almost desperately for a few moments, before Ithric pulled back just enough to cup Favian's face and draw him into a rough kiss, lips and teeth clashing. When they parted for breath, Ithric pressed their foreheads together. "Why would you *do* that?" he asked. "I never asked for that! I didn't *want* that sacrifice!"

Favian closed his eyes. "It's my body, Ithric. It's my choice. I *want* to be a priest. I want to help people, and serve the gods. And I want to be with you, but only if you accept my right to be who I was destined to be."

"I don't understand why you won't fight to change things," Ithric said. "It's *wrong*!"

Favian eased him back at arms' length to look at him, but it was Kathrael who answered.

"There's no honor in fighting a battle you can't possibly win," she said, thinking of the slaves she'd left behind in the south. The ones she'd vowed to save. "It's just another way to commit suicide."

Silence settled over the room for a long moment.

"Six years ago," Favian said slowly, "a eunuch couldn't enter into a handfasting, you know. Certainly, no one would have credited three people becoming bondmates, like my guardians did. And before Leader Magoldis of the Mereni rose to power, the idea of a female becoming the chieftain of a tribe would have been ludicrous."

He looked at Ithric as if willing him to understand. "It isn't time yet for this to change. When the time comes, it will happen."

Ithric looked at him, his anger drained away, leaving only sadness behind. "But, Favian, how will that time ever come if we don't stand up and say *no*?"

Favian could only shake his head, looking lost. "I don't know, Ithric. But… can we disagree about it, and still agree that… maybe… we were both wrong all those months ago in Draebard? I'm really not keen on getting my heart broken a second time — not when I've only just now gotten you back."

There was a pause as they looked at each other, finally seeing one another clearly, it seemed. Ithric appeared to deflate, all the fight draining from him, leaving behind only the weak, injured young man Kathrael had spent the last few days nursing back to health.

"Tell you what," he countered. "How about we start by agreeing that we're all knackered, and there's a very comfortable bed in this room that would be even more comfortable with company. We can fight again in the morning."

"I should probably leave you two alone," Kathrael said, surprised by the sharp ache that the words brought.

Ithric frowned. "Why?" he said, even as Favian looked at her with rueful eyes and said, "Er... no. You probably *shouldn't*. We don't have a good record when left to our own devices."

A thread of surprise wove through her pall of worry and loneliness. She glanced between the two of them, feeling something like hope trying to take hold in her breast.

"Stay, Little Cat," said Ithric. "Please. I've been without a pride for far too long. In fact, if you'll both forgive the presumption..."

He unfastened the borrowed robe he was wearing and turned around to let it drop. A moment later, the lion dropped onto all fours and slunk around to face them, snuffling the air curiously with a deep *whuff... whuff... whuff* noise.

Favian sagged, all of the tension flowing from his spine, leaving him propped against the wall, utterly limp. "Bastard," he whispered, his voice empty now of the bitterness that would have underpinned the word as little as an hour ago.

The lion butted up against him with its head, and Favian dropped to his knees, throwing his arms around the heavy shoulders and burying his face in the scruffy mane. He was trembling visibly.

The animal gazed up at Kathrael, serene, and she succumbed to her own need for reassurance.

When she knelt next to Favian and put a hand on his shoulder, he released his grip on Ithric with one arm and used it to pull her properly into the embrace. She came willingly, leaning against him, and against the lion's easy strength. The beast rubbed its head companionably against her body, a low rumble rolling through its chest.

"I'm sorry I dragged you into the middle of our mess, Kath," Favian said against her hair. "It wasn't my intention — truly."

"You didn't drag me, priest-boy," Kathrael pointed out, settling more fully against them. "I stuck my nose in because I wanted to. I make my own choices, remember?"

He choked on a huff of laughter. "Right. I know you do. You will stay with us, though?" There was a tentative note to the question, and she lifted her head enough to see his face.

"Are you sure you want me to? You've got him back now, Favian." She took a deep breath, the next words surprisingly difficult to get out. "You're not obligated to me, you know, just because we shared a blanket or a bed a few times."

Favian stared at her for a moment, his brow furrowed. "Kathrael. Do you really believe I can only care for one person at a time? If so, you've obviously forgotten who raised me. And you heard Ithric — he craves a pride of his own in the same way Senovo needs his pack around him. I... wasn't lying when I said that Ithric and I don't do well on our own."

She couldn't help the relief that bubbled up and flowed through her like an underground spring. She pressed the undamaged side of her face against Favian's chest to feel his heart beating, and whispered, "I'll stay, then."

The lion butted her again and slipped free of Favian's hold. It padded over to the low bed and jumped onto it with a lithe movement, settling among the mass of blankets. Bandages still circled its torso. The animal craned to sniff at them and chew at a loose edge.

"*Ah*! Don't, Ithric," Favian chided, pushing to his feet and offering Kathrael a hand up to follow him. "Leave them. Those bandages are there for a reason."

The lion curled a lip and shook its head in disgust. Kathrael couldn't stop the helpless smile that stretched her face. Favian saw the expression, and a shy, fond look slid over his own features.

"Gods," he said after a moment, rubbing a hand over his face, "I could sleep for a week. Maybe I *will* use some of the money Carivel gave us to send a messenger back to Draebard. I think we'd all benefit from a bit more time to recover before we try to travel."

"Not all of us — Rona doesn't have forever," Kathrael reminded him. "She needs to make a decision about the pregnancy soon."

Favian nodded. "Yes, you're right, of course. A day or two, then. That won't make much difference in the pregnancy, but it will give us a little more of a chance to rest, and for Ithric to heal."

"You think he'll come with us?" she asked.

"I hope so," Favian said, barely more than a breath, and turned to strip down to his linen shift and smallclothes. "Come on, Kathrael. Sleep. You need it, too."

It was true. Alone in her borrowed room, sleep had been slow to come and quick to leave as voices rustled around her, half-heard. She removed her outer layers and pinched the candles out before feeling her way to the bed. She wasn't sure what it said about her that she was more at ease with the idea of sharing a bed with a lion than she would have been at sharing it with Ithric in human form.

The lion-boy no more a danger to you than the priest is, came Vesh's ghostly voice from the shadowed, unseen corners of the room. *You're safer in their bed than you would be sleeping alone in yours*.

It was a startling realization. It was also something that Ithric must have understood inherently from the depths of his animal instincts. The pride. Safety in numbers. *Family*.

"Kath?" Favian asked, and she became aware that she must have frozen in place, staying quiet too long in the dark.

"Sorry," she said, shaking herself free. "Vesh just said something insightful, that's all."

"Oh, yes?" Favian replied. "What did he say?"

Kathrael worried her bottom lip for a moment. "I'll... tell you in a bit. I need to think about it for a minute, first."

She felt her way to the edge of the mattress. The lion was sprawled along the far side of the bed. Favian had arranged himself in the middle, and after a moment of fumbling, Kathrael pressed herself along the length of his back. She snuck an arm around him from behind, and he covered it with one of his own, holding her in place against him. She lay there for some time, the quiet of the room broken only by the raspy sound of the large cat's breathing.

"I've lost everyone I ever dared to get close to," she said slowly, feeling the truth of the words settle in her belly even as she said them. "I'd come to believe that I was fated to always be alone. But... even if there's always a chance of suffering more loss... I can still choose not to be alone. Even though it's hard. Even when it places my heart at risk. *We* can choose... not to be alone."

Favian was quiet for a long moment before he quoted softly, "*All who seek shelter shall find it. All the gods' children will receive solace.*"

Kathrael let the words soak into her, remembering a sweltering market square in Rhyth where she'd stared at a pair of rotten ground tubers and first decided to seek help at the temple. Those words had marked the beginning of a journey that she had expected — perhaps even hoped — would lead to bloody revenge followed by a quick death.

Instead they had led... *here*.

Where would they lead next?

Kathrael's dreams that night were strange, but not frightening. Wolves and lions lounged around on low divans in a sumptuously appointed Rhythian house, attending a feast while she and Vesh danced for them. Slaves cheered and slapped their thighs in appreciation from the corner, where they guarded the wealthy host and his family — bound and gagged, kneeling on the floor.

The music in the background faded away like mist as she groaned into wakefulness. She stretched, her muscles tingling pleasantly. Her eyes blinked open, to be greeted by early morning light slanting in through the small eastern window, painting everything gold.

Next to her, Favian slumbered on despite the jostling. It was, she suspected, the first full night of sleep he'd managed since they left Draebard, if not before. No wonder he was dead to the world. With a little jolt of surprise, she realized that Ithric, by contrast, was awake and in human form on Favian's other side, propped up on an elbow and looking down at him with a thoughtful, intent expression.

When he noticed her awake, his attention shifted to her and he gave a rueful smile. "Good morning, Little Cat. Sleep well?"

A hint of amusement lifted the corner of her mouth as she watched Favian drooling onto the bedclothes between them. "Perhaps not *quite* as well as Favian seems to be doing, but I can't complain. You?"

"I always sleep well," Ithric replied in a dismissive tone. "Lions are *champion* sleepers."

She let out a breath of laughter and rolled up on an elbow opposite him.

Ithric regarded her with interest for a long moment. "So," he said eventually. "I have to ask. You and Favian..."

She looked down for an instant before making herself meet his eyes again. "Bit of a long story. He wasn't lying—I really did put a knife to his throat and try to use him as a hostage to get to High Priest Senovo."

Ithric continued to stare at her as if trying to figure her out. "That probably wasn't the wisest choice of hostage on your part, you do realize."

"Well," Kathrael said, "in my defense… it sort of worked. The Wolf Patron *did* come."

"Yeah, I'll just bet he did," said Ithric. "With claws and fangs, no doubt. I'm surprised you're still in one piece."

She looked away again. "My own well-being wasn't high on my list of priorities at the time. Even if I'd known who Favian was, which of course I didn't."

"Hmm… I guess I've been in that place one or two times, myself," Ithric said, in a tone that made her think he probably had. His tone lightened deliberately. "So, afterward… let me guess. Favian immediately went all *mother hen* on you and wouldn't leave you alone?"

She looked at Favian's sleeping form and let the back of a finger stroke down the length of his upper arm. "Something like that, I suppose. To be fair, I was in pretty dire need of a mother hen. Or at least, of a friend. I still am, really."

"A friend who's a good kisser?" Ithric prodded, still eyeing her like she was a delicate wooden puzzle box and he wanted the key. "Or was that part just for the shock value?"

She couldn't help the faint blush that traveled up her neck. "Well... yes. It *was* for the shock value... but it's also true. I think we both needed someone for support. Not to worry, though, lion-boy. I know his heart lies with you. I've no intention of getting between you."

Ithric made a dismissive noise. "Don't be ridiculous, Little Cat. I've never understood the idea of ownership when it comes to love." He smirked. "In fact, if you ever *do* have the urge to get between us, I, for one, would be more than happy to oblige."

She snorted, though his words inspired a strange curl of sensation in her belly that was surprisingly pleasant. "I wasn't lying about being a prostitute either, lion-boy," she shot back. "So let's just say that if I *were* to take you up on that offer, it wouldn't be the oddest place I've ever been. Far from it."

Ithric raised an eyebrow. "Well, *well*. How intriguing," he teased. "Right now, though, I'd be interested in hearing more details about Favian's kissing skills. I'm a bit surprised that he was inclined, now that he's... you know."

"I'm a eunuch, Ithric. That doesn't mean I'm made of wood," came a sleep-roughened voice from below them.

Ithric looked down in surprise, but recovered quickly. "Well, certainly your prick isn't, I'm guessing. How long have you been awake?"

"Since somewhere in the vicinity of the *mother hen* jab," Favian said, peeling opening one bloodshot eye to glare up at him.

"Right. *No fighting*, you two," Kathrael insisted, pinning each of them with a meaningful look. "Not yet, anyway. It's far too early."

"Seconded," Favian agreed, and closed his eyes again.

Ithric rolled his eyes and said, "Fine. We'll fight later. Now, however, I have to test a theory. I assume it's not too early for this?"

With no further warning, he leaned down and caught Favian's lips in a sweet kiss that was completely at odds with their violent clash of teeth and lips the previous evening.

NINETEEN

Favian made a muffled noise of surprise that tailed off into a soft whine. The earlier curl of warmth in Kathrael's belly intensified, making her breathe in sharply. One of Favian's hands closed around her forearm as if to ground himself, while his other wrapped around the back of Ithric's head to hold him in place.

The kiss went on and on, as if all the words the pair could not say aloud were contained in it. Kathrael watched in fascination as a tear slipped free from the corner of Favian's closed eyes and trickled down his smooth temple.

When they finally parted and Favian spoke, his voice was unsteady. "No... never too early for that."

"Definitely better than fighting," Ithric agreed, his own voice hoarse.

Kathrael gently freed her arm from Favian's grip and thumbed away the little trail of salt water on the side of his face. "For the gods' sakes, you two, be *happy*, will you? You have a second chance now. Don't waste it."

On impulse, she leaned down and kissed Favian's warm, slick lips. He met her with a languid slide of mouth on mouth that turned the strange warmth in Kathrael's belly heavy and liquid.

When she pulled away with a final stroke of his cheek, he said, "I *am* happy." His gaze turned back to Ithric. "This is all I ever wanted, Ithric. Just this... just to be with you. I wondered for so many years if I would ever be able to have this kind of closeness with anyone."

There was still wariness behind Ithric's eyes. "As I recall, you used to want other things from me, as well — before you had that part of yourself cut out and thrown away like garbage." His voice grew rough on the final words.

Favian sighed out a slow breath and dragged himself into a sitting position. He took Ithric by the shoulders and met his challenging, almost *angry* gaze with sad blue eyes. "Ithric. What do I have to do to make you understand that I didn't join the priesthood as a way to spite you? *It wasn't about you.*" He shook his head as if to draw back some of the sharpness of his words, and started again. "I was already an acolyte in the temple when I first met you, you know. I knew even then that my life was destined for the gods' service. My urges for men — for *you* — terrified me."

"There's nothing *terrifying* about sex. Or lust," Ithric shot back. "Aren't you priests always on about it being one of the gods' greatest gifts to their children?"

A furrow formed between Favian's eyebrows. "Not everyone experiences desire the same way you do, Ithric. I was already having prophetic visions I couldn't escape — often showing terrible, tragic things that I was powerless to prevent. The last thing I needed was something else in my life that I couldn't control—my *own body* rebelling against me at the most inappropriate times."

"It was only a problem because you were constantly fighting yourself," Ithric insisted. "Denying yourself. *Don't* try to tell me you didn't like what we did when you finally stopped avoiding things and more or less jumped me."

A very faint worried tone had entered his voice. Despite her self-professed lack of interest in such things now that she no longer relied on sex to survive, Kathrael couldn't help wondering what, exactly, had passed between the two of them back in Draebard.

Favian was still frowning. "Ithric... we nearly tore each other apart. Before you left, we *did* tear each other apart. I don't want a lifetime of that."

Kathrael couldn't help adding, "I've seen how lust hurts other people. I've profited from offering my body as an outlet for lust, but I could never understand the way men seem oblivious to the harm it does."

Ithric shot her a hurt look that clearly said, *not you, too?* He straightened away from Favian's grip. "You're both wrong. Sex should be a source of joy and pleasure for everyone involved, whether it's tender or tempestuous. I never wanted to hurt you, Favian. I just wanted to be with you. But every time we got close, our rough edges grated together. And the closer we got, the deeper the wounds became. But I simply can't understand your desire to destroy that part of yourself rather than try to heal it."

Favian sighed and hooked a hand around the back of Ithric's neck. "It *is* healed now. This is what

I wanted, Ithric. I am… finally… as I was meant to be."

There was a considerable pause. "But you no longer desire me," Ithric said, as if the words were being pulled from him one at a time, and Kathrael got the feeling that they were finally getting to the heart of the complicated tangle between them.

Favian made a pained noise of negation and pulled Ithric forward to press another kiss to his lips. This time, Ithric was the one who looked to be on the verge of tears.

"Ithric," Kathrael said, when Favian released him and rested their foreheads together. "That's not true. If you'd seen him after he dreamed the vision about you… if you'd seen how frantic he was about getting to you… saving you… you wouldn't ever say such a thing. It was as if nothing else in the world existed for him, except the danger to *you*."

The shape-shifter looked at Favian with something akin to hope.

"I don't lust after you now, it's true," Favian said into the space between them. "But I still want to be close to you. In all ways, Ithric. In whatever way you want. Please don't run away from me again. *Please*."

Ithric's breath escaped in a rough hitch, as if he'd been punched. "Then don't make it sound like my desire for you is some sort of disease. Like it's hurting you."

Favian's hand gripped tighter. "Those were Kathrael's words, not mine. She and I have… something of a disagreement about matters of sex and desire. It's true that it hurt when I was younger, not to be able to feel desire for anyone society told me I was *supposed* to desire. I don't know. Maybe I wasn't as strong as you, or maybe it was easier for you since you desire men and women both.

"Whatever the case, I bought into the idea that I was broken, somehow, because I only felt lust for men. Maybe I shouldn't have bought into it. But, Ithric, don't you see? I'm a eunuch now. Nobody in Draebard cares if we're together. They might roll their eyes behind our backs and shake their heads in virtuous despair over us, but not a *single person* would object aloud."

Ithric's eyes were still closed. "I never asked you to make that sacrifice. I never *wanted* you to."

Favian reached up and kissed the pained crease between Ithric's brows. "No," he said. "You didn't. I chose to do it on my own. Now it's done, and I don't regret it, Ithric. I *don't*."

Silence stretched as Ithric digested this.

"Well," Kathrael said into the heavy atmosphere of the room. "That's not *completely* accurate, is it? He regretted it just a bit on the three-day horseback ride from Draebard to Teth."

The tension broke, and Ithric choked on a pained bark of laughter. "Yeah. I'll just bet he did." He ran a hand through his messy hair, leaving it in further disarray. "Gods, *look* at us. The shifter, the eunuch, and the girl who hates sex, all curled up together in bed."

Favian snorted through his nose and flopped, boneless, against the headboard. "When you put it like that…" He scrubbed a hand over his face, rubbing the sleep from his eyes. "I guess we probably deserve each other."

"No, Favian, you're wrong," Kathrael said, sobering. "I don't deserve any of this."

Ithric blinked at her. "Why ever not?"

Favian snaked an arm around her shoulders and pulled her down to rest against his side. "Yes, you do, Kath. You deserve life, and health, and happiness as much as any other person."

"I'm not sure I know how to be happy," she said slowly. "It seems... I don't know. *Selfish*, I guess, when there is so much wrong with the world."

Ithric reached across to hook a lock of her dark, sleep-tangled hair over her ear, and she felt a moment of surprise that the light touch did not make her flinch.

"Can't you find happiness in taking action to right those wrongs?" he asked. "Like when you rescued the twins, or helped free all of us from Turvick and Laronzo's clutches? There's nothing selfish about that."

She thought about his words, mulling them over for long moments. "I suppose... when I first met you and you convinced me to help Dex and Petra, I was too wrapped up in my own grief and desire for vengeance to feel much of anything. And when Turvick and his partner were taken away for punishment, I mostly just felt relief." She paused again. "But, it does make me happy to think of the two of you being reunited... maybe having the life together that you almost threw away."

"And kissing Favian?" Ithric asked in a sly tone. "Because that certainly makes *me* happy."

Favian blushed pink. "Doing it, you mean? Or watching *her* do it?"

"Both," Ithric said, as if the answer should be obvious.

Blood warmed Kathrael's face as well, and she wondered at it. Wondered that she should blush like a virgin over the idea of kissing when she had known such depths of depravity and humiliation throughout her short life.

"Yes. That did make me happy as well. You're right," she admitted quietly. "And... I think this would, too."

She sat up in Favian's embrace and leaned across his body, stretching out a hand to the lion-boy. Ithric's eyes lit with interest, and he followed her touch on his cheek willingly. She held her breath as their lips touched, a flash of worry piercing her chest that he would grab her and try to *take*, now that she had offered.

Instead, though, he kept the kiss as light and chaste as Favian had on that first night beside the campfire. Gradually, she relaxed, chiding herself as she realized that Favian would never have let Ithric press her too hard, assuming he had been inclined to do so in the first place. Even now, Favian's hand rested protectively between her shoulder blades, his thumb stroking back and forth as he watched her kissing his old lover.

After a few moments, Ithric pulled back a fraction in favor of rubbing his stubbled cheek along her scarred one. His lips brushed her ear, and he buried his nose in her hair for a moment before straightening away.

She caught her breath and looked at him—suddenly, painfully aware of the picture she made. Scarred face. Blind, milky eye. Unkempt hair in desperate need of a wash. Yet Ithric still looked at her with an appreciative gaze, not flinching away from the ugliness that she knew was there.

"My scars don't repulse you," she said with renewed wonder. "They didn't, even on that first night outside of Penth."

Ithric's brow furrowed. "Well, no. Why would they?"

"They repulse most people," she said, thinking of every person who had ever gasped and looked away, stepping back as if bad fortune and disfigurement might somehow be contagious.

"Yes," Ithric replied, "but you have to understand—most people are fools, in my experience." He reached out to brush fingertips over the patch of damaged flesh, sliding from her cheek, to her jaw, to her neck—following the trail where the vitriol had dripped down. "The lioness with scars on her face is always the most sought after. She's the strongest—she fought, and survived."

Kathrael caught her breath against the unexpected sob that tried to rise up. "I didn't fight," she said in a hoarse whisper. "I just ran. I've been running for half of my life."

"Kath. No. You *survived*," Favian reiterated, turning her head with a touch to her chin so she was forced to meet his gaze.

It was too much. She squeezed her eyes shut. "I take it back—I was wrong earlier. I'm sorry. Could you both go back to fighting now, please?"

Ithric huffed a breath of laughter through his nose. "Nope—not just now, I'm afraid. Maybe later. You were right—it's too early. In fact, if we're done with the soul baring for a bit, I'm going back to sleep. Might as well take advantage of being the invalid while I have the chance." He stretched carefully, several joints in his spine popping. "Someone wake me when there's food?"

"Shameless hedonist," Favian accused, affection underlying the insult.

"Yep, that's me," Ithric said, shuffling around to make himself as comfortable as he could with his wound still half-healed. He curled up on his side against Favian's hip and closed his eyes, humming in appreciation when Favian's fingers stroked through his hair.

They were quiet for some time, leaning against each other while Ithric dozed.

"I should see about hiring a fast rider this morning to take a message to Draebard for us," Favian said eventually. "They'll only be a few days ahead of us, but I'd like to avoid having search parties out for us if I can."

"Mmm," Kathrael agreed, half-asleep herself. A thought assailed her. "Do you think the priests would be willing to draw a bath and lend me some soap and hair oil? I'm tired of being grimy."

Favian shrugged, a look of interest lighting his pleasant features. "I don't see why not, especially if we haul our own buckets. I'll join you. It would be

340

nice to be clean, you're right." He poked Ithric, who groaned. "Ithric. Bath? You definitely need one."

Ithric batted his hand away. "Lemme sleep. Not s'posed to get the bandages wet, anyway. Bring me a bucket to wash in afterward or something."

"Do lions hate water as much as cats?" Kathrael wondered aloud.

"Eh. *Hate* is a strong word," Favian said, extricating himself from the tangle of blankets and limbs so the could rise. "*Dislike*, maybe. Though how it's any less savory than cleaning oneself with one's own tongue is something of an open question…"

"I'm not listening to this," Ithric mumbled.

"Of course you aren't," Favian agreed, and leaned over to run his fingers over Ithric's cheek in a brief caress. "Go to sleep. We'll be back later with food. And a bucket."

"*Mmph*," Ithric said, and fell asleep again.

She and Favian dressed quietly and left. Outside the door, Favian paused and let the wall take his weight, the night's events catching up with him. "He's still weak," he said. "That was a nasty wound."

"It's healing fast," Kathrael replied, and stepped close to wrap her arms around him. His chest rose and fell once within her grasp.

"Even so," he said, clearly thinking about how close Ithric had come to death. "A few inches lower, and…"

Around them, the temple was waking for the day. Kathrael pulled away and nudged Favian to move. "Hey. *Enough*," she said. "Come on. Bath first. You can fret later."

The novice priest who showed them where to find buckets, soap, and rags for washing was somewhat harried, and rushed off as soon as Favian thanked him.

"There's to be a public handfasting later to-day," Favian explained. "The couple are high in status, and I gather the priests are under pressure to make the ceremony a suitable spectacle for the crowd. In fact, I've been co-opted into distributing wine to the guests. The couple's families have a history of conflict, and apparently the High Priest believes that keeping everyone well-lubricated will reduce the chance of friction."

Kathrael snorted, placing a pair of water buckets onto metal hooks over the large hearth to heat them. "Right. Unless they get *too* drunk, and then all bets are off. Have fun straddling *that* fence."

Favian grinned, a sight Kathrael had sorely missed. "At least if the ceremony devolves into a brawl, I can just go back to Draebard afterward. That goes a long way toward taking the pressure off."

"True enough," she agreed. "Where's the hair oil? There must be some here…"

After a quick rummage, they located a vial of oil and a wooden comb on a small shelf opposite the bronze tub. Kathrael attacked the tangles matting her long hair to pass the time while the water warmed.

"There was a time not so long ago when I would have been appalled at the idea of my hair being dirty and unkempt," she said, the thought sitting oddly.

"I imagine it's different when you rely on your appearance for your livelihood," Favian offered. "But it's also hard to keep up with things like that when you're being dragged around from village to village by a half-crazed priest."

He moved to pick up a couple of buckets of cold water and dump them in the bronze washtub in an attempt to cover his obvious discomfort.

She raised an eyebrow. "I've told you, Favian. I make my own choices. Besides, it was far better than sitting around Draebard with no purpose beyond chopping vegetables for Brother Feldes and feeding the chickens."

He shot her a glance that was oddly shy. "Yes. Well. Thank you, anyway." He put the buckets aside and watched her fighting with a stubborn mat of hair. "Here. Let me? I think you'd better rub some oil into the snarls first or you're going to have chunks missing by the time you're done."

Again, Kathrael was taken aback by the unexpected offer—though perhaps she shouldn't have been. Maybe this was something else that was different in the north. Maybe men, or eunuchs, at least, really didn't see anything odd about cosseting a woman just for the sake of it. She slowly handed over the comb.

Favian took it and set it aside so he could work oil into the worst tangles. When he started methodically combing out her hair, starting near the bottom, the gentle tugging against her scalp sent strange tingles down Kathrael's spine. She closed her eyes, letting her guard down in a way she rarely had before, enjoying the pleasant, shivery sensation rather than questioning it.

It only took minutes for Favian to work out the final snags. The water in the buckets over the fire was not terribly hot, but they dumped it into the tub anyway rather than stand around waiting any longer. Favian filled another bucket to hang over the hearth while they washed — for Ithric, Kathrael presumed.

"You first," Favian said, a cheeky look crossing his face as he added, "You need it more."

Kathrael mock-glared at him. "I'd be offended if you weren't so obviously right about that." She checked the temperature, which was at least lukewarm rather than chilly, and removed her clothing to reveal flesh that was finally starting to fill out again after having been starved down to skin and bones for months.

To her surprise, rather than blushing and turning away, Favian was watching her. "You're looking much better than the first time you shed your clothing in front of me, Kath. I hope you're feeling better as well?"

Indeed, it was she who had to fight a blush. She stepped lightly into the tub and lowered herself into the water as she thought back to those horrible months of starvation.

"It's strange even trying to think back to those days," she said, after a thoughtful pause. "Hunger was an ache that never left. My guts cramped from all the worms in them, and my joints flared with pain at every movement. Even before the vitriol attack, I never really had enough to eat. Or else it was just parched grains, no meat or vegetables, and I would be hungry again in no time even if I ate until my stomach was full. This is the first time in my life that I've had all the nourishing food I could eat for months at a time."

Favian nodded. "Healer Sagdea says that without enough of the right kind of food, nothing in the body works the way it's supposed to." He paused to smile in amusement. "And Priest Feldes says that one cannot nourish the spirit without first nourishing the body."

Kathrael smiled as well. "Brother Feldes has a very fine spirit indeed." She began to wash herself, and hummed in appreciation when Favian brought over a rag to scrub at her back, along with a pitcher to pour water over her hair so she could soap it up and rub the soft strands together between her palms until they were squeaking.

"You know," she said idly, "Rhyth has some very fine bath houses. I only ever got to make use of them when I was working, but I do miss them sometimes. They were much grander than a metal tub sitting in a back room."

Favian made a noise of interest. "Oh yes? When we stayed in the palace at Rhyth, there was a huge tub in every guest room. We were all rather amazed by that, as I recall... though less so, once we realized that the buckets to fill them were hauled by child slaves." His voice grew sad at that, but he shook it off. "We didn't see much of the city outside the palace walls. It was beyond anything I've ever imagined, though. The scale of it was breathtaking."

"There are hot springs under parts of the city," Kathrael said, remembering. "Where they bubble up, the rich families built huge stone buildings full of mosaics and marble-lined pools big enough to swim in—at least some of them. There are steam rooms, with cold pools for dipping afterwards, and the whole place smells of cedar and fragrant herbs."

Favian watched her silently for a long moment before speaking. "You miss Rhyth, don't you. Even with everything that happened there."

She looked up at him, feeling vulnerable. "Your life has not been without pain either. Do you consider Draebard any less your home because bad things happened there?"

"No," he replied without hesitation. "I don't."

She nodded, and went back to rinsing herself off. Favian directed her head back with a light touch and poured water over her hair, setting off a new round of shivery tingles. After running a bit more oil through the dark strands and rinsing a final time, she sighed and gestured for a length of burlap toweling hanging nearby.

"Your turn," she said, and stepped out to dry herself.

Again, to her surprise, Favian merely nodded and stripped off his priest's robes and linen underthings, baring himself to her interested gaze with no apparent hesitation. His body was trapped somewhere between that of a muscular young man and that of a soft eunuch—not enough time had passed yet for his waist to thicken and his body hair to completely disappear.

Her gaze was caught by a twisted mass of scar tissue under his left collarbone, at the juncture of torso and shoulder. He glanced over, saw her looking, and smiled ruefully.

"I wasn't always a temple acolyte," he explained. "I probably had no business on a battlefield at that age, but I ended up on one just the same. Driving a chariot, to be precise. I failed to duck at the appropriate moment, and took an arrow through the shoulder. I'm afraid that's the only battle scar I have worth showing off, but at least it's a fairly impressive one."

Somehow, the imperfection made him seem more relatable, even though it had occurred under circumstances with which Kathrael had absolutely no experience. She shook herself free of her strange fascination, and pointed out, "You do have at least one other scar of interest now, you know."

At that, he huffed out a breath of laughter. "I'm not sure it's the sort of scar one shows off. And frankly, it's not much to look at as far as I can make out. It's surprisingly small."

"But surprisingly painful."

Favian shrugged, and stepped into the tub. "I think the arrow was worse, actually, though it didn't stay as bad for as long. Both of them were important steps toward the priesthood; I made the decision to leave the horse pens and join the temple not long after my shoulder injury."

Well," Kathrael said, feeling suddenly shy, "I for one, am glad you did. Even if Ithric isn't."

Favian grimaced and took up a soapy rag. "That's a very old argument, as I'm sure you gathered. I don't expect to break any new ground with it at this late date."

Kathrael gave herself a final scrub with the burlap and hung it back on its peg. Still naked, she padded over and dragged a chair to the head of the tub, so she could sit and return the favor of washing Favian's back.

"He's just scared that it means you don't want him any more, Favian," she said.

He frowned. "I told him I did. Twice."

"You told him, but I don't think he heard you. Not properly."

Favian didn't object when she freed his plait of blond hair and began unraveling it to wash.

"I thought I was completely clear," he said, the furrow between his eyebrows deepening.

Kathrael stopped running her fingers through his fine hair and leaned around to consider him. "Far be it from me to interfere, but I suspect actions will speak louder than words in this case."

He looked thoughtful for a moment. "Maybe you're right. The last time — the *only* time — we were together, it wasn't exactly what you'd call… subtle. Not that horny adolescents are generally known for their subtlety in such things."

"Not really, no," Kathrael agreed.

To her surprise, Favian reached up and drew her into a brief kiss. "Thank you. I wasn't exaggerating when I told you that the two of us are utter shite on our own. It really does help to have someone outside the quagmire available to throw us a rope. And it hasn't escaped me that we're only here in the first place because you engineered the whole thing."

"Least I could do," she said. "*I'm* only here because you two saved me."

He smiled and brushed wet fingers across her cheek. "I'm not at all sure that's true. But if it is, I consider the debt more than repaid."

She gave into the urge to press into his palm, soaking up the touch with closed eyes. "Everything will work out, Favian," she said. "You'll see."

>━∿⚜∿━<

A little while later, they returned to Ithric's sick room with supplies in tow.

"Food," Kathrael announced, setting the large bowl of stew on the table next to the low bed. She poked Ithric's shoulder when he only mumbled in response, and he pried open bleary eyes.

"Bucket," Favian added, setting down the heavy wooden pail full of steaming water. He had a couple of clean rags and a length of toweling slung over his shoulder. A small pot of soft lye soap nestled in his free hand, along with the stoppered vial of hair oil.

Ithric stretched, still somewhat gingerly. "Well, now," he said around a yawn. "I suppose I could get used to this."

"Best not," Favian shot back, "unless you're planning on getting skewered on a regular basis."

"Spoilsport," Ithric said, voice light.

"Come and eat, both of you," Kathrael commanded as she dragged the room's single chair over next to the small table. "I'm hungry, and if you don't want me to eat your shares as well, you'd better do something about it now."

That brought Ithric shuffling over to the edge of the bed immediately, and he took the wooden spoon she handed him with a smile. Favian followed a moment later. They huddled around the hot food, sharing the bowl with only a minimum of jousting and parrying for the choicest bits.

Favian lost interest before she and Ithric did, putting aside his spoon and leaving them to scrape up the rest of the thick stew. He wandered back to the bucket and untied the fastenings of his robes, removing both robes and shift until he was clad only in linen smallclothes, slung low on his hips.

Kathrael watched in something like amusement as Ithric, drawn to the movement in the corner of his eye, turned and did a rather comical double take.

His eyes narrowed warily. "What are you *doing*, Favian?"

Favian took up one of the rags and dipped it in the bucket. "What does it look like I'm doing? If I'm going to help you wash, I'd rather not splash water all over my robes."

With a look of consternation, Ithric rose slowly from his perch at the edge of the bed and stalked toward him. He was still naked except for the swathe of bandages after his transformation during the night—completely unselfconscious. Kathrael was treated to a fine view of the play of wiry muscles in his back and buttocks as he crossed the room. He stopped half a step too close to Favian, pressing into his space and looking down into Favian's blue eyes from his slight advantage in height.

"Oh?" he asked, his voice low and a little dangerous. "You're going to *help me wash*, are you?"

Favian did not back down. Kathrael knew that in his place, she would have been sorely tempted to do so under the force of that intense gaze. Instead, he merely widened his eyes into a clear *you're an idiot* expression and lifted the wet rag. "Well, *yeah*," he said. "I thought you were the one who wanted to play the invalid? Now turn around so I can start on your back."

They were a study in opposites, and Kathrael found she could not look away as she lounged back in the sturdy wooden chair. Ithric was lean and hungry, his wiry physique hinting at a surprising turn of strength and speed, given his lack of bulk. His mane of messy hair was dark, with ruddy highlights. Favian, by contrast, was sleek and well fed, the changes in his body already beginning to soften the angular lines of male muscle. His hair glinted gold in the sunlight streaming from the room's high window. His eyes were pale and deep like clear water as he and Ithric stared each other down.

Eventually, reluctantly, Ithric turned his back to Favian, revealing a haunted, hopeful expression to Kathrael's fascinated gaze. She let the corner of her lips curve up—a smile of reassurance that did nothing to ease Ithric's tension. At the first touch of the soapy rag, his eyes flickered closed. His brows were still drawn into an expression of the most exquisitely agonized desire.

Kathrael could not have explained what it was that caused her heart to beat faster in anticipation as she watched Favian wash the sweat and grime from Ithric's body with slow, deliberate strokes of the rag. He took infinite care around the bandages, and continued lower. When he reached around to slide the cloth along the crease of Ithric's hip, a hand shot out with catlike speed and grabbed his wrist in an uncompromising grip.

Ithric spun them around so Favian was facing him and growled, "If you're intending to stop any time soon, now would be a *very* good time to do so."

Still un-cowed, Favian met his eyes squarely. "I have *no intention* of stopping, you ass. Now either quit moping and take what you really want, or let me get back to what I was doing."

A low rumble rolled through Ithric's chest. A heartbeat later, the rag fell to the floor with a wet slap as Favian was summarily pinned on his back on the bed—the aurochs finally ready to be devoured. Kathrael held her breath, hypnotized by the sight.

"You should be careful what you ask for, Favian," Ithric said in a hoarse voice.

352

TWENTY

Favian arched up against him, testing the hold and falling back when it did not falter. "I've decided that *careful* isn't really my thing any more. Sorry to disappoint."

Ithric made another low noise and fell on Favian's throat, kissing and biting his way down the pale column of flesh. He loosed his grip on Favian's wrists, and Favian brought a hand up to the back of his neck to hold him in place. Ithric licked and nuzzled his way over Favian's chest and stomach, his hands scrabbling at the ties of the smallclothes that were now the only thing separating them. He rubbed his cheek against Favian's groin through the cloth and breathed in. Something jolted unexpectedly in Kathrael's belly, flaring into life at the sight.

"You smell different," Ithric accused, mouthing at Favian through the damp linen.

Favian's voice was a bit breathless. "They scent their soap differently here, I think."

The stubborn laces finally gave way to Ithric's fumbling and he tugged the underclothes down impatiently so he could get at Favian's skin directly. "No," he insisted. "*You* smell different."

"Really?" Favian asked, sounding curious but not alarmed. "Huh."

Ithric wrestled the smallclothes the rest of the way down and off. He resumed his place and shoved Favian's leg to the side, exposing him further. "Let me see you. I have to see what you did to yourself—"

"Ithric," Favian soothed, reaching down to run a hand through Ithric's hair. "There's not much to see. It's just a little scar, and an empty flap of skin…"

Ithric ran gentle fingers over Favian's cock. Favian closed his eyes in pleasure and let his head fall back, baring his neck. "You're not even *hard*," Ithric said, sounding as if the fact caused him physical pain.

Kathrael watched in silence, caught up in a way she never would have foreseen, mentally urging them to work it out—to come to an understanding after so many months of aching for each other.

Favian ran his hand down to Ithric's chin and made him look up, meeting his eyes. "I don't *need* to be hard. It's better this way, really. I want to feel *you*, Ithric… not my own desperation for release."

When Ithric didn't answer, Favian pulled him up the length of his body and sealed their lips together. Ithric made a noise somewhere between a whine and a sob into the kiss, before pressing him further down into the mattress.

When they finally parted for air, Favian met Ithric's eyes again. "I *do* still want you," he said, sounding as breathless as Kathrael felt. "*Please*. You *have* to believe me. Take me now, Ithric. Let me feel how much you want me in return."

354

Ithric looked so overwhelmed that it finally broke Kathrael free of her trance. She roused herself enough to get up from the chair and move to the discarded bathing supplies, where she picked up the vial of oil.

"You'll want this," she said, knowing well enough what was coming next after her long friendship with Vesh. "Take it slow. Don't... hurt him." Her voice went quiet on the final words, a note of pleading entering without her realizing it.

Ithric's hazel eyes flew to hers, but it was Favian who spoke. "Kath. He's not going to hurt me."

He lifted a hand to cup her cheek, making her look at him and see his expression of confident serenity. She felt another little shiver of reaction.

"No." Ithric had recovered enough for speech. "Little Cat... it's not going to be like that. I'd hurt myself long before I ever hurt him."

"Stay with us," Favian continued, still cupping her face. "Stay and watch. You'll see."

She hesitated for a long moment before nodding, still feeling shivery, her skin running hot and cold. She told herself it was only so she could be sure that Ithric wasn't too rough... that Favian hadn't taken on more than he expected. "All right," she said, and forced herself to quip, "Probably best to have a professional present, I suppose."

Ithric peered down at Favian with a strange expression. "So, how come you were never this uninhibited when you still had balls?" he asked.

Favian blushed, but actually appeared to give the question serious consideration. "I... suppose I didn't want to disappoint the people I respected, before. Now that I'm a eunuch, there's no one to disappoint. No one to shock."

"I think you shocked *him*," Kathrael pointed out, indicating Ithric with a flick of her eyes.

Favian smiled, and gave a little roll of his hips where they were pressed against Ithric's. "Well... maybe a bit. He'll get over it, though."

Ithric growled and thrust into the crease of Favian's hip. "I'm over it." He lifted his body away from Favian's so he could urge him to move.

Favian rolled over onto his stomach and hitched one leg up and to the side. His eyes sought out Kathrael, who was still more-or-less frozen next to the bed. "You're all right, though, Kath? Aren't you?"

She pulled her cynicism around her like a cloak and raised a supercilious eyebrow, despite the faint, tripping beat of her heart against her ribs. "Don't be daft. I doubt either of you could come up with anything that I haven't see dozens of times, priest-boy, if not hundreds. The rich men of Rhyth do *so* love their orgies."

With that, she returned to her perch on the chair near the bed, haughty as any queen. Of course, her sudden desire to sit down had *nothing* to do with the way her knees were turning to jelly. Ithric's eyes tracked her with interest for the span of a few breaths before he returned his attention to the bed.

"You know, Favian, I did actually manage to invite myself to a handful of those, and our Little Cat is not exaggerating." He poured a thin stream of oil over his fingers and trailed them along Favian's spine. "They have all sorts of interesting ideas about sex in the great houses." His fingers disappeared between Favian's buttocks and his forearm flexed. "Sometimes, though, the simplest things are still the best."

Favian hissed between his teeth, his eyes falling shut. His spine curved, and he scrabbled a bit against the tangled furs and blankets underneath him. Ithric poured more oil directly onto Favian's exposed flesh and set the vial aside. His free hand stroked up Favian's back and closed around his nape, steadying him.

Kathrael had tensed a bit in her chair at Favian's reaction to being breached, remembering well the unpleasant burn of being taken in that particular way. When Favian's eyes flew open, though, they were dark and pleasure-drugged, the pupils blown wide. The next sound torn from his throat was undeniably one of encouragement—a low groan.

Ithric looked every inch the hungry predator, yet despite his insistently throbbing prick leaving little smears of seed against Favian's hip, he merely continued to tease and work Favian open with unhurried movements. Kathrael made the mistake of looking at the shape-shifter's face, and the expression of desperate love there hit her like a blow.

The curl of shivery warmth in her belly burst into flame without warning, only to turn hot and liquid a moment later. It flowed down to the place between her legs and settled there, making her sex swell. On the bed, Favian gasped and keened as

Ithric pressed deeper, pushing back now against the fingers breaching him as if trying to get *more*. Kathrael *knew* Favian, and she knew that he was utterly incapable of putting on that kind of an act — his pleasure truly was real.

Kathrael's cunt pulsed at the realization, and some of the liquid heat squeezed out from between her swollen labia. She caught her breath audibly in surprise, wondering in a daze if she had somehow forgotten her moon time and started to bleed. This felt... *different*, though — slick, and wet, and oh-so-good against her suddenly sensitive inner lips.

Her small gasp of shock had attracted the others' attention. They stilled, and Favian dragged his wits back together to look at her with eyes that barely focused. "Kath?" he asked.

She didn't answer, unable to do more than stare at him with parted lips as her nipples hardened and rubbed deliciously against the linen of her shift.

Favian's eyes grew more intent, and Ithric was looking at her in worry now as well. She blushed scarlet.

"*Kath.*" Favian's voice was sharper now. "Say something. Have we upset you? Brought back bad memories, or — "

Suddenly, Ithric's nostrils flared. He breathed in slowly, as if scenting the air. His eyes lit with pleasant surprise. "No..." he said, drawing out the word. "It's all right, Favian. It looks like I spoke too soon earlier. I do believe our Little Cat is in heat for us after all."

Favian blinked, lifting his upper body to get a better view of her. The movement brought his back against Ithric's chest. Ithric looped a possessive arm around Favian's torso and grinned at her over his shoulder. The sight made a new pulse of wetness dampen the material of her underskirts.

"Kathrael?" Favian prompted yet again. "Is that true?"

She could only gape at them helplessly, swept away by her body's unexpected response. "I—" she managed eventually. "I don't know. I feel strange all of the sudden…"

"Good strange?" Ithric asked, as if he already knew the answer.

She nodded.

"Do you want us to stop what we're doing?" Favian said.

"No!" she said immediately. "No. Don't stop—"

Ithric's eyes went lazy and wicked. He reached down to close his teeth over the line of muscle running from Favian's neck to his shoulder, biting down. Kathrael's gaze fell on the small patch of skin with sudden, single-minded focus, and the sound Favian made went straight to her sex.

"Ithric!" he gasped, and batted the shape-shifter away.

Ithric backed off with a smug look and went back to regarding her. "Touch yourself, Little Cat. If you don't want to join in with us, you can watch and play with yourself while I take him."

Kathrael's heart was pounding now, but—

"I don't... I've never..." She trailed off, unable to manage a full sentence.

Ithric's brow furrowed. "You've never touched yourself?"

"I've never enjoyed it."

Favian's expression settled into a kind of gentle affection that did nothing whatsoever to quiet the whirlwind of emotions in her mind. "Try, if you want to," he said. "You might find that it feels different this time."

Ithric kissed the mark he'd made on Favian's skin and urged him back down on the bed, their attention returning to each other—much to Kathrael's relief. Could Favian have been right? Was this the pleasure he insisted so ardently that women could feel, as well as men?

"What about you, Favian? Can you still come?" Ithric asked, returning his fingers to Favian's slick opening.

Favian stretched like a cat. "I'm not sure," he said in a dreamy voice. "The other novices say that some eunuchs can, and some can't. As long as you keep doing *that*, I don't really care, to be honest."

"What, *this*, you mean?" Ithric asked, his wrist twisting.

Favian grunted and tried to press back against his fingers again. Kathrael's sex grew so full and heavy that it was almost uncomfortable. When she shifted against the hard seat of the chair to ease it, a new wave of pleasure skittered up her spine. She rocked her hips back and forth in tiny, instinctive movements, riding the little surges of liquid pleasure.

Ithric continued to stretch and tease Favian with his fingers, stopping at intervals to dribble more oil over the place he was breaching. Favian's mouth was open in an expressive *oh* of pleasure, the rest of his body gradually relaxing, growing heavy under the slow, merciless ministrations.

The tips of Kathrael's pebbled nipples ached terribly as they brushed against her chemise with every breath. With a groan, she pulled the laces free and tugged the loose material open, letting it fall over one shoulder until the breast on that side was exposed to the cooling air. She palmed the smooth globe with a soothing motion, trying to quell the fire, and breathed in sharply as a new jolt of pleasure rushed from the taut bud of flesh straight to her throbbing cunt.

Favian was moaning, now — his limp body wracked with tremors every few moments. "Please," he mumbled, "please... *Ithric.* Need you... I need you *right now.* Let me feel you. *Please...*"

Ithric looked nearly as undone as Favian did. He leaned down until his front pressed against Favian's back, and his lips were next to Favian's ear. "You'll have me," he said. His forearm flexed again, and Favian *keened*, arching off the bed.

The ache in Kathrael's sex was too great to ignore any longer. Feeling inexplicably wanton, she squeezed and pinched her exposed breast with one hand while hitching up her skirts an inch at a time with the other. On the bed, Ithric had pulled free of Favian's body and was oiling up his cock, which was hard and leaking. His gaze locked with

Kathrael's for an instant, their faces wearing mirrored expressions of need.

Favian turned over to lie on his back, and Ithric's gaze was drawn back to him as if pulled there by an inescapable force.

"I have to see you," Favian explained, still sounding half-gone.

Ithric crawled into the cradle of his spread legs. "I'm right here," he said. "I'm not going anywhere, Favian, I promise. Never again."

Favian surged up to kiss him, and Ithric groaned into his mouth. Kathrael pulled up the front of her skirts the final few inches until she could worm a hand underneath, and lifted her left leg to rest her foot on the edge of the bed. She cupped her swollen sex at the same moment Ithric curled his hips and pressed into the depths of Favian's body.

The thatch of hair between Kathrael's legs was soaked with the moisture her sex had produced. It was slick and warm, and a faint smell reminiscent of seaweed and musk floated to her nostrils. *This must be what Ithric smelled earlier*, she thought, and shivered. *He knew...*

Now, he and Favian were rocking together with lazy movements, never breaking the kiss as their bodies entwined, pressing ever closer. Ithric reached down to hook a hand under Favian's knee and pull his leg up. He thrust in again, and Favian gasped into the kiss.

Kathrael slid a fingertip between her outer lips, exploring the folds inside. Each movement sent shocks of pleasure through her body, growing sharper and more insistent when she touched the nub of flesh at the top that had always been painfully oversensitive before. Now, sliding a fingertip around it in slow circles felt like flying... felt like gliding up the side of a mountain, rising ever higher in hopes of seeing what lay on the other side.

"Missed you," Ithric was saying against Favian's lips. "Missed you so much, Favian. And *you*, Little Cat," he continued, and Kathrael made a needy noise upon hearing the endearment, "what you did... thank you... feels so good to have you both here..."

The warm desire in Kathrael's belly surged higher, a feeling like nothing she had ever experienced. Favian wrapped his arms around Ithric and pressed him close, skin to skin.

"Come for me," he whispered, and both Ithric and Kathrael cried out.

If Kathrael had been gliding before, now she was falling free, plunging into the warm depths of a welcoming sea as her sex throbbed and clenched, flooding her body with an ecstasy she had never even dreamed existed. She washed up on the shore long moments later, still sprawled in the chair, feeling dizzy and drugged with pleasure.

Favian still held Ithric as he twitched and shuddered in the aftermath of his own release, his face buried in the juncture of Favian's neck and shoulder.

"So beautiful," Favian said, "the pair of you."

Kathrael slowly drew her fingers away from her slick sex, jerking in surprise as the movement pulled another shivering aftershock from her spent body.

"Favian," she said after a long pause, her voice as raspy as if she'd been shouting, "I never *knew*..."

Ithric moved his head so that he could look at her while still resting his cheek against Favian's collarbone. His brows drew together. "Was that really your first time, Little Cat?"

Kathrael could only nod, a flush rising up her neck.

Ithric looked surprised for a moment, but then his face cleared and he smiled. "It's good, isn't it?" The smile transformed into a mischievous smirk. "Hey... maybe Favian's not so bad at this priest stuff after all."

Favian poked Ithric hard in the side—his *uninjured* side—and Ithric flinched. "Ow," he complained, lifting his upper body enough to glare down at his tormentor.

"He's right, though," Kathrael managed. "You're not bad at the priest stuff at all." She paused, taking stock of her body. "Only... am I supposed to feel like I'm a helpless puddle of warm mush afterward?"

"Oh, *definitely*," Ithric replied. "That's how you know you're doing it right."

"I guess that's good, then," she managed, sliding down a bit further in the chair.

Favian was still watching her, warm satisfaction on his face. "It's even better with someone else's arms around you afterward," he suggested.

She considered the offer, eyeing the warm bed piled with furs and blankets, along with the two

sated men curled up in it. Both of them were awaiting her response with interest, but no indication of
impatience. She realized that she was free to de-
cline, and they would treat her no differently than
if she accepted. She could *choose*, without fear of
losing them.

A soft voice whispered in her ear. *You're not
their whore, Kath. You're no one's whore. You're their
beautiful, scarred lioness, who fought and survived.*

A lump rose in her throat, and she swallowed
around it. Without a word, she rose on shaky legs
and untied her skirts. They fell to the floor by the
bed, leaving her clad only in her chemise, which
still gaped obscenely, half unlaced. Favian nudged
Ithric to move over and shuffled toward the center
of the mattress, leaving an inviting space next to
him.

When she curled up in it, Favian eased an arm
under her shoulders, supporting her head on his
chest. Ithric threw an arm and a leg over him from
the other side.

He was right. This was even better. She was
still mired in drowsy lassitude, but the slow brush
of fingers along the swell of her shoulder sparked a
pleasant tingle across her sensitized skin. She let
her own fingers trail across Favian's chest, and felt
gooseflesh rise in their wake.

"What about you, Favian?" Ithric mumbled
into Favian's neck. "Did you come?"

Favian was quiet for a moment, framing his response. "Not exactly. It's kind of hard to explain. It
feels quite a bit different now. Still very pleasur-
able, but it doesn't build in the same way it used to.

While I'm not sure I'd go out of my way to seek it out on my own, I definitely want this with you as often as you'd like. It makes me feel very close to you both. Very open."

Ithric's eyes were closed, though his expression appeared thoughtful. "Hmm... there's a joke in there somewhere about you being *opened*, but I'll restrain myself."

"How kind of you," Favian said, sounding deeply unimpressed. Kathrael snorted in amusement.

"I'm not sure how I feel about sharing a bed with a lover and not making them come," Ithric continued, still sounding half asleep. "Makes me feel selfish."

"Well, don't," Favian said, with a bit of asperity. "Because I'm enjoying getting something out of it beyond a few seconds of release and a mess of spend coating my belly. If you really need a project related to giving people orgasms, maybe you and Kath should talk."

Ithric smiled, his eyes still closed. "Maybe we should. Later, though. Sleep now."

"You've slept half the day already," Kathrael couldn't help pointing out, even though she was on the verge of dozing, herself.

"Invalid, remember?" Ithric muttered.

"You should both sleep," Favian said. "If I'm gone when you wake up, it's because I had to go help with the handfasting. I'll be back sometime this evening, though. If I'm feeling particularly charitable, I might even bring some leftover food and wine back with me."

Ithric yawned, arching his spine before settling back against Favian's side. "Mmm. Bring pork, if they have it. Or goat. Goat's good, too..."

Kathrael fell asleep to the rumble of Favian's soft chuckle under her cheek.

>~~ ☙ ~~<

The sound of a crying infant woke her some considerable time later, the noise persisting even as the dregs of the dream that had spawned it slipped away. She gasped and sat upright, disoriented. The last light of evening barely illuminated the room. There was a man next to her in the unfamiliar bed, sleeping with his back turned. He was naked, and the smell of sex permeated the air.

Without stopping to think, Kathrael scrambled back, half falling to the floor and crawling away until she fetched up against a wall, her daughter's anguished cries ringing in her ears. She slapped her hands against the sides of her head and squeezed hard, to no avail.

How could she have been so foolish as to fall asleep? Even now, the man was rolling over, her clumsy movements having awoken him. Had he paid her yet? Where was the money? Maybe she could get it and get away before he tried to fuck her again. The baby's cries grew into high-pitched screams, and she whimpered, unable to think clearly.

"Little Cat?" The question was tentative; the tone, worried. "Little Cat, what's wrong? Did you have a nightmare?"

The man rolled into a sitting position. A swathe of linen bandages crisscrossed his torso, and the sight penetrated her confused mind.

Ithric.

She let out a gasp of relief, still hazy on where she was and what was happening, but knowing deep in her bones that she was not in physical danger, at least.

"Kathrael," Ithric said, "Hey. You're scaring me now. Tell me what's wrong."

She shook her head, pressing fingers into her temples, unable to focus properly on both him and her baby. "I—I can't…"

Ithric was moving—rising from the bed and giving her a wide berth as he rummaged for small-clothes and a set of robes. "Right. I don't know what's happening, but I'm going to get Favian. Just stay here, Little Cat. Don't move. Don't do anything. Promise me."

She could only shake her head again, wishing with all her might that she could reach into her skull physically and rip those agonized cries out by force. She was only distantly aware of the door opening and closing as Ithric left.

The events from earlier in the day started to filter past the hazy veil of sleep and nightmare as she sat next to the wall, rocking back and forth. How could she have let herself feel such happiness while her baby's spirit was hungry and frightened? What kind of a person did that make her? She was surrounded by the dead—by people she had failed in *every conceivable way.* What *right* did she have to pleasure?

Time was meaningless, marked only by the jerky movements of her body as she continued to rock. Eventually, the door opened again, barely penetrating her awareness.

"She panicked out of the blue," Ithric was saying. "Stumbled out of bed and crawled over to the wall. She hasn't said a word, she just sort of whimpers. I didn't know what to do—"

"I'm not sure there *is* anything to do." Favian's voice that time, sounding grim. She tried to latch onto it, her eyes searching the deepening gloom for him.

Light flared as Ithric lit the lamp. Favian crossed to her and dropped to his knees. His soft hands covered her own and pulled them gently from her temples. "Kath," he asked, "is it your baby again?"

She nodded, still unable to speak, and leaned forward until her throbbing head rested against his sternum.

"Baby?" Ithric asked, from somewhere nearby. "Favian, what are you talking about? What's going on?"

Favian's chest expanded and fell in a deep breath. "For some reason, Kathrael attracts the spirits of the dead—people she's lost. They speak to her. Sometimes, they torment her. No one is quite sure why."

Kathrael choked on a sob, and one of Favian's arms came around her, holding her to him. She was dimly aware of movement as Ithric crouched at her side—close, but not touching.

"A baby, though?" Ithric asked, sounding appalled.

"M-my daughter," Kathrael managed in a quavering voice. "She d-died in my womb when I was —" She gulped, choking, and had to pause before she could go on. "When I was fourteen."

Ithric let his breath out.

Favian rubbed her back, and she shook with the need to somehow flee the painful reminder of her failure as a mother. As a woman.

"Kathrael says the baby's spirit is always hungry. Frightened," Favian said, still grim. "We've talked with the other priests, but so far no one has been able to come up with a way to help someone who's already dead."

Kathrael shuddered, and pressed back against Favian's light hold. "I-I need to *move*. I can't just sit here, I'll go mad!"

Favian's arms slipped away, but Ithric's hand fell on her shoulder. "Wait," he said. "Please, Little Cat — just for a minute. Help me understand. There's something that doesn't make sense to me. Why would a spirit feel hunger? You said your daughter died before she was born. How would she even know what hunger *is*?"

Kathrael hugged herself, torn between the desire to flee and the desire to collapse into their arms and shatter. "I don't *know*!" she said.

"What are you getting at, Ithric?" Favian asked. "Surely Kathrael is in a better position than either of us to judge?"

"It just doesn't make sense, Favian," Ithric repeated. "Think about it. *Frightened*... now *that* makes sense. Has anyone actually tried to help the poor kid?"

"*Help, how*?" Kathrael forced out, nearly at the end of her tether. "*She's dead!*"

"Ithric—" Favian began in a quelling tone.

"No. Just let me think out loud," Ithric interrupted. "She might be dead, but her spirit is *here*. I mean, how do you soothe any frightened baby? Has anyone *attempted* to offer her comfort?"

"How *can* I?" Kathrael nearly shouted, hating the hysterical undertone of her voice.

"We don't understand what you're suggesting, Ithric," Favian said, his calm at odds with her upset.

Ithric rose and urged Kathrael to shaky feet. "Just let me try something, you two. Please... give me your trust for a handful of minutes. Honestly, it doesn't look like anything we try could make the situation much worse than it already is, does it?"

Kathrael could only shake her head, trying not to latch onto false hope. Even so, it was easier to stop fighting and let herself be led, so desperate was she for *anyone* to proffer some sort of salvation from her private hell of self-loathing and despair.

"I think we're both open to any ideas you or anyone else might have," Favian said, echoing her thoughts. "But you'll still have to explain what you intend."

Ithric urged her toward the bed, and Favian added an arm to support her from the other side as well. "It's exactly what I said," Ithric offered. "What do you do when a baby cries, if it's not because of hunger? You soothe them."

Kathrael shuddered again. "I can't even touch her..."

Ithric guided her to the center of the bed and put a hastily folded blanket against the headboard for her to lean against. "No," he said, his voice sad. "But you can try to let go of your own pain over her loss, and be the comfort she needs. Babies always take their cues from their mothers."

That stopped her. Shock suffused her as the harsh truth of what he was saying cut through her haze of pain and self-hatred. No one in their right mind would hand a squalling baby to a person who was curled up rocking in the corner with their hands over their ears to block out the sound of the cries.

"Favian," Ithric urged, as Kathrael sat frozen on the bed in the wake of her epiphany. He gestured Favian to join her. Favian climbed in and sat next to her, shoulder to shoulder, his mouth twisting into a frown as she looked to him for guidance.

"As much as it pains me to say so," he said, "Ithric might just be onto something. Will you let him try to help?"

She nodded, still struck dumb. Her eyes slipped to Ithric as he crawled in to bracket her on the other side, only to squeeze shut a moment later when the wails echoing in her ears grew even more desperate.

"I'm so sorry, Kathrael," Ithric said. "I know it must hurt you. But she's just a baby. All she wants is to feel safe. To know that she's protected by people who care about her."

Tears rose up and spilled from Kathrael's good eye. "I couldn't protect her," she whispered.

Favian wrapped an arm around her and drew her close against him. "You're protecting her spirit. You're protecting her memory. You came to a place where other people could try to help. And, gods help me, I think you may have just stumbled on the person with the answer."

Unable to take any more, she buried her face against him and wept. All of the tightly held anguish she'd been caging in her chest escaped in a river of salt water that ran down her undamaged cheek. Ithric scooted up to rest against her back, one hand sliding up and down her arm in a soothing motion.

She cried for a long time. *I'm sorry, my precious daughter*, she thought. *I'm so sorry I tried to shut you out. To push you away. I didn't understand — I didn't know what else to do. I still don't, really. I love you, though. So much. I will always love you...*

Gradually, the sound of soft humming penetrated her awareness. She came back to her surroundings enough to realize that the low, soothing noise came from Ithric. He was still at her back, rocking her back and forth with tiny movements. Her chest settled, the rhythm of her congested breathing broken only by an occasional hitch as he started to sing in a surprisingly fine, clear tenor.

"I left my baby lying there,
lying there, lying there;
I left my baby lying there
To go and gather wineberries."

It was a lullaby; one she had not heard before. A new sob choked her, and she buried her face in Favian's linen robes.

"Ho-van, ho-van gorry o go,
Gorry o go, gorry o go;
I've lost my dearest baby-o..."

Favian stroked her head as she listened, the words of the song competing with the baby's cries. Cries that were slowly growing weaker.

"I saw the little yellow fawn,
yellow fawn, yellow fawn;
But never saw my baby.

"I found the otter on the lake,
on the lake, on the lake;
But could not find my baby."

Her daughter's cries subsided into soft whimpers, and Kathrael's heart skipped a beat, stealing her breath away for a moment.

"Ho-van, ho-van gorry o go,
Gorry o go, gorry o go;
I never found my baby-o.

"The faeries took my baby home,
baby home, baby home;
I'll see her when I'm dreaming."

The words trailed off, and Ithric returned to humming. Favian's light voice joined him, and a moment later, the voices of other unseen presences joined the harmony. Vesh. Her sister. Her mother. Even after Ithric and Favian's voices went silent, the lullabies continued — songs from the southern slave camps, songs from the temple.

Kathrael lifted her tear-stained face, looking around the room in wonder. Her daughter's spirit cooed and burbled quietly, the tiny, anguished wraith finally at peace.

"Kath?" Favian asked, his thumb coming up to brush away the tear track from her unscarred cheek.

Oh, my daughter, she thought. *My dearest baby. I think... I think... maybe... we don't have to be afraid any more.*

"Thank you," she whispered aloud. "Thank you both so much."

TWENTY-ONE

The three of them sat curled together in the flickering glow of the single lamp for a long time after the lullaby ended. The ghostly voices faded slowly into silence, the transition so gradual that Kathrael could not have said when they finally slipped back behind the unseen veil.

Favian insisted on leaving long enough to get them food, and watched carefully to ensure that Kathrael ate her share.

Afterward, they talked for *hours*. Kathrael learned that Ithric had turned into a lion for the first time seven years earlier, when bandits attacked his family on the road and killed his parents. He savaged one while in animal form, and the other three fled, leaving Ithric and his older sister alive.

"Alyndra tried to drag me to the temple as soon as we got back home to Venzor. She and the High Priest were both ignoring me, even though I was standing right there, talking about me becoming an acolyte like it was a foregone conclusion. So I waited until dark and ran away." He ran a hand through his ragged mane of hair, mussing it. "Alyndra was furious with me for leaving her alone before our parents could even have a proper funeral, and I was furious with her for trying to make me a prisoner of the Priests' Guild."

"It wouldn't have been like that," Favian interjected.

Ithric raised an eyebrow. "Wouldn't it?" he shot back in a deeply skeptical tone. "Not everyone in the northern temples shares Senovo's views on such matters, Favian. If he hadn't found me and taken me back to Draebard with him, I have no doubt that I would have been hounded into the temple if I'd ever dared show my face around people again."

Favian shook his head and breathed out sharply through his nose. Although he was practically radiating disagreement, Kathrael could see him rein himself in to avoid an argument.

"Anyway," Ithric continued, "things still aren't good between Alyndra and me. I heard she got handfasted a couple of years ago, but we haven't spoken since the summer after I ran away."

"Maybe it's time to try mending things," Favian offered. "I can't imagine being at odds with Frella for years on end. Life's too short. All three of us have learned that lesson far too well, I think."

"Maybe so," Ithric said.

In return for Ithric's story, Kathrael haltingly told him about her own life. When she spoke of her first disastrous meeting with the Wolf Patron, his eyes widened.

"Wait," he said. "*You're* the little slave girl from south of Rhyth?" His eyes flew to Favian, who nodded.

"Kath and I disagree to a considerable degree on the concept of prophecy," he said, "but I can't help thinking that our meeting — and everything that came after — was fated."

"Apparently I'm shorter in person than I was in his Seer's dream," Kathrael quipped, still uncomfortable with the idea that her actions had somehow been preordained.

"It's probably just because I was lying down in the dream," Favian replied, his lips quirking with rueful humor.

Ithric flopped back against the headboard of the bed, boneless, and shook his head. "Crazy — all of it. Completely demented, from start to finish." He reached over to grasp a cup of the rich wine Favian had brought them, and lifted it. "Ah, well — here's to fate."

Favian saluted him with his own cup, and Kathrael followed suit. "To fate," Favian said wryly.

"So," Ithric continued, "We're taking Rona, Nimbral, and Arnav to Draebard with us. Then what?"

Favian frowned, confused. "What do you mean, *then what*?"

"Well," Ithric said slowly, "I mean… I should probably have a word with Andoc about the state of things in the south, and I did promise Frella I'd teach her knife throwing. I expect there will be a fair amount of thoroughly enjoyable buggery in our future, Favian, and I'm definitely open to exploring new and exciting ways to make Kathrael come, if she's amenable."

Kathrael flushed. "I'm amenable," she mumbled.

Ithric made a *there you have it gesture*. "So, aside from all that, and singing the occasional lullaby as required... what's next? Little Cat? What are your plans now that you've successfully rescued everyone who was under old Turvick's thumb?"

Surprised, Kathrael flashed back to her so-called *plans* from when she started this unlikely journey. She couldn't stifle the snort of harsh, derogatory laughter that escaped.

"Oh... nothing much," she said in a voice laced with heavy sarcasm. "Once I'd traveled across the mountains and taken my bloody revenge on the Wolf Patron for abandoning the southern slaves, I was going to trek *back* across the mountains and lead a rebellion against the Masters in Rhyth without his damned help. Obviously."

Ithric's eyes lit with interest. "Oh? Were you now?" he asked, as if her ironic tone had bypassed him completely. "Hmm. All right—I'm in. Let's do that, then."

She blinked. "Ithric... I was out of my head at the time. Mad as a bag of weasels. One escaped slave girl can't lead a revolution—it's ridiculous."

Ithric only smiled at her, all innocence. "Oh... so you're saying you need a *shape-shifter* to help?" The smile sharpened—grew dangerous.

Kathrael's mouth opened, but no words came out.

Fortunately, Favian did not suffer from the same problem. "Ithric! Are you *soft in the head*? They *burn* shape-shifters in the south!"

"I know," Ithric said slowly, as if to an imbecile. "I was there. Don't you consider that a good reason to try and change things?"

"They also stone eunuchs who dare to step out from under the temple's protection," Kathrael said quietly.

"Yes. They do," Ithric agreed, sobering. "Favian, I don't think you understand how bad things are in Rhyth. The city is ready to tear itself apart. And if it falls, I don't think I have to tell you who's going to step in and take over."

"The Alyrions," Favian breathed.

"They're halfway there already," Ithric confirmed.

"More than that, I'd say," Kathrael said. "The cult of Deimok is growing in power all the time. The priests of the Old Religion are weak in the south. They will not stand against it for much longer."

"You're right, then—you *do* need to talk to Andoc," Favian said, sounding grim. "You both do. But, Ithric, he's not going to countenance starting a revolution."

Ithric raised an eyebrow. "I think you might be surprised."

"And how will starting a slave revolt even *help*, if the Alyrions are waiting for exactly that?" Favian asked.

Kathrael put her cup aside and laced her fingers together, looking down at them. "Almost half of the population is silenced right now, Favian. The slaves don't want to worship a foreign god. They don't want to bow down to an Emperor. They want the same thing you want in the north. Freedom. Dignity. A say in their own futures."

Favian flopped back into his chair as if he'd been pushed there by an unseen hand.

"Nothing more than all the gods' children deserve, surely. Would you disagree, Favian?" Ithric prodded.

There was a pause. "No," Favian said, very quietly. "Of course I don't disagree. Of *course* they deserve it. But where would three people even begin with such a thing?"

Kathrael's chest tightened at his words. *Three people*, he'd said. Was this really to be her life, now? Could it actually be true?

"I... don't have the faintest idea," she admitted. "I wasn't joking when I told you I was mad at the time."

Ithric smiled again. "Well, I suppose the *obvious* thing would be to talk to the leaders of the escaped slaves in the underground movement and see what they think. I know several of them — I suspect they'd have a few thoughts on the subject."

Both Favian and Kathrael stared at him with open mouths, and he shrugged.

"Hello? Spy, remember? What did you *think* I've been doing all these months?" He rose and stretched before leaning down to kiss first Kathrael, and then Favian. "First things first, though."

"Yes. Right," Favian said, once he'd managed to stop gaping. He shook his head, appearing to come back to himself with some difficulty. "Draebard. *Home*. Rona still needs help, Frella is almost certainly ready to strangle me for running off without her, and you two *definitely* need to speak with Andoc—*at length.*"

Ithric nodded, his expression agreeable. Kathrael felt suddenly light, unburdened, as if she might float away and soar into the sky at any moment.

"Yes. Draebard first," she echoed, nearly giddy with thoughts of the future. "And I want to do that orgasm thing again, too. *Lots.* That was really nice."

A grin split Ithric's face, and his eyes moved from one to the other of them with lazy affection. "Oh, *absolutely,*" he said. "As often as you like, Little Cat. Also, the buggery. Can't forget the buggery, can we?"

finis

Kathrael's story continues in

The Lion Mistress: Book 2.

For more books by this author, see www.rasteffan.com.

Made in the USA
Middletown, DE
15 May 2022

65801084R00231